1

The Soul of Golf

by Percy Adolphus Vaile

Copyright © 2/1/2016
Jefferson Publication

ISBN-13: 978-1523816521

Printed in the United States of America

Table of Contents

CHAPTER I

THE SOUL OF GOLF

Nearly every one who writes about a game essays to prove that it is similar to "the great game, the game of life." Golf has not escaped; and numberless scribes in endeavouring to account for the fascination of golf have used the old threadbare tale. As a matter of fact, golf is about as unlike the game of life as any game could well be. As played now it has come to be almost an exact science, and everybody knows exactly what one is trying to do. This would not be mistaken for a description of the game of life. In that game a man may be hopelessly "off the line," buried "in the rough," or badly "bunkered," and nobody be the wiser. It is not so in golf. There is no double life here. All is open, and every one knows what the player is striving for. The least deflection from his line, and the onlooker knows he did not mean it. It is seen instantly. In that other game it may remain unseen for years, for ever.

Explaining the fascination of anything seems to be a thankless kind of task, and in any case to be a work of supererogation. The fascination should be sufficient. Explaining it seems almost like tearing a violet to pieces to admire its structure; but many have tried, and many have failed, and there are many who do not feel the fascination as they should, because they do not know the soul of golf. One cannot appreciate the beauty of golf unless one knows it thoroughly.

Curiously enough, many of our best players are extremely mechanical in their play. They play beautiful and accurate shots, but they have no idea how or why they produce them; and the strange thing about it is that although golf is perhaps as mechanical a game as there is, those who play it mechanically only get the husk of it. They miss the soul of the game.

Golf is really one of the simplest of outdoor games, if not indeed the simplest, and it does not require much intelligence; yet it is quite one of the most difficult to play well, for it demands the greatest amount of mechanical accuracy. This, on consideration, is apparent. The ball is the smallest ball we use, the striking face of the club is the smallest thing used in field sports for hitting a ball, and, most important, perhaps, of all, it is farther away from the eye than any other ball-striking implement, except, perhaps, the polo stick, in which game we, of course, have a much larger ball and striking surface.

In all games of skill, and in all sports where the object is propelling anything to a given point, one always tries, almost instinctively, to get the eye as much in a line with the ball or missile and the objective point as possible. This is seen in throwing a stone, aiming a catapult, a gun, or an arrow, in cueing at a billiard ball, and in many other ways, but in golf it is impracticable. The player must make his stroke with his eye anywhere from four to six feet away from his little club face. One may say that this is so in hockey, cricket, and lawn-tennis. So, in a modified degree, it is, but the great difference is that in all these games there is an infinitely larger margin of error than there is in golf. At these games a player may be yards off his intended line and yet play a fine stroke, to the applause of the onlookers; while he alone knew that it was accident and not design.

The charm of golf is in part that its demand is inexorable. It lays down the one path—the straight one. It must be followed every step, or there is trouble.

Then there is in golf the sheer beauty of the flight of the ball, and the almost sensuous delight which comes to the man who created that beauty, and knows how and why he did it. There is at any time beauty in the flight of a golf ball well and plainly driven; but for grace and the poetry of flight stands alone the wind-cheater that skims away from one's club across the smooth green sward, almost clipping the daisies in its flight ere it soars aloft with a swallow-like buoyancy, and, curving gracefully, pitches dead on the green.

Many a man can play that stroke. Many a man does. Not one in fifty knows how he puts the beauty into his stroke. Not one in fifty would be interested if you were to start telling him the scientific reason for that ball's beautiful flight. "The mechanics of golf" sounds hard and unromantic, yet the man who does not understand them suffers in his game and in his enjoyment of it. That wind-cheater was to him, during its flight through the air, merely a golf ball; a golf ball 'twas and nothing more. To the other man it is a faithful little friend sent out to do a certain thing in a certain way, and all the time it is flying and running it is sending its message back to the man who can take it—but how few can? They do not know what the soul of golf means. So, when our golfer pulls or slices his ball badly, and then—does the usual thing, he cannot take the message that comes back to him. He only knows the half of golf, and he does not care about the other, because he does not know what he is missing. He is like a man who is fond of music but is tune-deaf. There are many such. He may sit and drink in sweet sounds and enjoy them, but he misses the linked sweetness and the message which comes to his more fortunate brother who has the ear—and the knowledge.

There is in England a curious idea that directly one acquires a scientific knowledge of a game one must cease to have an interest in it so full as he who merely plays it by guesswork. There can be no greater mistake than this. If a game is worth playing well, it is worth knowing well, and knowing it well cannot mean loving it less. It is this peculiar idea which has put England so much in the background of the world's athletic field of late years. We have here much of the best brawn and bone in the world, but we must give the brain its place. Then will England come to her own again.

England is in many ways paying now for her lack of thoroughness in athletic sports. Time was when it was a stock gibe at John Bull's expense that he spent most of his time making muscle and washing it. Then it was, I am afraid, sour grapes. England had all the championships. The joke is "off" now. The grapes are no longer sour. The championships are well distributed throughout the world—anywhere but in England; and we say it does not matter; that the chief end of games is not winning them. Nor is it; but we did not talk like that when we *were* winning them, and the trouble is not so much that we are losing, as the manner in which we are losing. The fact is that we are losing because our players do not, in many sports, know the soul of the game. The ideal is lost in the prosaic grappling for cups or medals, in the merely vulgar idea of success. Thus it comes to pass that many will not be content to get to the soul of a game in the natural way, by long and loving familiarity with it.

Hordes of people are joining the ranks of the golfers, and their constant cry is, "Teach me the swing," and after a lesson or two at the wrong end of golf, for a beginner, they go forth and cut the county into strips and think they are playing golf. Is it any wonder, when our links are cumbered with such as these, that those who have the soul of golf are in imminent daily peril of losing their own?

One who would know the soul of golf must begin even as would one who will know the soul of music. There is no more chance for one to gather up the soul of golf in a hurry than there is for that same one to understand Wagner in a week.

It is this vulgar rushing impatience to be out and doing while one is still merely a nuisance to one's fellows, which causes so much irritation and unpleasantness on many links; that prevents many from starting properly, and becoming in due course quite good players; for it is manifest that the "rusher" is starting to learn his game upside down, as, indeed, most professionals and books teach it. There can be no doubt that the right way to teach anything is to give the beginner the easiest task at first. About the easiest stroke in golf is a six-inch put. That is where one should start a learner. The drive is the stroke in golf that offers the greatest possibility of error, so he is always started with it. It is his own fault. "Teach me the swing" is the insistent cry of the beginner, who does not know that he is losing the best part of golf by turning it upside down. He will never enjoy it so much, or play so good and confident a game as he would were he to work his way gradually and naturally from his putter to his mashie, to his niblick, his iron, his cleek, his brassy, and his driver. Such a one may come to an intimate knowledge and love of the game. The rusher may play golf, but it will be a long time before he gets to the soul of the game.

A very good golfer in reviewing a golf book some time ago stated that he did not care in the least what happened while the ball was in the air, that all he cared about was getting it there. He has played golf since he was five years old, but he has clearly missed the soul of the game.

It is not necessary to dilate upon the wonderful spread of golf throughout the world. An industrious journalist some time ago marked a map of England wherever there was a golf club. It looked as though it had been sprinkled with black pepper. It is not hard to understand this marvellous increase in the popularity of the great game, for golf is undoubtedly a great game. The motor has, unquestionably, played a great part in its development. Many of the courses, particularly in the United Kingdom, are most beautifully situated. Many of the club-houses are models of comfort, and some of them are castles. The game itself is suitable for the octogenarian dodderer who merely wants to infuse a little interest into his morning walk, or it may be turned into a severe test of endurance for the young athlete; so no wonder it prospers.

There is a wonderful freemasonry among golfers. This is not the least of the many charms of the game, and to him who really knows it and loves it as it deserves to be loved, the sign of the club is a passport round the world.

Many a time and oft I see golfing journalists, when writing about the game, stating that something "is obvious." It has always seemed to me that it is impossible to say what is obvious to anyone in a game of golf. Writing of George Duncan, the famous young professional golfer, during the first half of the big foursome at Burhill, a great sporting paper said that a certain mashie shot was a "crude stroke." The man who wrote that article did not know the soul of golf. He saw the mashie flash in the air, some turf cut away, and a ball dropping on to the green. Just that and nothing more, and it was "obvious" to him that it was a crude stroke.

One who knew the soul of golf saw it and described it. It was a tricky green, with a drop of twenty feet behind it. To have overrun it would have been fatal. There was a stiff head-wind. The player would not risk running up. He cut well in under the ball to get all the back-spin he could. He pitched the ball well up against the wind, which caught it and, on account of the spin, threw it up and up until it soared almost over the hole, then it dropped like a shot bird about a yard from the hole, and the back-spin gripped the turf and held the ball within a foot of where it fell. It was obvious to one man that it was a crude shot. It was equally obvious to another, who knew the inner secrets of the game, that it was a brilliantly conceived and beautifully executed stroke. One man saw nothing of the soul of the stroke. He got the husk, and the other took the kernel.

Much has been made of the assumption that golf is the greatest possible test of a man's temperament. This has to a great extent, I am afraid, been exaggerated. It is one of those things in connection with the game that has been handed down to us, and which we have been afraid to interfere with. I cannot see why this claim should be quietly granted. In golf a man is treated with tragic solemnity while he is making his stroke. A caddie may not sigh, and if a cricket chirped he would be considered a bounder. How would our golfer feel if he had to play his drive with another fellow waving his club at him twenty or thirty feet away, and standing ready to spoil his shot?—yet that is what the lawn-tennis player has to put up with. There is a good deal of exaggeration about this aspect of golf, even as there is a good deal of nonsense about the interference of onlookers. What can be done by one when one is accustomed to a crowd may be seen when one of the great golfers is playing out of a great V formed by the gallery, and, needless to say, playing from the narrow end of it. Golf is a good test of a man's disposition without doubt, but as a game it lacks one important feature which is characteristic of every other field sport, I think, except golf. In these the medium of conflict is the same ball, and the skill of the opposing side has much to do with the chances of the other player or players. In golf each man plays his own game with his own ball, and the only effect of his opponent's play on his is moral, or the luck of a stymie. Many people consider this a defect; but golf is a game unto itself, and we must take it as it is. Certainly it is hard enough to achieve distinction in it to satisfy the most exacting.

When one writes of the soul of golf it sounds almost as though one were guilty of a little sentimentality. As a matter of fact, it is the most thorough practice which leads one to the soul of golf. Many a good professional can produce beautiful shots, such as the wind-cheater and the pull at will, but he cannot explain them to you; and no professional ever has explained clearly in book or elsewhere what produces these beautiful shots.

A famous professional once asked me quite simply, "How do I play my push-shot, Mr. Vaile?" I explained the stroke to him. He is as good a sportsman as he is a golfer, and would be ashamed to pretend to a knowledge which he has not. When I had told him, he said, "Thank you. Of course, I can play it all right, but I never could understand why it went like that. Now I shall be able to explain it better to my pupils."

Now it may in some measure sound incongruous, but I repeat that unless one knows the mechanics of golf one has missed the soul of the game. It is simply an impossibility for the blind ball-smiter to get such joy and gratification from his game as does the man who from his superior knowledge has produced results which are in themselves worth losing the game for. Many a golfer, or one who would like to be a golfer, will wonder at this. Many a game at billiards has been lost for the poetry of a fascinating cannon when the win was not the main object of the game; but in this respect billiards and golf are not alike. One is not, in golf, penalised for putting the soul and the poetry of the game into his shots, for they come of practice, and simply render one's strokes more perfect than they would otherwise be. So in the end it will be found that he who knows the game most thoroughly will have an undoubted advantage.

Therefore it behoves every golfer to strive for the soul of golf.

And now, as we must for a little while leave the soul of golf, let us consider its body, that great solid, visible portion which is the part that appeals most forcibly to the ordinary golfer. It is this to which the attention of players and writers has been most assiduously directed for centuries, yet it is safe to say that no game in the whole realm of sport has been so miswritten and unwritten as golf.

This is very strange, for probably there is no other game that is so canvassed and discussed by its followers. The reason may possibly be found in the fact that golfers are a most conservative class of people, and that they follow wonderfully the line of thought laid down for them by others. This at its best is uninteresting; at its worst most pernicious.

Another contributing cause is the manner in which books on sport are now produced. A great name, an enterprising publisher, and a hack-writer are all that are now required. The consequence is that the market is flooded with books ostensibly by leading exponents of the different sports, but which are, in many cases, written by men who know little or nothing of the subject they are dealing with. The natural result is that the great players suffer severely in "translation," and their names are frequently associated with quite stupid statements,—statements so foolish that one, knowing how these things are done, refrains from criticising them as they deserve, from sympathy with the unfortunate alleged author, who is probably a very good fellow, and quite innocent of the fact that the nonsense alleged to be his knowledge is ruining or retarding the game of many people. This is a most unscrupulous practice, which should be exposed and severely condemned, for it must not be thought that it is confined to any one branch of sport.

While we are dealing with the slavish following of the alleged thought of the leading golfers of the world, we may with advantage consider a few of the most pronounced fetiches which have been worshipped almost from time immemorial, fetiches which are the more remarkable in that they receive mental and theoretical worship only, and are, in actual practice, most severely despised and disregarded by the best players; but unfortunately the neophyte worships these fetiches for many years until he discovers that they are false gods.

Perhaps one of the silliest, and for beginners most disastrous, is the ridiculous assertion that putters are born, not made. In the book of a very famous player I find the following words:—

It happens, unfortunately, that concerning one department of the game that will cause the golfer some anxiety from time to time, and often more when he is experienced than when he is not, neither I nor any other player can offer any words of instruction such as, if closely acted upon, would give the same successful results as the advice tendered under other heads ought to do. This is in regard to putting.

Now this idea is promulgated in many books. It is, in my opinion, the most absolute and pernicious nonsense. The best answer to it is the fact that the writer of the words was himself one of the worst putters, but that by careful study and alteration of his defective methods, he became a first-class performer on the green. Also it will be obvious to a very mean intelligence that there is no branch of golf which is so capable of being reduced to a mechanical certainty as is putting.

The importance of removing this stupid idea will be more fully appreciated when one remembers that quite half the game of golf is played on the green, leaving the other half to be distributed among all the other clubs. It is well to emphasise this. A good score for almost any eighteen-hole course is 72. The man who can count on getting down in an average of 2 is a very good putter. Many professionals would throw away their putters if they were allowed to consider it down in 2 every time. This gives us 36 for puts. With this before us we cannot exaggerate the pernicious effect of the false doctrine which says that putting cannot be taught, that a man must just let his own individuality have full play, and similar nonsense; whereas the truth is that one might safely guarantee to convert into admirable putters many men who, from their conformation and other characteristics, would be almost hopeless as golfers. I must emphasise the fact that there is no department of the game which is so important as putting; there is no department of the game more capable of being clearly and easily demonstrated by an intelligent teacher; and there is no department of the game wherein the player may be so nearly reduced to that machine-like accuracy which is the constant demand, and no small portion of the charm, of golf.

Another very widely worshipped fetich, which has been much damaged recently, is the sweep in driving a ball. Trying "to sweep" his ball away for two hundred yards has reduced many a promising player to almost a suicidal frame of mind. Fortunately the fallacy soon exasperates a beginner, and he "says things" and "lets it have it." Then the much-worshipped "sweep" becomes a hit, sometimes a very vicious one, and the ball goes away from the club as it was meant to. It is becoming more widely recognised every day that the golf-drive is a hit, and a very fine one—when well played.

Perhaps the most pernicious fetich which has for many years held sway in golf, until recently somewhat damaged, is that the left arm is the more important of the two—that it, in fact, finds the power for the drive. Anything more comical is hard to imagine. There is practically nothing in the whole realm of muscular exertion, from wood-chopping to golf, wherein both arms are used, that is not dominated by the right, yet golfers have for generations quietly accepted this fetich, and it has ruined many a promising player. The votaries of this fetich must surely find one thing very hard to explain. If we admit, for the sake of argument, that the left arm is the more important, and that it really has more power and more influence on the stroke than the right, can they explain why the left-handed players, who have been provided by a benevolent providence with so manifest an advantage, tamely surrender it and convert their left hand into the right-handed players' right by giving it the lower position on the shaft? If this idea of the left hand and arm being the more important is correct, left-handed players would use right-hand clubs and play like a right-handed player, with the manifest advantage of being provided by nature with an arm and hand that fall naturally into the most important position. I think that this consideration of the subject will give those who put their faith in the fetich of the left, something to explain.

Almost from time immemorial it has been laid down by golfing writers that at the top of the swing the golfer must have his weight on his right leg. A study of the instantaneous photographs of most of the famous players will show conclusively that this is not correct. It is expressly laid down that it is fatal to sway, to draw away from one's ball during the upward swing; the player is specially enjoined on no account to move his head. A very simple trial will convince any golfer, even a beginner, that without swaying, without drawing his head away from the hole, he cannot possibly, if swinging correctly, put his weight on his right leg, and that at the top of his swing it must be mainly on his left—and so another well-worn belief goes by the board.

So it is with the exaggerated swing which for so many years dominated the minds of aspiring golfers to such an extent that many of them thought more of getting the swing than of hitting the ball. It is slowly but surely going.

The era of new thought in golf has dawned. It will not make the game less attractive. It will not make it any more exacting, for the higher knowledge cannot become an obsession. It sinks into a man, and he scarcely thinks of it as something beyond the ordinary game. It brings him into closer touch with the best that is in golf. He is able to obtain more from it than he could before. He is able to do more than he could formerly, for a man cannot get to the soul of golf except through the body, and love he not the body with the love of the truest of true golfers he will never know the soul.

This chapter originally appeared in *The Fortnightly Review* in the United Kingdom, and in *The North American Review* in the United States of America.

CHAPTER II

THE MYSTERY OF GOLF

There is no such thing as "the mystery of golf." One might reasonably ask, "If there is no such thing as 'the mystery of golf,' why devote a chapter to it?" But "the mystery of golf" should really be written "the mystery of the golfer," for the simple reason that the golfer himself is responsible for all the mystery in golf—in short, "the mystery of golf" may briefly be defined as the credulity of the golfer. Notwithstanding this, at least one enterprising man has produced a book entirely devoted to elucidating the alleged mystery of golf, wherein, quite unknown to himself, he proves most clearly and conclusively the truth of my opening statement in this chapter, that the mystery of golf is merely the credulity of the golfer; but of that anon.

There really is no mystery whatever about the game of golf. It is one of the simplest of games, but unquestionably it is a game which is very difficult to play well, a game which demands a high degree of mechanical accuracy in the production of the various strokes. It is apparent from the nature of the implements used in the game that this must be so. All the foolishness of nebulous advice, and all the quaint excuses which have been gathered together under the head of "the mystery of golf," are simply weak man's weaker excuses for his want of intelligence and mechanical accuracy. Until the golfer fully understands and freely acknowledges this, he is suffering from a very severe handicap. If, when he addresses his ball, he has firmly implanted in his mind the idea that he is in the presence of some awesome mystery, there is very little doubt that he will do his level best to perform his part in the mystery play.

We do not read anywhere of the mystery of lawn-tennis, the mystery of cricket, the mystery of marbles, squash racquets, or ping-pong. There are no mysteries in these games any more than there are in golf, and the plain fact is that the demand of golf is inexorable. It insists upon the straight line being followed, and the man who forsakes the straight line is immediately detected. In no game, perhaps, is the insistent demand for direction so inexorable as in golf. Perhaps also in no game is that demand so frequently refused, and, naturally, the erring golfer wishes to excuse himself. It is useful then for him to be told of the mysteries of golf—the wonderful mysteries, the psychological difficulties, the marvellous cerebration, the incredibly rapid nerve "telegraphing," and the wonderful muscular complications which take place between the time that he addresses the ball and hits it, or otherwise.

Now, as a matter of fact, this is all so much balderdash, so much falseness, so much artificial and indeed almost criminal nonsense. It would indeed almost seem as if the people who write this kind of stuff are in league with the greatest players of the world, who write as instructions for the unfortunate would-be golfer things which they themselves never dreamed of doing—things which would quite spoil the wonderful game they play if they did them.

PLATE I.

HARRY VARDON'S GRIP

Showing the overlapping of the first finger of the left hand by the little finger of the right. This is now the orthodox grip.

If there may be said to be any mystery whatever about golf, it is that in such an ancient and simple game there has grown up around it such a marvellous mass of false teaching, of confused thought, and of fantastic notions. No game suffers from this false doctrine and imaginative nonsense to the same extent as does golf. It is magnificently played. We have here in England the finest exponents of the game, both amateur and professional, in the world. If those men played golf as they tell others by their printed works to play it, I should have another story to tell about their prowess on the links.

Golf, in itself, is quite sufficiently difficult. It is quite unnecessary to give the golfer, or the would-be golfer, an additional handicap by instilling it into his mind that golf is any more mysterious than any other game which is played. The most mysterious thing about golf is that those who really ought to know most about it publish broadcast wrong information about the fundamental principles of the game. Innocent players follow this advice, and not unnaturally they find it tremendously difficult to make anything like adequate progress. Naturally, when some one comes along and explains to them in lengthy articles, or may be in a book, about the psychological difficulties and terrific complications of golf, they are pleased to fasten on this stuff as an excuse for their want of success, whereas in very truth the real explanation lies simply in the fact that they are violating some of the commonest and simplest laws of mechanics.

9

Here, indeed, I might almost be forgiven if I went back on what I have said about the mystery of golf, and produced, on my own account, that which is to me an outstanding mystery, and labelled it "the mystery of golf." This really is to me always a mystery, but I should not be correct in calling it "the mystery of golf," for it is more correctly described as the simplicity of the golfer. This mystery is that practically every writer about golf, and nearly every player, seems to labour under the delusion that there is a special set of mechanical laws for golf, that the golf ball flying through the air is actuated by totally different influences and in a totally different manner from the cricket ball, the ping-pong ball, or the lawn-tennis ball when engaged in a similar manner. That is bad enough, but the same delusions exist with regard to the conduct of the ball on the green.

Now it is impossible to speak too plainly about this matter, because I want at the outset to dispel the illusion of the mystery of golf. There is no special set of mechanical laws governing golf. Golf has to take its place with all other games, and the mechanical laws which govern the driving of a nail, a golf ball, or a cricket ball are fixed and immutable and well known, so that it is quite useless for any one to try to explain to intelligent persons that there is any mystery in golf or the production of the golfing strokes beyond that which may be found in other games. Some people might think that I labour this point. It is impossible to be too emphatic at the outset about it, for the simple reason that it is bad enough for the golfer to have to think at the moment of making his stroke about the things which actually do matter. If we are going to provide him with phantoms as well as solid realities to contend with, he will indeed have a sorry time. As a matter of fact, about seven-tenths of the bad golf which is played is due to too much thinking about the stroke *while the stroke is being played*. The golf stroke in itself may be quite easily learned; I mean the true golf stroke, and not the imaginary golf stroke, which has been built up for the unfortunate golfer by those who never played such a stroke themselves, and by those who write of the mystery of golf; but it is an absolute certainty that the time for thinking about the golf stroke, and how it shall be played, *is not when one is playing the stroke*.

As a matter of fact the golf stroke is in some respects a complicated stroke. Certain changes of position in the body and arms take place with extreme rapidity during the execution of the stroke. It is an utter impossibility for any man to think out and execute in proper order the component parts of a well-executed drive during his stroke. When a man addresses his ball he should have in his mind but the one idea—he has to hit that ball in such a manner as to get it to the place at which he wants it to arrive; but between the time of his address and the time that the ball departs on its journey his action should be, to use a much-hackneyed but still expressive word, practically sub-conscious; in fact, the way he hit that ball should be regulated by habit. If the result was satisfactory—well and good. If otherwise, he may analyse that shot in his armchair later on; but when once one has addressed the ball it is absolutely fatal to good golf to indulge in speculation as to how one is going to hit that ball, and if to that speculation one adds a belief in what is called "the mystery of golf," one had better get right away back to marbles at once, because it is a certainty that any one who believes in nonsense of this sort and practises it can never be a golfer.

The bane of about eighty-five per cent of golfers is a pitiful attempt to cultivate style. The most contemptible man at any game is the stylist. The man who cultivates style before the game is not fit to cumber any links. Every man should strive to produce his stroke in a mechanically perfect manner. A good style is almost certain to follow when this is done. Style as the result of a game produced in a mechanically perfect manner is most desirable, but style without the game is simply despicable. One sometimes sees misguided golfers, or would-be golfers, practising their follow-through in a very theatrical manner. It should be obvious to a very mean intelligence that a follow-through is of no value whatever, except as the natural result of a correctly executed stroke. If the stroke has been correct up to the moment of impact, the follow-through will come almost as naturally as a good style will be born of correctly executed strokes. Self-consciousness is the besetting sin of the golfer. It is hardly too much to say that the ordinary golfer devotes, unfortunately, too much thought to himself and "the swing," and far too little to the thing that he is there for—namely, to hit the ball.

In golf the player has plenty of time to spare in making his stroke, and he occupies too much of it in thinking about other things than the stroke. The essence of success at golf is concentration upon the stroke. The analysis has no right whatever to intrude itself on a man's mind until the stroke has been played. The inquest should not be held until the corpse is there. If this rule is followed, it will be found that the corpse is frequently wanting.

Golf is a very ancient game. Lawn-tennis is an absolute parvenu by its side, and there are many other games which, compared with golf, are practically infants. Golf stands alone as regards false instruction, nebulous criticism, and utter disregard of the first principles of mechanics. I have always been at a loss to understand this. It is not as though golf had not been played and studied by some of the keenest intellects in the land. We have had, as we shall see later on, men of the highest scientific attainments devoting their attention to the game, writing about it, lecturing about it, publishing things about it which exist solely in their imagination. This truly may be called a mystery.

I cannot leave the mystery of golf without giving some illustrations of the things which are published as instruction. For instance, I read lately that a good style results in good golf. This is the kind of thing which mystifies a beginner. The good style should be the result of the good golf, and not the golf of the style. I read elsewhere:

As a matter of fact most of the difficulties in golf are mental, not physical, are subjective, not objective, are the created phantasms of the mind, not the veritable realities of the course.

I find these things in Mr. Haultain's book entitled *The Mystery of Golf.*

There is no game where there are fewer mental difficulties than in golf. The game is so extremely simple that it can practically be reduced to a matter of physical and mechanical accuracy. The mental demand in golf—provided always, of course, that the man who is addressing the ball knows what he wants to do—is extremely small and extremely simple. "The created phantasms of the mind" are supplied by fantastic writers who have proved for themselves that these phantasms are the deadliest enemies of good golf. In another place I read the following passage:

You may place your ball how or where you like, you may hit it with any sort of implement you like; all you have to do is to hit it. Could simpler conditions be devised? Could an easier task be set? And yet such is the constitution of the human golfing soul that it not only fails to achieve it, but invents for itself multiform and manifold ifs and ans for not achieving it—ifs and ans, the nature and number of which must assuredly move the laughter of the gods.

Probably this is meant to be satirical, but it is merely a libel on the great body of golfers. It is not the "human golfing soul" which "invents for itself multiform and manifold ifs and ans for not achieving it." He who invents these ifs and ans is the author of the ordinary golf book on golf, written ostensibly by some great player, and the "ifs and ans" most assuredly, if they do not "move the laughter of the gods," are sufficient to provoke the derision and contempt of the golfer who feels that nobody has a right to publish statements about a game which must act in a detrimental manner upon those who attempt to follow them.

It is not the "human golfing soul" or the human golfing body which is so prone to error. Those who make the errors are those who essay to teach, and the time has now come for them to vindicate themselves or to stand back, to stand out of the way of the spread of truth; for one may be able to fool all the golfers some of the time and some of the golfers all the time, but it is a sheer impossibility to fool all the golfers all the time; and if the teaching which has obtained credence in the past were to be left unassailed, the result would be untold misery and discomfort to millions of golfers.

It is for this reason that I am dealing in an early chapter with the alleged mystery of golf, for I want to make it particularly clear that in the vast majority of cases those who attempt to explain the mystery of golf proceed very much on the lines of the octopus and obscure themselves behind clouds of inky fluid which are generally as shapeless in their form and meaning as the matter given off by the uncanny sea-dweller. In fact, the ordinary attempt to explain the mystery of golf generally resolves itself into the writer setting up his own Aunt Sally, and even then exposing how painfully bad his aim is.

Nearly every one who writes about golf claims for it that above all games it is the truest test of character, and in a degree unknown in any other game reveals the nature of the man who is playing it, and they proceed on this assumption to weave some of the most remarkable romances in connection with the simple and fundamental principles of the game. In the book under notice we are asked

... and yet why, *why* does a badly-played game so upset a sane and rational man? You may lose at bridge, you may be defeated in chess, you may recall lost chances in football or polo; you may remember stupid things you did in tennis or squash racquets; you may regret undue haste in trying to secure an extra run or runs in cricket, but the mental depression caused by these is temporary and evanescent. Why do foozles in golf affect the whole man? Humph! It is no use blinking matters—say what the scoffers may—to foozle at golf, to take your eye off your ball, cuts down to the very deeps of the human soul. It does; there is no controverting that.... Perhaps this is why golf is worth writing about.

It certainly is mysterious that any "sane and rational man" can write such stuff about golf. This is a fair sample of the kind of thing one gets from those who attempt to treat of golf from the physiological or psychological standpoint. I can hardly say too often that there is no such thing as the mystery of golf, any more than there is, in reality, such a thing as the soul of golf, but the mystery of golf is a meaningless and misleading term. The soul of golf means, in effect, the heart of golf—a true and loving understanding of the very core of the game.

It would be bad enough if the persons essaying to explain the alleged mystery of golf knew the game thoroughly themselves, but, generally speaking, they do not—in the case under consideration, the writer himself admits that he is "a duffer." Now taking him at his own valuation, it does indeed seem strange that one whose knowledge of the game is admittedly insufficient, should attempt to explain to players the super-refinements of a game at which he himself is admittedly incompetent. It may seem somewhat cruel to press this point, but in a matter such as this we have to consider the greatest good of the greatest number, and we must not allow false sentiment to weigh with us in dealing with the work of anyone who publishes matter which may prejudicially affect the game of an immense body of people.

The attempts to deal with the psychology and the physiology of golf are a mass of confused thought and illogical reasoning, but it is when the author proceeds to deal in any way with the practical side of golf that he shows clearly that his estimate of himself, at least in so far as regards his knowledge of the game, is not inaccurate. Let us take, for instance, the following passage. He says that William Park, Junior, has informed us that

... pressing, really, is putting in the power at the right time. You can hit as hard as you like if you hit accurately and at the right time, but the man who presses is the man who puts in the power too soon. He is in too great a hurry. He begins to hit before the club head has come anywhere near the ball.

This quotation, I may say, is not from William Park's book, but is taken from the volume I am quoting, and the last sentence—"He begins to hit before the club head has come anywhere near the ball"—shows clearly that the author has no idea whatever of even a mechanical analysis of the golf stroke, for it is impossible to begin the hit too soon. The main portion of the power of the drive in golf is developed (as indeed anyone with very little consideration might know) *near the beginning of the downward swing*. This is so simple, so natural, so apparent to any one who knows the game of golf that I feel it is almost unnecessary to support the statement; but there are so many people who follow the game of golf, and are willing to accept as gospel any remarkable statement with regard to the game, that I may as well refer doubters to James Braid's book on *Advanced Golf* wherein he shows clearly that anyone desiring to produce a proper drive at golf must be hard at it from the very beginning of the stroke. The author continues:

If in the drive the whole weight and strength of the body, from the nape of the neck to the soles of the feet, are not transferred from body to ball, through the minute and momentary contact of club with ball, absolutely surely, yet swiftly— you top or you pull or you sclaff, or you slice, or you swear.

It is almost unnecessary to tell any golfer that the whole weight of his body is not thrown at his golf ball, for this, in effect, would produce a terrific lunge and utterly destroy the rhythm of his stroke.

Here is another remarkable passage—"and as to that mashie shot where you loft high over an abominable bunker and fall dead with a back-spin and a cut to the right on a keen and declivitous green—is there any stroke in any game quite so delightfully difficult as that?" and my answer is "Certainly not, for there is no such stroke in golf." When one puts a cut to the right or to the left, one has no back-spin on the ball. The back-spin is only got by following through after the ball in a downward direction, and as to a mashie approach with a cut to the right—well, the cut on a golf ball in a mashie stroke is in practical golf *always* a cut to the left, which produces a run to the right. The shot as described by Mr. Haultain simply does not exist in golf. It probably is a portion of the mystery of golf which he has not yet solved.

Then we are told

... not only is the stroke in golf an extremely difficult one—it is also an extremely complicated one, more especially the drive, in which its principles are concentrated. It is, in fact, a subtle combination of a swing and a hit, the "hit" portion being deftly incorporated into the "swing" just as the head of the club reaches the ball, yet without disturbing the regular rhythm of the motion.

This again is another of the mysteries of golf, and a mystery purely of the inventive brain of the author. The drive in golf is played with such extreme rapidity that the duration of impact does not last more than one ten-thousandth of a second, yet we are asked to believe that the first portion of the stroke is a swing, but in, say, the five-thousandth of a second it is to be changed to a hit. Could the force of folly in alleged tuition go further than this?

We now come to an absolutely fundamental error in the golf stroke, an error of a nature so important and far-reaching that if I can demonstrate it, any attempt on the part of its author to explain anything in connection with the golf stroke mechanically, physiologically, psychologically, logically, or otherwise, must absolutely fall to the ground. We are told "the whole body must turn on the pivot of the head of the right thigh bone working in the cotyloidal cavity of the *os innominatum* or pelvic bone, the head, right knee and right foot remaining fixed, with the eyes riveted on the ball."

Now, put into plain English this ridiculous sentence means that the weight of the body rests upon the right leg. It is such a fundamental and silly error, but nevertheless an error which is made by the greatest players in the world in their published works, that I shall not at the present moment deal with the matter, but shall refer to it again in my chapter on the distribution of weight, for this matter of the distribution of weight, which is of absolute "root" importance in the game of golf, has been most persistently mistaught by those whose duty it is to teach the game as they play it, so that others may not be hampered in their efforts to become expert by following false advice.

Further on we are told, "in the upward swing the vertebral column rotates upon the head of the right femur, the right knee being fixed, and as the club head nears the ball the fulcrum is rapidly changed from the right to the left hip, the spine now rotating on the left thigh-bone, the left knee being fixed." Of course, I do not know on what principle the man who writes this is built, but it seems to me that he must have a spine with an adjustable end. None of the famous golfers, so far as I am aware, are able to shift their spines from one thigh bone to another. Moreover, to say that "the vertebral column rotates upon the head of the right femur" is merely childish unscientific nonsense, for it is obvious to any one, even to one who does not profess to explain the mystery of golf, that one's spine cannot possibly rotate within one, for to secure rotation of the spine it would be necessary for the body to rotate. This, it need hardly be pointed out, would be extremely inconvenient between the waggle and the moment when one strikes the ball.

We are told that in the downward swing "velocity of the club in the descent must be accelerated by minute but rapid gradations." For one who is attempting to explain the mystery of golf there could not possibly be a worse word than "gradations." The author, in this statement, is simply following an old and utterly obsolete notion. There is no such thing as accelerating the speed by minute gradations. Quoting James Braid in *Advanced Golf*, from memory, he says that you must be "hard at it" from the very moment you start the stroke, and even if he did not say so, any golfer possessed of common sense would know that the mere idea of adding to the speed of his golf drive by "steps," which is what the word "gradations" implies, would be utterly futile. The futility of the advice is, however, emphasised when we are told that these gradations come from "orders not issued all at once, but one after another—also absolutely evenly and smoothly—at intervals probably of ten-thousandths of a second. If the curves are not precise, if a single muscle fails to respond, if the timing is in the minutest degree irregular—the stroke is a failure. No wonder it is difficult."

It would indeed be no wonder that the golf drive is difficult if it really were composed as indicated, but, as a matter of fact, nothing of the sort takes place in the ordinary drive of a sane golfer. There is one command issued, which is "Hit the ball." All these other things which are supposed to be done by an incredible number of efforts of the mind are practically performed sub-consciously, and more by habit than by any complex mental directions. The drive in golf is not in any respect different from numerous other strokes in numerous other games in so far as regards the mental portion of it.

Now so far as regards the complicated system of mental telegraphy which is claimed for golf in the production of the stroke, absolutely the same thing happens in practically every game, with the exception that in most other games the player is, so far as regards the production of his stroke, at a greater disadvantage than he is in golf, for he has nearly always a moving ball to play at and much less time wherein to decide how to play his stroke. In golf he has plenty of time to make up his mind as to how he will play his stroke, and the operation, to the normal golfer, in so far as regards the mental portion of it, is extremely simple. His trouble is that he has so much nonsense of this nature to contend with, so much false instruction to fight. If he were given a correct idea of the stroke he would have no difficulty whatever with regard to his "gradations."

Braid has explicitly stated that this idea of gradually and consciously increasing the speed is a mistake, and I have always been especially severe on it as one of the pronounced fallacies of golf. I shall deal with it more fully in my chapter on "The Fallacies of Golf," but I may here quote Braid, who says:

Nevertheless, when commencing the downward swing, do so in no gentle, half-hearted manner such as is often associated with the idea of gaining speed gradually, which is what we are told the club must do when coming down from the top on to the ball. It is obvious that speed will be gained gradually, since the club could not possibly be started off at its quickest rate. The longer the force applied to the down swing, the greater do the speed and momentum become. But this gradual increase is independent of the golfer, and he should, as far as possible, be unconscious of it. What he has to concern himself with is not increasing his speed gradually, but getting as much of it as he possibly can right from the top. No gentle starts, but hard at it from the top, and the harder you start the greater will be the momentum of the club when the ball is reached.

Now this is emphatic enough, but it should not be necessary to quote James Braid to impress upon any golfer of average intelligence that this idea of consciously increasing his speed gradually as he comes down to the ball is the most infantile and injurious tuition which it is possible to impart. To encumber any player's mind with such utterly stupid doctrine is most reprehensible.

As an illustration of how little the author of this book understands the true character of the golf stroke, I may quote him again. In a letter recently published over his signature he says: "Mind and muscle—both should act freely and easily *till the moment of impact*; then, perhaps, the mind should be concentrated, as the muscles must be contracted, to the utmost." Now this is such utterly fallacious doctrine that I certainly should not notice it were it not that this book, on account of its somewhat original treatment of the subject, has obtained a degree of notice to which I do not consider it entitled.

This is so far from what really takes place in the drive at golf that I must quote James Braid from *Advanced Golf*, page 56. It will be seen from Braid's remarks that the whole idea of the golf drive from the moment the club starts on its downward course until the ball has been hit is that of supreme tension and concentration. It seems almost a work of supererogation to deal with a matter of such apparent simplicity, but when one sees matter such as that quoted published in responsible papers, one realises that in the interests of the game it is necessary to deal with statements which really, in themselves, ought to carry their own refutation.

Braid says: "Look to it also that the right elbow is kept well in control and fairly close to the side in order to promote tension at the top." Again at page 57 he says: "Now for the return journey. Here at the top the arms, wrists, body—all are in their highest state of tension. Every muscle and joint in the human golfing machinery is wound up to the highest point, and there is a feeling that something must be let go at once." On page 58 we read again: "No gentle starts, but hard at it from the very top, and the harder you start the greater will be the momentum of the club when the ball is reached." At page 60 again: "Keep the body and wrist under tension a little longer." At page 61 we read:

Then comes the moment of impact. Crack! Everything is let loose, and round comes the body immediately the ball is struck, and goes slightly forward until the player is facing the line of flight.

If the tension has been properly held, all this will come quite easily and naturally. The time for the tension is over and it is allowed its sudden and complete expansion and quick collapse. That is the whole secret of the thing—the bursting of the tension at the proper moment—and really there is very little to be said in enlargement of the idea.

Now here it will be seen that Braid's idea, which is undoubtedly the correct one, is that the golfer's muscles, and it follows naturally also his mind, are in a state of supreme tension until the moment of impact, *when that tension is released*. On the other hand, we are told by our psychologist that the moment which Braid says is the moment of the collapse of the tension is the moment for introducing tension and concentration. The statement is, of course, an extremely ridiculous one, especially coming, as it does, from one who presumes to deal with the psychology and physiology of golf, because nothing could be further from the truth than the statement made by him. It proves at the very outset that he has not a correct idea of the golf stroke, and therefore any attempt by him to explain the psychology of golf, if golf may be said to have such a thing as a psychology, is worthless.

Our author has also explained how, in the downward swing, the speed of the club is increased by extremely minute gradations. I have elsewhere referred to this fallacy, but the matter is so important that I shall quote James Braid again here. At page 57 Braid says:

Nevertheless, when commencing the downward swing, do so in no gentle, half-hearted manner, such as is often associated with the idea of gaining speed gradually, which is what we are told the club must do when coming down from the top on to the ball. It is obvious that speed will be gained gradually, since the club could not possibly be started off at the quickest rate. The longer the force applied to the down swing the greater does the speed of the momentum become, but this gradual increase is independent of the golfer, and he should, as far as possible, be unconscious of it. What he has to concern himself with is not increasing his speed gradually, but getting as much of it as he possibly can right from the top.

I am very glad indeed to be able to quote Braid to this effect, for if we may accept his statement on this matter as authoritative, it completely refutes one of the greatest and stupidest fallacies in golf, which is this particular notion of gradually increasing one's speed by any conscious effort of muscular regulation. Now if Braid's statement with regard to the muscular work in the downward portion of the drive is correct, it follows naturally that the explanation of the "mystery of golf" offered by the author is merely an explanation of a mystery which he has evolved from the innermost recesses of his fertile imagination; but it is needless for me to say that unless such an idea as this is absolutely killed, it would have a most pernicious effect upon the game of anyone who came within its influence.

It may seem, perhaps, that I attach too much importance to the writing of a gentleman who describes himself as "a duffer." It is not so. No one knows better than I do the influence of printed matter. I have lived amongst print and printers and newspapers for very many years, and needless to say I know as well as any man that not everything which one sees in print is true, but the remarkable thing about the printed word is that even with one who is absolutely hardened and inured to the vagaries and extravagances and inaccuracies of those who handle type, the printed word carries a certain amount of weight.

We can easily understand, then, that to those who are not so educated the printed word is much more authoritative. Therefore, even if the circulation of a book or a paper may be very little, it is always worth the while of one who has the interests of the game at heart to do his best not only to scotch, but absolutely to kill false and pernicious teaching of this nature, for the simple reason that even if a book circulates but a hundred copies, or a newspaper two hundred and fifty, which is giving them both a remarkably small circulation, it is impossible, or at least extremely improbable, that any man will be able, by his influence, *to follow each copy of that book or that newspaper*. There is a great fundamental truth underlying this statement. If one gives a lie a day's start, it takes a terrible lot of catching. This is particularly so in connection with printed matter, and I have had some very remarkable illustrations of the fact. So strongly, indeed, do I realise this fact, that although I believe that I am as impervious to adverse criticism as any one, I will never, if I can prevent it, allow criticism of that nature which I consider inimical to the interests of any subject with which I am dealing, to get the slightest possible start. Indeed, I have, on occasions, carried this principle still further, and when I have known that matter was to appear which I considered of a nature calculated to produce wrong thought in connection with a certain subject I have taken means to see that it did not appear.

It will be readily understood that I am not now referring to matters of personal criticism. I refer particularly to matters of doctrine published and circulated, even in the smallest way. If, for the sake of argument, the paper which spreads that false doctrine circulates only twenty copies, *one cannot follow every copy*, and to do one's work thoroughly and effectively it would be necessary to follow every copy of that paper in order to counteract the pernicious influence which it might otherwise exercise. Taking this view of the effect of printed matter, it should be apparent that I consider the time devoted to refuting injurious and false teaching well spent.

In the attempted explanation of the mystery of golf there are some amazing statements which tend to show clearly that the author of that work has not that intimate knowledge of sport generally which is absolutely essential to any man who would even essay satisfactorily to do what the author is trying to do. Let us examine, for instance, such a statement as this: "Indeed, the difficulties of golf are innumerable and incalculable. Take, for example, that simple rule 'Keep your eye on the ball.' It is unheard of in tennis; it is needless in cricket; in golf it is iterated and reiterated times without number, and infringed as often as repeated." Can anyone imagine a more wonderful statement than this? In tennis, by which from subsequent remarks it is clear that the author means lawn-tennis, and also indeed in tennis, it is, of course, a fundamental rule that one must keep one's eye on the ball. It is repeatedly drilled into every player, and even the most experienced players by neglecting it sacrifice points.

Lifting one's eye is one of the most prolific causes of missed smashes and ordinary volleys, while the half volleys which are missed through not attempting to follow out this universal rule are innumerable. We are told that it is "unheard of in cricket." This indeed is a marvellous statement. No coach who knows his duty in tennis, lawn-tennis, cricket, racquets, or in fact any game where one plays at a moving ball, could possibly have gone more than about half a dozen lessons, if so many, without impressing upon his pupil the extreme importance of endeavouring to watch the ball until the moment of impact. This, of course, is a counsel of perfection, and is not often perfectly carried out, for various reasons which I shall deal with in my chapter on "The Function of the Eyes."

For one who has attempted a critical analysis of the psychology of golf the author makes some wonderful statements. Speaking about "looking" *versus* "thinking," and keeping one's eye on the ball, the author says: "As a matter of fact, instead of *looking*, you are *thinking*, and to *think*, when you ought to *play*, is the madness of mania." It should be fairly obvious to anyone who does not even profess to be capable of analysing the emotions of a golfer that to look it is necessary to be thinking—to be thinking about looking, in fact; that it would be impossible to look without thinking; that indeed the looking is dependent upon the thinking, or, as our author would probably put it, he must will to look—not only must he will to look, but he must will to hit. Those are the two important things for him to will—to look and to hit. Now those things cannot be done without thinking, and yet we are told that to *think* when you ought to *play* is "the madness of mania."

The author goes on to give what he calls a very "simple and anatomical reason" for this inability to see one's ball when one is thinking instead of looking. He says:

Everybody has heard the phrase "a vacant stare." Well, there actually is such a thing as a vacant stare. When one's thoughts are absorbed in something other than the object looked at, the eyes lose their convergence—that is to say, instead of the two eyeballs being turned inwards and focussed on the thing, they look straight outwards into space, with the result, of course, that the thing looked at is seen indistinctly. I am convinced that this happens to many a grown-up golfer. He thinks he is looking at his ball, but as a matter of fact he is thinking about looking at his ball (a very different affair), or about how he is going to hit it, or any one of a hundred other things; and, his mind being taken off that supreme duty of doing nothing but *look*, the muscles of the eye are relaxed, the eyeballs resume their natural position and stare vacantly into space.

It will probably not be news to most of us that there is such a thing as "a vacant stare." We probably remember many occasions when, "lost in thought," our eyes have lost their convergence, but it will indeed be news to most of us that it is the supreme duty of the eyes to do nothing but *look*.

We are now face to face with this fact according to this analysis. The author quotes the great psychologist, Höffding, as saying, "We must will to see, in order to see aright." We now, by a natural and logical process of reasoning, have the golfer settled at his ball, his address duly taken, his eye fixed on the ball, and he is in the act of "willing" to see as hard as he can. So far so good. Let us presume that he *is* seeing. Now we are told that to think when he ought to play is the madness of mania. We must presume that it will now be impossible to proceed with his stroke unless he "wills" to move. How will he "will to move" without thinking? If anybody can explain to me how a golfer can play a stroke without willing to hit as well as to look, I shall indeed consider that he has explained at least one mystery in golf.

We are told that

... if during that minute interval of time which elapses between the commencement of the upward swing of the club and its impact with the ball, the golfer allows any one single sensation, or idea to divert his attention—consciously or unconsciously—from the little round image on his retina, he does not properly "perceive" that ball; and of course, by consequence, does not properly hit it.

Notwithstanding this statement, we see that the author tries to implant in the mind of the golfer the idea that during his downward stroke arms and hands are receiving innumerable orders "at intervals probably of tens of thousandths of a second," and that at the moment of impact with the ball the mind has to become suddenly concentrated and the muscles suddenly contracted. He surely will allow that in this advice he is trying to impart at least one single sensation or idea which is sufficient to ensure that he will "not properly perceive that ball, and of course, by consequence, that he will not properly hit it."

Here is another paragraph worthy of consideration: "But if one tautens any of the muscles necessary for the stroke, the stroke is spoiled." I think I have already quoted James Braid on the subject of tension in the drive, to show that this statement is utterly fallacious, and that without very considerable tautening of the muscles it would be impossible to produce a golf drive worthy of the name.

The strangest portions of this alleged explanation of the mystery of golf are always when it comes to the question of practical golf. Let us consider briefly such a statement as the following:—

Both sets of stimuli must be intimately and intricately combined throughout the whole course of the swing; the wrists must ease off at the top and tauten at the end. The left knee must be loose at the beginning, and firm at the finish, and the change from one to the other must be as deftly and gently, yet swiftly wrought, as a crescendo passage from pianissimo to fortissimo on a fiddle.

We have already seen what James Braid says about the golf stroke—that from the top of it right to the impact the muscles must be in a state of the fullest tension; while it is of course well known now that the left knee is never at any time in the stroke what is described as loose, for from the moment that a properly executed golf drive begins, the weight proceeds towards the left foot and leg, and therefore it would be impossible to play a proper drive with the left knee "loose." I deal fully with this subject in my chapter on "The Distribution of Weight."

PLATE II.

HARRY VARDON

Stance and frontal address in short put.

As we proceed with the consideration of this work we find that golf is indeed a mystery to the author. We are informed that "the golf stroke is a highly complex one, and one necessitating the innervation of innumerable cerebrospinal centres; not only hand and eye, but arms, wrist, shoulders, back, loins, and legs must be stimulated to action. No wonder that the associative memory has to be most carefully cultivated in golf. To be able, without thinking about it, to take your stance, do your waggle, swing back, pause, come forward, hit hard, and follow-through well over the left shoulder, always self-confidently—ah! this requires a first-class brain, a first-class spinal cord, and first-class muscles"; and—if I might be pardoned for adding it—a first-class idiot. Nobody but a first-class idiot could possibly do all these things without thinking of them, except probably that brilliant follow-through "well over the left shoulder!"

I have heard many things enunciated by people who considered themselves possessed of first-class brains, but this is absolutely the first time that I have ever heard of a good follow-through "well over the left shoulder." A good follow-through "well over the left shoulder" generally means a most pernicious slice. Any follow-through at any game goes after the ball. What happens when that is finished is merely a matter of individual style and the particular nature of the stroke which has been played. The club, in some cases, may come back over the left shoulder; in other cases it may point right down the course after the ball; in another it may swing practically round the body. It is little touches such as these which show the lack of practical acquaintance with the higher science of the game. No one acquainted with the inner secrets of golf could possibly refer to that portion of a stroke which is coming back from the hole as "the follow-through."

As an instance of absolutely ridiculous nonsense I may quote the following:

What the anatomists say is this, that, if the proper orders are issued from the cortex, and gathered up and distributed by the corpora striata and the cerebellum, are then transferred through the crus cerebri, the pons varolii, the anterior pyramid and the medulla oblongata, down the lateral columns of the spinal cord into the anterior cornua of grey matter in the cervical, the dorsal and the lumbar region, they will then "traverse the motor nerves at the rate of about 111 feet a second, and speedily excite definite groups of muscles in definite ways, with the effect of producing the desired movements."

Of course this to the ordinary golfer is absolute nonsense, but to the skilled anatomist and student of psychology, who may also be a golfer, it is worse than nonsense, for the simple reason that assuming that the measurement of the speed at which these orders travel has been even approximately measured as proceeding at the rate of "about 111 feet a second," it is obvious that such a rate of progression would be, by comparison with the speed at which the golf stroke is delivered, merely a gentle crawl.

One might be excused if one thought that this book was merely a practical joke perpetrated by a very ingenious person at the expense of golfers, but I do not think we should be justified in assuming that, for then we should have to speak in a very much severer manner than we are doing; for when one reads about such things as "the twirl of the wrists, the accelerated velocity, and the hit at the impact," one is justified in assuming that even if the psychology of the author were sound, his knowledge of the mechanical production of the golf drive is extremely limited. He says:

Psychologists are, I believe, agreed that there is in the mind a faculty called the Imagination. Indeed, there has been a whole essay written and printed on "The Creative Imagination."

Even if psychologists are not agreed on this subject we could, I think, take as irrefutable evidence of the existence of the "creative imagination" the work under notice.

It is curious to find one who is endeavouring to analyse matters which are psychologically abstruse exhibiting the greatest confusion of thought. Let us take an illustration. He says: "We misuse words; we construct an artificial and needless barrier between mind and matter. By 'matter' we simply mean something perceptible by our five senses." Let us consider this statement. It would be impossible to imagine a more sloppy definition of matter. According to this definition of matter, glass is not matter, for it is not perceptible by our sense of hearing, smelling, or tasting. It is evident that the author means—which in itself is erroneous—to define matter as something which is perceptible by one of the five senses, but in an analytical psychologist so overwhelming an error is inexcusable. It is manifest that he is not equal to the task which he has set himself in any way whatever. He says that "The golfer, strive as he may, is the slave of himself." Here again we have a gross libel on the poor golfer. The ordinary golfer is not the slave of himself. He is the slave of thoughtless persons who write about things which they do not understand, and, in some cases, the bond-servant of those who write without understanding of the things which they do very well.

Elaborating this idea, the author proceeds: "It is not a matter of want of strength or want of skill, for every now and again one proves to oneself by a superlative stroke that the strength and the skill are there if only the mind could be prevailed upon to use them." This truly is a marvellous statement from one who essays a critical analysis of anything. It is undoubtedly possible that a player might be set at a tee blindfolded, and provided his caddie put down sufficient balls for him to drive at and he continued driving long enough, he would unquestionably hit "a superlative stroke." Would this prove that the strength and the skill are there? I wonder if our author has ever heard of such a thing as "a ghastly fluke"?

A little later on we read: "Time and time again you have been taught exactly how to stand, exactly how to swing," and he then proceeds to wonder how it is that the unfortunate golfer is so prone to error. The reason is not far to seek. It is found in the work of such men as our author, and others who should know much better than he; it is found in the work of men who teach the unfortunate golfer to stand wrongly, to swing wrongly. These, in company with our author, will be duly arraigned in our chapter on "The Distribution of Weight." That is the plain answer why golfers do not get the results which they should get from the amount of work and thought which they put into their game, for golfers are, unquestionably, as a class, the most thoughtful of sportsmen. If they were not, a book such as I am dealing with could not possibly have secured a publisher. Continuing his argument on this subject he says:

... and yet how often it has taken three, four, and even five strokes to cover those hundred yards! It would be laughable were it not so humiliating—in fact, the impudent spectator does laugh until he tries it himself; then, ah! then he, too, gets a glimpse into that mystery of mysteries—the human mind—which at one and the same time wills to do a thing and fails to do it, which knows precisely and could repeat by rote the exact means by which it is to be accomplished, yet is impotent to put them in force. And the means are so simple. So insanely simple.

To which I say, "And the means are indeed so simple, so sanely simple." It is writers who do not understand the game at all who make them insanely complex. As a definite illustration of what I mean let me ask the man who writes that the golfer who desires to drive perfectly "could repeat by rote the exact means by which it is to be accomplished" where, in any book by one of the greatest golfers, or in his own book, the golfer is definitely instructed that his weight must not at any time be on his right leg. In fact the author himself, in common with everybody who has ever written a golf book, *deliberately misinforms the golfer in this fundamental principle.*

How, then, can a man who claims to be possessed of an analytical mind say that the ordinary golfer could repeat by rote the exact means by which anything is to be accomplished when it is now a matter of notoriety that practically the whole of the published teaching of golf is fundamentally unsound?

Speaking of the golfer's difficulties in the drive the author says, "The secret of this extraordinary and baffling conflict of mind and matter is a problem beyond the reach of physiology and psychology combined." Yes, there is no doubt that it is; but it is a matter which is well within the reach of the most elementary mechanics and common sense.

It will probably seem that I am dealing with this attempt to explain the mystery of golf very severely, but I do not feel that I am treating the matter too strictly. Golf is enveloped and encompassed round about with a wordy mass of verbiage. All kinds of men and some women, who have no clearly defined or scientific ideas, have presumed to put before the unfortunate golfer directions for playing the game which have landed him in a greater maze of bewilderment than exists in any other game which I know. It is obvious that if a man is both "a duffer" and a slow thinker it will be unsafe for him, until he has improved both his game and his mental processes, to attempt to explain the higher science of golf for anyone. It should be sufficient for him to study the mechanical processes whereby he may improve his own game until at least he has been able to take himself out of the class which he characterises himself as the duffers. To explain golf scientifically in the face of the mass of false doctrine which encumbers it, it is necessary that one should be, if not at least a quick thinker, an exact thinker, and that one should know the game to the core.

It seems to me that there is possibly a clue to the remarkable statements which we get in this book in the following quotation, which I take from the chapter on "Attention":

When I first rode a bicycle, if four or five obstacles suddenly presented themselves, these to the right, those to the left, I found I could not transfer my attention from one to the other sufficiently quickly to give the muscles the requisite orders—and I came a cropper ... and so with the golf stroke.

It seems to me that here we have the key of the author's difficulty. His mind was fixed on the obstacles—some to the right and some to the left. In similar circumstances most budding cyclists, and I have taught many, confine their attention to the clear path right ahead, and consequently the obstacles "these to the right, those to the left" do not trouble them. This, psychologically speaking, is a curious confession of the power of outside influences to affect the main issue. It seems to me that right through the consideration of this subject the author, like many other golfers, has been devoting his mind far too much to the things which he imagines about golf, instead of to the things which are, and they are the things which matter. No wonder, then, that he has "come a cropper."

There is a chapter called "The One Thing Necessary," which starts as follows: "But, since I stated that my own belief is that only one thing can be 'attended' to at a time, you will probably be inclined to ask me what is the most important thing? what precisely ought we to attend to at the moment of impact of club with ball? Well, if you ask me, I say *the image of the ball.*" This is really an astonishing statement. "At the moment of impact of club with ball" the image of the ball does not really matter in the slightest degree. As I shall show later on, the eye has fulfilled its functions long before the impact takes place. Also, of course, to the non-analytical mind it will be perfectly obvious that *the image of the ball* could be just as well preserved if the golfer had lifted his head three to six inches, but his stroke would have been irretrievably ruined.

Now, as a matter of fact, by the time the club has arrived at the ball it is altogether too late to attend to anything. All the attention has already been devoted to the stroke, and it has been made or marred. As we have clearly seen from what James Braid says about the stroke the moment of impact is the time when the attention and the tension is released, so it will obviously be of no service to us to endeavour forcibly to impress upon our minds in any way the image of the ball. If there is any one thing to think of at the moment of impact, the outstanding point of importance must be that the eyes should be in exactly the same place and position as they were at the moment of address.

Here is a most remarkable sentence:—

It is a pity that so many literary elucidators and explicators of the game devote so many pages to the subsidiary circumstances.... I wonder if they would pardon me if I said that, as a matter of simple fact, if one *attended to the game* (with all that that means), almost one could stand and strike as one chose, and almost with any kind of club.

There is a large amount of truth in this; but it comes most peculiarly from the author of this book, for of all the literary obfuscators whom I have ever come across I have never met his equal in attention to the "subsidiary circumstances" and neglect of the real game. Much time is wasted in an analysis of the nature of attention. Now, attention, psychologically, is somewhat difficult to define from the golfing point of view, but as a matter of simple and practical golf there is no difficulty whatever in explaining it. Attention in golf is merely habit acquired by practice and by starting golf in a proper and scientific manner. I shall have to deal with that more fully in my next chapter, so I shall not go into the matter here. Suffice it to say that lifting the eye at golf is no more a lack of attention than is lifting the little finger in the club-house. It is merely a vice in each case—a bad habit, born probably of the fact that in neither case did the man learn the rudiments of the game thoroughly.

We are told that "the arms do not judge distance (save when we are actually touching something), nor does the body, nor does the head. The judging is done by the eyes"; but we must not forget that the arms accurately measure the distance.

CHAPTER III

PUTTING

The great mystery to me, not about golf, but about the work of the greatest golfers, is the attitude which they all adopt with regard to putting. Now, putting may quite properly be said to be the foundation of golf. It really is the first thing which should be taught, but, as a matter of fact, it is generally left until the last. Practically all instructors start the player with the drive. It is beyond question that the drive is the most complex stroke in golf, and it is equally beyond question that the put is the simplest. There can be no shadow of doubt whatever that the only scientific method of instructing a person in the art of playing golf is one which is diametrically opposed to that adopted by practically all the leading players of the world. Instead of starting the beginner at the tee and taking him through his clubs in rotation to the putting-green, the proper order for sound tuition would be to start him six inches from the hole and to back him through his clubs to the tee.

This is so absolutely beyond argument that I need not labour the point here, except in so far as with it is bound up the important question of attention—that is, of riveting one's eye and one's mind on the ball for the whole period employed in making the stroke. As I said in the preceding chapter, attention is habit. Attention includes the habit of keeping the eye on the ball and the head still until the stroke has been played. The best way of inculcating the vices of lifting the head and the eye during the stroke is to teach the player the drive first. It stands to reason that if a player is started, say, with a six-inch put, that he has at the moment of making his stroke both the ball and the hole well within the focus of his eyes, so that it is absolutely unnecessary for him to lift his eye in order to follow the ball. It therefore follows that he is not tempted to lift his eye.

Now, no player should be allowed to go more than two or three feet from the hole until he has learned to hole out puts at that distance with accuracy and confidence. By the time he is allowed to leave the putting-green, he will have acquired the habit of attention.

It will be clearly seen that, starting now from the edge of the green with his chip shot, he is much more certain of striking the ball and getting it away than he would be were he put on to the more uncertain stroke in the drive; so by a gradual process of education the player would come in time to the drive, and by the time he arrives at the most complicated stroke in the game—the stroke wherein is the smallest margin of error—he has cultivated the habit of attention, which includes keeping one's head still.

Of course, this is a counsel of perfection which one does not expect to find carried out, although a similar course is followed by all good teachers in every trade, profession, science, or game, but as I have said before, in golf there is a tremendous amount of false teaching which is generally followed. It is, however, a certainty that any beginner who has the patience, perseverance, and moral courage to educate himself on these lines, will find golf much easier to play than it would be if he had started, as nearly everybody wants to start, with "the swing." It is bad enough that putting should be relegated to the position it is, but the attitude of the great writers, or perhaps I should say the great golfers who have written books about golf, aggravates the offence, and forms what is to me the greatest mystery in connection with golf literature.

I shall give here what Braid, Vardon, and Taylor have to say about putting. Let me take Vardon first. At page 143 of *The Complete Golfer* he says:

For the proper playing of the other strokes in golf, I have told my readers to the best of my ability how they should stand and where they should put their feet. But except for the playing of particular strokes, which come within the category of those called "fancy," I have no similar instruction to offer in the matter of putting. There is no rule and there is no best way.

The fact is that there is more individuality in putting than in any other department of golf, and it is absolutely imperative that this individuality should be allowed to have its way.

And now comes a very wonderful statement:

I believe seriously that every man has had a particular kind of putting method awarded to him by Nature, and when he putts exactly in this way he will do well, and when he departs from his natural system he will miss the long ones and the short ones too. First of all, he has to find out this particular method which Nature has assigned for his use.

Again on page 144 we read that when a player is off his putting

... it is all because he is just that inch or two removed from the stance which Nature allotted to him for putting purposes, but he does not know that, and consequently everything in the world except the true cause is blamed for the extraordinary things he does.

Let us now repeat what James Braid has to say on the important matter of putting. On page 119 of *How to Play Golf* he says:

It happens, unfortunately, that concerning one department of the game that will cause the golfer some anxiety from time to time, and often more when he is experienced than when he is not, neither I nor any other player can offer any words of instruction such as, if closely acted upon, would give the same successful results as the advice tendered under other heads ought to do. This is in regard to putting.

Further on we are informed that "really great putters are probably born and not made."

So far we must admit that this is extremely discouraging, but there is worse to follow.

Let us now see what Taylor has to say about putting. At page 83 in his book, *Taylor on Golf*, and in the chapter, "Hints on Learning the Game," he says:

Coming back to the subject of actual instruction. After a fair amount of proficiency has been acquired in the use of the cleek, iron, and mashie, we have the difficulty of the putting to surmount. And here I may say at once it is an absolute impossibility to teach a man how to putt.

Even many of the leading professionals are weak in this department of the game. Do you think they would not improve themselves in this particular stroke were such a thing within the range of possibility? Certainly they would. The fact is that in putting, more than in aught else, a very special aptitude is necessary. A good eye and a faculty for gauging distances correctly is a great help, indeed, quite a necessity, as also is judgment with regard to the requisite power to put behind the ball. Unfortunately, these are things that cannot be taught, they must come naturally, or not at all.

All that is possible for the instructor to do is to discover what kind of a putting style his pupil is possessed of, offer him useful hints, and his ultimate measure of success is then solely in his own hands.

It is easy to tell a pupil how he must needs hold his clubs in driving or playing an iron shot, but in putting there is hardly such a necessity. The diversity of styles accounts for this, and in this particular kind of stroke a man must be content to rely upon his own adaptability alone.

Now in the same book on page 240, in the chapter on "The Art of Putting," we read:

The drive may be taught, the pupil may be instructed in the use of the cleek, the iron, or the brassie, but in putting he must rely upon his own powers of reducing the game to an actual science. The other strokes are of a more or less mechanical character; they may be explained and demonstrated, but with the ball but a few feet distant from the hole there are many other things to be considered, and hints are the only things that can be offered. The pupil may be advised over the holding and grip of the putter, but as far as the success of the shot is concerned it remains in his own hands.

In passing, I may remark that it seems to me that in this latter respect the put is not vastly different from any other stroke in golf, or indeed, for the matter of that, in any other game.

Continuing, Taylor says:

Putting, in short, is so different to any other branch of the game that the good putter may be said to be born, not made.

That this is really the case is proved by the fact that many of the leading players of the day, professionals and amateurs alike, are very frequently weaker when playing with the putter than when performing with any other of their clubs. Speaking solely of professionals, is it at all probable that this would be so were they capable of improving themselves in this particular department? Certainly not.

Now it will be admitted that this is a very gloomy outlook for him who desires to learn how to put. He is thrown entirely on his own resources. I must quote Taylor once again with regard to putting. He says:

And yet it is none the less true that to putt perfectly should be the acme of one's ambition. Putting is the most important factor of success, for it happens very frequently that a man may meet a stronger driver, or a better performer with the iron clubs, and yet wrest the leadership from him when near the hole.

There can be no doubt whatever of the truth of what Taylor says in this last paragraph—"Putting is the most important factor of success"; yet we are confronted with the amazing statement made by the three greatest masters of the game, men who between them have accounted for fourteen open championships, men whose living depends upon playing golf and teaching it, that "the most important factor of success" cannot be taught. There is no possible doubt about their ideas on this subject. They deliberately tell the unfortunate golfer, or would-be golfer, that good putters are born and not made, that putting cannot be taught, and that each person must be left to work out his own salvation.

It is admitted that putting is practically half the game. It has been well illustrated in the following way:—Seventy-two strokes is a good score for almost any course. The man who gets down in two every time is not a bad putter. This allows him thirty-six strokes on the green, which is exactly one-half of his score. Now what does this statement which is made by Braid, Vardon, and Taylor amount to? It is an assertion by them that they are unable to teach half of the game of golf, and *that* the most important half, for, as we have seen, Taylor says that it is "the most important factor of success." Now surely there is something wrong here. As a matter of fact it is the most absolute nonsense which it is possible to imagine. Putters are not born. They are made and shaped and polished to just as great an extent as any metal putter that ever was forged. Putting is the simplest and easiest thing in golf to learn and to teach, and it is positively wrong for men of the eminence in their profession which these players enjoy to append their names to statements which cannot but have a deleterious effect on the game generally, and particularly on the play of those who are affected by reading such absolutely false doctrine.

There are certain fundamental principles in connection with putting which cannot be disregarded. It is quite wrong to say that the first thing to consider is some particular idiosyncrasy which a man may have picked up by chance. The idea of Nature having troubled herself to allot any particular man or men, or, for the matter of that, women or children, any particular styles for putting is too ridiculous to require any comment. Needless to say, very many people have peculiarities which they exhibit in putting, as well as in other matters, but in many cases it is the duty of the capable instructor not to attempt to add the scientific principles of putting to a totally wrong and ugly foundation. The first duty of one who knows the game and how to teach it is to implant in the mind of his pupil the correct mechanical methods of obtaining the result desired. If, after he has done this, it be found that his natural bent or idiosyncrasy fits in with the proper mechanical production of the stroke, there is no harm in allowing him to retain his natural style; but if, for the sake of argument, it should be found that his natural method is unsuitable for the true production of the stroke, there is only one thing to do, which is to cut out his natural method, and make him put on the lines most generally adopted.

Nor is this difficult to do, for it stands to reason that anyone who is a beginner at golf has not already cultivated a style of his own.

The statements of these three great golfers are absolutely without foundation—in fact, they are indeed so far from the truth that I have no hesitation whatever in saying that in at least ninety per cent of the cases which come before a professional for tuition, if the subject is properly dealt with by an intelligent teacher, putting is, without any shadow of doubt, the easiest portion of golf to teach and to learn. In the face of the mischievous statements which have been so widely circulated in connection with the difficulty of learning the art of putting, one cannot possibly be too emphatic in stating the truth. In doing this, let it be understood that I am not stating any theory or publishing any idea which I am not prepared fully to demonstrate by practical teaching. It is a curious thing, but one to which I do not wholly object, that those who read my books seem to consider that they have a personal claim on my services as well, and it is no uncommon thing for me to receive visits from men who are in trouble about their putting, their drive, or their approach, and I have not, as a rule, any very great trouble in locating the seat of the difficulty.

The pernicious influence of such teaching as that which I have just quoted repeatedly comes before me. I know men who seem to consider that the chief art of putting in golf is bound up in another art, namely, the art of the contortionist, whereas, of course, nothing could be further from the truth. Putting, as I shall show later on, is an extremely simple operation. In fact its simplicity is so pronounced that little children, almost without instruction, do it remarkably well, because they do it naturally. It is only when people come to the game possibly rather late in life, and perhaps with habits acquired from other games, and in addition to this are told that they must evolve their own particular style, that we find the difficulty, for the style which is evolved is, in the vast majority of cases, no style at all, and the stroke is played unnaturally.

That is what I have to say with regard to the "difficulty" of putting. I shall, later on, deal with the principles involved in putting. It will, in the meantime, be sufficient for me to consider and criticise these statements generally. If this were my own uncorroborated opinion, it is possible that the definite statements of three men like Braid, Taylor, and Vardon might outweigh what I have said, although I do not believe that even in that case they would; for what I have quoted is such obvious nonsense that it would indeed be to me a mystery if any golfer possessed of ordinary common sense could accept any view of the matter other than that which I put forward.

However, when dealing with names like these, it is worth while to reinforce oneself. Let us see what James Braid has to say about the matter in *Advanced Golf*. At page 144, chapter x., dealing with "Putting Strokes," Braid says: "Thus practically any man has it in his power to become a reasonably good putter, and to effect a considerable improvement in his game as the result." Here is the message of hope to the putter. It will be remembered that Taylor states that the good putter may be said to be born, not made, and that Braid practically said the same thing. This, of course, is nonsense, and if any refutation were necessary, James Braid himself is the refutation. The first time I saw Braid putting, he was trying a Vaile putter for me at Walton-on-Heath. He came down on the ball before he had come to the bottom of his swing, and finished on the green quite two inches in front of the spot where the ball had been. Before I had reflected in the slightest degree, I came out quite naturally with the question, "Do you always put like that?" "Yes," said Braid in his slow, quiet way, "and it is the best way." By this time I had remembered who Braid was, and I did not pursue the subject any further, but I thought a good deal. I thought that Braid would, in due course, find out that it was not the best way, and I fully understood why he was such a bad putter.

Since then Braid has found out that his method was wrong. He has altered it, and now plays his puts in the only proper way, which I shall refer to later on. As everybody knows, Braid is now a very fine putter—*but he was not born so*. If ever there was an illustration of a fine putter made out of a bad putter, James Braid is the outstanding example, and James Braid is the answer to Taylor's question as to whether a professional can improve his putting or not. Any professional whose putting is bad can improve it by using his brains, because when a professional puts badly it is rarely a question of his hands, his eye, or his wrist being wrong. The seat of the deficiency is much deeper than that.

Let us now see what James Braid has to say about putting. At page 146 of *Advanced Golf* he practically eats his own words. This is what he says:

Of course, they say that good putters are born and not made, and it is certainly true that some of the finest putters we know seem to come by their wonderful skill as a gift, and nowadays constantly putt with an ease and a confidence that suggest some kind of inspiration. But it is also the fact that a man who was not a born putter, and whose putting all through his golfing youth was of the most moderate quality, may by study and practice make himself a putter who need fear nobody on any putting green. I may suggest that I have proved this in my own case. Until comparatively recently there is no doubt that I was really a poor putter. Long after I was a scratch player I lost more matches through bad putting than anything else. I realised that putting was the thing that stood in the way of further improvement, and I did my best to improve it, so that to-day my critics are kind enough to say that there is not very much wanting in my play on the putting green, while I know that it was an important factor in gaining for me my recent championship.

So I may be allowed the privilege of indicating the path along which improvement in this department of the game may best be effected; and what I have to say at the beginning is, that putting is essentially a thing for the closest mathematical and other reckoning. It is a game of calculations pure and simple, a matter for the most careful analysis and thought.

Now here at least we have common sense with regard to putting. Braid holds himself out as an example of the bad putter turned into the good putter. He does not, it is true, tell us why he was a bad putter and how he changed his bad methods to his present excellent method, but I have already given the key to that. I shall, however, deal with it more fully when I come to the question of the practice of putting. Braid says on page 147 of *Advanced Golf*, still speaking of putting, that "the mechanical part is comparatively simple." He continues: "Putts most generally go wrong because the strength or the line, or both, were misjudged, and they were so misjudged because the different factors were not valued properly, and because one or two of them were very likely overlooked altogether."

I think very few golfers will be inclined to dispute the opening statement that "Putts most generally go wrong because the strength or the line, or both, were misjudged." I may say that I never heard of a put which went wrong for any other reason. If the strength and the line are both right, one always has an excellent chance of ending in the tin! Braid tells us again on page 148

... that what I call the mechanical part of putting—the hitting of the ball—is simple and sure in comparison with the other difficulties that are presented when a long putt has to be made; yet it is hardly necessary to say to any experienced golfer that there are absolutely thousands of players who fail in their putting, not because of any lack of powers of calculation or a good eye, steady hand, and delicacy of touch, but simply because they have fallen into a careless way of performing this mechanical part, and of almost feeling that any way of hitting the ball will do so long as it is hit in the right direction and the proper degree of strength is applied.

Again Braid says on page 149:

Absolutely everything depends on hitting the ball truly, and the man who always does so has mastered one of the greatest difficulties of the art of putting. A long putt can never be run down except by a fluke when the ball has not been hit truly, however exactly all the calculations of line and strength have been made.

Now the point which I am making, and I hope making in such a manner that no one will ever dare even to attempt to refute it, is the fact that the mechanical operation of putting is one of extreme simplicity, entirely devoid of mystery, and capable of acquirement by persons even of a very low order of intelligence. I want to make it plain beyond the possibility of doubt that putting is the foundation of golf and that it can be very easily learned, provided always that the instructor has a proper idea of the mechanics of the put. Generally speaking, when one uses the word "mechanics" a golfer is afraid that he is about to receive some abstruse lecture illustrated by diagrams and mathematical formulæ, but it is not so. It is essential to a thorough knowledge and enjoyment of the game of golf that the golfer should understand the mechanics of putting.

James Braid says that it is a matter of mathematics and calculation, and he is not far wrong; but the mechanics of the put are of such extreme simplicity that no golfer or would-be golfer need be discouraged because one refers to the elementary science which is involved in the making of the perfect put. Rather let him be thankful that he has James Braid's corroboration of the fact, which I have for many years past tried to impress upon golfers, that the main thing to strive at in connection with improving their game is a proper understanding of the mechanical principles involved in producing the strokes. Until the ordinary golfer has this he will not progress so rapidly as he may desire.

I think that we may now consider that it *is* possible to teach people how to put; so, having disposed of this fable, let us consider the most important features of putting. I do not propose here to illustrate the manner in which the stroke is to be played. I have done that fully in *Modern Golf* and in other places. I am here concerning myself mainly with the fundamental principles. When these are properly grasped, and these I may say are practically all arm-chair golf, any person of ordinary intelligence should be able to go on to a putting green, and by carrying them out become quite a good putter.

Let us first consider the manner of propulsion of the ball. Provided, for the sake of argument, that the putting-green were an enlarged billiard table with a hole in the middle of it, and one were given a penny to put into that hole from the edge of the table, how would one endeavour to do it? There can be but little doubt one would try to *roll* the coin into the hole. Now that is the way one must try to put. The ball must be rolled up to the hole. At first sight this seems an entirely superfluous direction. The reader may say: "In what other way may puts be sent into the hole than by rolling?" Practically, there is no other way. It was the idea that there was another and a better way of holing puts than by rolling them into the hole which made James Braid in the old days such a bad putter, for in those days James Braid putted with what is commonly called "drag." It is no uncommon thing to hear men who play a very fine game of golf advise players to "slide" their long puts up. Put in another way this simply means—advice to play a long put with what is known as "drag."

PLATE III.

HARRY VARDON

23

At the top of his swing, showing his weight mainly on the left leg. This characteristic is very marked in Vardon's play.

It is well known that at billiards one can hit very hard and direct one's ball very well by playing with a large amount of drag, and golfers have carried this notion on to the putting-green, but, it must be admitted, in a very thoughtless manner. In billiards the ball is very heavy in proportion to its size. It moves on a perfectly level and practically smooth surface, the tip of the cue is soft and covered with chalk, which gives a splendid grip on the ball, and the blow is delivered very far below the centre of the ball's mass, and is concentrated on a particular point. In golf it is impracticable in putting to get very much below the centre of the ball. It can be done, of course, with a club which is sufficiently lofted, but the moment this is done there is a tendency to make the ball leave the green, which is not calculated to make for accuracy. Moreover, be it remembered that the contact here is between two substances which are not well calculated to enter into communion, namely, the comparatively hard and shiny surface of a golf ball, and the hard and frequently unmarked face of a putter. Moreover, the golf ball is frequently marked with excrescences called brambles or pimples.

It is obvious that in many cases the first impact will be on one of these pimples, and also in many cases certainly not in a line dead down the centre of that bramble and in a line coinciding with the intended line of run of the ball. When the impact takes place in this manner it is obvious that, according to the simplest laws of mechanics, the put must be started wrongly. It is also obvious that if there is this tendency to go crookedly off the face of the club the ball will have more opportunity of getting out of the track, which it makes for itself in the turf, if it is lifted in any degree from the turf by a lofted club.

It is apparent that a golf ball on a putting green sinks into the turf. It is equally apparent that it will, on its way to the hole, make for itself a track or furrow of approximately the same depth as the depression in which it was resting when stationary. That furrow, to a very great extent, holds the ball to its course and minimises very much the faulty marking of a great many of the golf balls of to-day, so that it will be seen that the object of the player should be not in any way whatever to lift his ball from the green in the put, which is the invariable and inevitable tendency of attempting to put with drag by means of a lofted club. It is an extremely common error to suppose that a put played with drag hugs the green more than one played in the ordinary way, or with top. As a matter of incontrovertible fact, no put hugs the green more than a topped put. It would be easy enough to demonstrate this were it necessary to do so, but it is a matter which comes in more in the dynamics of golf, and possibly I shall have the space to treat of it further there. We may, for our immediate purpose, content ourselves with the fact that James Braid has abandoned putting with drag, and now rolls his ball up to the hole with, if anything, a little top, although, be it clearly understood, there is no apparent intention on his part to obtain this top, nor does he in *Advanced Golf* advocate that any attempt should be made to obtain top; but there can be no doubt whatever that the manner in which he plays his put tends to impart a certain amount of top to the ball, and this, of course, causes it to run very freely.

Now with regard to putting drag on a long put, it should be obvious to any one that, considering the roughness of the green, the extreme roughness of the ball and its comparatively light weight in proportion to its size, it would be impossible to make that ball retain any considerable measure of back-spin over any appreciable distance of the green. The idea is so repugnant to common sense and practical golf that it has always been a matter of astonishment to me to think that it could have prevailed so much as it has. However, there can be no doubt that putting under this utterly wrong impression has done a very great amount of harm to the game of players who might otherwise have been many strokes better. Let our golfer understand that there is one way, and one way only, in practical golf to put the ball, and that is to roll it up to the hole.

There is generally an exception to prove the rule, and if I can find an exception to this rule, it must be when one is trying to bolt short puts. Practically every one has experienced the difficulty of holing short puts, especially when the green is extremely keen. It is here that the delicacy of the stroke allows the ball and the inequalities thereof and any obstructions on the turf to exercise their fullest power to deflect the ball from the line to the hole. James Braid, in these circumstances, advises bolting one's puts. Needless to say, he explains that one should put dead for the middle of the hole, and by bolting, of course, is meant that one should put firmly so as to give the ball sufficient strength of run to overcome its inequalities or those of the turf.

This, unquestionably, is good advice; but if one puts at the hole in this manner and does not get it cleanly enough to sink into the tin at once, the ball with top will run round the edge of the tin and remain on the green. This is the only case in golf that I can call to mind where there is any use in putting drag on a put, and the reason for this is that the distance from the ball to the hole and the nature of the green is such that the ball is able to retain a very considerable portion of its backward spin, and upon contact with the rim of the hole, instead of having a forward run on it which enables it to hold up and so get away from the hole, the back-spin gets a grip on the edge of the hole and the ball falls in.

So far as I can remember, this is absolutely the only case in which drag of any sort may be considered useful in a put. When I say drag of any sort I am not, of course, referring to cutting round a put, or negotiating a stymie with back-spin, for neither of these strokes comes within the scope of my remark.

Having arrived at a decision as to the best method of sending the ball on its journey to the hole, we have now to consider a point of supreme importance in golf, and one which is not sufficiently insisted upon by instructors. This is, that at the moment of impact the face of the putter shall form a true right angle with the line of run to the hole. That is the fundamental point in connection with putting; but it is of almost equal importance that the right angle shall be preserved for as long a time as possible in the swing back, and also in the follow-through—in other words, the head of the putter should be in the line of run to the hole as long as possible both before and after the stroke. With this extremely simple rule, and it will be apparent that this can be just as well learned in an arm-chair as anywhere else, almost anyone could put well.

There is another point of outstanding importance. I have said that the head of the putter should form a right angle to the line of run to the hole. I shall be more emphatic still. Let us consider the line of run to the hole as the upright portion of a very long letter T laid on the ground. The top of the letter T will then be formed by the front edge of the sole of the putter, so that it will be seen that not only does the putter face form a dead right angle to the line of run to the hole, but that the line of run to the hole hits the putter face dead in the centre. For all ordinary putting, that is the one and only way to proceed. One reads in various books about putting off the heel, putting off the toe, and putting with drag. This is, comparatively speaking, all imbecility and theory. There is no way to put in golf comparable with the put that goes off the centre of the club's face. If we may treat the face of the putter as a rectangle, bisect it by a vertical line and also by a horizontal line, the point where these two lines cross each other will be the portion of the putter which should come into contact with the ball.

These are extremely elementary matters; but it is impossible, although they are so elementary, to exaggerate their importance, and it is amazing, considering their simplicity, how much neglected they are in all books of instruction, and, generally speaking, by all instructors. For instance, James Braid, at page 149, tells us:

Hitting the ball truly is simply a question of bringing the putter on to it when making the stroke to exactly the same point as when the final address was made, and of swinging the putter through from the back swing to the finish in a straight line.

This statement would be correct if the address had been made correctly in the first instance, but unless one has it in one's mind to make one's putter the top of the T—that is, the completion of the right angle to the line of run to the hole—the chances are that one's original address was wrong. Then it will be clearly seen that it is not "simply a question of bringing the putter on to it when making the stroke to exactly the same point as when the final address was made." The important point is to see that the final address is correctly made; but in no book which I have read—and I have read practically every book on golf which deserves to be read—do I find any simple and explicit directions for the mechanical portion of the put, which, as James Braid truly observes, is extremely simple.

Now for the idea of the stroke: The player will, of course, have learned his grip from some of the books on golf, or from a professional. He will in all probability have adopted the overlapping grip, for that grip tends, more than any other, to bring both wrists into action together; and there can, I think, be little doubt that for most people it is the better grip. Having obtained a good general idea of the simple mechanical operations involved in the contact of the club with the ball, the player now has to consider how that club moves where it is, if we may so express it, bound to him. Well, if he has even a rudimentary idea of mechanics, he will know that if he wishes to swing that club so that it may hit the ball in an exactly similar manner every time, he should suspend it on a single bearing, so that it would swing in a similar manner to the pendulum of a clock.

The perfect put, from a mechanical point of view, is made by a motion which is equivalent to the swinging of a pendulum. If, instead of allowing the weight of the pendulum to be, as it generally is, in the plane of the swing, it were turned round so that the flat side faced towards the sides of the clock, we should have a rough mechanical presentment of the golf club in the act of making a put. This is, of course, a counsel of absolute perfection. It is an impossibility to the golfer, both on account of his physical and physiological imperfections, and on account of the fact that the golfer practically never puts with an upright putter.

We are frequently told that a put is the only true wrist stroke in golf. As a matter of fact there is no true wrist stroke in golf, for it is evident that if one played the put as a true wrist stroke with a club whose lie is at a considerable angle to the horizontal, the centre of the circle formed by the club head will be away from the ball to such an extent that the instant the club head leaves the ball it must leave the line of run to the hole, and equally as certainly will it leave the line of run to the hole immediately after it has struck the ball.

Now this is not what we require, so it has come to pass that the put at golf is to a very great extent a compromise. It must, above everything, be a deliberate stroke with a clean follow-through. There must be no suggestion of reducing the put to a muscular effort. The idea of the pendulum must be preserved as much as possible, and the strength of the put regulated to a very great extent by the length of one's backward swing.

It is of the first importance that the body should be kept still during the process of putting, and it stands to reason that the wrists must also be kept as much as possible in the same place. If one finds that one has a marked tendency to sway or to move the body about, standing with one's feet close together will frequently correct this.

I have referred to the fact that the put is not a wrist stroke. As a matter of fact, the wrists must in all good putting "go out after the ball." By this is meant that at the moment of impact the wrists must in the follow-through travel in a line parallel with the line of run to the hole, and they must finish so that the club head is able, at the finish, to stay over the line of run to the hole. To do this, it is obvious that the wrists, after impact, must move forward. No true follow-through in the put can be obtained from stationary wrists. This may sound a little complicated. As a matter of fact it is nothing of the sort, and the action is very simple, very natural, and when properly played the ball goes very sweetly off the club and with splendid direction.

There is one good general rule for regulating the distance which one should stand from the ball in putting. When one addresses one's ball, one should be in such a position that the ball is right underneath one's eyes. To put it so that there can be no possible mistake as to what I mean, I may say that in most cases the eyes, the ball, and the hole should form a triangle in a plane at a right angle to the horizon. Now I know how hard it is for some people to follow a remark which refers to planes and right angles and horizons, so as this is a matter of extreme importance, and a matter where many beginners go absolutely wrong, I shall make it so plain that there is no possibility of misunderstanding what I mean.

Let us imagine a large, irregularly shaped triangle with the apex at the hole. We shall suppose, for the sake of argument, that this triangle is composed of cardboard, that it is a right-angled triangle, and that its base is 4' 6" wide. This triangle, then, is laid on the green so that its base is vertical, and the corner which is remote from the hole represents the ball, the upper corner of the base being, of course, the player's eyes.

I believe this to be a matter of very great importance, for here it will be seen that we have the eyes, the ball, and the hole all in the same plane. Some people like putting with very upright putters. For the purpose of experiment I had a perfectly upright putter made, but upright putters are, I think, open to this objection—one's body hangs too far over them, so that at the moment of striking the ball one is looking inwards towards the ball, for one's head projects beyond the line of run to the hole for a considerable distance. It will thus be seen that one is looking down one line to the hole, and putting over another. Needless to say, this cannot be good for direction. The eye, the ball, and the hole should undoubtedly be in the same plane, and that plane at right angles to the horizon.

As regards the position of the ball in relation to the feet there is some slight difference of opinion, but generally it may be said that about midway between the feet is the best position. If anything, the ball should perhaps be a little nearer to the left foot than to the right, but this is a matter upon which we cannot lay down any hard and fast rule. The main point for the player to consider will be how he can best secure the mechanical results which I have stated as being the fundamental requisites of good putting. The matter of an inch or two in his stance, nearer the hole or farther from it, is not of very great importance compared with this. Some players have an idea that they can secure a better run on their ball when putting by turning over their wrists at the moment of impact. This is one of the most dangerous fallacies which it is possible to conceive. The idea is absolutely and fundamentally erroneous.

If one desires to put any run on one's ball more than is obtained by the method of striking it which I have stated, it is always open to one to play the put a little after the club has reached the lowest point in its swing,—that is to say, as the putter is ascending, but this is practically unnecessary. If one requires a little more run on the ball it is best obtained by making the stroke a little stronger. Any attempt whatever to do anything by altering the angle of the face of the club during impact is utterly beyond the realm of practical golf.

There are many refinements in the art of putting which go somewhat beyond the fundamental principles laid down in this chapter, in that they call for cut of a particular kind; but for about ninety-five per cent of the puts which one has to play, practically nothing more need be known by the golfer than is here set out.

I am not here going to describe the method in which one cuts round a stymie, for I have done that very fully elsewhere; and, moreover, this does not so completely come within the scope of this work, for it enters much more into the region of practical stroke play than do the matters which I have treated of and which I intend to treat of in this book.

There is, however, one stroke which is played on the putting-green, yet is not truly, of course, a put. It is a stroke which I myself introduced into the game several years ago. This is the stroke which is now known as the Vaile Stymie Stroke. It is unique among golf strokes in that it is not an arc. Every known golf stroke before I introduced this stroke into the game was an arc of a more or less irregular shape, but it was an arc. The essence of my stroke is that it is produced in practically a straight line. For all ordinary stymies it is without doubt the most delicate and accurate stroke which can possibly be played, and the manner of playing it, after a golfer has once conquered the force of habit which tends to make him raise his club from the earth immediately he leaves his ball, is very simple. The mashie is drawn back from the ball in a perfectly straight line, and with the sole of it practically brushing, or no more than just clearing the green. It is then moved sharply forward, but instead of coming up with the ball after it has hit it, it passes clean forward down the intended line of flight in a perfectly horizontal line, provided always, of course, that the green is level, so that it finishes some inches down the line to the hole and practically touching the green. No attempt must be made to strike the ball or to take turf. The idea in one's mind should be to divide the ball from the green with the front edge of the sole.

Many mashies are not suitable for this shot, because the sole is not cut away enough on the back edge, as indeed the sole of every mashie should be; so it will frequently be found that the best club for negotiating stymies is the niblick, for its sole being cut away so much enables the front edge of the club to get well in underneath the ball. This is a matter of the very greatest importance in playing stymies, for the simple reason that it enables the player to put so much more of his force into elevation than is possible when the front edge of his mashie is cocked up, as it frequently is, by the breadth of the sole of the mashie; for in many cases when one is trying to play a stymie the rear edge of the sole of the club makes contact with the green first and tilts up the front edge, so that it is at least a quarter of an inch higher than it should be, and instead of striking the ball almost at the point where it is resting on the turf, it gets it fully a quarter of an inch to half an inch higher up. The consequence of this is that too much of the force of the blow goes into propulsion instead of elevation.

This means that if the stymie is close to the hole and there is only a very short run after the ball has got over the obstacle, the player invariably finds that with his imperfectly constructed mashie he cannot put enough stop on the ball, nor play the shot delicately enough to give it a chance to get into the hole, because the run is in many cases far too strong. Every golfer who desires to play a stymie well should see to it that he has a mashie with a very fine front edge, and that the sole is not flat in any part, but begins to curve away immediately it leaves the front edge. With the mashie constructed on these lines all ordinary stymies absolutely lose their terror if the shot is played as described.

The delicacy and accuracy of this stroke are remarkable. The direction is an astonishing illustration of the importance of the rule for putting which I have laid down, of keeping the front edge of the putter at a right angle to the line of run to the hole, both before and after impact. As the whole essence of playing this stymie stroke correctly consists of the straight movement of the face of the club sharply down the intended line of flight and run to the hole, the wrists have naturally to follow the head of the club in a line parallel with that made by the head of the club, and so accurate is the result that in any ordinary stymie if a wire were stuck on the top of the intervening ball, I would guarantee to hit the wire every time.

This stroke was a revelation to me of the importance of the principles which I am now enunciating, although, of course, I was well aware of their soundness before I discovered this stroke.

The usefulness of this stroke is not confined merely to playing stymies, but it makes a magnificent and accurate chip shot; or if one has a bad portion of green to put over one can, with this stroke, rely upon going as straight through the air as one can in the ordinary course over the green.

Lest anyone should think that this is merely a theoretical stroke, let me tell how I came to introduce it into the game of golf. I had used the stroke myself for some time. One afternoon I was in the shop of George Duncan, the famous young Hanger Hill professional. It was raining heavily, and to pass the time I was knocking a ball about on the mat. Presently I set up a stymie and said to Duncan:

"Show me how you play your stymie, George."

"Oh, just in the usual way," said Duncan.

"Well, show me," I said.

Duncan took his mashie and played the stymie shot perfectly, "just in the usual way."

"There is a much better way of playing a stymie than that," I said, and I set up the shot and showed Duncan how I played it by my method. Very few people can give George Duncan any points with the mashie. He got hold of the stroke at once, and he would hardly wait for the rain to stop before he went out on to the green to try it there. He plays the shot perfectly now, and maintains, as indeed I show in *Modern Golf*, that there is no stymie stroke to compare with it, and of that I have myself absolutely no doubt. In fact, so accurate is the stroke that if I found myself badly off my game with my putter, I should take my mashie and play this stroke, for as regards the fundamental principle of putting it is a wealth of instruction in itself.

Cutting round a stymie is nearly always included in the chapter on putting, but it is practically always a mashie stroke, and in the majority of cases is a very short pitch with a large amount of cut. On account of the loft of the mashie the club gets well in underneath the ball, and as the head of the club at the moment of impact is travelling in a line which runs at a fairly sharp angle across the intended line of flight and run of the ball it imparts a strong *side roll* to the ball. The cut on a golf ball in such a stroke as I am now describing resembles almost exactly the off-break spin in cricket. This means that the ball has a strong side-spin, so that the moment it hits the earth it endeavours to roll sideways, but the force of propulsion fights this tendency, and the resulting compromise is a curve which enables the ball to get round the intervening obstacle, and, if the stroke is well executed, to find the hole.

Almost all golf books instruct the player wrongly about this stroke. He is told to draw his hands in towards him at the moment of impact, and in some cases, even where the author calls his book *Practical Golf*, he is told to draw his hands in after impact. Both of these instructions are utterly wrong. There must be no conscious drawing in of the hands at the moment when one is trying to cut a put. All the cut must be done by the natural swing of the club across the intended line of run of the ball: in other words, the cut is a continuous process from the time that the club begins its swing until the time that it ends it. The fact that the ball is in the way of the face of the club as it crosses the intended line of run to the hole may be said to be merely an incident in the passage of the club head. Any attempt whatever to interfere with the natural swing of the club or to juggle with the ball during impact, or, more futile still, after impact, must result in irretrievably ruining the stroke.

The stymie shot which I have described will also be found of use a little farther from the green, and by means of it an excellent run-up shot, with most accurate direction, can be played. There is another way of negotiating a stymie which I have never seen described. It is pulling round a stymie. It will be obvious to any one acquainted with the game that cutting round a stymie is merely another form of slice; although of course the run of the ball is obtained in a different manner from the curve of the slice in the air, yet the method of production of the stroke is practically similar. So is it with pulling a put. There is no doubt that this can be done; but I think there is also no doubt that it is the most difficult method of negotiating a stymie which there is. The stroke is played, to all intents and purposes, as is the pulled drive. Some people imagine that it may be obtained by turning over the wrist at the moment of impact. This is quite an error, and is absolutely destructive of accuracy. As, in the cut put, the head of the club is travelling from outside the line across it, towards the player's side of the line at the moment of impact, so, in the pull, the head of the club must be travelling from the player's side of the line across and away to the far side of the line at the moment of impact. That is the secret of the pull either in the drive or the put.

I cannot refrain from quoting Vardon again. He says on page 148:

There should be no sharp hit and no jerk in the swing, which should have the even gentle motion of a pendulum. In the backward swing, the length of which, as in all other strokes in golf, is regulated by the distance it is desired to make the ball travel, the head of the putter should be kept exactly in the line of the putt. Accuracy will be impossible if it is brought round at all. There should be a short follow-through after impact, varying, of course, according to the length of the putt. In the case of a long one, the club will go through much further, and then the arms would naturally be more extended.

This is wisdom as regards the put. There can be no doubt whatever about this being practical golf of the highest order, but Vardon rather spoils it by the following sentence in which he says, "In the follow-through the putter should be kept well down, the bottom edge scraping the edge of the grass for some inches."

Now, if that means anything at all, it means that although Vardon's conception of the put and its execution in many ways is excellent, yet he has been making for years the error which made James Braid a bad putter—in other words, he has been putting with drag. It is well known that for a very long time Vardon's weakness was his putting; and I firmly believe that the secret of his bad putting was this low follow-through with his put. I think that Vardon's follow-through in his put is now not so low as it was, and the consequence is that his putting has improved.

Vardon continues:

It is easy to understand how much more this course of procedure will tend towards the accuracy and delicacy of the stroke than the reverse method, in which the blade of the putter would be cocked up as soon as the ball had left it.

What is more natural, then, than that the blade of the putter should be cocked up immediately after the ball has left it? That is exactly what should happen in the perfectly played put. Vardon has already told us that the put is to be played with the "even gentle motion of a pendulum." Let us suppose for a moment that it was the weight of the pendulum turned side-wise which had struck the golf ball. It stands to reason that immediately the weight, which in this case answers to the face of the golf club, has struck the ball and sent it on its way to the hole, the face begins to "be cocked up."

Vardon here makes a totally erroneous claim. He claims greater delicacy and accuracy for the put played with drag as against that played as Braid now plays his puts. There can be no shadow of doubt that the put played with drag, or with a low follow-through "scraping the top of the grass for some inches," partakes much more of the nature of a tap than does the put which is played with top or a perfectly horizontal blow. If Vardon has not completely realised this, as I think he has, he will, ere long, do so, as James Braid already has done.

I need not here deal with complicated puts; that is to say, puts of such a nature that one has to traverse one, two, or more slopes on the way to the hole. These puts do not, in themselves, contain any of the fundamental principles of golf. Each one stands entirely by itself, and these are absolutely matters in which nothing but practice on the green can be of any use. It will be obvious to any schoolboy that if he has to run across five little hills on his way to the hole, and that three of these slant one way and two the other; and if we say for the sake of example that they are all practically equal in their width and slope, that it will be a case of four of them cancelling out on the good old plus and minus system of our schoolboy days, and we shall then be left practically to calculate how much we will have to allow for putting across the incline of one slope. This is not a case which I should think of giving myself. I merely give it because I came across such an illustration given in a book which is supposed to cater for those who desire the higher knowledge of golf, but as a matter of practical golf these situations but seldom occur.

Allowing for the drop in a green when one is putting across the slope, requires a lot of practice, and is most absolutely and emphatically not a thing that can be learned in an arm-chair, or in any golf school. It must be learned on the green itself.

Although James Braid has remodelled his putting with such success, he still, to a certain extent, clings to his own idea of putting with drag. On page 154 of *Advanced Golf* he says:

For general use I am a strong believer in a putter having just a little loft. I know that some players like one with a perfectly straight face which does not impart the slightest drag to the ball, their theory being that such putters are capable of more delicate work than others, and that the ball answers more readily to the most delicate tap from them. There may be considerable truth in this, though, obviously, great skill and confidence on the part of the player are taken for granted.

And again he says:

The strength of long putts can generally be more accurately regulated with a lofted putter than with a straight-faced one.

He continues:

This is the kind of putter that I might recommend for what might be called a medium or average green, if there can be said to be such a thing; but I wish to point out that the putter that is the best suited to such a green is not so well suited to either a very fast green or a very slow one, and that in each of the latter cases the club best adapted to the circumstances is one with considerably more loft on it.

On page 56 he says:

Now in both these cases, when the greens are very slow and when they are extremely fast, the best putter for them is one with very considerable loft on the face, and it will often be found that there is nothing better than a fairly straight-faced iron, or an ordinary cleek, if it is big enough in the face to suit the player. With this club and its great dragging power, the effect seems to be practically to reduce the distance between the ball and the hole. Such is the drag that the ball is simply pushed over a considerable part of the way, and it is only when it is quite near to the hole that it begins, as it were, to run in the usual way. The fact is that for the first part of the journey the ball does not revolve regularly upon its axis, as it does when approaching the hole, but simply skates over the turf, and it will be found that with a little practice the point at which it will stop skating can be determined with very considerable exactness. When it does so stop there is still so much drag on it that it is very quickly brought to a standstill. Thus in both cases, of the very fast and the very slow green, the ball can be played without fear right up to the hole when the putter is so well lofted as I have recommended.

Here we are told that the ball "simply skates over the turf." As I have shown before, this is one of the greatest fallacies in golf. It is impossible to obtain any results by drag in a long put, which are not better obtained by simply rolling the ball up. Braid says that "with a little practice the point at which it will stop skating can be determined with very considerable exactness," and he goes on to say that "when it does so stop there is still so much drag on it that it is very quickly brought to a standstill."

This is obviously nonsense. It is the drag on the ball which makes it do any skating which may take place. It is obvious that when the skating has ceased the drag has stopped exerting its influence. How, then, is it going to stop the ball from rolling in a natural manner?

We see here the mistake of importing into golf the well-known phenomena of billiards, but one would have thought that the experience of the billiard-table would have been sufficient to show the fallacy of this statement. The billiard player uses drag to enable him to play his ball fast and accurately, and there is no doubt that by means of this drag he does obtain very considerable accuracy, but directly the ball has ceased to "skate" he knows that that is the time when the drag has entirely departed from it, and that the momentum has conquered the friction caused by the back-spin; in other words, the drag having accomplished its work has gone out of business, and all the run that is on the ball is derived from the remains of the momentum imparted to it.

I cannot say too emphatically that in my opinion this idea of putting with drag, or with any club having a loft more than that which barely enables one to see the face of it when it is properly soled, is dangerous and calculated to produce bad putting on the part of anyone who attempts it, even as it did in the case of James Braid himself.

There is one remark which James Braid makes about stymies which I should like to refer to here. Braid says: "Given complete confidence, the successful negotiation of a stymie is a much less difficult matter than it is imagined to be, though in the nature of things it can never be very easy." I must say that I differ entirely from Braid in this respect. I maintain that in the nature of things most ordinary stymies, when played in the manner which I advocate, are very easy. The difficulty of the stymie, provided one's club is properly built—and later on I shall refer to the construction of the mashie—is much exaggerated. Eight of ten stymies should present no more difficulty than an ordinary put. The only time a stymie should present a difficulty to the golfer is when the intervening ball is much nearer to the hole than to the ball which is stymied, so that the force required to get over the obstacle is so much that the player, after landing on the far side of the stymie, has too much power in his ball to give it a chance to settle in the hole, but even such a stymie as this may, if the ground be suitable, be overcome by lofting one's ball so as to drop on the hither side of the stymie, bound over it on its first bound, and continue on its way to the hole. This, probably, is one of the most difficult ways of negotiating a stymie; but as showing that it is eminently a matter of practical golf, I may say that I was illustrating the shot one day to a man who had practically just started golf. I showed him how to obtain the shot, and he did it at his first attempt. I advised him not to try again that day.

Braid continues:

I need not say that the pitching method is only practicable—and then it is generally the only shot that is practicable—when both balls are near the hole, and are so situated in relation to each other and to the hole that the ball can reach the latter as the result of such a stroke as enabled it to clear the opponent's ball.

Braid is, I think, referring to a clean pitch into the hole, although the photograph leaves this open to doubt. The pitching method is practicable when one is stymied in almost any position on the green, provided always, as I have said, that one has any chance whatever of pulling up in time to get into the hole after having got over the stymie. Let me give an example:— Supposing my ball were fifteen yards from the hole, that the green was absolutely level, and that I had a stymie ten inches or ten feet in front of me. I should not hesitate for a moment to use the shot which I have described as the best stymie stroke in the game. The ball in front of me, so far from being an obstruction, or in any way whatever putting me off, would, if anything, serve as a good line to the hole. I am aware that to many golfers who do not know this stroke, and comparatively few do, this will sound like exaggeration. I am prepared at any time to demonstrate the practical nature of what I am writing to any one of my readers who cannot obtain the results which I get with this stroke.

At the time that I introduced this stroke there was much controversy about it, and it was claimed that it was not a new stroke, but that it was exactly the same as the stroke played by all golfers when stymied. This, however, is quite an error. Speaking of the stymie shot, James Braid says

... it is just an ordinary chip up, with a clean and quick rise, the fact being remembered that the green must not be damaged. To spare the latter the swing back should be low down and near to the surface, which will check the tendency to dig. The thing that will ensure the success of the shot, so far as the quick and clean rise is concerned—and often enough success depends entirely upon that—is the follow-through. Generally, if the club is taken through easily and cleanly, all will be well.

It is obvious from this description that the stroke in Braid's mind is totally different from my stymie stroke. With the stroke as I play it, it is an absolute impossibility to "dig" into the green. One has no need to have any anxiety whatever about the green, for as the club travels parallel with the surface of the green all the time, it is obvious that no damage can ensue. If there is any deflection whatever from the straight line, it would be at the moment of impact, but even here it stands to reason that there is practically no deflection whatever; for even in a stroke played, relatively speaking, so slowly as is this shot, any alteration of the line of the stroke after it has once been decided upon, is quite improbable, but the dominant idea in the player's mind must be to insert the front edge of his mashie between the ball and the grass, and above everything to keep his follow-through as straight and as low along the surface of the green as was his swing back. It is this straight and low follow-through which gives the ball its "quick and clean rise," as Braid calls it. Curiously enough, the follow-through which Braid shows for his stymie shot, wherein the head of the club is raised from the green, will not give anything like so quick a rise or such delicacy of touch as will the stroke played in the manner which I have described, and, above everything, with the very low follow-through insisted upon by me.

PLATE IV.

HARRY VARDON

At the top of his swing in the drive. This is a fine illustration of Vardon's perfect management of his weight, which is mainly on his left foot. Observe carefully the wrists, which are in the best possible position to develop power.

I may mention that George Duncan never uses any other stroke than this when playing a short stymie. Indeed, he went so far as to say, when I was having him photographed for my illustrations in *Modern Golf*, that it was useless to take any exposures of the ordinary stymie shot, for the stroke introduced and described by me had practically put it out of the game.

Speaking of cutting round a stymie, James Braid says: "Whichever way I wish to make the ball curl, either round the other ball from the left-hand side, or from the right, I hit my own with the toe of the club, drawing the club towards me in the former case so as to make a slice, and holding the face of it at an angle—toe nearer the hole than the heel—in the latter, in order to produce a hook." And he adds: "You cannot do anything by hitting the ball with the heel of your putter," to which I would rejoin, nor can you do anything by hitting the ball with the toe of your putter, that you cannot do better by hitting it absolutely in the middle, which is the only proper part wherewith to hit a golf ball.

In the illustrations Braid is shown cutting the put with an aluminium club. One has no more chance of cutting round a stymie with a club of this nature than one would have with a bar of soap, for the simple reason that on account of the breadth of its sole—for if it be not an aluminium club, it is at least shaped on the same lines—it is impossible to get the face of the club sufficiently underneath the ball for the loft to get to work so as to impart that side roll which is of the essence of cutting

31

round. Braid says at page 171: "But remember that you can never get any work on the ball if the green is stiff." Now if this is so, I should like to know what use there is in attempting to put with drag?

I quite agree with Braid that it is practically impossible to get any work whatever on the ball with the club he is shown using. With such a club it would be still more difficult, if not absolutely impossible, to obtain any appreciable drag, but if, as Braid says, "you can never get any work on the ball when the green is stiff," how can he advise one to attempt to put with drag on a stiff green? To my mind this is absolutely bad and misleading advice.

In my chapter on the "Construction of Clubs" it will be seen that I advocate a short putter for short puts. In *Advanced Golf* James Braid has some interesting things to say about gripping low down. He says:

Many golfers grip very low down, even half-way between the leather and the head. If their putting when done this way is first class, nobody can say anything to them, but if it is not first class it may be pointed out to them that the system is absolutely bad. It may be allowed to pass for holing-out purposes; but for a putt of any length it cannot be good, for the club is not swung in the ordinary easy manner by which distance can be so accurately gauged. The ball is more or less poked along. When a man putts in this way he is putting largely by instinct, and even though he may generally putt well, his work on the greens cannot be thoroughly reliable. No putting is so good and consistently effective as is that which is done with a gentle even swing, which can be regulated to a nicety, and such putting is only possible when there is enough shaft left below the grip to swing with.

I am quite in accord with what James Braid says about this method of putting, and I do not for one moment think that the short grip should be used for approach puts, but I am sure the nearer one gets to the hole the closer one should get down to the ball. Braid deals further on with the question of shortening one's putter. He says:

As to the length of the shaft, many players, because they find that they always grip their putters a foot or so from the end of it, proceed in due course to have the best part of that foot cut off, or in purchasing a new putter they have the shaft cut very short. Are they quite satisfied that it is not better to have a fair amount of shaft projecting up above the place where they grip when that place is very low down?

The answer to this is that in many cases the wood which projects above the grip is very much in the way of true putting. Any golfer who is foolish enough to cut anything like a foot off any club without any compensation to the head in the way of balance must be expected to pay the penalty for his ignorance, and anyone having a club constructed for him on such a principle, or, rather, want of principle, will inevitably pay for it. Braid goes on to say:

Often enough no consideration is given to this point; it is not imagined that the shaft above the grip can serve any useful purpose. Yet it is constantly found that a putter cut down is not the same putter as it was before, not so good, and has not the same balance; and, again, many players must have been surprised sometimes, when doing some half-serious putting practice with a cleek, iron, or driving mashie, each club with its long shaft, to find out what wonderfully accurate work could be done in this way. The inference from all experience, having theoretical principle to back it, is that the top or spare part of the shaft acts as a kind of balance when the putter is gripped low down, and tends materially to a more delicate touch and to true hitting of the ball. A very little reflection will lead the reader to believe that this is so, and in some cases it may lead him towards a revision of his present methods.

Personally, I should not think that even "a very little reflection" would be necessary to induce anyone to believe that the top part of the shaft acts "as a kind of balance" when the putter is gripped low down, but it is quite obvious that it is possible to build a putter, let us say, for the sake of example, two-thirds of the length of an ordinary putter, which is just as perfectly balanced as the long club. This is not any question of theory—it is a matter of absolutely proved and tried practice in golf. One may have a perfect putter which will be ruined by taking a few inches off the shaft. The balance of that putter is probably irrevocably destroyed, unless, perchance, the owner is lucky in adding weight to the head in some way, but dealing with a putter like this is tricky work for one who does not understand it. The main point in connection with this matter of Braid's, which I have quoted, is that he gives a kind of qualified approval to the idea of the short putter for short puts. Personally, I think it is the soundest of sound golf, and I am inclined to think that before many years we shall see the shorter clubs used in their proper place when their value is more clearly understood.

Vardon has some very interesting things to say in his book, *The Complete Golfer*, on "Complicated Putts," while dealing with what he calls "one of the most difficult of all putts—that in which there is a more or less pronounced slope from one side or the other, or a mixture of the two." As he truly says, "In this case it would obviously be fatal to putt straight at the hole." He continues: "I have found that most beginners err in being afraid of allowing sufficiently for the slope"; and I have found that nine champions of ten make exactly the same error. It is as bad a fault at golf as it is at bowls to be "narrow," by which, in golf, is meant not to allow enough for the slope of the green, for it is obvious that if one is narrow one does not give the hole a chance any more than one does when one is short; so we may add to the stock maxim in putting "Never up, never in," another one, which is just as sound, "Never be narrow."

Vardon goes fully into the general principles underlying these complicated puts, but as I have already indicated, this is unquestionably a matter which can only be settled by practice on the green; but he also goes into the question of the manner in which the stroke should be played, and here we have a subject which legitimately comes within the scope of this work. He continues:

But there are times when a little artifice may be resorted to, particularly in the matter of applying a little cut to the ball. There is a good deal of billiards in putting, and the cut stroke on the green is essentially one which the billiard player will delight to practise, but I warn all those who are not already expert at cutting with the putter to make themselves masters of the stroke in private practice before they attempt it in a match, because it is by no means easy to acquire. The chief difficulty which the golf student will encounter in attempting it will be to put the cut on as he desires, and at the same time to play the ball with the proper strength and keep on the proper line. It is easy enough to cut the ball, but it is most difficult, at first at all events, to cut it and putt it properly at the same time. For the application of cut, turn the toe of the putter slightly outwards and away from the hole, and see that the face of the club is kept to this angle all the way through the stroke. Swing just a trifle away from the straight line outwards, and the moment you come back on to the ball draw the club sharply across it. It is evident that this movement, when properly executed, will give to the ball a rotary motion, which on a perfectly level green would tend to make it run slightly off to the right of the straight line along which it was aimed.

There are one or two points in this statement which are of very great importance. Vardon says: "For the application of cut turn the toe slightly outwards and away from the hole, and see that the face of the club is kept to this angle all the way through the stroke." This is absolutely unsound golf, for Vardon is advising his reader to play the put with the toe of the putter slightly outwards and away from the hole. It stands to reason that following this advice will put the face of the club in such a position that at the moment of impact it will be impossible for it to be at a right angle to the intended line of run to the hole, and this rule is, for all purposes of practical golf, invariable. It is obvious that coming on to the ball in the manner suggested must tend to push it away to the right—that is to say, it would have a strong tendency to go away to the right from the very moment of impact, which is not what is generally wanted in a good put; also playing the put in this manner tends quite naturally to decrease the amount of cut put on it. The idea that cut mashie shots and cut puts are played in this manner has arisen from the fact that very frequently the golfer addresses the ball with the toe of his club laid back a little, but by the time he has come on to the ball again he has corrected this. In many cases, if it were not for laying the toe of the club back a little in this manner, golfers would be inclined, although as a matter of strict and accurate golf they should not be, to drag the ball across towards the left of the hole.

Vardon says: "Swing just a trifle away from the straight line outwards, and the moment you come back on to the ball draw the club sharply across it." Now here again we see this outstanding error of practically every man who ever put pen to paper to write about golf, which is that in producing the cut, whether it be in a put or a sliced drive, something is done intentionally to the ball during the period in which the ball and the club are in contact. This is absolutely wrong. I have explained before that the cut put, and indeed all cut strokes at golf, are produced by the club swinging across the intended line of flight or run at the moment of impact, and the amount of cut depends entirely upon the angle and the speed at which the club head is travelling across the intended line of flight or run. It is obvious that the amount of cut must also, to a certain extent, depend on the amount of loft of the club, for the greater the loft of the club the greater assistance will the golfer who is applying the cut obtain from the weight of the ball.

Vardon goes on to say: "It is evident that this movement, when properly executed, will give to the ball a rotary motion, which on a perfectly level green would tend to make it run slightly off to the right of the straight line along which it was aimed"; but as I have already shown, the unfortunate part of it is that a put so played would not go down the straight line which every golfer desires that his put shall go on; nor indeed on anything like it.

Also it is a delusion that it is possible with any of the ordinary putters to obtain a cut of a sufficiently pronounced degree to remain on the ball, especially on the bramble balls, for any appreciable distance. Vardon supposes a case of a steep but even slope all the way from the ball to the hole, and he gives instructions as to how to put across this slope with cut so as to hold the ball up against the slope. He says:

But we may borrow from the slope in another way than by running straight up it and straight down again. If we put cut on the ball, it will of itself be fighting against the hill the whole way, and though if the angle is at all pronounced it may not be able to contend against it without any extra borrow, much less will be required than in the case of the simple putt up the hill and down again.

In the first place, I may remark that we do not generally borrow from a slope "by running straight up it and straight down again." The path of the ball is generally, almost from the time it is hit, a curve, and a gradual curve, in which one sees to it that the ball is at its farthest from the straight line to the hole somewhere about midway to the hole. But this idea of putting cut on the ball with a putter, which is sufficient to hold the ball up against the hill for any appreciable distance, is practically a delusion. I can easily understand that if Vardon plays the cut put as he himself directs it to be played, that he thinks that cut administered to a ball by an ordinary putter may have a very great effect in holding the ball up against the side of a hill for a considerable distance, but this really is not so. Putting, however, as Vardon instructs one to put for obtaining cut, would in itself punch the ball up against the slope of the hill, and I can easily believe that anybody who plays the put like this, thinking that he is obtaining cut by so doing, will be under the impression that cut is a very useful thing for holding the ball up against the slope in this manner, whereas he is in effect simply punching the ball up against the slope—in other words, he is playing a put, which if the green were perfectly level, would be yards off his line to the hole and to the right of it.

Vardon goes on to say:

Now it must be borne in mind that it is a purely artificial force, as it were, that keeps the ball from running down the slope, and as soon as the run on the ball is being exhausted and the spin at the same time, the tendency will be, not for the ball to run gradually down the slope—as it did in the case of the simple putt without cut—but to surrender to it completely and run almost straight down.

There is a fundamental error here, for Vardon states that practically the spin on the put and the run on the ball will be exhausted at the same time, but it is an utter impossibility to calculate with any exactness whatever as to what happens in such a case. Vardon knows no more about it than any other golfer, and all that any golfer knows about this is extremely little, so that to advise anyone to attempt to hold his ball up against a slope by the application of cut with any ordinary putter, particularly a broad-soled putter, is to invite him to play his shot blindfolded.

Vardon does not mention the length of the put which he considers it possible to play with this cut, but in his diagram he shows a put which would conceivably be quite a long put, let us say for the sake of argument fifteen or sixteen feet, but the theory would be just as bad if it were much less. He says:

Our plan of campaign is now indicated. Instead of going a long way up the hill out of our straight line and having a very vague idea of what is going to be the end of it all, we will neutralise the end of the slope as far as possible by using the cut and aim to a point much lower down the hill—how much lower can only be determined with knowledge of the particular circumstances, and after the golfer has thoroughly practised the stroke and knows what he can do with it. And instead of settling on a point half-way along the line of the putt as the highest that the ball shall reach, this summit of the ascent will now be very much nearer the hole, quite close to it in fact. We putt up to this point with all the spin we can get on the ball, and when it reaches it, the forward motion and the rotation die away at the same time, and the ball drops away down the hill, and, as we hope, into the hole that is waiting for it close by.

Vardon may well say "as we hope," for the put described by him has no more chance of being brought off on a putting-green than Vardon has of winning another open championship from an aeroplane. To speak of putting a ball in this manner, and treating it with such magic that when it gets up by the hole the forward motion and the rotation die away at the same time, is not practical golf, but absolute moonshine, for it would be an utter impossibility to persuade any golf ball which has ever been made to receive from any known form of golf club sufficient cut to make it behave in the manner described. The theory of the thing on paper is to a very great extent right, with the exception that the cut described would require to be obtained by a club with a much greater loft than any ordinary putter; but it is evident that putting with putters such as those which Braid or Vardon use, it would be an utter impossibility to get cut on the ball which would stay with the ball during a long put and exert much influence in holding the ball up against any appreciable slope, for with these putters, which have not much loft, it is evident that any spin whatever which is imparted to them by drawing the putter across the line of run at the moment of impact will be mainly about a vertical axis which is, in effect, the spin of a top. It is evident that as the ball progresses across the green there will be a very strong effort indeed on the part of the ball, following its friction on the green, to wear down this vertical motion and convert it into the ordinary roll of a naturally hit put.

Even when one is putting with a highly lofted club and with a tremendous amount of drag on a perfectly flat green, the drag goes off the ball in a wonderfully short space of time, and here, of course, one is using a spin which is analogous to the drag of the billiard player, for it is pure back-spin which is fighting in the same plane the forward roll of the golf ball. Therefore it is reasonable to suppose, and indeed it is undoubted that the ball would be more likely to retain this pure back-spin for a much longer time than would the ball with the side-spin imparted by the putter, for the spin which is imparted by the putter does not directly fight the forward progress of the ball as it is spinning across the plane of the roll which the ball desires to take, whereas, as I have before pointed out, the ball played with drag is absolutely fighting the forward roll of the golf ball. It therefore would for a very short distance skid over the putting-green, but those who only theorise about these matters have a ridiculously exaggerated idea of the influence of drag on the golf ball.

I have made it very plain, and I cannot emphasise the matter too strongly, that any attempt whatever in long puts to use drag or cut of any kind is to be deprecated.

There is another matter which Vardon refers to that I should like to notice here. He says:

One of the problems which strike most fear into the heart of the golfer is when his line from the ball to the hole runs straight down a steep slope and there is some considerable distance for the ball to travel along a fast green. The difficulty in such a case is to preserve any control over the ball after it has left the club, and to make it stop anywhere near the hole if the green is really so fast and steep as almost to impart motion of itself. In a case of this sort I think it generally pays best to hit the ball very nearly upon the toe of the putter, at the same time making a short, quick twitch or draw of the club across the ball towards the feet. Little forward motion will be imparted in this manner, but there will be a tendency to half lift the ball from the green at the beginning of its journey, and it will continue its way to the hole with a lot of drag upon it. It is obvious that this stroke, to be played properly, will need much practice in the first place, and judgment afterwards, and I can do little more than state the principle upon which it should be made.

I need hardly do more here than repeat what I have said in the case of the other puts. Any attempt to jump a ball at the beginning of the put on a steep, fast green is about as bad a method of starting it as one could possibly imagine. There is nothing for it but the smooth, steady roll. Few greens, of course, are so steep that the ball will run off them unless it has been very violently played, so the ordinary principles of putting still hold good here—there is one way to play that put, and that is not from the toe, but from the centre, of the club, and as straight as may be for the hole, having due regard to the slope or slopes of the green. Of course, as I have before indicated, if one is very near to the hole, certainly not more than two to three feet at the utmost, one may be excused for putting straight at the hole with drag, because a ball can be made to carry its drag for about this distance.

CHAPTER IV

THE FALLACIES OF GOLF

The fallacies of golf, as it has been written, are so numerous and so grave that it would be impossible to deal with them fully in a chapter, so I must here content myself with dealing generally with them, and specifically with a few of the minor mistakes which are so assiduously circulated by authors of works on golf. I shall take them as they come, in their natural order. We shall thus have to deal with them as follows: slow back, the distribution of weight, the sweep, the power of the left hand and arm, the gradually increasing pace of the sweep, the action of the wrists, and the follow-through.

We have then to consider, in the first place, the oft-repeated and much-abused instruction to go "slow back." The rhythm of many a swing is utterly spoilt by this advice, for the simple reason that, generally speaking, it is tremendously overdone. Anyone who has ever seen George Duncan's swing could surely be excused for thinking that slow back must be a delusion. It is not, however, given to everybody to be able to swing with the rapidity and accuracy which characterise Duncan's wonderful drive. In fact, the most that can be said in favour of going slowly back is that all that is necessary in the way of slowness is that the player shall not take his club up to the top of his swing at such a rate that in his recovery at the top of the swing he will have any unnecessary force to overcome before he begins his downward stroke.

It stands to reason that there must be at the top of the swing a moment wherein the club is absolutely stationary. The whole object of slow back is to ensure that at this moment, which is undoubtedly a critical portion of the swing, there shall be no undue conflict of the force which brought the club head up to the top of the swing and that force which the golfer then exerts to start the club on its downward journey. When this has been said, practically all that need be said about slow back has been said.

It is almost a certainty that slow back, as one of what Vardon calls the parrot cries of the links, has done more to unsettle the drives of those who follow it, and the tempers of those who follow them, than any other of the blindly followed fetiches of golf. Let it be understood then, once and for all, that undue slowness is almost as great a vice as undue quickness. What the player must, in every case, strive after is the happy medium. It is an absolute impossibility to preserve the rhythm of a swing that goes up with the painful slowness and studied deliberation which we so frequently see as the precursor of a tremendous foozle.

Incorporated in this overdone injunction, "slow back," we have the idea of swinging the club away from the ball. In various places we are told plainly that the club is not to be lifted away from the ball, but that it must be swung back, whereas, of course, there can be no doubt whatever that the club is lifted back, and is started on its journey by the wrists.

It is obvious that no swing can be started from the lowest point in an arc. If, for example, we take the pendulum of a clock which is hanging motionless, it will be impossible to swing it one way or the other without lifting it. Equally obvious is it that the golf club must be lifted away from the ball.

"As you go up, so you come down" is another revered fallacy. We are clearly, and probably rightly, instructed, when driving, to take the club away from the ball in the line to the hole produced through the ball.

We do this going back comparatively slowly until we are compelled to leave the line, or rather the plane, of the ball's flight. So at the moment of making our first divergence from the straight swing back, we import into our arc a sudden and pronounced curve. On the return journey, the downward swing, we travel all the way at express speed. He would indeed be credulous and unanalytical who could believe that the arc of the downward swing coincides with that of the upward, when the upward swing is carried out according to the generally published theory, which, of course, it generally is not. The theory is only good in so far as it goes to inculcate the idea of remaining in the line to the hole both before and after impact as long as possible.

The next fallacy which we have to deal with is the matter of the distribution of weight in the drive. Practically every book that has been published misinforms the golfer on this point, which is a matter of fundamental importance in the game; in fact, it is of such great importance that I shall not deal with it fully here, but shall reserve it for my next chapter wherein I shall give the views of the leading exponents of the game on this all-important subject, and shall then show wherein I differ from them.

Let us consider that we have now arrived at the top of the swing. Every author of a golf book insists upon the fact that the drive at golf is a sweep and not a hit. James Braid, in chapter viii. of *How to Play Golf*, writing of "The Downward Swing," says:

The chief thing to bear in mind is that there must be, in the case of play with the driver and the brassie, no attempt to *hit* the ball, which must be simply swept from the tee and carried forward in the even and rapid swing of the club. The drive in golf differs from almost every other stroke in every game in which the propulsion of a ball is the object. In the ordinary sense of the word, implying a sudden and sharp impact, it is not a "hit" when it is properly done.

The impact in the golf drive has been measured by one of our most eminent physicists to occupy one ten-thousandth of a second. I think we may take this as "implying a sudden and sharp impact." Braid goes on to say, "when the ball is so 'hit' and the club stops very soon afterwards, the result is that very little length, comparatively, will be obtained, and that, moreover, there will be a very small amount of control over the direction of the ball."

This might be right, but it seems almost unnecessary to point out that when a ball has been struck at the amazing speed which such a brief contact indicates, there is extremely little probability that the club will stop "very soon afterwards"—in fact, it would be almost a matter of impossibility to induce a club which had been used for delivering a blow at the rate which this brief time indicates, to stop very shortly afterwards. The head of a golf club at the moment of impact with the golf ball is travelling so rapidly that a camera timed to take photographs at the rate of one twelve-hundred-and-fiftieth of a second's exposure, gets for the club head and shaft merely a vague swish of light, while the ball itself, if it is caught at all, appears merely to be a section of a sperm candle, so rapid is its motion. I am speaking now of a photograph taken at this extremely rapid rate when the photographer is facing the golfer who is making the stroke, but so rapid is the departure of the ball from the club that even when the photographer is standing in a straight line directly behind the player, the ball still presents the appearance of a white bar.

It should then be sufficiently obvious to anyone that so far as regards the stroke "implying a sudden and sharp impact," the golf stroke, probably of all strokes played in athletics, is, at the moment of impact, incomparably the most rapid. It has, therefore, always seemed to me a matter for wonder to read that this stroke is a sweep and not a hit.

Braid here says one thing which is of outstanding importance as exploding another well-known fallacy. It is as follows:

While it is, of course, in the highest degree necessary that the ball should be taken in exactly the right place on the club and in the right manner, this will have to be done by the proper regulation of all the other parts of the swing, and any effort to direct the club on to it in a particular manner just as the ball is being reached, cannot be attended by success.

This is so important that I must pause here to emphasise it, because we are frequently told, and even Braid himself, as I shall show later on, has made the same mistake, that certain things are done during impact, by the intention of the player during that brief period, in order to influence the flight of the ball. There can be no greater fallacy in golf than this. No human being is capable of thinking of anything which he can do in this minute fraction of time, nor even if he could think of what he wished to do, would it be possible for his muscles to respond to the command issued by his mind.

To emphasise this, I must quote from the same book and the same page again. Braid says:

If the ball is taken by the toe or heel of the club, or is topped, or if the club gets too much under it, the remedy for these faults is not to be found in a more deliberate directing of the club on to the ball just as the two are about to come into contact, but in the better and more exact regulation of the swing the whole way through up to this point.

That is the important part in connection with this statement of Braid's. Many a person ruins a stroke, as, for instance, in endeavouring to turn over the face of the putter during the moment of impact, through following, in complete ignorance, the teaching of those who should know better, and they then blame themselves for their want of timing in trying to execute an impossibility, whereas the remedy is, as Braid says, not in trying to do anything during the moment of impact "but in the better and more exact regulation of the swing the whole way through up to this point."

Braid is here speaking of the drive, but what applies to the drive applies to every stroke in the game, with practically equal force. He continues:

The object of these remarks is merely to emphasise again, in the best place, that the despatching of the ball from the tee by the driver, in the downward swing, is merely an incident of the whole business.

"Merely an incident of the whole business." It is impossible to emphasise this point too much. The speed of the drive at golf is so great that the path of the club's head has been predetermined long before it reaches the ball, so that, as I have frequently pointed out in the same words which Braid uses in this book, the contact between the head of the club and the ball may be looked upon as merely an incident in the travel of the club in that arc which it describes.

The outstanding truth of this statement will be more apparent when we come to deal with the master strokes of the game. Braid's remarks here are so interesting that I must quote him again:

The player, in making the down movement, must not be so particular to see while doing it that he hits the ball properly, as that he makes the swing properly and finishes it well, for—and this signifies the truth of what I have been saying—the success of the drive is not only made by what has gone before, but it is also due largely to the course taken by the club after the ball has been hit.

In this paragraph Braid is making a fallacious statement. It will be quite obvious to a very mean understanding that nothing which the club does after it has hit the ball and sent it on its way, can have any possible effect upon the ball, and, therefore, that the success of the drive cannot possibly in any way be "due largely to the course taken by the club after the ball has been hit." The success of the stroke must, of course, be due entirely to the course taken by the club head prior to and at the moment of impact. What Braid would mean to express, no doubt, is that if the stroke has been perfectly played, it is practically a certainty that what takes place after the ball has gone, will be executed in good form.

I have frequently seen misguided players practising their follow-through without swinging properly, whereas it is, of course, obvious that a follow-through is of no earthly importance whatever except as the natural result of a well-played stroke; and provided that the first half of the stroke was properly produced, it is as certain as anything can be that the second half will be almost equally good, but it is certain that nothing which the club does after contact with the ball has ceased can possibly influence the flight or run of the ball. It is, for instance, obvious that if a man has played a good straight drive clean down the middle of the fair-way, his follow-through cannot be the follow-through of a slice, because the pace at which he struck that ball must make his club head go out down the line after the ball. Similarly, if a man has played a sliced stroke, it stands to reason that after the ball had left his club, his club head could not, by any possible stretch of imagination, follow down a straight line to the hole.

These things are so obvious to anyone who is acquainted with the simplest principles of mechanics that it is strange to see them stated in the fallacious manner in which Braid puts them forth. Braid here says:

The initiative in bringing down the club is taken by the left wrist, and the club is then brought forward rapidly and with an even acceleration of pace until the club head is about a couple of feet from the ball.

Now here we see that Braid subscribes to the idea of "the even acceleration of pace," but it will be remembered that in a previous chapter I quoted him as saying that there must be no idea of gaining speed gradually; that one must be "hard at it from the very top, and the harder you start the greater will be the momentum of the club when the ball is reached." Here there is no notion whatever of even acceleration of pace. It is to get the most one can from the absolute instant of starting, but notwithstanding this, Braid tells us on page 57 of *How to Play Golf*: "When the ball has been swept from the tee, the arms should, to a certain extent, be flung out after it."

We observe here that Braid speaks of the ball as having been "swept from the tee," notwithstanding that in *Advanced Golf* at page 58 we read: "But when he has got all his movements right, when his timing is correct, and when he has absolute confidence that all is well, the harder he *hits*, the better." I have italicised the word "hits."

Now here we have the practical golf of the drive, and I cannot do better, in disposing of the fetich of the sweep, than re-echo Braid's words that for a golfer who wants to get a good drive, when he has everything else right, "the harder he hits the better."

As a matter of simple practical golf, provided always that a golfer executes his stroke in good form, it is impossible for him to hit too hard. This amazing fallacy of the sweep ruins innumerable drives, and renders many a golfer, who would possibly otherwise play a decent game, merely an object of ridicule to his more fortunate fellow-players who know that the golf drive is a hit—a very palpable hit—and not in any sense of the word a sweep.

Taylor also subscribes to the fetich of the sweep. At page 186 of *Taylor on Golf* he says:

In making a stroke in golf the beginner must feel sure that the correct method of playing is not the making of a hit—as such a performance is understood—but the effort of making a sweep. This is an all-important thing, and unless a player thoroughly understands that he must play in this style I cannot say I think the chance of his ultimate success is a very great one; it is an absolute necessity this sweep, and I cannot lay too much stress upon it.

He continues:

As a more practical illustration of my meaning, I will suppose that the player is preparing to drive. His position is correct, he is at the exact distance from the ball. All that is then necessary is that with a swinging stroke he should sweep the ball off the tee. But, if in place of accomplishing this sweep, the ball is *hit* off the tee—well, that may be a game, but it certainly does not come under the heading of golf.

Now we have already seen that James Braid in *Advanced Golf*, which was published after *How to Play Golf*, has abandoned the idea that the golf drive is a sweep. Taylor is wonderfully emphatic about the sweep, but I think it will not require much to convert any golfer, who is in doubt about the matter, to my views, for the comparative results obtained will speak for themselves. Moreover, if there is any one man more than another who is a living refutation of the sweep notion that man is J.

H. Taylor. It is impossible to watch him driving, and to know the power which he gets from his magnificent forearm *hit*, without being absolutely convinced that the true nature of the golf drive is a hit and not a sweep.

I do not find that Vardon subscribes to this idea of the sweep so definitely as does Taylor, and as did Braid in *How to Play Golf*, but he does unquestionably subscribe to the notion of the club gradually gathering speed in its downward course, for he says at page 69 of *The Complete Golfer*:

The club should gradually gain in speed from the moment of the turn until it is in contact with the ball, so that at the moment of impact its head is travelling at its fastest pace.

This, of course, in itself is correct, but there should be no conscious effort of gradually increasing the pace. As Braid says, "one must be 'hard at it' right from the beginning." The gradual and even acceleration of pace must unquestionably be left to take care of itself, and it has no more right to cumber the golfer's mind than has the idea when he is throwing a stone that his hand should be moving at its fastest when the stone leaves it.

PLATE V.

J. H. TAYLOR

At the top of his swing in the drive. Note here the position of Taylor's wrists. This is a matter of the utmost importance. Taylor is at times inclined to get a little on to his right leg, but probably here the weight is at least equally distributed, if not mainly on the left.

One of the most pronounced and harmful golfing fallacies is what I call "the fetich of the left." All of the leading writers and players do their best to instil into the minds of their pupils the idea that the left hand is the more important. This is a fallacy of the most pronounced and harmful nature, but it is of such great importance to the game that I shall not deal with it particularly here, but shall reserve it for a future chapter.

We now have to deal with the question of gradually increasing the pace in the drive. I have already, to a certain extent, dealt with this matter. Nearly all writers make a strong point of this fallacy. James Braid at page 54 of *How to Play Golf* says:

The initiative in bringing down the club is taken by the left wrist, and the club is then brought forward rapidly, and with an even acceleration of pace until the club head is about a couple of feet from the ball.

Here it will be seen clearly that Braid gives the idea that the player is, during the course of the downward swing, to exercise some conscious regulation of the increase of the speed of the head of the club.

Braid then goes on to say:

So far, the movement will largely have been an arm movement, but at this point there should be some tightening-up of the wrists, and the club will be gripped a little more tightly.

Anyone attempting to follow this advice is merely courting disaster. To dream of altering the grip, or of consciously attempting in any way to alter the character of the swing, or to introduce into the swing any new element of grip, touch, control, or anything else whatever, must be fatal to accuracy. Braid is much sounder on this matter in *Advanced Golf* where he makes no assertion of this nature, but tells the golfer that he must not bother himself with any idea of gradually increasing his pace.

This is what Braid says. It is worth repeating:

Nevertheless, when commencing the downward swing, do so in no gentle, half-hearted manner, such as is often associated with the idea of gaining speed gradually, which is what we are told the club must do when coming down from the top on to the ball. It is obvious that speed will be gained gradually since the club could not possibly be started off on its quickest rate. The longer the force applied to the down swing, the greater do the speed and the momentum become, but this gradual increase is independent of the golfer, and he should, as far as possible, be unconscious of it. What he has to concern himself with is not getting his speed gradually, but getting as much of it as he possibly can right from the top. No gentle starts, but hard at it from the very top, and the harder you start the greater will be the momentum of the club when the ball is reached.

That, I take it, is absolutely sound advice, for herein there is no stupid restriction whatever, nor should there be, for the golfer, from the time his club leaves the ball till it gets back to it, should have nothing whatever wherewith to cumber his mind but the one idea, and that is to *hit* the ball. Braid is surely wide of the mark when he says "but this gradual increase is independent of the golfer, and he should, as far as possible, be unconscious of it."

Firstly, it seems to me that this gradual increase is entirely dependent on the golfer, and secondly, that he should be extremely conscious of it, and the necessity for the production of it; but this is one of the many things in golf which, when once it is thoroughly learned, becomes so much a matter of second nature that the golfer does it instinctively. He knows perfectly well that he *will* gradually increase his pace until he hits the ball, but he will not have it in his mind that he *has* to do so. All this is bound to be in the hit. The man who drives the nail does not worry himself about gradually increasing the pace of the hammer head until it encounters the head of the nail. He knows he is doing it, but he does not worry himself about it as the golfer does about his similar operation. If the golfer would remember that nothing matters much except to hit the ball hard and truly, and would disregard a lot of the absolute nonsense about the domination of either one hand or the other, the gradual acceleration of speed, and many other items of a similar nature, he would find that his game would be infinitely improved.

I could quote pages from leading authors dwelling upon this matter of the gradual increase of speed, but I shall content myself with the passage which I have here quoted from James Braid, together with the remarks that I have made in former portions of this book, and may make in later chapters. Braid, in *Advanced Golf*, is sufficiently emphatic about this matter, and I think we may take it that in *Advanced Golf* he has given up the idea expressed in his smaller and less important work *How to Play Golf*, that one should trouble oneself with the even acceleration of speed. Whether he has or not, it is an absolute certainty that any idea of consciously regulating the speed of the club's head in the drive, will result in a very serious loss of distance, for it will be found an utter impossibility for anyone so to regulate the speed of the club without seriously detracting from the rate at which the head is moving through the air, and as every golfer knows, or should know, the essence of the golf stroke is, that the club shall be travelling at the highest possible speed when it strikes the ball. I am, of course, now speaking with regard to the drive, and obtaining the greatest distance possible, for that is generally the object of the drive.

The point which must be impressed upon the golfer is, that from the moment he starts his downward swing until he hits the ball, he has nothing whatever to think of except hitting that ball. Everything which takes place from the top of the swing to the moment of impact should practically be done naturally, instinctively, sub-consciously—any way you like, except by the exercise of thought during that process as especially applied to any particular portion of the action, for it is proved beyond doubt that the human mind is not capable of thinking out in rotation each portion of the golf drive as it should be played, during the time in which it is being played.

Probably there is more ignorance about the action of the wrists in golf than about any other portion of the golf stroke, yet this is a matter of the utmost importance, a matter of such grave importance that I must in due course deal with it more fully and examine the statements of the leading writers on the subject.

It is laid down clearly and distinctly by nearly all golf writers and teachers that the golfing swing must be rhythmical, that there must be no jerking, no interruption of the even nature of the swing—in fact, we have seen that according to many of them the stroke is a sweep and not a hit, yet we are told distinctly that at the moment of impact a snap of the wrists is introduced. This must tend, of course, to introduce a tremendous amount of inaccuracy in the stroke at a most critical time, and it is therefore a matter worthy of the closest investigation.

We have already dealt with the fallacy of the sweep. It is a curious thing that although the leading golfers and authors pin their faith to the sweep as being the correct explanation of the drive in golf, yet nearly all of them, when it comes to a question of the stroke with the iron clubs, say that it is a hit. Now the stroke with the iron clubs is identical with the stroke with the wooden clubs, with the exception, of course, in many cases, that it has not gone back so far; but the action of the wrists is, or should be, the same. The club head travels, stroke for stroke, relatively in exactly the same arc; the beginning of the stroke and finish of the stroke is the same, and all the other laws, *mutatis mutandis*, apply. It would, indeed, be hardly too much to say that there is at golf only one stroke, and that every other stroke is a portion of that stroke, that stroke being, of course, the drive. If we take the drive as the supreme stroke in golf, and examine the nature of the stroke, we shall find that in that stroke is included practically every stroke in the game. That being so, it seems to me extremely hard to differentiate between a cleek shot and a drive—in fact, in so far as regards the production of the shot it is impossible to differentiate between them. If the one is a hit, the other is, and as a matter of fact, every stroke in golf, with the possible exception of the put, is a hit.

While we are speaking of hits and fallacies, it will not be out of place to devote a little attention to a point of extreme importance, and at the same time one which is very much neglected in most books dealing with the game. It is the ambition of many a golfer to get what he imagines to be "the true St. Andrews swing." They try this in numberless cases, where, from the stiffness of their joints and their build generally, it is impossible in the nature of things that they can obtain a very full swing. It is bad enough in these cases, for I speak now of people who have taken to the game when their frames have become so set that it is practically an impossibility for them to obtain anything in the nature of a full swing, but the attempt to obtain a long swing is not, however, confined to those who have taken to the game late in life, although it is with them naturally a greater error than it is with those who started the game when their limbs were more supple and their frames more easily adapted to the stroke.

If I allow myself to take my natural swing, I can nearly always see the head of the club at the top of my swing, and at the finish it is hanging nearly as far over the right shoulder as it was at the top of the swing over the left shoulder. There can be no doubt that with a swing like this, when one can control it sufficiently, one gets a very long ball, and there is a very delightful feeling in getting a perfect drive with such a swing, but from the very nature of the stroke it stands to reason that it must be less accurate than a much shorter and less showy effort.

Harry Vardon, in *The Complete Golfer*, asks: "Why is it that they like to swing so much and waste so much power, unmindful of the fact that the shorter the swing the greater the accuracy?" There can be no doubt whatever that in the very full swing, such as I have described, there is a waste of power and a sacrifice of accuracy. The rule which is true of the put, "Keep the head of the club in the line to the hole as long as you can, both before and after impact," is, *mutatis mutandis*, just as applicable to the drive.

Vardon continues:

Many people are inclined to ask why, instead of playing a half shot with the cleek, the iron is not taken and a full stroke made with it, which is the way that a large proportion of good golfers would employ for reaching the green from the same distance. For some reason, which I cannot explain, there seems to be an enormous number of players who prefer a full shot with any club to a half shot with another, the result being the same or practically so.

This is a curious remark to come from a golfer of the ability of Harry Vardon. I should have thought that the reason is sufficiently obvious. In playing a full shot the ordinary golfer feels that he has simply to get the most that his club is capable of. He therefore has no necessity to exercise any conscious muscular restraint. He plays the shot and trusts the club for his regulation of distance, but on the other hand, in playing a half shot he knows that he must exercise a good deal of judgment in applying his strength. It seems to me that there can be very little doubt that this is the reason why most golfers prefer the full shot. However that may be, it is beyond doubt that the desire, as Vardon puts it, "to swing so much" is the root cause of a vast amount of very bad golf.

"The shorter the swing, the greater the accuracy." This statement is as true of one's wooden clubs as it is of the iron. It should be printed as a text and hung in every golf club-house in the world, for there can be very little doubt that if the value of this advice were thoroughly realised, it would make golf pleasanter and better for every one. The blind worship of the full swing has been carried to a lamentable extent, and golfers who devote any thought to their game are beginning to understand that beyond a reasonable swing back, the surplus is so much waste energy, and, which is more important still, simply imports into the stroke a very much greater risk of error.

Many years ago I had a very remarkable illustration of the value of the short swing. A club mate of mine who was an adept at most games, and a champion at lawn-tennis and billiards, took it into his head to play golf. He was in the habit of thinking for himself. Of course, directly he started to learn golf, every one wished to make him tie himself into the usual knots, but he refused to be influenced by other people's ideas. He was content to work out his own salvation. He had watched many of the unfortunate would-be golfers contorting themselves in their efforts to reproduce what they took to be "a true St. Andrews swing," but determined that he would not follow their example.

He had conceived the idea that a drive was only an exaggerated put, and he made up his mind that he would proceed to exaggerate his put by degrees until he had reached the limit of his drive, and had found that no further swinging back would give him extra distance. He found that he got no farther with his drive when he carried his club right round to what is known as the full swing, than he did when his club head came from about the same height as his lawn-tennis racket did in playing the game which he knew so well.

When he had ascertained this he resolutely refused to increase the length of his swing. His club mates laughed at him and told him that it was not golf, that he was playing cricket, and many other pleasant little things like this. It had no effect whatever on him, for he knew that he was producing the stroke, in so far as he played it, exactly according to the best-known methods of the leading golfers of the world. He was content, in this respect, to follow known and accepted methods, but he would not in any way adopt the prevalent idea of a long swing.

Of course, he was laughed at and told that it was extremely bad form, but before long he "had the scalps" of his detractors. Then they were unable to say much about his golf, and he had very much the best of the argument when within a remarkably short space of time he won the championship of his Province. He proved quite conclusively to his own satisfaction, and to the great chagrin of many of the other players, the truth of Vardon's statement, "The shorter the swing the greater the accuracy."

There can be very little doubt that for those who take to golf late in life, especially if they have not played other games, the orthodox swing is a trap. A very great number of them get the swing, but not the ball. Many of them are, I am afraid, under the impression that the swing is of more importance than getting the ball away. Needless to say, they do not improve very much.

For those who take to golf late in life, I am sure that the great principle which makes for length and direction in any ball game that is, or ever was played, namely, keep in the line of your shot as long as you can both before and after impact, will be found as sound to-day as it always has been. Probably it will be found, and before very long too, that what is true for the late beginner is equally true for the greatest experts. As a matter of fact, some of our leading professionals are beginning to realise this already, particularly with regard to their iron play.

There are several very important points in connection with the short swing—points which, I believe, are of very great advantage to the golfer when once he has thoroughly grasped them. It is obvious that the shorter the swing is, the less necessity will there be for disturbing the position of one's feet. This naturally means that there is less likelihood of any undue swaying. Secondly, the shorter swing is naturally much more upright than the orthodox swing, and it comes more natural to a player to hit downwards at his ball when using it.

The first point which we have made is that the shorter swing produces less disturbance of the feet, because it is generally more upright than a corresponding length of the orthodox swing. In the flat swing there is less need to move the feet than there is in the upright swing. It is in the latter that one feels *soonest* the necessity for lifting the heel of the left foot, but in the short swing there is not the same necessity for balancing and pivoting on the toes as there is in the orthodox drive, for the swing back is not extended enough to require it. It should be apparent then that with the short swing much of the complexity of the golf drive is taken away.

I must make this a little clearer: practically all the golf books tell us that the left heel must come away from the earth when the arms seem to draw it. Anyone who follows this out in practice will find that it is impossible to preserve the rhythm of his swing. As a matter of practical golf the left heel must come away from the earth as soon as the head of the club leaves the ball. The motions are practically simultaneous. This matter of the management of the feet is probably the greatest contributing cause to the complexity of the golf drive, and the many erroneous descriptions of it which are given by our leading players. The principal reason for this is that it is the latitude given to the body by this shifting of the heels which accounts for the wrong transference of the weight to the right foot, and the equally wrong *lurching* on the left foot.

One would not, of course, for a moment advocate that the golfer's heels should be immovable, although James Braid does maintain, quite wrongly, I think, that the position of the feet at the moment of impact should be exactly the same as at the moment of address—that is, that the heels should be firmly planted on the ground. Although he says this, the instantaneous photographs of him in the act of driving show conclusively that he does not carry his theory into practice. Many of our greatest golfers are beginning now to see that the firmer the foundation, the more fixed and immovable the base, the steadier must be the superstructure—to wit, the chest and shoulders—and therefore the more constant will be the centre, if I may use the word in a general sense, of the swing.

41

The importance of preserving this "centre" cannot be overestimated, for golf is a game which demands a wonderful degree of mechanical accuracy, and it is only by observing the best mechanical principles that the best results can be obtained.

In the ordinary drive of the ordinary golfer there is usually an excessive amount of foot and ankle work, and, generally speaking, this foot and ankle work is not carried out in the best possible manner. There is, as a matter of fact, imported into the drive far too great an opportunity for the player to move his weight about. He takes full advantage of this, and the usual result is that he transfers his weight, when driving, to his right leg, which, as we shall see later on, is a very bad fault for the golfer to acquire. In the shorter swing there is much less temptation for the golfer to make the errors which are usually attendant on faulty footwork.

The other point of importance which I have mentioned in connection with the short swing, is that it comes much more naturally to the player to hit downwards. Probably not one golfer in a hundred realises that the vast majority of his strokes are made in a manner wholly opposed to the best science of golf. They are, generally speaking, *hit upwards*, whereas the most perfect golf drive should be hit downwards, and this statement is, in perhaps a less degree, true of nearly all golf strokes which are not played on the green.

The best way to get any ordinary ball into the air is to hit it upwards, but this general rule does not apply to the golf ball, for it is always stationary and is generally lying on turf. However, few players will trust the loft of the club to perform its natural function. They seem to forget that each club has been made with a loft of such a nature that, given the ball is struck fairly and properly, the loft may be relied on to do its share of the work. Consequently, as they will not trust the club to get the ball up, they hit upwards, and so, to a very great extent, minimise the amount of back-spin which might come from the loft, were the club travelling in a horizontal line at the moment of impact.

It is very much harder, however, to hit upwards with a short swing, or perhaps it would be more correct to say that there is a much greater tendency to hit the ball before the club head has got to the lowest point in its swing. We must emphasise this point, for it is of great importance, as back-spin is of the essence of the modern game, and particularly of the modern drive. If, therefore, we can show that the short swing tends more naturally to produce back-spin than does the full St. Andrews swing, and at the same time to give greater accuracy as regards direction, it need hardly be stated that it will not be long before we have the scientific players giving the stroke the place to which it is undoubtedly entitled in the game of golf.

CHAPTER V

THE DISTRIBUTION OF WEIGHT

The distribution of weight is of fundamental importance in the game of golf. If one has not a perfectly clear and correct conception of the manner in which one should manage one's weight, it is an absolute certainty that there can be no rhythm in the swing. One often sees references to the centre of the circle described by the head of the club in the golf swing. It will be perfectly apparent on giving the matter but little thought that the head of the golf club does not describe a circle, but it is convenient to use the term "centre of the circle" when referring to the arc which is described by the head of the club.

The all-important matter of the distribution of weight has been dealt with by the greatest players in the world. Let us see what Taylor, Braid, and Vardon have to say about this subject, for it is no exaggeration to say that this is a matter which goes to the very root of golf. If one teaches the distribution of weight incorrectly, it does not matter what else one teaches correctly, for the person who is reared on a wrong conception of the manner in which his weight should be distributed, can never play golf as it should be played. It is as impossible for such a person to play real golf as it would be for a durable building to be erected on rotten foundations.

Now let us see what the greatest players have to say about this. Vardon, at page 68 of *The Complete Golfer*, says:

The movements of the feet and legs are important. In addressing the ball you stand with both feet flat and squarely placed on the ground, the weight equally divided between them, and the legs so slightly bent at the knee-joints as to make the bending scarcely noticeable. This position is maintained during the upward movement of the club until the arms begin to pull at the body. The easiest and most natural thing to do then, and the one which suggests itself, is to raise the heel of the left foot and begin to pivot on the left toe, which allows the arms to proceed with their uplifting process without let or hindrance. Do not begin to pivot on this left toe ostentatiously, or because you feel you ought to do so, but only when you know that the time has come, and you want to, and do it only to such an extent that the club can reach the full extent of the swing without any difficulty.

While this is happening it follows that the weight of the body is being gradually thrown on to the right leg, which gradually stiffens, until at the top of the swing it is quite rigid, the left being at the same time in a state of comparative freedom, slightly bent in towards the right, with only just enough pressure on the toe to keep it in position.

That is what Vardon has to say about this important matter.

At page 53 of *Great Golfers*, speaking of the "Downward Swing," Vardon further says:

In commencing the downward swing, I try to feel that both hands and wrists are still working together. The wrists start bringing the club down, and at the same moment, the left knee commences to resume its original position. The head during this time has been kept quite still, the body alone pivoting from the hips.

It is obvious that if the pivoting is done *at the hips* it will be impossible to get the weight on the right leg at the top of the swing without some contortion of the body, yet we read at page 70 of *The Complete Golfer* that "the weight is being gradually moved back again from the right leg to the left." Thus is the old fatal idea persisted in to the undoing of thousands of golfers.

I have already referred to the wonderful spine-jumping and rotating which is described in *The Mystery of Golf*. Many might not understand the jargon of anatomical terms used in this fearful and wonderful idea, so I shall add here the author's corroboration of my interpretation of his notion.

At page 167 he says: "The pivot upon which the spinal column rotates is shifted from the head of the right thigh-bone to that of the left."

I have always been under the impression that the spinal column is very firmly embedded on the os sacrum—that, in fact, the latter is practically a portion of the spinal column, and that it is fixed into the pelvic region in a manner which renders it highly inconvenient for it to attempt any saltatory or rotatory pranks.

We are, however, told that the pivot on which the spinal column rotates "shifts from the right leg to the left leg." If the spine were "rotating," which of course it cannot do in the golf stroke, on any "pivot," which, equally of course, it does not, that "pivot" must be the immovable os sacrum. What then does all this nonsense mean?

James Braid, at page 56 of *Advanced Golf*, says:

At the top of the swing, although nearly all the weight will be on the right foot, the player must feel a distinct pressure on the left one, that is to say, it must still be doing a small share in the work of supporting the body.

Taylor, in *Taylor on Golf*, at page 207, says:

Then, as the club comes back in the swing, the weight should be shifted by degrees, quietly and gradually, until when the club has reached its topmost point the whole weight of the body is supported by the right leg, the left foot at this time being turned, and the left knee bent in towards the right leg. Next, as the club is taken back to the horizontal position behind the head, the shoulders should be swung round, although the head must be allowed to remain in the same position with the eyes looking over the left shoulder.

At page 30 of *Practical Golf* Mr. Walter J. Travis says:

In the upward swing it will be noticed that the body has been turned very freely with the natural transference of weight almost entirely to the right foot, and that the left foot has been pulled up and around on the toe. Without such aid the downward stroke would be lacking in pith. To get the shoulders into the stroke they must first come round in conjunction with the lower part of one's anatomy, smoothly and freely revolving on an axis which may be represented by an imaginary line drawn from the head straight down the back. Otherwise, the arms alone, unassisted to any appreciable extent, are called upon to do the work with material loss of distance.

At page 88 of *Golf* in the Badminton Series, Mr. Horace G. Hutchinson says:

Now as the club came to the horizontal behind the head, the body will have been allowed to turn, gently, with its weight upon the right foot.

We here have the opinions of five golfers, whose words should undoubtedly carry very great weight. The sum total of their considered opinion is that in the drive at golf the weight at the top of the swing must be on the right leg. I have, however, no hesitation in saying that this idea is fundamentally unsound and calculated to prove a very serious hindrance to anyone attempting to follow it. So far from its being true that the weight of the body is supported by the right foot at the top of the swing, I must say that entirely the opposite is true, and that at the top of the swing the weight of the body is borne by the left foot and leg in any drive of perfect rhythm.

This may possibly be going a little too far, so we shall, in the meantime, content ourselves with *absolutely denying* that the weight at the top of the swing goes on to the *right* leg, and with *insisting* that at the top of a perfectly executed swing *the main portion of the weight must be borne by the left foot and leg*. In so positively making this statement I am confronted by a mass of authority which would deter many people from essaying to disprove such a well-rooted delusion in connection with the game, but I think that before we have finished with this subject we shall be able to show very good reason for doubting the statements of these eminent players.

There is no possible doubt as to the rooted nature of this belief in the minds of these players. James Braid, in fact, emphasises it in some places. He says in *How to Play Golf*:

When the swing is well started, that is to say, when the club has been taken a matter of about a couple of feet from the ball, it will become impossible, or at least inconvenient and uncomfortable to keep the feet so firmly planted on the ground as they were when the address was made. It is the left one that wants to move, and consequently at this stage you must allow it to pivot. By this is meant that the heel is raised slightly, and the foot turns over until only the ball of it rests on the ground. Many players pivot on the toe, but I think this is not so safe, and does not preserve the balance so well. When this pivoting begins, the weight is being taken off the left leg and transferred almost entirely to the right, and at the same moment the left knee turns in towards the right toe. The right leg then stiffens a little and the right heel is more firmly than ever planted on the ground.

It seems to me that these famous golfers are confronted by a mechanical problem in this matter. The veriest tyro at golf is familiar with the axiom that it is absolutely necessary for him to keep his head still. Many authors tell one that the swing is conducted as though the upper portion of the body moved on an axis consisting of the spine. All golfers, authors, and professionals, who know anything about the game, will tell one that the habit of swaying, which means moving the head and body away from the hole, is fatal to accuracy.

Harry Vardon, at page 67, says: "In the upward movement of the club the body must pivot from the waist alone and there must be no swaying, not even to the extent of an inch." A little further down on the same page, we read: "In addressing the ball you stand with both feet flat and securely placed on the ground, the weight equally divided between them."

Now it seems fairly obvious that if one starts the golf drive with the weight practically evenly distributed between the right foot and the left foot, and seeing that it is an axiom of golf that one must not move one's head, it is impossible for one to get the weight of the body on to the right foot and leg without absolutely contorting one's frame. Let us make this clearer still. We have our golfer set at his ball, his address perfect, and his weight evenly distributed between his two feet. As he knows that it is wrong for him to move his head, we can, without interfering with his drive in the slightest degree, stretch tightly a wire at a right angle to the line of flight to the hole and pass it across within a quarter of an inch of his neck, below his right ear.

The position of this wire will not in any way hamper the golfer in his drive, but in order to fulfil the instructions which are laid down with the utmost persistence by every golf book, that it is of fundamental importance to keep the head absolutely still, it will be necessary for our golfer to play his drive without allowing his head or neck to touch this wire; but if he can do this, and at the same time get the weight of his body, at the top of his swing, on to his right leg, as advised by Taylor, Braid, and Vardon, and by Messrs. Hutchinson and Travis, without making himself both grotesque and uncomfortable, he will indeed have performed an unparalleled feat in the history of golf, for, to put the matter quite shortly, it is nonsense to suppose that it can be done. The thing is mechanically impossible.

If a man starts with his weight equally distributed between his legs, and then uses his spine or any other imaginary pivot to turn his body upon in the upward swing, it will be impossible for him to shift his weight so that it goes back on to his right leg. I am not, of course, allowing for a person who has an adjustable spine, such as that described by Mr. Arnold Haultain in *The Mystery of Golf*, which rotates, according to the author, first on one thigh bone and then on another. This spine is of such a remarkable nature that I must devote, later on, a little time to considering its vagaries. At present I am, however, dealing with a matter of practical golf and simple mechanics, about which there is absolutely no mystery but a vast amount of misconception.

When I first stated in *Modern Golf*, which, so far as I am aware, was the first book wherein this fundamental truth was laid down, that the left was the foot which bore the greater burden, it was regarded as revolutionary teaching, but there is not a professional golfer of any reputation whatever who now dares to teach that at the top of the swing the weight is to be put on the right. There is, however, no harm in fortifying oneself with the opinion of at least one of the triumvirate expressed elsewhere. Personally, I think that the mechanical proposition is so extremely simple and incontrovertible, as I have stated it, that it is unnecessary to go further, but such is the veneration of the golfer for tradition that as a matter of duty to the game I shall leave no stone unturned, not only to scotch, but absolutely to kill, this mischievous idea which is so injurious to the game.

In *Great Golfers*, Harry Vardon says, speaking of his address and stance: "I stand firmly, with the weight rather on the right leg." At page 50 of the same book he says, speaking of the top of the swing: "There is distinct pressure of the left toe and very little more weight should be felt on the right leg than there was when the ball was addressed." We see clearly here that Vardon's statement in *Great Golfers* that at the top of the swing "very little more weight should be felt on the right leg than there was when the ball was addressed" does not agree with his statement in *The Complete Golfer* wherein he states that "the weight of the body is being gradually thrown on to the right leg." The unfortunate part about this contradiction is that *Great Golfers* was published before *The Complete Golfer*, so that we are bound to take it as Vardon's more mature and considered opinion that the weight at the top of the stroke is thrown mainly on the right leg.

PLATE VI.

HARRY VARDON

The finish of his drive, showing how the weight goes forward on to the left foot.

This leaves us apparently as we were, but seeing the contradiction in Vardon's statement, we may with advantage turn to action photographs of him taken whilst actually playing the stroke. Here we see most clearly in such photographs as those shown on pages 86 and 87 of *Great Golfers*, that the body, instead of going away from the hole, has, if anything, gone forward. This is sufficiently marked in the photographs which I am now referring to, but in *Fry's Magazine* for the month of March 1909 there appeared a remarkable series of photographs showing ten drives by Harry Vardon. These photographs are, unquestionably, of very great value to the game, for they show beyond any shadow of doubt whatever, that Vardon's weight is never, at any portion of his drive, mainly on his right leg. The first photograph showing him at the top of his swing is a wonderful illustration of the fact that at the top of the swing in golf the main portion of the weight goes forward on to the left foot.

Before leaving this portion of our consideration of the distribution of weight, I must refer again to the description given of this matter in *The Mystery of Golf*. The author says:

The whole body must turn on the pivot of the head of the right thigh bone working in the cotyloidal cavity of the "os innominatum" or pelvic bone, the head, right knee, and right foot, remaining fixed, with the eyes riveted on the ball. In the upward swing the vertebral column rotates upon the head of the right femur, the right knee being fixed; and as the club head

45

nears the ball, the fulcrum is rapidly changed from the right to the left hip, the spine now rotating on the left thigh bone, the left knee being fixed; and the velocity is accelerated by the arms and wrists in order to add the force of the muscles to the weight of the body, thus gaining the greatest impetus possible. Not every professional instructor has succeeded in putting before his pupil the correct stroke in golf in this anatomical exposition.

For which we may be devoutly thankful, for if ever there was written an absolutely ridiculous thing about golf which could transcend in stupidity this description, I should like to see it.

As a matter of fact, the statement does not merit serious notice, but the book is published by a reputable firm of publishers, and no doubt has been read by some people who do not know sufficient for themselves to be able to analyse the alleged analysis of the author.

Let us now subject his analysis to a little of the analysing process. We are told that "the whole body must turn on the pivot of the head of the right thigh bone working in the cotyloidal cavity of the 'os innominatum' or pelvic bone." This is merely another way of saying that the right leg and foot is supporting the whole weight of the body, although the head must remain fixed. We have already considered the similar statements expressed in *The Mystery of Golf*, and by much more important people in the golfing world than the author of this book, so we need not labour this point, but he goes on to reduce his directions to the most ludicrous absurdity. We are told that in the upward swing the vertebral column rotates upon the head of the right femur.

Of course, I am not personally acquainted with Mr. Haultain, and he may be speaking from his own practice, but assuming for the sake of argument that he is a normally constructed man, the base of his vertebral column never gets anywhere near his right femur, nor is it possible for anybody's vertebral column to rotate unless the person is rotating with it, which one is inclined to think would prove rather detrimental to the drive at golf if indulged in between the stance and address and impact.

As though we had not already had sufficient fun for our money, we are told that "as the club head nears the ball the fulcrum is rapidly changed from the right to the left hip, the spine now rotating on the left thigh bone."

So far as one can judge from our author's description he must have been in the habit of playing golf amongst a race of men who have adjustable spines, the tail end of which they are able to wag from one side of the pelvic bone to the other. Personally, I have yet to meet golfers of this description. One feels inclined to ask the author of this remarkable statement what is happening to the os coccyx whilst one is wagging one's spine about in this remarkable manner.

This statement is about the funniest thing which has ever been written in golf, and it has absolutely no relation whatever to practical golf. It is merely an imaginative and absolutely incorrect exposition of the golf drive, not only from a golfing, but from an anatomical, point of view; and it is to me an absolute wonder how anyone, even one who labels himself "a duffer," can attach his name to such obviously inaccurate and foolish statements. One really would be inclined to be much more severe than one is in dealing with such a book were it not for the amusement which one has derived from a perusal of such fairy tales as a rotating spine which, during the course of the golf drive, jumps from one thigh bone to the other, steeplechasing the pelvic bone as it performs this remarkable feat.

I have referred in other places to the looseness of Mr. Haultain's descriptions in all matters of practical golf. At page 89 he confirms one's impression, if confirmation were required, that his idea of the fundamental principle of the golf swing is as ill-formed as are his notions of anatomy, for he says: "The left knee must be loose at the beginning and firm at the finish." At no time during a stroke in golf, of any description whatever, should there be any looseness of the body. During the production of the golf stroke the body is practically full of tension and attention. It is the greatest mistake possible to imagine that because one portion of the body is doing the work, any other portion may "slack." One who makes this statement has not a glimmering of the beginning of the real game of golf. I can readily believe that to such an one golf is a "mystery."

The left knee is in harness from the moment the ball is addressed until long after it has been driven, and it is a certainty that the left knee has far more work to do than has the right, so for anyone to cultivate an idea that the left knee may, at any time during the production of the golfing stroke, "be loose," is a very grave error.

While we are considering the matter of the distribution of weight, it will be advisable for us to devote our attention to the disposition of the weight at the moment of impact. Speaking of the management of the weight at this critical time, Vardon says:

When the ball has been struck, and the follow-through is being accomplished, there are two rules, hitherto held sacred, which may at last be broken. With the direction and force of the swing your chest is naturally turned round until it is facing the flag, and your body now abandons all restraint, and to a certain extent throws itself, as it were, after the ball. There is a great art in timing this body movement exactly. If it takes place the fiftieth part of a second too soon the stroke will be entirely ruined; if it comes too late it will be quite ineffectual and will only result in making the golfer feel uneasy, and as if something had gone wrong. When made at the proper instant it adds a good piece of distance to the drive, and that instant, as explained, is just when the club is following through.

It is evident from this statement, that Vardon is under the impression that the timing of this body movement should be so performed as to come in when the club is following through. I have shown before that the follow-through of a stroke is of no importance whatever except as the result of a perfectly executed first half of the stroke, if one may so describe it. It must be obvious to anyone who knows but little either of golf or mechanics that nothing which the body or the club does after contact between the ball and the club has ceased can have any influence whatever upon the flight of the ball, either as to distance or direction. Practically everything which takes place after the ball has left the club is the natural result of what has been done before impact. This cannot be too forcibly impressed upon golfers, for it is not at all uncommon to find men deliberately stating that the follow-through exerts a tremendous influence on the stroke. It should be perfectly manifest that this cannot be so. It is no doubt of very great importance to have a good follow-through, but the good follow-through must be the result of a good stroke previously played, otherwise it will be worthless.

Harry Vardon states that this timing of the body movement takes place immediately after impact, for that is "just when the club is following through." He has himself provided the best possible refutation of this obviously erroneous statement. The timing of the body on to the ball in the manner mentioned by him practically commences, in every drive of perfect rhythm as are so many of Vardon's, from the moment the stroke starts, for the body weight which is put into the golf drive comes largely from the half turn of the shoulders and upper portions of the body from the hips in the downward swing. This half turn and the slight forward movement of the hips are practically one and the same. If they are not, something has gone wrong with the drive.

Absolute evidence of the correctness of this statement is provided by Vardon himself in *Fry's Magazine* for March 1909. Here we see the remarkable series of ten drives by Vardon which I have already referred to. The first photograph shows most clearly that at the top of the swing the main portion of his weight is on his left foot. As a matter of carrying golf to the extreme of scientific calculation it is quite probable that there is much more than Vardon's physical weight on his left leg, for the rapid upward swing of his club is suddenly arrested when considerably nearer the hole than his left shoulder, so that the leverage of the head of the club will have thrown more weight than that which the left actually bears on it as its share of Vardon's avoirdupois. This, of course, is undoubted as a matter of practical mechanics, but it is not of sufficient importance to enter into fully in any way here.

It is, however, of importance for us to consider the photographs which follow, for here we see quite clearly that very early in the downward swing Vardon raises his right heel and bends his left knee slightly forward, and in the third, fourth, and fifth photographs we see very clearly that he is executing that turn of his body which carries his weight forward on to the ball in a very marked degree. This point is very clearly brought out in the instantaneous photographs of both Vardon's driving, and in that of George Duncan's. It is positively futile to say that the timing of the body weight in the follow-through is done when the club is following through, because it is obvious that this would not be "at the proper instant," and that it could not, by any stretch of imagination, add "a good piece of distance to the drive."

It is curious to note in this connection that on page 53 of *Great Golfers* Harry Vardon says:

Almost simultaneously with the impact, the right knee slightly bends in the direction of the hole, and allows the wrists and forearms to take the club right out in the direction of the line of flight, dragging the arms after them as far as they will comfortably go, when the club head immediately leaves the line of flight and the right foot turns on the toe. This allows the body to turn from the hips and face the hole, the club finishing over the left shoulder.

Here it will be seen that Vardon brings the timing of this very important forward movement back a little to "almost simultaneously with the impact." Now this phrase may mean immediately prior to, or immediately after, impact, and there can be no possible doubt which it is. It must be *prior* to impact if it is to exert any beneficial effect whatever upon the stroke. To add any distance to the drive, it is obvious that what was done in the way of timing the body on to the ball must have been done *prior to impact*, and merely continued after the ball had gone away, so that the finish was perfectly natural.

Now Vardon shows quite clearly in his drive that in his follow-through his weight goes forward until it is practically all on his left leg. So, for the matter of that, do the instantaneous photographs of nearly every famous golfer, but some of them have a very peculiar misconception of the disposition of weight at the moment of impact.

Let us, for instance, see what James Braid has to say about the matter at page 53 of *Advanced Golf*. Dealing with this all-important moment, he says:

I would draw the reader's very careful attention to the sectional photographs that are given on a separate page, and which in this form show the various workings of the different parts of the body while the swing is in progress as they could not be shown in any other way. They have all been prepared from photographs of myself, taken for the special purpose of this book. In some cases, in order to show more completely the progress of the different movements from the top of the swing to the finish, the position at the moment of striking is included. Theoretically, that ought to be exactly the same as the position at the address: and even in practice it will be found to be as nearly identical as possible, in the case of good driving, that is. Therefore, for the sake of precision, the third photograph in each series of four is a simple repetition of the first, and is not a special photograph.

I may mention that this is a common idea of illustrating a golf stroke. The author of the book shows the stance and address. He then shows the top of the swing, and after that the finish, and he thinks that he has then done his duty by his reader. As a matter of fact, these are all positions in the swing where there is practically "nothing doing" as the American puts it.

To illustrate the various movements in the drive, I took for *Modern Golf*, and used, eighteen different positions, and there was not one too many. It is quite impossible to illustrate the drive in golf by three positions; and it is absolutely erroneous to attempt to illustrate the moment of impact by a repetition of the photograph taken for stance and address. From the golfing point of view it is almost impossible to imagine two positions which are so entirely dissimilar. From the point of view of a mere photographer there may be some slight similarity, as indeed there is in all photographs of golfers, but to compare stance and address with the position at the moment of impact with the ball, is mere futility.

Let us quote Braid's remarks with regard to stance and address:

When in position and ready for play, both the legs and the arms of the player should be just a trifle relaxed—just so much as to get rid of any feeling of stiffness, and to allow of the most complete freedom of movement. The slackening may be a little more pronounced in the case of the arms than with the legs, as much more freedom is required of them subsequently. They should fall easily and comfortably to the sides, and the general feeling of the player at this stage should be one of flexibility and power.

Everything is now in readiness for making the stroke, and the player prepares to hit the ball.... While he is doing this he will feel the desire to indulge in a preliminary waggle of the club just to see that his arms are in working order, waving the club backwards and forwards once or twice over the ball.... Obviously there is no rule in such matters, and the player can only be enjoined to make himself comfortable in the best way he can.

Now we see here that the main idea of the player at the moment of address is to make himself comfortable—in other words, to get into as natural a position as he possibly can in order to execute his stroke. The whole idea of the stance and address is to get into a perfectly natural position, and one that is quite comfortable and best calculated to enable one to produce a correct stroke. We see clearly that this is what Braid considers to be necessary at the moment of address.

Let us turn now to *Advanced Golf* at page 61, which we have already quoted. Braid, at that page and on the preceding pages, explains clearly that the whole idea of the golf stroke is supreme tension, and that at the moment of impact the tension is greatest. He says: "Then comes the moment of impact. Crack! Everything is let loose, and round comes the body immediately the ball is struck and goes slightly forward until the player is facing the line of flight." Is it possible to imagine two more diametrically opposed conditions of the human frame than those which I have described in Braid's own words? Yet we find this fine player producing, for the guidance of golfers as to what takes place at the moment of impact, the same photograph which he shows them for stance and address!

Moreover, Braid himself clearly shows in his action photographs that such a statement as this is quite wrong. If we had any doubt at all about the matter, we might examine the photographs of Braid himself, which show clearly that the positions taken up by him when addressing the ball and when hitting it, are, as might easily be believed, widely different, for at the moment of impact there is the supreme tension and power which he advises as being a necessity for the production of a long drive. It is true that James Braid's feet, particularly his right foot, do not move from the ground so much as do those of Harry Vardon or George Duncan; but it is nevertheless true that the movement of his legs, arms, and shoulders show, at the moment of impact, a position totally different from that taken up by him during his stance and address.

It might seem that these things are not of sufficient importance to warrant the critical analysis to which I am subjecting them, but there can be no doubt that there are a vast number of people to whom golf is of infinitely more importance than political economy, and to these it is a matter of most vital importance that they should know what they are doing and what they ought to do at this critical period; and in dealing with the books which have been produced in connection with the game of golf they have such a mass of contradictory and fallacious teaching to wade through, that it is small wonder that they are, as a rule, utterly befogged as to the proper principles upon which to proceed.

Let us, for instance, examine these two statements with regard to the follow-through. At page 55 of *How to Play Golf*, in his chapter on "Finishing the Stroke," James Braid says:

The second that the ball is hit, and not before, the player should begin to turn on his right toe, and to allow a little bend of the right knee, so as to allow the right shoulder to come round until the body faces the line of flight of the ball. When this is done properly the weight will be thrown on to the left foot, and the whole body will be thrown slightly forward. The whole of this movement needs very careful timing, because it is a very common fault with some players to let the body get in too soon, and in such cases the stroke is always ruined. Examine the photographs.

Let us now turn to page 62 of *Advanced Golf*. Here we read:

As for the follow-through, there is very little that can be said here, which is not already perfectly understood, if it is not always produced. After impact, and the release of all tension, body and arms are allowed to swing forward in the direction of the flight of the ball, and I would allow the right knee to give a little in order to remove all restraint. But the weight must not be entirely taken off the right foot. That foot must still be felt to be pressing firmly on the turf, showing that although the weight has been changed from one place to another, the proper balance has not been lost.

Braid here says that the weight must not be entirely taken off the right foot. Well, to all intents and purposes, it is entirely taken off the right foot, as will be shown by photographs of any of the leading players in the world at the finish of the stroke, and, indeed, of James Braid himself. Braid says: "Examine the photographs," and I have examined them. At pages 57 and 59 of *How to Play Golf* Braid is shown finishing a full drive or brassy shot. Here, without any possible doubt, his weight is all on his left foot. At page 61 of *Advanced Golf* there are some photographs of Braid's boots and trousers from the knee downwards, entitled "Leg action in driving." One of these is entitled "Finish." Here it will be seen that the whole of the weight is unmistakably on the left leg.

If one looks at the instantaneous photographs of James Braid in this book and in *Great Golfers* one will see quite clearly that in all finishes his weight goes unmistakably on to his left leg.

Braid makes a very wonderful statement in *Great Golfers* at page 175. Writing there of the downward swing, he says: "My body does not commence to turn till the club head is about two feet from the ball—namely, at the point when the wrists come into the stroke." As a matter of fact James Braid's body begins to turn almost simultaneously with the beginning of the downward stroke, and as another matter of practical golf the wrists also come in at the very beginning of the stroke. With this latter point I shall, however, deal later on.

Let me here emphasise the fact that the body turn must commence very early in the stroke, as indeed is quite natural. It is obvious that if anyone were to postpone the turning of the body until the club head "is about two feet from the ball" the rhythm of the stroke would be utterly destroyed. In this matter I am contradicting Braid flatly about his own practice. Therefore, I must refer any reader who doubts the accuracy of my statement, and Braid himself, if he cares to challenge it, to *Fry's Magazine* for May 1909, wherein are shown eight drives by James Braid. No. 1 shows Braid at the top of his swing; No. 2 shows him before his club head has travelled a foot, and even in this short distance we see that his body has already turned very considerably. Any attempt whatever to follow out what Braid says here and to postpone the turn of the body until the club head is two feet from the ball, must prove disastrous.

Braid continues on the same page:

At this moment the left knee turns rather quickly, as at the moment of striking, I am firm on both feet; the quickness of the action makes it difficult to follow with the eye, but I am convinced this is what happens. Immediately after impact I commence turning on the right toe, bending the right knee slightly. This allows the right shoulder to come round till the body is facing the hole. It is most essential that this should be done, and then no thought will be given as to how the club will finish, as the speed at which the club head is travelling will naturally take it well through.

Here we have, at least, very important corroboration of the fact that one need not worry about the follow-through if the first portion of the stroke has been correctly played. Braid says that at the moment of striking "the player is quite firm on both his feet and faces directly to the ball, just as he did when he was addressing it before he began the upward swing. Anyone who thinks out the theory of the swing for himself will see that it is obviously intended that at the moment of impact the player shall be just as he was when he addressed the ball, which is the position which will afford him most driving power and accuracy."

This statement is so amazing that I must give definite instructions as to where to find it. It is on page 54 of *How to Play Golf*, and I think it proves conclusively that the idea which Braid is endeavouring to impart to his pupils and readers is entirely wrong, and is not the method which he himself follows in practice. Confirmation of my opinion can be obtained from a study of the third picture in the series of drives by James Braid in the May number of *Fry's Magazine* for 1909, which I have just referred to. Here we see clearly that the positions, from a golfing point of view, are utterly dissimilar, as indeed is most natural.

Braid states that immediately after impact he commences "turning on the right toe, bending the right knee slightly." I think it will be found that even with James Braid, who certainly uses his legs in a somewhat different manner from many of the leading professionals, the right foot begins to lift before impact with the ball. I am inclined to think that both Braid and Taylor are more flat-footed at the moment of impact than most of the other professional golfers; but there can be little doubt that the body is swung into the blow before impact, otherwise it would be a matter of practical impossibility for them to obtain the length which they do; while it is a certainty that for the ordinary golfer it would be fatal to attempt to keep his weight in any way whatever on his right leg at the finish of his drive.

This rooted fallacy with regard to the distribution of weight so that at the top of the swing it shall be on the right foot, has obtained its hold in a very peculiar manner. At the top of the swing the right leg is practically perfectly straight, and, naturally, as the foot is firmly planted on the ground and therefore held at both the heel and the toe while the leg has turned with the body, there is a very considerable amount of torsional or twisting strain on the leg. This torsional strain, added to the fact that the leg is perfectly straight, has led to the idea that a great deal of the weight is on the right leg.

This idea has been confirmed to a very great degree by the manner of contact of the left foot with the earth. At the top of the swing the golfer pivots on the left foot, practically from the ball of the big toe to the end thereof, or on that portion of his boot representing this space. This naturally makes his contact with the earth *appear light*. These two causes, taken together, have produced the fallacy with regard to having the weight on the right foot and leg at the top of the swing. In the one case it is a physical cause, namely, the stiffness and torsional strain on the right leg, and in the other case it is a visual deception. It stands to reason that, provided the two surfaces will bear the strain, as much weight could be borne on a point as on a surface immeasurably greater, but in the second case there would be a greater *appearance* of weight. This is exactly what has happened with regard to the golf drive. It is executed extremely quickly, and those who have attempted to explain it have not been able to follow the motions with sufficient rapidity and intelligence, nor have they been able to explain them accurately either from a mechanical or anatomical point of view.

Until we can get some golfer who can pass the test suggested by me, and play his stroke without touching the wire strained within a quarter of an inch of his neck, after having taken his stance with his weight evenly distributed between his legs, and at the same time play it without contortion with his weight on his right leg, we may take it that this tremendous fallacy with regard to the distribution of weight at the top of the swing has been exploded.

CHAPTER VI

THE POWER OF THE LEFT

The fetich of the left is, amongst golfers, only second, if indeed it is second in its injurious nature, to the idea that the weight should be put on the right foot at the top of the swing. It is very hard indeed to trace the origin of the idea that the left hand and arm is of more importance in the golf stroke than the right, but that it is a very rooted idea there can be no doubt whatever.

To those who are not acquainted with the literature of golf and the remarkable ideas which many golfers have of the nature of their game, it would seem almost superfluous to go very fully into this matter, for one would think that it is sufficiently obvious that the right hand and arm are the dominant factors in producing the golf stroke. It is, however, useless to deny that there is a large body of opinion, backed by most influential authority, in favour of the left hand and arm being more important than the right.

Let us see, before we go any further in the matter, what the leading professionals have to say about it.

Harry Vardon, it is true, does not explicitly state that the right hand is the more important, but by implication he does assert so right throughout *The Complete Golfer*. Let me quote a few of his remarks with regard to the left hand. On page 61 Vardon says:

The grip with the first finger and thumb of my right hand is exceedingly firm, and the pressure of the little finger on the knuckle of the left hand is very decided. In the same way it is the thumb and first finger of the left hand that have most of the gripping work to do. Again, the palm of the right hand presses hard against the thumb of the left. In the upward swing this pressure is gradually decreased, until when the club reaches the turning point there is no longer any such pressure; indeed, at this point the palm and the thumb are barely in contact.

We see here clearly that, as indeed Vardon has stated elsewhere, at the top of the swing the grip of the right has opened up until it may almost in a measure be said to have ceased to direct operations.

Vardon continues:

This release is a natural one, and will or should come naturally to the player for the purpose of allowing the head of the club to swing well and freely back. But the grip of the thumb and first finger of the right hand, as well as that of the little finger upon the knuckle of the first finger of the left hand, is still as firm as at the beginning.

From this it will be seen that the grip at each side of the hand is apparently as firm as it was at the beginning of the stroke, but in some mysterious manner it has eased up in between the forefinger and the little finger. We need not, however, go any further into that matter at the present time, but we may continue the consideration of Vardon's statement here. He goes on to say: "As the club head is swung back again towards the ball, the palm of the right hand and the thumb of the left gradually come together again. Both the relaxing and the retightening are done with the most perfect graduation, so that there shall be no jerk to take the club off the straight line. The easing begins when the hands are about shoulder high and the club shaft is perpendicular, because it is at this time that the club begins to pull, and if it were not let out in the manner explained, the result would certainly be a half shot or very little more than that, for a full and perfect swing would be an impossibility. This relaxation of the palm also serves to give more freedom to the wrist at the top of the swing just when that freedom is desirable."

We might, for a moment, leave this statement, and turn to page 126. Speaking here of the approach shot with the mashie Vardon says: "This is one of the few shots in golf in which the right hand is called upon to do most of the work, and that it may be encouraged to do so the hold with the left hand should be slightly relaxed"; and again at page 147 in dealing with putting Vardon says: "But in this part of the game it is quite clear that the right hand has more work to do than the left."

In these statements it is quite evident that Vardon wishes to express the idea that, generally speaking, the left hand is in command of the stroke.

Reverting for a moment, and before I proceed to consider what the other authorities have to say on this subject, to Vardon's remark that "This is one of the few shots in golf in which the right hand is called upon to do most of the work," I may say that Vardon does not, in the whole of *The Complete Golfer*, explicitly describe any one stroke wherein he shows that the left hand "is called upon to do most of the work," nor, for the matter of that, does any other professional golfer or author, although the statement is common to nearly all books on the game.

James Braid, on page 55 of *How to Play Golf*, says:

A word about the varying pressure of the grip with each hand. In the address the left hand should just be squeezing the handle of the club, but not so tightly as if one were afraid of losing it. The right hand should hold the club a little more loosely. The left hand should hold firmly all the way through. The right will open a little at the top of the swing to allow the club to move easily, but it should automatically tighten itself in the downward swing.

Here again we see the idea that the left is in charge, because although we are told that in the address the left hand should "just be squeezing" the club, yet we are told clearly and definitely that "the left hand should hold firmly all the way through." It is somewhat difficult to reconcile these directions, and it is obvious that if the right is going to "open a little at the top of the swing" the club will certainly move easily—in fact it will move so easily that the accuracy of the stroke will be very considerably interfered with.

Let us for a moment turn to *Advanced Golf*. There, James Braid, speaking of the top of the swing, says: "Now for the return journey. Here at the top, arms, wrists, body—all are in their highest state of tension." Let me pause here for a moment to ask how it is possible for "arms, wrists, body" all to be "in their highest state of tension," if the right hand is to "open a little at the top of the swing to allow the club to move easily"; and how is it possible for the right hand to "automatically tighten itself in the downward swing" if it was already in its "highest state of tension" when it was at the top of the swing?

It will be apparent that it is utterly impossible for the arms and wrists to be tighter than they are when they are "in their highest state of tension." Therefore, we must take it that James Braid's advice at page 55 of *How to Play Golf* is over-ridden by his advice at page 57 of *Advanced Golf*, for I think that we are entitled to consider that *Advanced Golf* represents Braid's last word with regard to the science of golf.

Quoting still from the same passage, page 57 of *Advanced Golf*, Braid says: "Every muscle and joint in the human golfing machinery is wound up to the highest point." It is impossible to get away from that. We are told that at the beginning of the downward swing "every muscle and joint in the human golfing machinery is wound up to the highest point."

Now the student of golf who desires to start his swing on a firm and sure foundation must mark this statement well. I repeat it for the third time: "Every muscle and joint in the human golfing machinery is wound up to the highest point," and let it be remembered that Braid is now speaking *of the start of the downward swing.*

We will now turn to *Taylor on Golf*. At page 193 Taylor says:

My contention is simply this: that the grasp of the right hand upon the club must be sufficiently firm in itself to hold it steady and true, but it must not be allowed on any account to over-power the left. The idea is that the latter arm must exercise a predominant influence in every stroke that may be played. As regards my own position in the matter, my grip with either hand is very firm, yet I should hesitate before I told every golfer to go and do likewise.

Here we see that Taylor distinctly says that "the idea is that the latter arm (*i.e.* the left) must exercise the predominant influence in every stroke that may be played," and although he says explicitly that his own grip with both hands is very firm, he puts the utterly false idea of the predominance of the left into the minds of those who are influenced by his teaching.

Taylor, at page 107 of *Great Golfers*, says in dealing with the "Downward Swing":

The club is brought down principally by the left wrist, the right doing very little until the hands are opposite the right leg, when it begins to assert itself, bringing the full face of the club to the ball.

It is almost unnecessary to say, especially in view of Taylor's statement that he holds very firmly with both hands, that he does not carry out this dangerous teaching. Harry Vardon says to attempt it is fatal, and I am pleased to add my corroboration.

This amazing fallacy is wonderfully deeply rooted. A friend of mine some time ago was in trouble about his iron shots. He consulted a professional, who endeavoured to cure him by telling him when playing his stroke to hold so lightly with his right hand that at any time during the stroke he could slide it up and down the shaft.

Oh no! He is not a duffer, nor is he mentally unbalanced. He is merely a professional golfer who plays for England and suffers from the hallucination handed on to him by more famous players than he.

What could be stronger than this? Let me quote Taylor again. At page 90 of *Taylor on Golf* he says:

The right hand is naturally the stronger of the two—much more powerful in the average man than the left—and the learner is just as naturally prone to use it. But in the game of golf he must keep in front of him at all times the fact that the left hand should fill the position of guide, and it must have the predominating influence over the stroke.

51

That this is rather unnatural I am perfectly willing to admit. Its being unnatural is the basis of its great difficulty, but it is a difficulty that must needs be grappled with and overcome by any man who desires to play the game as it should be played.

But Taylor will not give in to this idea himself! Is not this wonderful?

Harry Vardon says of the grip that one should "remember that the grip with *both* hands should be firm. That with the right hand should not be slack as one is so often told." This is valuable corroboration, for it must be remembered that Vardon only subscribes to the fetich of the left *by implication*. Nowhere, I think, can we convict him of actually preaching it.

Now let us turn to the volume on *Golf* in the Badminton Library contributed by Mr. Horace G. Hutchinson. At page 85 Mr. Hutchinson says:

Since, as will be shown later on, the club has to turn in the right hand at a certain point in the swing, it should be held lightly in the fingers, rather than in the palm, with that hand. In the left hand it should be held well home in the palm, and it is not to stir from this position throughout the swing. It is the left hand, mainly, that communicates the power of the swing; the chief function of the right hand is as a guide in direction.

At page 87 Mr. Hutchinson continues:

So much, then, for the grip. Now, when the club, in the course of its swing away from the ball, is beginning to rise from the ground, and is reaching the horizontal with its head pointing to the player's left, it should be allowed to turn naturally in the right hand until it is resting upon the web between the forefinger and the thumb.

We see here that this distinguished amateur is an out and out adherent of the fallacy of the left. He tells us distinctly that it is the "left hand, mainly, that communicates the power of the swing, and that the chief function of the right hand is as a guide in direction," but notwithstanding the fact that "the chief function of the right hand is as a guide in direction," we see that at the top of the stroke it turns loosely in the hand until it is "resting upon the web between the forefinger and the thumb."

PLATE VII.

HARRY VARDON

The finish of the drive—a little later than in Plate VI., showing the weight completely on the left foot.

Of course, in the circumstances, it will be very hard indeed for us to follow out James Braid's idea of everything at this point being in supreme tension, but it is interesting to see what Mr. Hutchinson thinks about the matter.

We have here the opinions of the three most distinguished professionals in the world, backed by that of one of the distinguished amateurs in the game, a man who has distinguished himself both by his play and his writing. In the face of this weight of authority it may seem rash to venture to state plainly and explicitly that as a matter of practical golf the right hand and arm is the dominant partner, and that it is the duty of every normal golfer to have this idea firmly implanted in his mind when he settles down to his address.

As the right is the dominant partner in the golf drive, so must the predominance of the right be the dominant idea in one's mind, but the domination of the right must not be abused, as we shall show later on.

It is, of course, proper for a golfer to have clearly fixed in his mind the fact that the right is the more important member of the two, but when he has once got that fact carefully and well stowed away in his mind, it will be no more trouble to him than it is at present to every normal person to use his knife in his right hand with which to cut his meat, for it is an absolutely natural proceeding. The trouble with the fetich of the left is that not only is it a perfectly unnatural proceeding, but it is also, on that account, something extra for the golfer to cumber his mind with during his swing. If he plays his stroke naturally and without any thought of the mismade maxims of unpractical persons, he will inevitably let the right hand and arm take charge of the stroke, but the right will not at any time endeavour to do more than its proper share, and therefore the left will be given every chance to do a fair amount of the work. It is the interference with Nature by putting the left forward into a place which it has no right to occupy, which ruins so many golf strokes.

Let us now turn to *The Complete Golfer*. Here, at page 60, Harry Vardon says:

We must now consider the degree of tightness of the grip by either hand, for this is an important matter. Some teachers of golf, and various books of instruction, inform us that we should grasp the club firmly with the left hand and only lightly with the right, leaving the former to do the bulk of the work and the other merely to guide the operations.

It is astonishing with what persistency this error has been repeated, for error I truly believe it is. Ask any really first-class player with what comparative tightness he holds the club in his right and left hands, and I am confident that in nearly every case he will declare that he holds it, nearly, if not quite, as tightly with the right hand as with the left. Personally, I grip quite as firmly with the right hand as with the other one. When the other way is adopted—the left hand being tight and the right hand simply watching it, as it were—there is an irresistible tendency for the latter to tighten up suddenly at some part of the upward or downward swing, and, as surely as there is a ball on the tee, when it does so there will be mischief.

If we sum up the advice of Vardon and Taylor, and of Braid as shown in his latest work *Advanced Golf*, we see clearly that although they subscribe to the idea of the predominance of the power of the left hand and arm, they do not themselves carry it out in practice. Taylor says that his grip with both hands is very firm, yet he should hesitate before recommending other people to follow his methods. I think we may take it for granted that a method which has resulted in four open championships may be considered good enough to follow.

Vardon, as we have seen, only subscribes to this notion inferentially, and nobody could be more emphatic than he is with regard to the distribution of force in the grip. His words "Ask any really first-class player with what comparative tightness he holds the club in his right and left hands, and I am confident that in nearly every case he will declare that he holds it, nearly, if not quite, as tightly with the right hand as with the left," present the case exactly. Any man who plays golf properly will find it impossible to tell you how he distributes the force of his grip on his club, and what proportion of power the grip of the left bears to the right. As a matter of fact, the man who plays golf properly has no time to think of such nonsense as this. This is a matter which is regulated for him by common sense and nature.

The trouble steps in when he is advised to interfere with the ordinary course of Nature, and to put the left hand in a position of authority which it has no right whatever to try to exercise. I say advisedly "try" to exercise, because it never can exercise the power which it is supposed to have. It stands to reason, therefore, that any attempt whatever to make it exercise a power superior to the more powerful arm must result in interfering with the proper functions of the hand and arm which should be naturally in command of the stroke.

We have seen that James Braid in *Advanced Golf* has quite altered the opinions which he expresses in *How to Play Golf*, and he also agrees that at the top of the swing, and until the stroke is played, it is right to grip the club as hard as one can with both hands—in fact, he says as plainly as it is possible for anyone to say anything, that during the whole of the downward swing the muscles are in a state of supreme tension, and fortunately he does not repeat the common error, the error which he himself makes in *How to Play Golf*, of advising the player to encumber his mind with any idea of regulating the increase of speed of the club head.

Vardon puts the matter splendidly when he says:

Personally, I grip quite as firmly with the right hand as with the other one. When the other way is adopted—the left hand being tight and the right hand simply watching it, as it were—there is an irresistible tendency for the latter to tighten up suddenly at some part of the upward or downward swing, and, as surely as there is a ball on the tee, when it does so there will be mischief.

This is such an important statement that I must, in passing, emphasise it, although I hope to deal with it again later on, for Vardon here strikes a deadly blow to the absurd nonsense which most books lay down about regulating the grip during the upward and downward swing. As Vardon truly says, any attempt to apportion the respective power of the grip of the left and right during the golf swing must inevitably result in disaster, for there will unquestionably be, as he well remarks, a pronounced tendency to tighten up at some part of the swing in a jerky manner. The only way to guard against this is to be, as James Braid says in *Advanced Golf*, in a state of supreme tension from the moment the downward swing starts.

It must be remembered that Vardon himself advocates easing up with the grip of the right at the top of the swing, although he says that he grips as firmly with the right as the left. It stands to reason that if Vardon does ease up with his right at the top of the swing, he must during his downward stroke restore the balance of power. It seems perfectly clear that in doing this there is a very great danger of what he describes as an "irresistible tendency for the latter," that is the right hand, "to tighten up suddenly."

I cannot see that, because Vardon starts with his grip equally firm with each hand, and then relaxes the firmness of his grip with his right hand at the top of the stroke, trusting to regain his firmness by the time he has reached the ball again, he removes from his swing the danger of the sudden tightening-up which he shows will threaten the swing of anyone who attempts to let the left hand have the predominant grip. It seems to me perfectly clear that this danger must be even in Vardon's downward swing, but we know quite well that Vardon, as a stroke player, is a genius, and that even if it is not a danger for him, it would be for ninety-five of every hundred golfers.

The truth is, with regard to the golf grip, although none of the leading professionals or authors are courageous enough to state it, that for the ordinary golfer—aye, and even for the extraordinary golfer—there is only one way to apportion the force of the left and right in the grip, and that is *not to think about it at all when one is doing it*, but to grip very firmly with both hands, and leave any apportionment of force which may be necessary to Nature, and the golfer who follows this advice and instruction will find that Nature can attend to it infinitely better than he can.

In golf we frequently find that one fallacy is built up on another, and it is quite an open question if the fallacy of the power of the left hand and arm is not founded on another fallacy, namely, the fallacy of the present overlapping grip. Now this sounds like rank heresy, and I may as well say at once that I am not prepared to assert that the present overlapping grip is a fallacy, but it is at least open to argument if it is the best grip which can be taken of a golf club.

There is no such thing as standing still in golf or any other game—either we are progressing or we are going backwards. In golf, notwithstanding the vast amount of false teaching which is published, we are unquestionably advancing. It must not be thought from this that it is of no importance that most of the matter which is published about golf is entirely misleading, for that is not so. This misleading matter is followed by an enormous army of golfers who are not able to think out the matter for themselves, but there are a very great number of golfers who absolutely disregard the published tuition of the greatest experts in the world and play golf as it should be played, and in no case is this more pronounced than in the persons of leading professional golfers, for they write one thing, but do absolutely the other themselves.

In the old days, when Vardon and all the other champions used the two-handed grip, it would have been rank folly for any person other than Vardon to have asserted that it was better to get the grip of the right hand off the club, as the overlapping grip does to a very great extent, but this grip was tried by Vardon, and it very soon became almost universal. However, I think we are justified in asking if this grip is undoubtedly the best that it is possible for us to get. Before the overlapping grip became fashionable both hands had their full grip on the shaft of the club, and in those days men played great golf, and there are many of them who still play great golf with the same hold, which they have refused to alter.

At page 194 of *Taylor on Golf*, speaking of the grip, Taylor says:

To sum up the matter, I should describe the orthodox manner of gripping with the right in the following words: The fingers must close around the club in such a way that provision is made for the thumb to cover and cross the shaft, the first joints of the fingers, providing this is done, being just in sight. Nothing more or nothing less. This is the grip generally accepted as being orthodox, and the one generally favoured by the majority of those who decide to follow up the game properly. But, as is the case with everything which is favoured by any considerable number of enthusiasts, there are those who, untrammelled by tradition, break away and hold the club differently, with one hand at least.

Take, as for instance, the case of Mr. John Ball, jun. This gentleman—one of the leading golfers of the day—holds the club firmly, not to say tightly, in the palm of his right hand. Well, he has discovered that this does not detrimentally affect his play, so I presume that may be taken as a satisfactory proof that the orthodox way may sometimes be departed from. Then, after Mr. Ball, I might mention the name of Mr. Edward Blackwell. He is almost certainly the most consistently good long driver we possess now, and his unorthodox method of grip with the right hand has not affected his play.

Taylor, of course, uses the overlapping grip, which is to-day the orthodox grip.

Taylor speaks here of "those who, untrammelled by tradition, break away and hold the club differently, with one hand at least," but it seems to me that the two golfers quoted are not those who are breaking away from the traditional hold. Rather does it seem to me that it is we of the orthodox grip of to-day who have broken away from the best traditions of golf, and taking best and best of those who have adopted the modern grip and those who have maintained the old grip, there is practically "nothing in it." Looking at the grip of men like Mr. H. H. Hilton, Mr. John Ball, and Mr. Edward Blackwell, it would, I think, to-day, require a person almost bereft of intelligence to imagine for one moment that the power of the stroke in the play of these golfers is obtained from their left arms and hands, and I do not suppose for a single moment that any one of these players would dream of asserting that he gets his length or direction from the left arm.

We are now confronted with the fact that one at least of these players with the two-handed grip is at practically no disadvantage against the best golfers in the world, and we must take it for granted in the face of what we have said, that his power of stroke and his command thereof is obtained from his right hand and arm. Now that being so, let us say for the sake of argument that he desires to improve his play by bringing the action of his wrists into greater harmony by adopting the overlapping grip. Surely one is confronted with this question—should one overlap the left hand with the right, or should one overlap the right with the left. In the present overlap the left hand takes the first grip of the club, and the right hand overlaps it, and in so doing is taken, to a very great extent, off the shaft of the club.

55

The question now arises, Should not one first take one's grip with the right hand, the dominant hand, the guiding hand, and the hand which is operated by the stronger arm, and having got this grip, proceed to overlap with the left, always allowing, of course, for the necessary insertion of the thumb of the left between the shaft and the palm of the right hand?

This may sound revolutionary, but I assure my readers that it is not one half so revolutionary as the change from the old two-handed grip to the present overlapping grip, for in that change the right hand was, to a very great extent, deprived of its pride of place. I think there is very little doubt that a player who became accustomed to the right-handed grip with the left overlap, would find that he produced a better game than he was able to do with the present overlapping grip. The fact is that we are inclined to take a much too complimentary and optimistic view of our exploits. Golf has now come to such a pass that it is played almost perfectly by a few of the best players, so that we have come to consider a five by a leading player as a serious lapse; but we must not judge the great body of golfers by the perfect players. These men would probably play very well under any conditions which could exist in the game. We have to consider the greatest good of the greatest number—in other words, the object of our search is to ascertain and understand perfectly what is the best way, and although I am stating this proposition with regard to the golf grip quite tentatively, and am laying it down as a subject for argument, I have very little doubt indeed that it will be found in the future that the right-handed grip is the best grip for playing golf.

I think there is very little doubt that the most important change in the next decade will be in the right hand and arm coming into their kingdom. It need not be thought that this will happen in a day, or a month, or a year. For very many years the great game of golf was played, and was well and truly played by men who never dreamed of putting part of one hand beneath the other—who would have scouted the overlapping grip and the levering of the right hand off the shaft as sacrilege—but some one introduced the idea, because it brought the wrists closer together so that they worked more in harmony than with the old grip. Harry Vardon tried it and found it good, and it went into the game of golf and the history thereof.

And to see Vardon use it, one might well say, "What more can you want?"; but that is not argument. Probably the one who asked that question would have asked the same question had he seen Vardon playing when he was using the old grip, when one wrist was fighting the other; so we must not be deterred from our speculation, from peering into the future. Of course, the essence of the overlapping grip is that it reduces the conflict of the wrists, and so conduces to greater accuracy and to less interference with the rhythm of the swing. It stands to reason that in the old days of the two-handed grip this conflict was worse than it would be now, for then the fetich of the left had not been weakened, and it was a distressful thing to have a hefty left in possession of the end of one's shaft and interfering with the proper functions of the right in an unwarrantable manner.

Scientific golfers have, however, now come to the conclusion that the right hand and arm are the dominant partners in the production of the golf stroke, although there are many of the old school who still pathetically retain and exhibit their allegiance to the old tradition of the left being the master.

If we have established the fact that the right is the dominant factor in the production of the drive, it seems to me that it follows quite naturally that the place of honour on the shaft should be allotted to it, and that it should be allowed the full grip, and not as it is at present, pushed off the shaft so that the grip of the dominant hand is practically reduced to that of the thumb and the first and second fingers. If this point is conceded the right hand obtains the full benefit of its undoubtedly superior power, for it obtains a firm and natural grip, whereas the present overlapping grip is a most unnatural hold and a difficult one for beginners to acquire, although very few players who have once used it return to the old grip.

Not only is the proposed grip more solid and natural, and productive of greater power and accuracy than the present overlapping grip, but it unquestionably carries the main idea of the overlapping grip to its logical conclusion, as it reduces the stroke much more to a one-wrist shot than does the present grip.

There will always be found many people who are prepared to condemn utterly anything which they do not understand. Some of these are sure to exercise themselves on this subject, so I shall give them some additional food for thought. Some time ago, a golfer who was capable of removing Mr. John Ball from the Amateur Championship Competition, lost his left thumb at the second joint. After his misfortune he took to driving a much longer ball than he had been in the habit of doing before his accident.

Now there must have been some reason for this. The only one which I can suggest is that his accident put the right hand more into its proper and natural place on the shaft than it had been before. Curiosity led me to try to reproduce this grip as much as possible. I used the ordinary overlapping grip, with the exception that I allowed my thumb to remain out and to rest on the back of my right hand in a line with the knuckle of the little finger. I was astonished to find how closely it seemed to bring the wrists together. The injured golfer would probably have the ideal golf grip if he overlapped his right with his left forefinger instead of using the ordinary overlap, for he would have a perfectly free and full right-hand grip, no interference by the thumb of the left hand, and a natural overlap with the left forefinger on the little finger of the right hand.

There is surely food for thought in these considerations, and I am sure that many who take to golf late in life could do much better with this grip and the short swing than they do with the grip which is most in vogue, and with much striving after an exaggerated swing. It is not wise for us to think that there is nothing to discover or to improve on in the grip. There is in this suggestion much room for experiment and argument, and unless I am very much mistaken we shall, in the future, see the relative position of the hands on the shaft altered.

I may here refer again to the remarks made on the power of the left by Mr. Horace Hutchinson. It will be remembered that he said:

Since, as will be shown later on, the club has to turn in the right hand at a certain point in the swing, it should be held lightly in the fingers, rather than in the palm, with that hand. In the left hand it should be held well home in the palm, and it is not to stir from this position throughout the swing. It is the left hand, mainly, that communicates the power of the swing; the chief function of the right hand is as a guide in direction.

Notwithstanding Mr. Horace Hutchinson's statement with regard to the function of the right hand, there is given on page 86 of the Badminton *Golf* an illustration entitled "At the top of the swing (as it should be)." Here we see a player in about as ineffective a position for producing a drive as one could possibly imagine, for the right elbow is considerably above the player's head and is pointing skyward. It would be an impossibility from such a position to obtain either adequate guidance or power from the right hand, and it is a matter of astonishment to find the name of such a fine player and good judge of the game as Mr. Horace Hutchinson attached to an illustration which must always be a classical illustration of "The top of the swing (as it should *not* be)."

We may here for the time being disregard the fundamentally unsound position of the right arm, for Mr. Horace Hutchinson has apparently altered his mind since, as we find him in *Great Golfers* photographed at the top of his swing with the right elbow in an entirely different position. We see there clearly that he had come to realise the importance of keeping his elbow well down and as much as possible in the plane of force indicated by the swing and the shaft of the golf club. These photographs are very interesting. Mr. Horace Hutchinson says that the golf club "should be held well home in the palm, and it is not to stir from this position throughout the swing," yet at the top of Mr. Horace Hutchinson's swing illustrated on page 296 of *Great Golfers* we see clearly that at the top of his swing the club is barely held in the fingers of the left hand—as a matter of fact the forefinger of the left hand is raised and the club is merely resting in the three other fingers, which appear to be curved on to the club and hardly exerting any pressure whatever.

It is abundantly clear from this photograph that Mr. Hutchinson, who is the most pronounced adherent to the fetich of the left, is driving his ball with a grip which is, to all intents and purposes, a right-handed stroke. This photograph was taken in action and at the rate of about one twelve-hundred-and-fiftieth of a second, so that there cannot be much doubt as to the fact that Mr. Horace Hutchinson is merely another exemplification of the fact that the golfers who write for the public tell them one thing, while they themselves practise another.

Before concluding this chapter on the power of the left, I may mention that Mr. H. H. Hilton in Mr. John L. Low's book *Concerning Golf*, subscribes to the idea of attempting to regulate the force of the grips taken by the hands. He says on page 78 of that book:

When the main object of a shot is to obtain length, hold tight with the left hand. The left hand will then do most of the work in taking up the club. The right hand comes in on the down swing to add force to the shot, and all parts of the player's anatomy cohering together, the impetus will carry his shoulders round, and unless he arbitrarily checks the motion, he will finish his shot with his arms and club thrown forcibly away from him; in short, he will have followed through.

It will be seen that this fine player distinctly advises a stronger grip with the left than with the right hand when one's object is distance. In the drive the object, of course, generally is distance, and we are distinctly advised by Mr. Hilton to play our stroke in a manner which Harry Vardon has clearly laid down as almost certain to lead to irretrievable disaster, for starting with a firm grip with our left, which we are to put practically in command of the club on the upward swing, we are then to bring the right into play "on the down swing to add force to the shot."

It will be clearly seen here that Mr. Hilton is under the impression that the left is performing the more important portion of the work, for he speaks of the right hand as coming in to add force to the shot, whereas, in fact, the main portion of the force is provided by the right, and if there is any question of either hand and arm *adding* force to the shot, that will be done by the left hand and arm, and not by the right.

I do not think it is necessary for me to go any further in order to show how deeply rooted and how widespread is this delusion about the power of the left. It is another one of those pernicious fallacies which absolutely strike at the root of the game of the great body of golfers, and it is impossible for one to take too much trouble in discrediting it to such an extent that it will soon be recognised as not being practical golf.

I can hardly close this chapter better than by a quotation from a letter received by me from the professional of an American club as far afield as San Antonio, Texas. He writes:

It has taken me years of persistent effort to bury the many prejudices against the proper use of the right arm, but they must go, and I am glad to see you voiced sentiments strong enough to make men stop and think over the situation. Let us hope they will act.

CHAPTER VII

THE FUNCTION OF THE EYES

One of the commonest of the many excuses advanced for missing one's drive is, "I lifted my eye." If the player only knew it he could lift his eye with impunity. That is not what matters. It was lifting his head which caused the trouble.

"Keep your eye on the ball" is, without question, the soundest of sound golf maxims, but it is both abused and misused. We need not waste time arguing the question as to whether or not keeping one's eye on the ball at the moment of impact is absolutely essential to success in driving. Every golfer knows that for all purposes of practical golf one absolutely must keep one's eye on the ball, and that to do any other thing with the eyes at the moment of striking the ball is, to put it mildly, quite inconvenient.

The trouble in connection with lifting one's eye is that one's eyes are in one's head. The seat of the machinery which works the golf drive is in the same place. If one relaxes for a moment the mental effort which has to be made whilst the golf stroke is being executed, the eyes quite naturally wander in the direction in which the ball is about to go. That in itself would not be so bad. The eyes unfortunately do not wander without carrying the head with them. The head is attached to the portion of the body where, roughly speaking, the centre of the swing is situated. Immediately the head moves, the centre of the circle, if it may for purposes of illustration be so called, is affected. Hopeless inaccuracy is the result. It is a matter of the most vital importance in golf that the eyes must not move. Keeping the eyes in the one position from the moment when one has finally addressed the ball until the moment of impact practically ensures the proper management of one's weight; for it stands to reason that if the eyes do not move it is impossible for the head to move, and if the head does not move it will be impossible to sway, and therefore to get the weight on to the right leg at the top of the swing, as do so many golfers who follow the misleading directions given with regard to the distribution of weight in the golf drive.

Keeping one's head perfectly still is a matter of far greater importance than keeping one's eye on the ball; for it will be obvious that it is quite possible for a golfer, after having taken his address, to keep his eye on the ball until he has driven it, but he may in the meantime have lifted his head three or four inches. Lifting his head three or four inches will not have caused him to take his eye off the ball for an instant, but it will have been sufficient to have ruined his drive. Therefore, we see that the really important thing is to keep one's head and eyes in the same position for the impact as they were at the moment of address. When I say the same position it is manifest that there will be a fractional alteration, but it must be the aim of the scientific golfer to have his eyes, at the moment of impact, almost exactly in the same position as they were at the moment of address.

Keeping one's eyes steady in this manner means, as has already been pointed out, that one preserves the centre, if it may be so called, of the swing much better than if one allows one's weight to move from one leg to the other. Preserving the centre of the swing in this manner means that the rhythm of the swing must be very much better than if it has a moving "centre." A moving centre must import into the stroke of any golfer far greater inaccuracy than there would be if his centre had remained constant, as it will do if he keeps his head in the same place.

Some time ago a good professional golfer asserted that the well-known maxim "Keep your eye on the ball" was a delusion, and that it was possible to play perfectly good golf blindfolded, provided one had first taken one's stance and judged one's swing at the ball. In due course a match was arranged between this professional, blindfolded, and an amateur, and the professional was very badly beaten, as he did not, I believe, win a single hole. This result naturally tended to discredit his ideas very considerably.

As a matter of practical golf, what he wished to establish is perfectly correct. Although "Keep your eye on the ball" is the soundest of sound practical golf, it is to a very large extent preached in a manner which is in itself entirely fallacious—for two reasons: Firstly, the player is told that it is absolutely essential to his stroke that he must keep his eye on the ball up to the moment of impact, and not only must he keep it there until the moment of impact, but that he should keep on gazing at the turf where the ball had lain after the ball has gone on its way.

Now our professional golfer, who essayed the task of playing blindfolded golf, was perfectly correct in stating that it is not necessary to keep one's eye on the ball in playing golf, for the simple reason that the eye has fulfilled its function and has gone out of business, so far as regards that stroke, long before the head of the club has come into contact with the ball. It is this fact which makes us so prone to lift our eyes, and with them our heads, which of course is fatal to good golf. I go so far as to say that if Vardon in his drive could be automatically blindfolded when his club was two feet from his ball, and that he could accustom himself to keeping his head still after he was blindfolded, it would not affect his drive in the slightest degree, for the very simple and all-sufficient reason that the eye has finished its function in connection with the golf stroke for a very considerable period before impact takes place. It has assisted the golfer to take his proper stance and address, and has aided him in judging his distance, but the arc of the golf stroke is practically settled almost from the instant that it starts on its downward path.

The duration of impact in a drive at golf has been measured by the most competent authority to be one ten-thousandth of a second. Photographs of the impact of the golf club with the golf ball taken at the one twelve-hundred-and-fiftieth of a second, are merely blurs. There is no clear definition of the club whatever. We can see from this that the rate of speed at which the golf club is travelling is extreme, even had we not the scientific measurement of the exact amount of time consumed during the contact. It will be obvious to a very ordinary understanding that when a club is travelling at this terrific pace it would be impossible for anyone to impart into the line of travel of the club head a new direction at, say, two feet from the ball, without ruining both the force and the direction of the ball. Therefore, it is evident that if one could close one's eyes when the club head was two feet from the ball and still keep one's head in exactly the same position, the impact would be practically not affected at all.

This is the undoubted fact in so far as regards the work of the eye. It fulfils its duty very early in the stroke; but although the explanation of the function of the eye is so incorrectly given, still "Keep your eye on the ball" is, and ever will be, a sound golfing maxim, for it is not given to golfing man to be able to lift his eye and at the same time to keep his mind concentrated on his stroke, and to keep his head in the same place as it was in when he addressed his ball. Therefore, although it is not so absolutely necessary to keep one's eye on the ball as is generally laid down, it is expedient to preach to the fullest extent and to insist on what Harry Vardon calls "the parrot cry of the links."

Most writers who deal with the matter of keeping one's eye on the ball are not satisfied with exhorting the player to keep his eye on the ball until after the moment of impact; they go further still and insist upon the fact that he must continue to gaze at the piece of turf whereon the ball lay, long after the ball has departed to the hole. This, again, is an absolute fallacy. It is only excusable on the principle that the greater includes the less, and that by insisting on one gazing at the turf long after the ball has sped on its way, one may be able to make the player do what he should do, and that is just to keep his eye on the ball until the moment of impact, for if we follow the advice given by many notable men of continuing to gaze at the turf after the ball has been driven, there can be no doubt whatever that we do much to spoil the rhythm and effectiveness of the drive.

To preserve these we have been told that the head must be kept immovable throughout the golf drive, and that one must keep one's eye on the ball until it has been driven, and on the place where it was after it has been driven. However, following Vardon's explanation of the drive and taking what we know of this stroke ourselves, it will be remembered that at the moment of impact, "simultaneously," Vardon says, the body moves down the line of flight to the hole. It follows, therefore, that if one continues turf-gazing after one has hit the ball, that one's body is going on its way towards the hole whilst one's head is being held backward in the opposite direction to the travel of the body. This is absolutely bad golf, and Vardon does not do this himself.

The truth with regard to the proper management of the eye in the golf stroke is that it should move simultaneously with the ball, for if there be any attempt whatever to drive the ball and to keep the head in the same position as it was at the moment of address, this will inevitably result in preventing the right shoulder getting through and the body following it as it ought to do, for a rigid head and neck will prevent any follow-through.

Vardon is very explicit about the value of timing the body so that it goes forward down the line of flight towards the hole at the moment the stroke is made. He shows us, as a matter of fact, that this forward movement is practically simultaneous with the impact of the club on the ball. It will be obvious, then, to anyone, that this turf-gazing after one has hit the ball, which is recommended by the leading authorities of the game, is absolutely bad golf, for it must inevitably interfere with the follow-through.

At page 174 of *The Complete Golfer* Vardon says:

Keep your eye on the ball until you have hit it, but no longer. You cannot follow through properly with a long shot if your eye remains fastened on the ground. Hit the ball and then let your eye pick it up in its flight as quickly as possible. Of course this needs skilful timing and management, but precision will soon become habitual.

It was by the merest chance that I saw this passage after I had written my chapter on "The Function of the Eyes," although I am now incorporating it herein.

I am very glad to have Vardon's authority to back me up in discrediting the silly idea about turf-studying; but although I have him with me I cannot hold him guiltless of spreading the error, for he has been photographed *repeatedly* illustrating it in a style which he never uses in actual play. This may be seen in the series of photographs in *Fry's Magazine* already referred to, and also at pages 89 and 97 of *Great Golfers*, wherein this great player is shown in positions which in actual play he would not understand how to get into; but people who know no better, and have not the real power of comparative analysis and close thinking, are led away and suffer for this kind of foolishness merely because it is associated with a great name.

PLATE VIII.

EDWARD RAY

This plate shows the champion's tremendous finish in the drive. Ray, at the top of his stroke, gets much of his weight on his right foot, but does not advise others to do so.

In connection with this matter of the function of the eye there is an interesting point which I have not seen mentioned in any golf book—a point which makes it, if anything, more necessary for one to insist upon the vast importance of the maxim "Keep your eye on the ball," although it is fallaciously preached both before and after impact. This point is that there is just before impact a very considerable portion of the travel of the head of the golf club during which the ball is practically never seen by the golfer. This is what I may call the golfer's "blind spot." It exists in practically all ball games where the ball is struck by a bat or other implement of that kind. Its existence, of course, is well known in cricket. I have played lawn-tennis for twenty years, and I do not believe that I have at any time during that period seen my racket hit the ball when actually playing. I have seen it do it when I have made up my mind to watch the ball and forget other matters, but in actual play one does not do this. One plays the stroke with the utmost naturalness. The ball is coming towards one and one gauges the distance and strikes. One knows that whatever happens one's stroke is made for good or ill, and there is in many strokes a blind spot of fully six to nine inches in length.

I have had some wonderful photographs of this blind spot wherein it is shown most clearly that the lawn-tennis player is looking right away from his ball long before he has struck it. I think it is beyond question that this same blind spot exists in golf. I have no doubt whatever that, perfect player as he is, there is in Harry Vardon's stroke a blind spot of at least five inches. Few people who have not studied this question can realise the incredible rapidity with which the head of a golf club travels. I am well aware that there are many photographs of Harry Vardon in existence, which show him carefully studying the turf after the ball has gone on its way. I am also well aware that these photographs were taken to illustrate the fact that he does engage in turf-studying after the ball has gone on its way. I am also well aware that in actual play he does nothing of the kind, and that his beautiful, free, and natural finish is as different from the stiff and constrained photographs shown when he does not lift his head, as chalk is from cheese.

I have watched Harry Vardon many and many a time, and I am absolutely certain that in his natural play he has no thought whatever in his mind of gazing at the turf after his ball has gone away. There is nothing whatever to be gained by doing so, and there is much to be lost. Any attempt whatever to anchor the head by gazing at the turf after the ball has gone away, and then afterwards to allow it to resume its place, together with the shoulders, in the swing of the follow-through, is mere futility, and must result in absolutely spoiling the rhythm of the swing and a proper follow-through.

There is no player in the world who could be taken as a finer example than Harry Vardon, of the fact that in the golf swing and at the moment of impact there must be no restraint whatever on the movement of the shoulders and the head. They must work together with the club head and the ball. If they do not all move at the same time something is out of gear.

In the game of blindfolded golf which I have referred to, the professional player took his stance, addressed his ball, and was then blindfolded with a handkerchief, an operation which naturally took some considerable time, but even as it was, he played some astonishingly good shots even when his whole swing was blindfolded. He should have had a pair of spectacles lined with cotton wadding or some similar material and fastened with an elastic band, which could have been lifted up whilst he was taking his address and closed down the moment he was ready to make his stroke. This would have given him a better chance to demonstrate what he desired to, which, as I have already said, was in itself practically sound.

I have spoken of Harry Vardon's blind spot, and I have said that it is a matter of five inches. As a matter of fact it may quite well often be double that; but it seems to me perfectly plain that nothing whatever that Vardon can do when his club is within a foot of the ball, so long as he keeps his head steady or still, is likely to alter the path of the club head—I am speaking now, of course, of any normal golf stroke. This consideration of the matter brings us back to the statement which I have made time and time again, and in which I am supported by James Braid, that once the golf stroke is commenced, the fact of it connecting with the ball is merely an incident in the path of the club head; and that after the club head has proceeded a certain distance on the way to the ball it is beyond the power of the player to alter the character of that stroke, for his force has been irretrievably directed, in so far as regards that particular stroke, in a particular manner.

Speaking of the position of the head in driving, Taylor says:

The head is maintained in exactly the same position as the arms are brought down again, and so it remains until the ball has been swept from the tee. The arms and body for all practical purposes go through the same action, but in the reverse way as in the upward swing, the body being held in a similar position, but with the head turned and eyes looking over the right shoulder at the finish of the stroke.

During the progress of this downward movement the weight of the body is again transferred, passing from the right leg to the left, until when the finish arrives the whole of the weight has been placed upon the left foot, while the right has assumed the position previously held by its neighbour.

We see here in a very marked degree the fallacy of the distribution of the weight so that at the top of the swing the greater portion of it is on the right leg; for Taylor, although he tells us that "the head is maintained in exactly the same position," says that "during the progress of this downward movement the weight of the body is again transferred, passing from the right leg to the left."

It is a very natural question for us to ask, "How can all this shifting of the body be going on if the head is to be kept perfectly still?" As a matter of fact it is a physical impossibility; and it is also obvious that it would be impossible to keep the head still, rigidly fixed, as we are told it should be, at the moment of impact, and yet to get a true follow-through.

Let us read a little farther on, and we see that Taylor says: "If the ball has been struck there must be no semblance of checking or snatching at the club. The player must not check himself or allow premonitory symptoms of a check to make themselves felt even in the slightest degree. He must allow the club head to follow the line of flight of the ball as straight and as far as is possible." It stands to reason that if one's head remains fixed for an instant after the impact of the club with the ball, that instant the club head must feel the tendency to be drawn out of the straight line to the hole, and the follow-through down the line to the hole, which is so properly insisted on by all great golfers, is ruined.

Taylor continues: "The arms must be thrown forward freely and naturally, and as a consequence the right shoulder must be allowed to swing forward too." This should effectually dispose of the idea of holding the head still after the ball has left the ground, for the simple reason that if the head and neck be held still, it will be a matter of utter impossibility for the right shoulder to go through and down the line to the hole as it should.

I must emphasise this matter a little more strongly by Taylor's own words, for it is of very great importance in the golf drive. Continuing, he says, in reference to the fact that the arms must be allowed to go forward freely and naturally and that therefore the right shoulder must be allowed to swing forward:

By doing this the involuntary checking of the swing is rendered impossible; but if arms and shoulders were to be held tightly under control and as rigid as steel, the stroke would be finished as soon as the head of the club had been brought into contact with the ball. Every stroke in golf must be played freely, every muscle of the body must be allowed to do its full share of the necessary work.

That is undoubtedly so; but if one arbitrarily fixes the position of one's head as a stationary point in the golf swing after the ball has gone on its journey, one prevents the right leg doing its share of the work in shifting the weight forward down the line towards the hole, and therefore one, to a very great extent, ruins one's follow-through. This is a point which, in my mind, is of very great importance to the drive, and it is, in so far as regards the function of the eyes, one of the most pronounced fallacies of the many fallacious statements with which unfortunate golfers are loaded.

This blind spot which I have referred to, exists, as I have already said, in practically every game wherein the ball is struck with an implement. It is found in lacrosse, racquets, tennis, cricket, lawn-tennis, polo, base-ball, hockey, ping-pong, and even in billiards; but the probability is that the farther the striking surface of the club or other implement is from the eye, the less is the blind spot; and this is very fortunate for the golfer, for his margin of error is so small that it is of great importance to him to reduce this blind spot to a negligible quantity. But on the other hand, as a matter of scientific and accurate golf, he will make nearly as great a mistake in his golf if, in his endeavour to follow out the well-known and useful maxim, "Keep your eye on the ball," he acquires the habit of turf-gazing after the ball has gone on its way to the hole.

I have before had occasion to refer to the book entitled *The Mystery of Golf*, and I have already, in part, touched upon some of the author's curious ideas with regard to the analysis of the golfing stroke. At page 159 he tells us that "the arms do not judge distance (save when we are actually touching something) nor does the body, nor does the head. The judging is done by the eyes." I am afraid that we cannot deny that the judging is, in all cases, done by the eye, because it is obvious that if we had not the use of our eyes, we should not be able to see the ball; but the author seems to overlook the somewhat important fact that although the arms do not judge distance, yet they *measure* it, and this matter of measurement is a matter of extreme importance, as is exemplified in the case of play out of a bunker where one has to measure the distance without grounding the club.

On the same page the author says: "If the eyes look up before the ball is hit, the muscles do not receive the proper orders to hit, and the most important part of the stroke is done blindly. That is my theory"; and a most remarkable theory it is too. The muscles received their proper orders to hit at the moment the stroke was begun, and lifting the eyes a moment before impact would not affect the stroke if the head remained in the same position. Lifting the eyes is in nearly every case, as I have already pointed out, an action following on lifting the mind. The mind has been allowed to come off the stroke because the player's mental picture of the stroke has been completed long before the physical act. In other words, he has got ahead of his stroke. Then his head comes up, which of course is fatal to good golf.

It is a very remarkable circumstance that the attempted analysis by the author of *The Mystery of Golf* shows clearly that he has entered upon his task with but a very faint idea of sport generally, and he is in this respect much handicapped in his efforts. Let us consider what he has to say with regard to lifting the eye in golf. We read on page 164:

I have sometimes thought that there are two simple and especial reasons for this difficulty of keeping one's eye on the ball: first, because there is nothing to stimulate the attention; second, because one has to attend so long. In cricket, tennis, racquets, as I have shown, the stimulus is extreme; by consequence, your eye follows the ball like a hawk. In billiards there is no stimulus, but you rarely, if ever, take your eye off your ball in billiards. Why? I think because (1) the ball is so near to the eye—and, therefore, the stimulus strong; (2) because the period of time requisite for the stroke is so short. In golf there is no stimulus and the period is always long: you have to look at your ball for more than the whole period of the upward and downward swings.

This remarkable statement shows very clearly, as I have before said, that the author is not practically acquainted with games generally, for lifting the eye is common in practically every game where a ball is used. And it is amazing to find anyone attempting to analyse such a stroke as the golf stroke and at the same time making the statement that "you rarely, if ever, take your eye off your ball in billiards"; and he proceeds to give reasons why one rarely takes one's eye off one's ball in billiards, whereas the game of billiards is an outstanding illustration of the fact that one does take one's eye off the ball. To a very great extent one plays one's stroke at billiards with a most pronounced blind spot every time, in that, just prior to the moment of striking the cue ball, one always looks at the object ball and practically one never sees one's cue on to one's own ball.

Also, it is open to doubt if the golf stroke takes, on the average, from the time the club leaves the ball in its upward swing until the moment of impact, any longer than the billiard player takes in playing his stroke. If it does, the difference is not a matter which need enter into any practical comparison of the strokes.

The curious thing is that in the game instanced by the author as possessing the greater stimulus, that is those games wherein the ball is moving, as in cricket, tennis, racquets, the tendency to lift the eye from the ball is much more pronounced than in those games where the ball is stationary, and this, I think, is by no means unnatural. The operation of the eye is incredibly swift. It catches the flight of the oncoming ball and one plays the stroke to meet it. In playing a stroke at a moving ball, it stands to reason that one has, all other things being equal, less time between the beginning of the stroke and impact than one would have in executing a similar blow where the ball is stationary, for here we have merely the pace of one moving object to deal with, whereas we have in the other case the pace of the two moving objects added together.

It seems to me clear, therefore, that the eye has been able to ascertain much more rapidly what will happen in the case of the two moving objects, and having decided definitely that the stroke must be played in a certain way, the mind has given to the muscles the necessary orders, and the eye has then gone out of business so far as regards that particular stroke, and we get the astonishing result that we find famous players at lawn-tennis playing their strokes with a blind spot of, in many cases, as much as nine inches. This is beyond the region of doubt, and can be proved to demonstration by numerous photographs, so it will be seen that even if there were anything whatever in the suggested comparisons, they are fundamentally unsound in their premises, and therefore absolutely useless for any purposes of practical golf.

We are told at page 166: "If you *don't* keep your eye on the ball, your stroke is cut short the moment you take your eye off." This is obviously an error. Let us imagine that the golfer has played his stroke perfectly accurately up to within three inches of his ball and then takes his eye away from it, will any practical golfer believe that if he keeps his head still the fact of moving his eye is going to alter that stroke in any way whatever? I think not.

Again we are informed at page 167 that: "It is at all events indisputable that any photograph showing a good follow-through shows the player looking at the spot where the ball was, after the ball had left it; proving that he was really looking at the ball when he hit." Personally, I may say that I have never yet seen a photograph of a good follow-through which did show the player looking at the spot where the ball was after the ball had left it, for photographs of that nature which I have seen showed most clearly that if one desires to absolutely prevent oneself from following through, one of the best methods of doing it is to cultivate the habit of studying the turf after the ball has gone on its way to the hole.

In this we know that we have Vardon entirely with us. His corroboration is valuable for the point is of great and practical importance to the game.

CHAPTER VIII

THE MASTER STROKE

In his chapter on "Special Strokes with Wooden Clubs" Vardon discusses the question of the master stroke in golf. At page 86 of *The Complete Golfer* he says:

Which, then, is the master stroke? I say that it is the ball struck by any club to which a big pull or slice is intentionally applied for the accomplishment of a specific purpose which could not be achieved in any other way, and nothing more exemplifies the curious waywardness of this game of ours than the fact that the stroke which is the confounding and torture of the beginner who does it constantly, he knows not why, but always to his detriment, should later on at times be the most coveted shot of all and should then be the most difficult of accomplishment. I call it the master shot, because to accomplish it with any certainty and perfection, it is so difficult, even to the experienced golfer, because it calls for the most absolute command over the club and every nerve and sinew of the body, and the courageous heart of the true sportsman whom no difficulty may daunt, and because, when properly done, it is a splendid thing to see, and for a certainty results in material gain to the man who played it.

Here we have a very definite statement by one of the greatest stroke players in the world, that the master stroke at golf is "the ball struck by any club to which a big pull or slice is intentionally applied for the accomplishment of a specific purpose which could not be achieved in any other way."

It is to me a most extraordinary thing to find a golfer of the ability of Harry Vardon classing the pull and the slice as practically equal in order of merit. Anyone who is acquainted with golf must know that the pull is an infinitely more difficult stroke to play correctly than the slice. The slice is a stroke which is comparatively easy, but no one can truthfully say the same thing of the pull.

Before we proceed to a consideration of the question of the master stroke, it will be interesting to quote what Taylor has to say on the subject. At page 88 of *Taylor on Golf* he says:

Still it is not advisable, neither do I look upon it as being golf in the truest sense of the word, for the knack of pulling or slicing to be cultivated, as I am afraid it is by a great many players. No compromise should be made with a fault.

Here we see that what Harry Vardon regards as the master strokes of the game, are looked upon by Taylor as faults.

I may say at the outset that I am not inclined to agree with Vardon at all in this matter of the master stroke in golf. If there is one stroke which stands out above and beyond all others in its demand for accuracy, and a perfect knowledge of the method of applying spin, also a supreme ability perfectly to apply that knowledge, it is the stroke which is commonly called a "wind-cheater"; that is to say a long low ball which flies very close to the earth for the greater portion of its journey, and rises towards the end of its flight to its greatest height.

Although this ball is called the wind-cheater, it is just as effective and just as useful on a perfectly still day as it is against a howling gale, for this stroke is, in my opinion, without any doubt whatever, the master stroke in golf, and if a man has this stroke he should be very willing to allow anybody else to have all the pulls and slices in golf. The supreme importance of this stroke is so pronounced that I have always wondered at the comparatively unimportant position which has been given to it in every book on golf, with the exception of my own works. Pulling and slicing, as golfing shots, may be said to be practically unnecessary if a man has full command of the plain drive without back-spin and the wind-cheater.

Very frequently when a man is called upon to pull or to slice, it is to remedy a previous error, and there can be no doubt that with the pull and the slice it is an utter impossibility to keep on the line in the same manner as can one who uses back-spin in the drive. The secret of the greatest golf of the future lies, in my opinion, in the proper application of back-spin in the drive.

I do not intend here to go fully into the effect of spin on the flight of the ball, as I shall do that at length in my chapter on "The Flight of the Golf Ball." Suffice it to say that the tremendous advantage of the ball with back-spin is, that being hit as the club is descending, and the hands at the time of impact with the ball being a little in front of the ball, the loft of the club is, to a certain extent, minimised, so that the ball is, in effect, struck with a club which has much less loft than would be the case if it were driven in the ordinary manner. This means that for the first part of the carry, the flight of the ball is very low, and as the club was not at the lowest portion of the swing when it struck the ball, the wind-cheater acquires a large amount of back-spin which asserts itself later on, and causes the ball to reach the highest point in its trajectory towards the end of its flight.

One of the greatest of the many merits of this ball is that the method of producing it almost commands a follow-through down the intended line of flight. This in itself tends to give better direction than any of the ordinary golf strokes. The pull and the slice, as is well known, curve very much in their flight, and especially in a wind. It is utterly impossible for the best golfer in the world to say within twenty yards as regards direction, and that, of course, means much more than twenty yards—in fact, practically double that—where the ball will come to rest; but this is not so with the wind-cheater, for although the ball has been sent on its way with a very heavy back-spin, so much of it has been exhausted in lifting the ball at the end of its flight, that by the time the ball strikes the earth there is little, if any, retarding power in the back-spin, so that the ball is frequently a very good runner. I must, however, devote a little attention here to the method of production of the pull and the slice.

There is a wonderful amount of misconception about these strokes, even in the minds of the greatest golfers. Let me, before I proceed to examine what Harry Vardon has to say about the production of the pull, state the general principles upon which the production of all spin is produced. Spin is imparted to a golf ball, as we shall see more clearly later on, merely by the fact that the face of the club, instead of following through after the ball in the intended line of flight, crosses the line of flight at a more or less acute angle; for the slice the club head comes from the far side of the line of flight across towards the player's side of the line of flight; for the pull the process is reversed, and the club head, coming from the player's side, swings right out across the line of flight; in the wind-cheater the club passes downwards along the intended line of flight. There is, of course, no such thing in practical golf as top-spin, so we need not consider that.

There is one other important point which I must mention here. At the moment of impact the face of the club must be, to all intents and purposes, at a right angle to the intended line of flight. For instance, in a slice, any attempt to produce the slice by laying back the toe of the club, or any tricks of this nature, must result in disaster. It is impossible for the person playing the stroke *to time* anything to be done by him *during impact*, and it stands to reason that nothing will affect the ball except what takes place during impact. This, then, resolves the stroke into the fact that the contact between the ball and the club is, as I have frequently insisted, and, as we have seen, James Braid declares, merely an incident in the travel of the club's head in the arc which it is describing.

Although I have said that the face of the club must be at a right angle to the line of flight of the ball, this is not exactly correct, although it is so for all purposes of practical golf. The reason I say that it is not correct, is that practically every well played slice starts off on the line to the hole a little to the left of the true line of flight, so that it is probable that at the moment of impact the face of the club is not at a dead right angle to the initial portion of the flight of the ball. However, it is unquestionably necessary that the face of the club should be as nearly as possible at a right angle to the intended line of flight at the moment that the impact takes place. If this point is not attended to as carefully in the pull and the slice as it is in other strokes, the result must be inaccuracy of direction, and very pronounced inaccuracy too.

Let us now turn to Harry Vardon's directions as to how to play the pull. He says:

Now there is the pulled ball to consider, for surely there are times when the making of such a shot is eminently desirable. Resort to a slice may be unsatisfactory, or it may be entirely impossible, and one important factor in this question is that the pulled ball is always much longer than the other—in fact, it has always so much length in it that many players in driving in the ordinary way from the tee, and desiring only to go straight down the course, systematically play for a pull and make allowances for it in their direction.

He then gives instructions for the stance, and proceeds:

The obvious result of this stance is that the handle of the club is in front of the ball, and this circumstance must be accentuated by the hands being held even slightly more forward than for an ordinary drive. Now they are held forward in front of the head of the club. In the grip there is another point of difference. It is necessary that in the making of this stroke the right hand should do more work than the left, and therefore the club should be held rather more loosely by the left hand than by its partner.

We may pause for a moment here to remark that this is another one of those very noticeable instances wherein Vardon infers that it is usual for the left to do more work than the right, and we may also note that he here gives advice which he has in other portions of his book condemned—that is, attempting to hold more loosely with one hand than with the other, for it is obvious that if, as he has told us will be the case, we attempt to give the right hand a watching brief over the left, the right will come in too suddenly at some portion of the swing, and it is also equally obvious that if we follow out Vardon's advice here and allow the left to hold the watching brief, it will similarly misconduct itself.

I must emphasise again, before I pass on, the very pronounced inference which Vardon here makes that, generally speaking, the left is the dominant partner. Vardon then continues: "The latter," that is the right hand, "will duly take advantage of this slackness," that is the slackness of the left hand, "and will get in just the little extra work that is wanted of it. In the upward swing carry the club head just along the line which it would take for an ordinary drive."

This, I may say, is remarkable advice, for it is well known that in playing the pull the club head begins to move away from the ball, inwards, the moment it is lifted from the ground. This, of course, is natural, for generally speaking, the club goes back to the ball in the way in which it comes up, and as the ball is played by an outward glancing blow, it stands to reason that it will not be taken back straight from the ball as Vardon states here. That, however, is by the way.

Let us now continue with what Vardon has to say:

The result of all this arrangement, and particularly of the slackness of the left hand and comparative tightness of the right, is that there is a tendency in the downward swing for the face of the club to turn over to some extent, that is, for the top edge of it to be overlapping the bottom edge. This is exactly what is wanted, for, in fact, it is quite necessary that at the moment of impact the right hand should be beginning to turn over in this manner, and if the stroke is to be a success the golfer must see that it does so, but the movement must be made quite smoothly and naturally, for anything in the nature of a jab, such as is common when too desperate efforts are made to turn over an unwilling club, would certainly prove fatal.

We have here Vardon's description of how to obtain a pulled ball which he regards as one of the master strokes of the game, but his conception of this stroke is absolutely erroneous. We are told by Vardon that in making this stroke "in the upward swing" we are to carry the club head just along the line which it would take for an ordinary drive. Now, at page 88, Vardon refers to "the inflexible rule that as the club head goes up so will it come down."

It is now established beyond any doubt whatever that the pull is played by an outwardly glancing blow, the converse of the inwardly glancing blow of the slice, but if to obtain a pull we are to follow Vardon's advice and take the club straight back away from the ball, how are we going to come back by the same track as we went up, which is straight down the line of flight, and at the same time to obtain an outwardly glancing blow? The thing is a manifest impossibility, and, as a matter of fact, is not practical golf. This idea of turning over the wrists at the moment of impact is an utterly erroneous notion which I must deal with somewhat more fully. I shall show that James Braid originally had this idea himself, but that he has now, in all probability, abandoned it.

It is evident that Vardon has but a hazy idea of the correct method of production of the pull, although, as we well know, he is a master of the art of producing this stroke. At page 92 of *The Complete Golfer* he gives his description of the manner in which he thinks one of the master strokes of the game is produced. I must quote him again fully, for it is necessary to do this in order that my readers may follow the trend of his mind:

It is necessary that in the making of this stroke the right hand should do more work than the left, and therefore the club should be held rather more loosely by the left hand than by its partner. The latter will duly take advantage of this slackness, and will get in just the little extra work that is wanted of it. In the upward swing carry the club head just along the line which it would take for an ordinary drive. The result of all this arrangement, and particularly the slackness of the left hand and comparative tightness of the right is, that there is a tendency in the downward swing for the face of the club to turn over to some extent, that is for the top edge of it to be overlapping the bottom edge. This is exactly what is wanted, for, in fact, it is quite necessary that at the moment of impact the right hand should be beginning to turn over in this manner, and if the stroke is to be a success the golfer must see that it does so.

It will be seen from this quotation that Vardon is under the impression that in playing the pull the club goes straight back from the ball in the same manner as it would be taken were one playing an ordinary drive. We notice, too, that he commits

65

himself to the statement, that it is necessary that the top edge of the face of the club should be practically overlapping the bottom at the moment of impact. This, in effect, means that the club is actually deprived of its loft at the moment of impact.

It will be apparent to anyone who understands very little about the ordinary principles of mechanics that it would be an impossibility to play an effective shot in this manner. Indeed it would be impossible to raise the ball from the ground, and any attempt whatever to give this turn over of the wrists at the moment of impact would inevitably result in a very large proportion of foundered balls.

It must be remembered that Vardon is advising the player to consciously attempt to regulate the loft of his club during an impact which lasts for no more than the ten-thousandth of a second. Golf is at all times a game calling for a remarkable degree of mechanical accuracy, but it is obviously asking, even of the most perfect player, far too much when we request that he shall, by the action of his hands and wrists, regulate the loft of his club in an impact which lasts for such an extremely short time. We must remember that if the shot were played as Vardon describes it, the loft of the club face is continually changing during, let us say, the foot before it gets to the ball and the foot after it has passed it.

The whole idea of the stroke in golf, in so far as regards loft, ought to be that at the moment of impact the player has nothing whatever to do with the loft, his duty being confined to hitting the ball in a certain way and allowing the loft to do its own work, and to take the angle at which it will naturally come down, but any attempt consciously to regulate the loft of the club during impact, especially on the lines laid down by Vardon, must inevitably result in disaster. Vardon tells us that at the moment of impact it is necessary that the club face should be turning so that it will be practically overlapping at least the moment after the ball is struck.

His error is by no means an uncommon one. The same thing exists in lawn-tennis in the lifting drive, where about ninety per cent of the players who try the lifting drive under the impression that it is got by a turn over of the wrist, do the turn too soon and founder the ball—in other words, put it into the net. If the pull were to be played in the way Vardon describes it, the result would be exactly the same. The ball would simply be topped or absolutely foundered.

I cannot emphasise too strongly the fact that this turn over of the wrists in the pull has nothing whatever to do with the production of the stroke, although Vardon says that it has. This turn over of the wrists will, if it precedes the moment of impact, ruin the stroke. It must come naturally long after the ball has gone on its way, and it must come not by any voluntary or conscious effort on the part of the player, but as the natural result of the correctly played first portion of the stroke.

In my chapter on "The Flight of the Ball," I shall go more fully into the mechanical principles of the production of the pull. It will be sufficient for me to say here that the pull is produced by an upward, outward, glancing blow, but there must be no attempt whatever to alter the loft of the club at the moment of impact.

In so flatly contradicting such a master of stroke play as Harry Vardon, it may be as well for me to fortify myself by evidence taken from the work and photographs of another famous golfer who was himself originally under the impression that the pull was obtained in this manner, but who has apparently since abandoned this idea. I feel sure that for the great majority of players who know anything whatever of elementary mechanics, it will be unnecessary for me to do this, but there is a vast number of players who are not well acquainted with even simple mechanical problems, and it is for these that I take the trouble to bring forward James Braid to give evidence against this idea of turning over the wrist at the moment of impact.

We must remember that Braid himself has stated in *How to Play Golf* that the striking of the ball is merely an incident in the travel of the club's head, and we must remember that this book *How to Play Golf* was written long after the quotation which I am now about to give from *Great Golfers* at page 175. There James Braid tells us that "in playing for a *pulled ball* the right wrist turns over at the moment of impact." This is emphatic enough, and Braid here commits himself to the same statement as Vardon does, that is to say, that the right wrist turns over *at the moment of impact*. This is what I absolutely deny.

It is natural to suppose that Braid's book, *Advanced Golf*, contains the author's last word with regard to the science of playing the pulled ball, one of the balls, let us remember, which Harry Vardon considers the master stroke in the game. Let us therefore turn to Braid's illustration of playing for a pull in the four photographs following page 78. Braid here fortunately illustrates the actual moment of impact in the pull, and it will be seen on examining his club that it is apparently perfectly soled, that is to say that the club is lying as truly and flatly as it is at the moment of address. This is very important and quite incontrovertible as being Braid's considered opinion, because this stroke is a posed photograph for the purpose of illustrating the impact in the pull. We see quite clearly from this photograph that there is absolutely no turning over of the wrists, but that on the contrary, the right hand is, if anything, well back on the shaft, and showing no sign whatever, as I have already said—not even a symptom—of beginning to turn over. Nor, as a matter of fact, should it do so. The club does not begin to turn over in the manner described until it has reached practically the full extent of its outward swing on the far side of the line of flight.

This photograph is, in itself, quite sufficient evidence to show us that Braid has abandoned his idea with regard to the necessity for turning over the right wrist at the moment of impact in the pull, but it is instructive to note that there is in the whole of *Advanced Golf* not one word about turning over the wrists at the moment, of impact in the pull, so that we may take it as definitely settled that James Braid has, since the publication of *Great Golfers*, found out his error in this matter, for, against his one sentence in *Great Golfers* that "in playing for a *pulled ball* the right wrist turns over at the moment of impact," we have not only his statement in *How to Play Golf* that the impact is a mere incident in the travel of the club head, but the still more eloquent fact that in *Advanced Golf* he says no word whatever in support of this theory, and that he most expressly and emphatically by his own photographs contradicts the idea.

We need not consider what Taylor has to say in connection with the production of the pull, for we see clearly that his idea of both the slice and the pull is that they are merely errors in golf and not to be encouraged.

Let us turn now to a consideration of the slice. The same misconception which is so prominently shown by nearly every writer about golf with regard to the pull obtains also in connection with the slice. This is clearly shown by James Braid in *Great Golfers*, for following the quotation which I have already given with regard to the pulled ball, he says: "But for a sliced ball I cut a little across the ball, the wrist action being the reverse of that for a pull, viz., the right hand is rather under than over."

PLATE IX.

JAMES BRAID

Here, in spite of what Braid says, it will be seen that his weight at the finish goes almost entirely on to the left foot.

Braid tells us that for a pulled ball he turns his right wrist over *at the moment of impact*. Well, as the wrist action for the slice is the reverse of this, it follows that *at the moment of impact* he turns his right wrist under. This is a very common misconception. It is one which is held by an astonishing number of practical players. Mr. Walter J. Travis in his book on *Practical Golf* repeatedly makes the error of thinking that this turn under of the wrist has any effect whatever on the stroke,

67

but it is just as great an error to think that this turn under of the wrist has anything to do with the production of the slice, as it is to think that the turning over of the wrist has anything whatever to do with the pull. Both of these actions quite naturally *follow* the correct production of the strokes referred to.

The slice is an inwardly glancing blow, if anything, with a suspicion of downward action, whereas, as I have already explained, the pull is an outward, upward, glancing blow. There must be no attempt whatever to turn the right wrist under or downward at the moment of playing the slice, as Braid says he does in *Great Golfers*, although I have not been able to find the same statement in *Advanced Golf*, where we should naturally expect to see it if Braid still has this idea. The curious thing is that in James Braid's illustrations in *Advanced Golf* for playing a slice the right hand is much further forward on the club than it is in those showing the grip for the pull; in fact were it not that the stance shows clearly that the photographs are correctly marked, one would be much inclined to think that they had been wrongly entitled. In playing for the slice, Braid's hand is well over the club, whereas in the pull it is almost underneath it. In *Advanced Golf* this grip for a slice is extremely pronounced, in fact very much more so than in his illustrations of the stance and address for this stroke which he gives in his book *How to Play Golf.*

The popular misconception about the slice is well instanced by what Harry Vardon has to say in connection with the cut mashie approach. He says at page 129 of *The Complete Golfer*:

It is also most important that at the instant when ball and club come into contact the blade should be drawn quickly towards the left foot. To do this properly requires not only much dexterity, but most accurate timing, and first attempts are likely to be very clumsy and disappointing, but many of the difficulties will disappear with practice, and when at last some kind of proficiency has been obtained, it will be found that the ball answers in the most obedient manner to the call that is made upon it. It will come down so dead upon the green that it may be chipped up in the air until it is almost directly over the spot at which it is desired to place it.

I have no hesitation whatever in saying that this is absolutely bad golf. In all cases where cut is applied to the golf ball there must be no attempt whatever to introduce anything into the stroke during the period of contact between the ball and the club. I am here dealing with Vardon's statement with regard to the mashie approach, but it is apparent that all cut shots are, in effect, slices, and if one gets the idea into one's mind that the slice is obtained by anything which is done consciously during impact and timed by the player to be done in that space of time, it must militate severely against one's chance of producing a successful shot.

A little farther down on the same page Vardon says:

At the moment of impact the arms should be nearly full length and stiff, and the wrists as stiff as it is possible to make them. I said that the drawing of the blade towards the left foot would have to be done quickly because obviously there is very little time to lose; but it must be done smoothly and evenly, without a jerk, which would upset the whole swing, and if it is begun the smallest fraction of a second too soon the ball will be taken by the toe of the club, and the consequences will not be satisfactory. I have returned to make this the last word about the cut, because it is the essence of the stroke and it calls for what a young player might well regard as an almost hopeless nicety of perfection.

Here it is quite evident that Vardon thinks that the cut on a mashie approach is played by something imported into the stroke *during impact*, whereas the truth is that the club in a good shot properly played never alters from the line of the arc mapped out by the mind from the very beginning of the stroke. Vardon says that the cut "must be applied smoothly and evenly without a jerk, which would upset the whole swing." It is obvious that if the head of the club has travelled in a certain line down to within a fraction of an inch of the ball, and is then suddenly pulled across the ball, *there must be a jerk.*

This, however, is not what happens when the stroke is well played. The club face simply passes across the intended line of flight of the ball with the front edge of the sole approximately at a right angle to such intended line of flight, but the club head proceeds across the line in an uninterrupted arc. If what Vardon, Mr. Travis, and many other people lay down, were correct, a drawing of the stroke would show the club head proceeding to the ball in a curve, then a sudden jump inwards towards the player with a continuation approximating to the follow-through of the first half of the stroke, but it is almost needless to say that nothing of this kind takes place either in this modified slice or the true slice at golf, which we shall have to deal with more particularly later on.

Speaking of this shot—the cut mashie stroke—Vardon says: "It will come so dead upon the green that it may be chipped up into the air until it is almost perfectly over the spot at which it is desired to place it."

This may be so. I have played the shot myself repeatedly, and I have repeatedly seen perhaps the greatest master in the world of the cut mashie approach, to wit J. H. Taylor, playing this shot, and there cannot be any doubt whatever that this particular class of mashie approach nearly always gives the ball a considerable run from left to right. This, indeed, is perfectly natural, for one goes right in underneath the ball and gives it a tremendous side roll tending to make it swerve in the air from left to right, and when it strikes the green, to run in the same direction. So pronounced indeed is the swerve and run of this ball that I have seen J. H. Taylor playing at Mid-Surrey when the green was practically completely obstructed by a large tree, play this shot so that it curved round the tree on to the edge of the green and then ran in almost to the pin.

The shot which stops so dead at the hole, as Harry Vardon mentions, must of necessity have much more in the nature of back cut which produces back-spin than has the ball played by the stroke which he describes.

Vardon refers to the pull and the slice as being the master strokes in golf. I have already said that if I had to pick any one stroke which could be called the master stroke in golf, it would be the wind-cheater, and it is open to question if the long plain drive is not entitled to greater respect than either the pull or the slice. Be that as it may, there is in my mind very little doubt about the respective merits of the wind-cheater and the other strokes referred to. The wind-cheater is the ball which is produced with a large amount of back-spin. Harry Vardon describes it at page 105, and he explains that in order to make the push shot perfectly "the sight should be directed to the centre of the ball, and the club should be brought directly on to it (exactly on the spot marked on the diagram, page 170)." I may remark here that the spot shown on the ball at page 170 of *The Complete Golfer* for a push shot is absolutely above the centre of mass of the ball, and that at page 106 Harry Vardon gives a diagram of "The push shot with the cleek." In this diagram he shows that the face of the cleek at the moment of impact is perpendicular.

It is quite certain that even if one could hit the ball above the centre of its mass with a perpendicular face, it would be impossible to get the ball off the ground in this manner. The push shot with the cleek must be played with loft on the club, and indeed it does not matter what club is used for this shot, there must be *loft* on the face of the club *at the moment of impact* if one is to obtain a satisfactory result, and not only must there be loft on the face of the club, but it is a certainty that the impact of the club with the ball must be *below* the centre of the ball's mass, and not as Vardon shows it at page 170 of *The Complete Golfer*, above it.

Vardon, for playing this push shot, uses a cleek with a shorter handle and with more loft than his ordinary cleek. This, indeed, is quite natural, for the shot is, in the nature of it, a very straight up and down shot in the line to the hole, and also as it is desirable that the ball shall be hit by the club before the club head has reached the lowest point in its swing, Vardon naturally has his hands forward of the ball at the moment of impact. This, of course, to a certain extent, counteracts the loft of the cleek, but in no case does it counteract it to the extent shown by Vardon in the diagram at page 106 of *The Complete Golfer*, for were the blow made as shown by these diagrams, it would be a mechanical impossibility to obtain the result described by Vardon.

The reason for keeping the hands forward of the ball is, as I have indicated, that the club head may make impact with the ball before it has reached the bottom of its swing, and Vardon's reason for playing with a club of greater loft than is usually employed is that this greater loft helps to make up for the fact that his hands are forward of the ball at the moment of impact. Playing this stroke with an ordinary cleek would rob the cleek of so much of its loft that the probability is that the flight of the ball would in its initial stages be too low to give a satisfactory result.

Vardon says at page 106: "The diagram on this page shows the passage of the club through the ball as it were, exactly," but the trouble is that it does not show the passage of the club through the ball "as it were, exactly," because at the moment of impact with the ball the club must have sufficient loft on its face to lift the ball, and, moreover, the face of the club must make its first contact at a point at most as high as the centre of the ball, but preferably much lower, so that the force of the blow has an opportunity of exerting itself upwardly through the centre of the ball's mass. Vardon plays this shot perfectly, but he does not describe it as well as he plays it. He says at page 106 of *The Complete Golfer*:

I may remark that personally I play not only my half cleek stroke, but all my cleek strokes in this way, so much am I devoted to the qualities of flight which are thereby imparted to the ball, and though I do not insist that others should do likewise in all cases, I am certainly of opinion that they are missing something when they do not learn to play the half shot in this manner. The greatest danger they have to fear is that in their too conscious efforts to keep the club clear of the ground until after impact, they will overdo it and simply top the ball, when, of course, there will be no flight at all.

There can be no doubt that this stroke is an extremely valuable one, particularly with the cleek, and it is a stroke which will well repay anyone for the time spent in practising it. There is, indeed, as Vardon says, a great danger of the player topping the ball if he tries to keep too far away from the ground until after the impact, but he must at all costs get out of his mind the idea of hitting the ball where Vardon says it should be hit, viz. above the centre of the ball's mass. This never was golf. It is not golf now, and it never will be golf.

It is almost incredible, but is a fact, that a golf journalist who presumed to say that he knew what was "at the back of his (Harry Vardon's) head" stated in an article in a sporting magazine in London, that this push shot, one of Vardon's most beautiful and accurate strokes, is obtained by thumping the ball on to the earth—in fact that the stroke is almost what one might term a "bump ball," to use the cricket term. Any idea more abhorrent to the true golfer than the notion of producing his finest cleek shots and approach shots by banging the ball on to the earth can hardly be imagined, nor anything more incorrect.

The wind-cheater is an invaluable stroke, but there can be no doubt that it is a stroke calling for a very considerable degree of skill in order to play it perfectly, or indeed very well, and in connection with this matter there was a very peculiar but entirely mistaken idea that for the production of this stroke it was necessary at the moment of impact to turn over both wrists. This idea obtained for years, and notwithstanding my repeated explanations, the deeply rooted notion was persevered in and used in such a manner by many players that it seriously interfered with their game.

Some of the criticism which I had to put up with at the time that I was instructing golfers in these matters was very remarkable. I must give one instance which seems almost incredible. I had explained in the pages of *Golf Illustrated*, the leading golfing journal of London, how the pull is produced, and I had therein indicated as clearly and decidedly as I now do that it was impossible to produce the pull by the method indicated by Harry Vardon. Mr. A. C. M. Croome, the well-known international player, solemnly asserted in the *Morning Post* that he had himself seen Harry Vardon produce the shot in the manner which I said was an impossibility, and that in effect an ounce of practice was worth a pound of theory.

I took the trouble to explain that a cinematograph with about 400 pictures, or perhaps a good many less per second, was sufficient to deceive an ordinary man into thinking that he saw a continuous picture. I explained that the camera which took the photographs for my purpose was timed to give an exposure of one twelve-hundred-and-fiftieth of a second, and that this was, therefore, at least three times as rapid as the machine which deceives an ordinary man into thinking that he sees a single picture, but notwithstanding that the camera was so tremendously rapid in its exposure, the golf club beats it to such an extent that at the moment of impact the club is represented by a swish of light or movement on the plate, and the ball immediately after impact is represented by something resembling a section of a sperm candle. So extremely rapid is its flight that it is impossible to obtain even by so short an exposure anything resembling clear definition.

I showed clearly that an implement which was moving so fast as to absolutely beat the machine which was three times as fast as the machine which deceived the human being, was not likely to be able to be followed accurately by the human eye unaided in any way whatever. Still, that was the kind of criticism which I had to undergo.

I was told exactly the same thing when I explained that in the push shot there must be no attempt whatever to turn over the wrists at the moment of impact, that in this shot as in all other strokes at golf, there must be no attempt whatever made to interfere with, or alter, during impact, the angle of the loft taken at the time of address, for any such attempt as this must end in trouble.

It was some years after this controversy that Mr. A. C. M. Croome produced a column in the *Morning Post* entitled "Justice," in which he referred to the matter as follows:

MR. VAILE RIGHT

It is common talk that Sherlock has improved a great deal since he migrated from Oxford to Stoke Poges, and for once common talk is right. His driving, at least when the ground is hard, is distinctly longer than it used to be, but the increased length has not been purchased at the expense of steadiness. The ball still flies from his wooden clubs along a line ruled straight to the hole. Even more valuable to him than the gain in length is the acquisition of all that range of shots which, if correctly played, leave the striker posed with his arms straight out and the back of his right hand uppermost.

A few years ago I, in common with many other misguided golfers, believed that the movement of the right hand was the cause, not the consequence, of correct execution. Consequently a large percentage of the shots attempted to be played in this way went anywhere but to the desired place. We turned the key in the lock too soon. So far as I know Mr. P. A. Vaile was the first publicist to set forth the truth. I have differed from him on many points and found myself unable to follow the more abstruse of his treatises. It is a pleasure to acknowledge a debt to him, and it is a heavy debt, for a misconception of the work done by the right hand in holding the ball up against left hand wind is fraught with disastrous consequences. Sherlock was performing this feat most exactly on Tuesday and hitting the ball monstrous far with his irons forbye.

I was very pleased to see this statement by Mr. Croome, for several reasons. It was a sportsmanlike acknowledgment of error, and a fine instance of what I call "the detached mind," which is extremely rare in England. The majority of controversialists are too much taken up with the personal aspect of the controversy, to remember that the controversy if it is worth entering upon, must always be of more importance than the controversialists, but beyond this, it is always of importance, especially for one who is in the habit of writing golf, to know the game to the core, for such an one can do much to spread a correct knowledge of the game, and this misconception of the action of the wrists has been responsible for millions of foundered shots.

I cannot help thinking, however, that in Mr. Croome's generous acknowledgment of error, he was, to a certain extent, committing another error, for when he spoke of "all that range of shots, which if correctly played, leave the striker posed with his arms right out and the back of his right hand uppermost" he referred naturally to balls which have been played in the main with back-spin, but a little later on he proceeded to say:

It is a pleasure to acknowledge a debt to him, and it is a heavy debt, for a misconception of the work done by the right hand in holding the ball up against a left hand wind is fraught with disastrous consequences.

Here it will be evident that Mr. Croome is referring to a pulled ball, but at no time when one has obtained a pulled ball by a stroke properly played, will the finish be such as that described by Mr. Croome. The finish described by him is the characteristic finish of the wind-cheater type of ball, but, notwithstanding this, the point is that Mr. Croome has acknowledged the error with regard to the turn over of the wrists; as he very well puts it, "we turned the key in the lock too soon." That very succinctly summarises the matter, and it will be sufficient for our purpose in this chapter.

I must quote again a passage in Mr. Croome's article. He says: "Even more valuable to him than the gain in length is the acquisition of all that range of shots which, if correctly played, leave the striker posed with his arms straight out and the back of the right hand uppermost." This is a somewhat curious sentence. As a matter of fact, anyone who acquires this range of shots will acquire with it extra distance, for the finish, as I have already stated, but cannot state too often or too emphatically, is the characteristic finish of the wind-cheater—a ball which carries the beneficial back-spin of golf, the secret at once of length and direction.

CHAPTER IX

THE ACTION OF THE WRISTS

There is no doubt that a proper wrist action in the drive is of very great importance, and it is just as undoubted that the real secret of wrist action has been enshrouded in mystery by anyone who has in any way attempted to deal with it. Indeed, so great a master of the game as James Braid, absolutely confesses that he does not know where the wrists come in during the drive. As Braid has already stated that it is almost impossible to teach putting, it really looks as though there is quite a considerable gap in golf which must be left to his pupils' imagination, but this is not really so. These great golfers really know golf and teach it much better than their published works would lead one to believe, and as a matter of fact in very many instances the matter which I am criticising so plainly is, I believe, not their own. I cannot believe that much of the ridiculous nonsense which is published in association with the greatest names of the world would be upheld by them in an ordinary lesson—in other words, I am firmly convinced that they suffer in the interpretation by persons whose knowledge of golf is extremely limited.

It will, however, be interesting to see what the great golfers have to say with regard to wrist work. Let us turn first to Harry Vardon at page 70 of *The Complete Golfer*. There he says:

Now pay attention to the wrists. They should be held fairly tightly. If the club is held tightly the wrists will be tight, and *vice versa*. When the wrists are tight there is little play in them and more is demanded of the arms. I do not believe in the long ball coming from the wrists. In defiance of principles which are accepted in many quarters, I will go so far as to say that, except in putting, there is no pure wrist shot in golf. Some players attempt to play their short approach with their wrists as they have been told to do. These men are likely to remain at long handicaps for a long time. Similarly there is a kind of superstition that the elect among drivers get in some peculiar kind of "snap"—a momentary forward pushing movement—with their wrists at the time of impact, and that it is this wrist work at the critical period which gives the grand length to their drives, those extra twenty or thirty yards which make the stroke look so splendid, so uncommon, and which make the next shot so much easier. Generally speaking, the wrists, when held firmly, will take very good care of themselves; but there is a tendency, particularly when the two V-grip is used to allow the right hand to take charge of affairs at the time the ball is struck, and the result is that the right wrist, as the swing is completed, gradually gets on to the top of the shaft instead of remaining in its proper place.

There are several important statements in this paragraph. Vardon says, "I do not believe in the long ball coming from the wrists," and I say that there is no doubt whatever that in the ordinary acceptation of the term the long ball no more comes from the wrists than it does from the feet, for as Vardon indicates here, in a drive of perfect rhythm there is no such thing as getting the wrists into the work at, or about, the moment of impact, as is so frequently advocated by authors who preach what they do not themselves practise.

Vardon says that "except in putting there is no pure wrist shot in golf." I have already shown that not even in putting is there such a thing as a pure wrist shot in golf, unless, indeed, the player should be playing with a putter which has an absolutely perpendicular shaft. In this case, and in this only, is it possible to play a pure wrist shot in golf if one follows out correctly the instructions which are recognised as being the soundest guide in good putting.

Before quoting from James Braid in *Advanced Golf* I must draw particular attention to what Vardon has said about the "snap" of the wrists at the moment of impact. He says that "there is a kind of superstition that the elect among drivers get in some peculiar kind of 'snap'—a momentary forward pushing movement—with their wrists at the time of impact, and that it is this wrist work at the critical period which gives the grand length to their drives." It is surely not to be wondered at that this, as Vardon terms it, "superstition" exists, when we read in a book such as *Advanced Golf*, which was published several years after Vardon's *Complete Golfer*, statements to this effect:

Then comes the moment of impact. Crack! Everything is let loose, and round comes the body immediately the ball is struck, and goes slightly forward until the player is facing the line of flight. The right shoulder must not come round too soon in the downward swing but must go fairly well forward after the ball is hit. If the tension has been properly held all this will come quite easily and naturally; the time for the tension is over and now it is allowed its sudden and complete expansion and quick collapse. That is the whole secret of the thing—the bursting of the tension at the proper moment—and really there is very little to be said in enlargement of the idea. At this moment the action of the wrists is all-important, but it cannot be described. Where exactly the wrists begin to do their proper work I have never been able to determine exactly, for the work is almost instantaneously brief. Neither can one say precisely how they work except for the suggestion that has already been made. It seems, however, that they start when the club head is a matter of some eighteen inches from the ball, and that for a distance of a yard in the arc that it is describing they have it almost to themselves, and impart a whip-like snap to the movement, not only giving a great extra force to the stroke, but, by keeping the club head for a moment in the straight line of the intended flight of the ball, doing much towards the ensuring of the proper direction. It seems to be a sort of flick—in some respects very much the same kind of action as when a man is boring a corkscrew into the cork of a bottle. He turns his right wrist back; for a moment it is under high tension, and then he lets it loose with a short, sudden snap. Unless the wrists are in their proper place as described, at the top of the swing, it is impossible to get them to do this work when the time comes. There is nowhere for them to spring back from.

Here it will be seen that in a work of James Braid which is entitled *Advanced Golf* and which was published several years after Harry Vardon's *Complete Golfer* and by the same firm, we have advice and information given to us which is diametrically opposed to the ideas of Harry Vardon. There can be no doubt whatever that Vardon's opinion with regard to this matter is much sounder than Braid's, and in order that I may assist anybody who is in doubt as to which opinion to be influenced by, I shall analyse Braid's statement.

We must, before we begin to consider Braid's advice, remember that he himself admits that he does not know where the wrists come in.

This reminds me of an incident which occurred a short time ago. An unfortunate golfer who had an idea that a golf ball should be hit in much the same manner as a cricket ball, or any other common sort of ball, came to me in my office one day and asked me to show him what was wrong with his swing. I put down a ball for him on a captive machine, handed him a golf club and said: "Let me see you hit it?" He proceeded to hit it, but the instant his club head moved away from the ball it was apparent to me that he had not a rudimentary idea of the golf stroke. His left wrist began to turn outwards instead of inwards and downwards. I showed him at once how wrong he was in the fundamental principles of the golfing stroke, for, as is quite usual, he had no idea whatever of the proper distribution of his weight, having been taught by his professional that it must, at the top of the swing, be on his right leg. But the main point to which I want to draw attention is contained in his plaintive remark to me:

"Yes, that is all right now you show it to me, and I can feel that it is better, but it is when I come to play the ball and have to remember all these things that I make a mess of it."

My reply to him was: "My dear fellow, the man who understands how to teach golf does not teach you how to remember all these things. He teaches you how to forget them—in other words, he so instructs you that everything you do between the moment that you address the ball and the time that you hit it, is done practically without any strain on your mind whatever. It is done by habit or second nature. Anyone who teaches you in such a manner that you have to remember each of the things which you think go to make up a perfect drive *while you are making that drive* is no use whatever to you as a teacher," and he was immensely relieved even at the bare idea of this revolutionary teaching.

Nevertheless, in effect, this is the only true and scientific tuition for the golfing drive. We want to make the golfer handle his club in such a manner that all these things which the ordinary book tells him about as being necessary to be done and to be considered seriatim, fall into their places as naturally as one foot comes after another in a walk. To do this we have, unquestionably, to go through an enormous amount of elimination of utterly false doctrine, and the quotation I have just given from *Advanced Golf* is an excellent illustration of what a true teacher has to do in the way of beating down and clearing away harmful doctrine.

Here we have published with the authority of a great player like James Braid, and in absolute opposition to the advice of an equally great player, Harry Vardon, a statement to the effect that the wrists come into the drive and influence the stroke for eighteen inches before and after impact. We are told that "at this moment the motion of the wrists is all-important, but it cannot be described." We need not wonder that the action of the wrists cannot be described, for at the moment referred to by James Braid, there is, as a matter of practical golf and undoubted fact, no wrist action whatever. If one had any doubt whatever about this, one would only have to look at Braid's photographs in *Advanced Golf* showing how he plays for a pull and a slice respectively.

In both of these strokes Braid uses identically similar photographs to show his stance and address. Personally, as I have already stated, I consider that he is, from a golfing point of view, utterly wrong in doing such a thing, for there can be no doubt that the positions are extremely different. Indeed, it would be quite ridiculous to suppose that they were not so, but taking these photographs as Braid's mental picture of what he does at the moment of impact, we see there clearly that the wrists are, at the moment of impact, in exactly the same position as they were at the moment of address.

Taking this in conjunction with the fact that Braid says in the extract which I have just quoted "Where exactly the wrists begin to do their proper work I have never been able to determine exactly, for the work is almost instantaneously brief," we are quite justified in coming to the conclusion that Braid himself does not, in this critical portion of the swing, use any wrist work whatever.

Now Braid says that he has never been able to determine exactly where the wrists begin to do their proper work, so I must explain for his benefit, and for the benefit of the great body of golfers, where the wrists really begin to do their work, and where they do the most important part of their work, and that is absolutely at the beginning of the downward stroke. It is here that the wrists have the greatest life and "snap" in them, for the weight of the club and the strain of the development of the initial velocity fall across the wrist-joints in that position which gives them their greatest resistance—that is, in the way in which the wrists bend least; but it must not be forgotten that although the wrist bends least sideways, still, the bend that the wrist is capable of in that direction provides a tremendous amount of strength. This is particularly evident in all games which are played with rackets.

I must here give an illustration of the power that is obtained in this position. I have before referred to Mr. Horace Hutchinson's illustration of the proper position at the top of the drive which he gives in the Badminton volume on *Golf*. Here the player is shown with the right elbow pointing skywards, and the left, if anything, too much out the other way.

An unfortunate golfer who had tried to put these principles into execution came into my office one day, and told me that he could get no length whatever in his drive. I handed him a club and said: "Let me see you swing?" At the top of his swing he got into this position which is now considered the classical illustration of how it should not be done, and after I had allowed him to swing several times from this position I said to him: "Now swing again, but stop at the top of your swing." He stopped at the top of his swing, and I then went and stood behind him almost in a line with his right shoulder and the hole and about a club's length from him, and I addressed him as follows: "Will you kindly forget for the moment that that thing which you have in your hands is a golf club, and will you also consider, ridiculous as it may seem, that for the nonce my head is a block of wood, and that you have in your hands now an axe instead of a golf club, with which you desire to split my head in two. Would you now, if you had to strike this block of wood, use your arms as you are doing?"

"Why, no," came the answer instantly. "I should do this," and down dropped both elbows underneath the club. Then I said to this searcher after the truth:

"I do not think I shall ever again have to tell you where to put your elbows," and he answered, apparently overwhelmed by my supernatural cleverness:

"That is a wonderful illustration. I never thought of it like that before."

I am giving this as an illustration of the vagueness with which people treat an utterly simple proposition such as this. This man was a chartered accountant, and really, in his way, a particularly clever fellow, but he was overwhelmed with admiration because I was able to show him that with his golfing club he was doing, or trying to do, a thing which no one but an idiot would have dreamed of trying to do with a hammer or an axe. This is the kind of thing for which we have to thank the people who write vague generalities about things which they do not understand.

Let us analyse this most important pronouncement of Braid's a little further. He continues:

Neither can one say precisely how they work, except for the suggestion that has already been made. It seems, however, that they start when the club head is a matter of some eighteen inches from the ball, and that for a distance of a yard in the arc that it is describing they have it almost to themselves and impart a whip-like snap to the movement, not only giving a great extra force to the stroke, but, by keeping the club head for a moment in the straight line of the intended flight of the ball, doing much towards the ensuring of the proper direction.

The real truth of this matter is that there is no portion of the arc of the drive wherein the wrists exert less influence, or are *so completely out of business* as they are in that portion of the drive wherein James Braid *says they are predominant*.

The wrists have a tremendous amount to do with the development of the speed of the stroke, but particularly in the initial stage of the downward stroke. This will be most clearly seen by a study of George Duncan's wrist action at plate 64 of *Modern Golf*, wherein the wrists are shown turning over when the club has gone about half-way on its downward swing. Of course, they begin to turn over much sooner than this, but the truth is that the turn-over of the wrist or, more correctly speaking, the roll of the forearms in the downward swing is such a wonderfully gradual and natural process that it would be utterly impossible for anyone to say at what particular period in the downward swing it happens, and if anyone can say, or, rather, does say, at what particular period the wrists come in to the downward stroke, he is not only an ignorant golfer, but an enemy to golf, for it is a matter which cannot be described except to say that the wrist action begins absolutely with the beginning of the stroke, and is then a continuous and natural turn until the club gets very close to the ball, by which time there is practically nothing left for the wrists to do, as the club has reverted to the position in which it was at the moment of address, or perhaps I should say that it ought to have reverted to that position, as indeed, in so far as regards the club itself, is properly shown by James Braid in his photographs of stance and address and impact.

We have now to deal with the space of eighteen inches in the follow-through, wherein James Braid asserts the wrists still have it all to themselves. This eighteen inches is in all properly executed straight drives, and by straight drives, I mean drives which are not intentionally pulled or sliced, taken up by a clean follow-through down the line of flight after the ball, and this follow-through is, of course, associated with the forward movement of the body on to the left leg which is so well and clearly shown in the instantaneous photographs of James Braid and Harry Vardon, but is, by Braid in *Advanced Golf*, stated to be inadvisable in his text, but clearly shown as advisable in his photographs.

There can be no doubt whatever that any attempt to introduce into the drive for eighteen inches before and after impact, anything whatever in the nature of a "whip-like snap" would absolutely ruin the rhythm of the swing, for it is evident that the introduction of a "whip-like snap" into something which we have been told is "a sweep," would absolutely upset the general character of that "sweep." It is impossible to have a sweep, and in that sweep to sweep the ball away and at the same time to get the ball away by a "whip-like snap." Either we have the sweep or we have the whip-like snap, admitting for the sake of argument that either of these statements is correct, which is not the fact, as the ball is hit away and neither "swept" nor got away with a "whip-like snap," but the would-be learner is presented with this mass of confused thought, instead of having nothing whatever to think of with regard to hitting the ball more than he would have in his mind if he stood still in the road and tried to smite an acorn with his walking-stick.

Let me make this matter perfectly plain. We will consider that the beginner has taken his stance and addressed his ball perfectly. Let him now take his club back from the ball in the manner which the text-books describe for an ordinary drive. Let him swing it thus back from the ball for a foot and let him swing it back against that ball and for a foot on the way to the hole. Let him do this once, twice, ten times, a hundred times, aye a thousand times, if so many be necessary for him to get absolutely and firmly settled in his mind the fact that this swing of one foot back and one foot forward is almost an exact replica of what happens every time he hits a good straight drive in actual play; that it is approximately a correct sample of the club action in that section of the swing back, downward swing, impact, and follow-through. This idea, and this idea only, is what the golfer must have in his mind, and when he has got this into his mind he will see clearly that the whole importance of using the wrists properly in golf is to get them to do their chief work in the early development of the power of the golf drive, but that by the time the ball is reached by the club head they have absolutely gone out of business and do not again come into operation until in the natural order of things they turn the club over, and pull it off the line of flight to the hole in the follow-through.

PLATE X.

HARRY VARDON

Finish of a drive, showing Vardon's perfect management of his weight.

Braid is wonderfully hazy in this matter. He continues: "It seems to be a sort of flick, in some respects very much the same kind of action as when a man is boring a corkscrew into the cork of a bottle. He turns his right wrist back; for a moment it is under high tension and then he lets it loose with a short sudden snap." This really is very sad. We are repeatedly told that the golf stroke is a swing or a sweep, and that it must be of an even character from beginning to end, and yet we have James Braid in *Advanced Golf* telling us that the impact in the drive "seems to be a sort of flick." Well, all I can say is that I wish any golfer who goes into the flicking business much joy and great improvement, but I have not much hope that he will get it until he finds out that flicking is no portion of the game of golf.

Braid's idea of this most important portion of the drive is most remarkable. His haziness in connection with the matter extends even to his illustration. He says that this wrist action is "in some respects very much the same kind of action as when a man is boring a corkscrew into the cork of a bottle. He turns his wrist right back; for a moment it is under high tension and then he lets it loose with a short sudden snap."

This is, mechanically, a marvellous statement. I do not profess to be a great authority on the subject of corkscrews, bottles—or their contents, but even in this respect I may confess to being a trifle more than theoretical, and I may say that I have inserted many a corkscrew into many a cork, but I have never yet used a corkscrew wherein I turned my wrist over as the right wrist turns over in the downward swing of the golf club. As a matter of fact, I never inserted a corkscrew into a cork where I did not turn my wrist from left to right. All the tension in putting a corkscrew into a cork is on the backward journey, or that which corresponds to the upward swing in golf. There is no tension whatever on the return, or that portion of the screwing process which corresponds to the downward swing in golf, whereas in golf the main portion of tension is in the downward swing; but I believe Braid is a teetotaller, so we may forgive him if in this respect his theory is unsound, and I think we can say that although he may be entirely theoretical in this, his theory is, in this instance, not more unsound than it is in regard to what he professes to describe as the wrist action in the golf drive.

Braid says that "unless the wrists are in their proper place, as described, at the top of the swing, it is impossible to get them to do this work when the time comes. There is nowhere for them to spring back from." This is correct and absolutely sound; the wrists must, unquestionably, be in their right place at the top of the swing, the right place being, as I have already indicated, and as indeed practically every respectable book on golf, with the exception of the Badminton volume, shows, underneath the shaft of the club at the top of the swing, but it is quite wrong to speak of any such thing as there being no place "for them to spring back from."

There must be no "spring." It is more a question of swinging than springing, although, as my readers know, I am opposed even to the idea of a swing in the golfing stroke. The stroke in golf is one of the finest hits in the whole realm of athletics, and I object entirely to it being called a swing or a sweep, or anything but that which it is legitimately entitled to be called.

Braid says at page 62: "After impact and the release of all tension, body and arms are allowed to swing forward in the direction of the flight of the ball." This sentence gives us pause. We have seen, according to Braid, that for the space of a yard, that is for eighteen inches before and after impact in the drive, the wrists come into the swing and do something with a "whip-like snap"—something that is a sort of a "flick." We see that this "whip-like snap," and this "sort of a flick," are kept up for eighteen inches after impact, but we are told a little farther on that at the moment of impact "everything is let loose, and round comes the body immediately the ball is struck."

How is it possible to imagine this kind of thing taking place within a swing of perfect rhythm? It is evident that Braid has a very rooted notion about this wrist movement. I must quote again from him, this time from *How to Play Golf*. On page 54 he says:

The initiative in bringing down the club is taken by the left wrist, and the club is then brought forward rapidly and with an even acceleration of pace until the club head is about a couple of feet from the ball. So far the movement will largely have been an arm movement, but at this point there should be some tightening-up of the wrists, and the club will be gripped a little more tightly. This will probably come about naturally, and though some authorities have expressed different opinions, I am certainly one of those who believe that the work done by the wrists at this point has a lot to do with the making of the drive.

Personally, I believe that Braid is wrong in speaking about the initiative in bringing down the club being taken by the left wrist. I believe that the left wrist has no more to do with it than the right wrist, and I do not believe that one practical golfer in a hundred could tell which wrist he uses, and the chances are that if he could tell he would not be a very good golfer, for these are things with which a golfer has no right to cumber his mind. They are things which can quite well be left to Nature. It is an act of supreme folly for the ordinary man to think in the slightest degree of apportioning to either hand the share of its work in the drive. That absolutely must never be on his mind when beginning his stroke.

Braid here emphasises his idea that the wrists come into the golf drive at about two feet from the ball. In *Advanced Golf* he says eighteen inches. In this matter I must unhesitatingly be with Harry Vardon, and if I had not Harry Vardon's support,—if I stood against the authority of the world of golfers—I should still be just as positive as I am with the important corroboration which Vardon gives me, for there can be no doubt that as a matter of practical golf, there is no portion of the stroke in golf wherein the wrists are more quiescent than in the impact. I must not be misunderstood when I say this. It is obvious that the wrists at the moment of impact will be braced to receive the shock of the blow, but the speed of the blow has been developed long before impact, and the wrists have approximately resumed their normal position as at the moment of address.

Although Harry Vardon is so positive in combating the notion of the wrists coming into the drive at the moment of impact, I find him at page 53 of *Great Golfers* saying, when writing of the downward swing with the driver and brassy:

In commencing the downward swing I try to feel that both hands and wrists are still working together. The wrists start bringing the club down, and, at the same moment, the left knee commences to resume its original position. The head during this time has been kept quite still, the body alone pivoting from the hips. When the left knee has turned, I find I am standing firmly on both feet and the arms are in position as in the upward swing, before the left knee started to bend. From this point the speed of the wrists seems to increase, and the impact is thus made with the club head travelling at its highest velocity.

I would here draw attention to the fact that Harry Vardon says: "The wrists start bringing the club down." This, I consider, is very important. I have already referred to Braid's statement about the left wrist taking the initiative. It is of very great importance for the golfer or would-be golfer to know that the left wrist has not any right whatever to claim precedence of the right wrist at this critical moment in the development of the power in the drive.

The other point in this extract to which I desire to draw attention is that Vardon says, speaking of a point in the swing which he describes, and which is practically the same spot wherein Braid says the wrists exert their influence, that is to say, two feet from the ball: "From this point the speed of the wrists seems to increase, and the impact is thus made with the club travelling at its highest velocity." It is quite possible—in fact, it is nearly certain that the speed of the wrists will increase from that point, and that the impact will be made with the club travelling at its highest velocity, but in describing it in this manner Vardon is very nearly guilty of falling into the same error as James Braid has; for this reason, that he is directing the mind to the speed of the wrists at a critical portion of the stroke, whereas there is only one point whose speed has to be considered, and that is the point that does the business, which is the centre, if one may call it so, of the face of the golf club, and it stands to reason that if this is coming down at an ever-increasing speed, what Vardon says of this point would be as true of any other point in the downward swing, but it is bad golf to direct the attention of the student or the golfer to the speed of his connecting link instead of to the business end of the club, at any period during his swing. The golfer's mind must be centred on his ball and his club head.

Taylor, so far as I remember, does not fall into this very grave error, but he, in common with most of the great professionals, is under the impression that the wrists are largely used at the moment of impact to influence the stroke. This is one of the gravest errors in golf. Speaking of lofting a stymie Taylor says: "Then, exactly as the club strikes the ball, the wrists must be turned in an upward direction smartly. The result of this is that the ball is lofted over the other, and if hit properly it will run on and go out of sight as intended." It is a very curious thing that nearly every author or great golfer thinks that in lofting a stymie the best way is to turn the wrists upwards, whereas in fact, and in practical golf, absolutely the best and most certain way of lofting a stymie is to turn neither the wrists, nor, as naturally follows, the face of the club, upwards, at the moment of impact. That must always tend, in a stroke of very great delicacy, which is a natural characteristic of many stymies, to put too much power into propulsion instead of elevation. The best stymie stroke which can be played, is played without lifting the mashie or the niblick by so much as a fraction of an inch after the ball has been hit. I have illustrated this stroke very fully, both by diagram and photograph in *Modern Golf*, and it is unquestionably superior in every way to the ordinary method of playing a stymie.

Let us now glance at the Badminton *Golf* and see what Mr. Horace Hutchinson has to say with regard to this wrist action. At page 90 we read:

Now as the club comes near the ball, the wrists, which were turned upward when the club was raised, will need to be brought back, down again. It is a perfectly natural movement, but where many beginners go wrong with it is that they are too apt to make this wrist-turn too soon in the swing, and thereby lose its force altogether. The wrists should be turned again, just as the club is meeting the ball—otherwise the stroke, to all seeming perhaps a fairly hit one, will have very little power.

It is quite evident that Mr. Hutchinson is an adherent of the "whip-like snap" and the "flick" theory at the moment of impact, for he tells us that the wrists must be turned again just as the club is meeting the ball.

I need not deal fully with this statement, for I have already sufficiently analysed the same idea which is held by James Braid. The only difference is that Mr. Horace Hutchinson's is very much worse than Braid's, in that he thinks the turn-over of the wrists should be executed at the moment of impact, which of course would import into the golf stroke a very much greater risk of error than already does exist in it, and it is unnecessary for me to assure golfers that there is already quite sufficient chance of error without our endeavouring to add to it in any way whatever. But I should like to pause to raise one question.

Mr. Hutchinson, like nearly every other writer on golf, is a disciple of one of the most pronounced fallacies in the game, viz.: "As you go up, so you come down," naturally, of course, all things being reversed. Let us then consider this point. We are informed by Mr. Horace Hutchinson that the wrists should be turned again just as the club is meeting the ball. Following our hoary fallacy of "As you go up, so you come down" I presume from this that immediately the club leaves the ball, the wrists begin to turn backwards. This would indeed give us a peculiar start for our drive.

From an anatomical point of view I think there is very little doubt whatever that the wrists have finished their distinctive function much earlier in the production of the golf stroke than is generally thought to be the case, and what is commonly miscalled wrist action is, in effect, merely the natural roll of the forearm, as it is, I believe, called, at any rate in the case of the left arm, its supination. There can be no doubt that in the majority of cases where writers refer to wrist action, they are confusing the natural turn of the forearms with wrist action.

Before closing this chapter I may perhaps be excused if I refer again to that remarkable volume *The Mystery of Golf*. At page 167 we are told:

At the bottom of the swing, therefore, the club head is, or should be, moving in a straight line. Probably it is when the greatest acceleration in the velocity of the club, and the strongest wrist action in the swing of the arms occur in this straight portion of the stroke, that the follow-through is most efficacious.

For one who essays to explain the mystery of golf, this is a very marvellous statement. Probably at no portion whatever of the golf stroke is the club head proceeding in a straight line. It may be taken for an absolutely settled fact that it is always proceeding in an arc. Also it is quite clear that the author is making the sad mistake, which has been made by so many other people, of thinking that the wrist action is most in evidence immediately before and after the period of impact. Most of the leading golfers fall into the error of stating that cut is obtained by something which is done by the wrists at the moment of impact, but this is unquestionably an error. I have dealt with that already in other places so fully that I think that it will not be necessary for me to do more here than to state that in all good shots the cut is decided upon practically the moment the club begins its downward journey, for the amount of cut which is administered to any ball depends entirely upon the speed, and the angle at which the club head passes across the intended line of flight of the ball, provided always, of course, that the club is properly applied.

CHAPTER X

THE FLIGHT OF THE GOLF BALL

The flight of the ball, and particularly of the golf ball, exercises a strange fascination for many people to whom the phenomena of flight exhibited by a spinning ball travelling through the air, are not of the slightest practical importance. That is to say, there is an immense number of people who take merely a scientific, and one might almost say an artistic interest in the effects produced by the combined influence of spin and propulsion. Scientific men have been for many years well aware of the causes which produce the swerve of a ball in the air. By swerve I mean, of course, a curve in the flight of the ball which is due to other causes than gravitation, and in the word swerve I do not include the drift of a ball which has been perfectly cleanly hit, but which, in the course of its carry, has been influenced by a cross wind. This does not legitimately come under the heading of swerve. It is more correctly described as drift, and will be dealt with in due course.

In the *Badminton Magazine* of March 1896, the late Professor Tait published an article on "Long Driving." Professor Tait was a practical golfer and a very learned and scientific man. He proved most clearly that a golf ball could not be driven beyond a certain distance. He proved this absolutely and conclusively by mathematics, but, so the story runs, his son, the famous Freddie Tait, proved next day with his driver, that his father's calculations were entirely wrong, for he is alleged to have driven a golf ball over thirty yards farther than the limit which his learned parent had shown to be obtainable. Naturally, Professor Tait had to reconsider his statements, and he then arrived at the conclusion that there must have been in the drive of his son, which had upset his calculations, some force which he had not taken into consideration. He soon came to the conclusion that this was back-spin, and he dealt with this matter of back-spin, which is a matter of extreme importance to golf, in a most erudite article, which is much too advanced for the ordinary golfer, so I shall content myself here with referring to just a few of the most important points in connection with it. It is necessary that I should, in dealing with the flight of the ball, give those of my readers who are not already acquainted with the simple principles of swerve, some idea of what it is which causes the spinning ball to leave the line of flight that it would have taken if it had been driven practically without spin.

The explanation is very simple. If a ball is proceeding through the air, and spinning, the side which is spinning *towards the hole* gets more friction than the other side which is spinning *away from the hole*. It is well known that a projectile seeks the line of least resistance in its passage through the air. It follows that the greater friction on the *forward spinning* half causes the ball to edge over towards the side which is spinning away from the hole. This, in a very few words, is the whole secret of swerve.

Professor Tait stated in his article that Newton was well aware of this fact some 230 years before the publication of the professor's article, and that he remarked when speaking of a spinning tennis ball with a circular as well as a progressive motion communicated to it by the stroke, "that the parts on that side where the motions conspire must press and beat the contiguous air more violently, and there excite a reluctancy and reaction of the air proportionately greater."

This really is an extremely simple matter and a very simple explanation. I have taken care to explain it so simply, for swerve is, by a very great number of people, looked upon as an abstruse problem—in fact, my book on *Swerve, or the Flight of the Ball*, is catalogued as a treatise on applied mathematics, instead of, as I intended it to be, simply a practical application of the ascertained facts to the behaviour of the ball in the air.

Professor Tait's article has enjoyed a wonderful vogue. Although it was published nearly twenty years ago it is quite frequently quoted at the present time. There are, however, in it some errors which one would not have expected to have found in such a scientific article. Speaking of the golf ball shortly after it has left the club, Professor Tait said:

It has a definite speed, in a definite direction, and it *may* have also a definite amount of rotation about some definite axis. The existence of rotation is manifested at once by the strange effects it produces on the curvature of the path so that the ball may skew to right or left; soar upwards as if in defiance of gravity, or plunge headlong downwards instead of slowly and reluctantly yielding to that steady and persistent pull.

There is, in this statement of Professor Tait's, a fundamental error in so far as regards the flight of the ball. He said: "The existence of rotation is manifested at once by the strange effects it produces on the curvature of the path." This is incorrect from a scientific point of view, and it is also badly stated. The existence of rotation is not manifested "at once"; in very many cases, practically in all, the ball proceeds for quite a long distance before the effect of rotation is seen. This is more particularly so when it is a matter of back-spin, but it is equally true of the pulled ball or the sliced ball. Both of these proceed for a considerable distance before the effect of spin is noticeable. In fact it is well known to all golfers that the spin begins to get to work as the velocity of the ball decreases. Also it seems as though it is incorrect to refer to the strange effects it (rotation) produces on the curvature of the path, for it is the rotation itself which produces the curvature.

Professor Tait then said:

The most cursory observation shows that a ball is hardly ever sent on its course without some spin, so that we may take the fact for granted, even if we cannot fully explain the mode of its production. And the main object of this article is to show that long carry essentially involves under-spin.

I shall deal with these two statements later on.

Professor Tait said:

To find that his magnificent carry was due merely to what is virtually a toeing operation—performed no doubt in a vertical and not in a horizontal plane, is too much for the self-exalting golfer!

The fact, however, is indisputable. When we fasten one end of a long untwisted tape to the ball and the other to the ground and then induce a good player to drive the ball (perpendicularly to the tape) into a stiff clay face a yard or two off, we find that the tape is *always* twisted in such a way as to show under-spin; no doubt to different amounts by different players, but proving that the ball makes usually from about one to three turns in six feet, say from forty to a hundred and twenty turns per second, this is clearly a circumstance not to be overlooked.

It is wonderful how easily a scientific man, as Professor Tait was, can be led astray when he sets out to find the thing he has imagined. Professor Tait, by a footnote to his article in the *Badminton Magazine*, to my mind entirely discounts the value of his experiments. His footnote is so important that I must quote it fully. He says:

In my laboratory experiments, players could not be expected to do *full* justice to their powers. They had to strike as nearly as possible in the centre, a ten-inch disc of clay, the ball being teed about six feet in front of it. Besides this pre-occupation, there was always more or less concern about the possible consequence of rebound, should the small target be altogether missed.

It will be apparent even to anyone who is not possessed of a scientific or analytical mind that Professor Tait *compelled* his players to endeavour to play their strokes in such a manner that the ball had to travel down a line decided on by Professor Tait. I do not know at what height Professor Tait placed his clay disc from the earth, but it is evident that if he put it very low down it would involve the playing by the golfer of a stroke which would naturally produce back-spin, and in any case the trajectory was arbitrarily fixed. In experimenting with such a stroke as this, and in such a manner as this, it should be evident that there should have been no restriction whatever as to the player's trajectory. If it was decided that it was necessary to catch the ball in a clay disc, that disc should have been so large that it was impossible for the golfer's ball to escape it. It should not have been necessary for the golfer *to aim* at the disc. The mere fact of his aiming at the disc and the ball being teed so near as six feet to the disc, all tended to produce the shot which would give the results which Professor Tait was looking for, but that does not prove that the ordinary stroke at golf is produced in a similar manner, and I do not for one moment believe that it is.

In speaking of *the stroke proper* Professor Tait said:

The club and the ball practically share this scene between them; but the player's right hand, and the resistance of the air, take *some* little part in it. It is a very brief one, lasting for an instant only, in the sense of something like one ten-thousandth of a second.

We may note here that Professor Tait said: "*The right hand and the resistance of the air* take *some* little part in it." One would be inclined to think from this that Professor Tait was, as indeed was probably the case, an adherent of the fetich of the left, for there can be no doubt that in "the stroke proper" the right hand does much more than take "*some*" little part in it.

I think that Professor Tait is wrong in his idea that under-spin, or, as I prefer to call it, back-spin, is essential to a long carry. I firmly believe that a ball which is hit with practically no spin whatever, can have a very long carry. However, as the paper which I am now about to consider follows in many ways very closely on the lines of Professor Tait's article, I shall leave this matter for consideration when I am dealing with that paper.

The paper which I am now referring to is one which was read at the weekly evening meeting of the Royal Institution of Great Britain on Friday, 18th March 1910, by Professor Sir J. J. Thomson, M.A., LL.D., D.SC., F.R.S., M.R.I., O.M.; Cavendish Professor of Experimental Physics, Cambridge; Professor of Physics, Royal Institution, London; Professor of Natural Philosophy, Royal Institution, and winner of the Nobel Prize for Physics, 1906. The title of this paper was "The Dynamics of a Golf Ball." It will be observed that neither the Institution under the auspices of which this lecture was delivered, nor the lecturer, is inconsiderable. Professor Thomson is, without doubt, a very distinguished physicist, and we must therefore receive anything he writes with a certain amount of respect. There are, however, in this paper, so many remarkable statements that it is necessary for me to deal with it quite fully.

Professor Thomson tells us very early in the lecture that Newton was well aware of the cause of swerve which I have already set out, some 250 years ago, and that he remarked that in a spinning tennis ball the "parts on that side where the motions conspire, must press and beat the contiguous air more violently, and there excite a reluctancy and reaction of the air proportionately greater."

Professor Thomson says at the beginning of his lecture:

There are so many dynamical problems connected with golf that a discussion of the whole of them would occupy far more time than is at my disposal this evening. I shall not attempt to deal with the many important questions which arise when we consider the impact of the club with the ball, but shall confine myself to the consideration of the flight of the ball after it has left the club.

I may say here that Professor Thomson, although he announces his intention of doing this, is later on in his paper, as we shall see, tempted into considering the questions of impact, and, in my opinion, making several grave errors therein. We may, however, in the meantime, pass this by.

Professor Thomson continues:

This problem is in any case a very interesting one, which would be even more interesting if we could accept the explanations of the behaviour of the ball given by some contributors to the very voluminous literature which has collected around the game. If this were correct, I should have to bring before you this evening a new dynamics and announce that matter when made up into golf balls obeys laws of an entirely different character from those governing its action when in any other condition.

This, at the outset, is an extremely remarkable statement to come from so eminent a physicist, for I may say that Professor Thomson, after making a remark of this nature, proceeds to explain the phenomena of swerve on exactly the same links which I have set out fully and explicitly in my book *Swerve, or the Flight of the Ball*. That, however, is a matter of small importance. It may be that Professor Thomson has not had the opportunity of perusing this book. It may indeed be that Professor Thomson has been unfortunate enough only to have read articles wherein an erroneous explanation of the well-known phenomena of the flight of the ball is given. Be that as it may, there can be no doubt that the explanation which has been given of the causes of swerve has been adequate and accurate, and there would not have been any necessity whatever for Professor Thomson to bring before the learned Institution whose fellows listened to his address "a new dynamics." It would have been sufficient if he had correctly explained the phenomena of the flight and run of a golf ball according to the well-recognised laws which govern the flight and run of all balls. This, however, he quite failed to do.

Professor Thomson says: "If we could send off the ball from the club as we might from a catapult, without spin, its behaviour would be regular, but uninteresting." It is quite possible to send a golf ball off a club without spin. It is just as possible, from a practical point of view, to send a golf ball away without spin from the face of a driver as it is from the pouch of a catapult. The catapult is a machine, and it is a certainty that it can be made to propel a golf ball without any initial spin whatever. A machine can be made to drive a golf ball with just as little spin, and as a matter of practical golf, by far the greater number of golf balls are driven without appreciable spin—that is to say, without spin which has any definite action on the flight of the ball.

The learned lecturer says: "A golf ball when it leaves a club is only in rare cases devoid of spin." It is impossible to prove or disprove this statement, for practically no ball goes through the air with the same point always in front. We may see this quite clearly if we care to mark a lawn-tennis ball, and to hit it perfectly truly, and slowly, so that it goes almost as a lob across the net. We shall see even then that the marked part of the ball moves from one place to another. In fact, even if a golf ball were driven by a machine which did not impart to it any initial spin, it is almost a certainty that that ball would not have proceeded far before it had acquired sufficient motion to justify one in technically calling it spin. Spin, however, is a delightfully indefinite word, but this much one may at least say, and it is, in effect, a contradiction of Sir J. J. Thomson's assertion, namely that in the vast majority of balls hit with golf clubs, especially by skilled players, the effect of spin on the stroke *unless designedly applied*, which is comparatively rare, is practically negligible.

Professor Thomson says that

... a golf ball, when it leaves the club, is only in rare cases devoid of spin, and it is spin which gives the interest, variety, and vivacity to the flight of the ball; it is spin which accounts for the behaviour of a sliced or pulled ball; it is spin which makes the ball soar or "douk," or execute those wild flourishes which give the impression that the ball is endowed with an artistic temperament and performs these eccentricities, as an acrobat might throw in an extra somersault or two for the fun of the thing. This view, however, gives an entirely wrong impression of the temperament of a golf ball, which is, in reality, the most prosaic of things, knowing while in the air only one rule of conduct which it obeys with an intelligent conscientiousness, that of always following its nose. This rule is the key to the behaviour of all balls when in the air, whether they are golf balls, base-balls, cricket balls, or tennis balls.

The idea of a spherical object having a nose is so unscientific and so inexact that it is not necessary for me to dwell very strongly on it here, and I should not do so were it not that this looseness of description is of considerable importance in dealing with Professor Thomson's ideas. He continues:

Let us, before entering into the reasons for this rule, trace out some of its consequences. By the nose on the ball we mean the point on the ball furthest in front.

It will be obvious to my readers that this description is scientifically extremely inaccurate, for if we take a line through the ball from the point of contact with the club to the point on the ball farthest in front, which Professor Thomson calls its nose, we shall find that the flight of that ball will always be in that same line produced, whereas in the spinning ball it is nothing of the sort. The whole trouble here is that Professor Thomson wants to have the "nose," as he calls it, of the ball, both a fixed and a moving point. This, obviously, is most unscientific. If the nose of the ball is the point that is farthest in front, I cannot say too emphatically that it stands to reason that the ball in flight will go straight out after that point, but the fact is that the point in front is continually changing; moreover, the fact that the ball goes the way it is spinning is not explained by any tendency of the ball to wander that way on account of the spin irrespective of the friction of the air.

It will thus be seen that Professor Thomson's explanation in this matter is incorrect and misleading. This is about the most unscientific explanation which could be given of this matter, and it is one which is calculated to mislead people who would otherwise understand the matter quite clearly, so we shall drop Professor Thomson's idea of giving the ball a "nose" which is always in the front of it, but which is also supposed to be continually travelling sideways. It is obvious that Professor Thomson cannot have it both ways.

It is very clear indeed that Professor Thomson is not well acquainted with the method of applying spin to balls which are used in playing games. He says:

A lawn-tennis player avails himself of the effect of spin when he puts "top-spin" on his drives, *i.e.* hits the ball on the top so as to make it spin about a horizontal axis, the nose of the ball travelling downwards as in figure 4; this makes the ball fall more quickly than it otherwise would, and thus tends to prevent it going out of the court.

I have played lawn-tennis for more than twenty years, and I am the author of three books on the game, one of which is supposed to be the standard work on the subject, and I can assure Professor Thomson that no lawn-tennis player would dream of doing anything so silly as to hit a lawn-tennis ball "on the top" in an attempt to obtain "top-spin."

The scientific method of obtaining top-spin is to hit the lawn-tennis ball on what Professor Thomson, if he were driving the ball over the net to me, would call its nose—that is to say, I should hit the ball on the spot which was farthest from Professor Thomson. I should hit it there with a racket whose face was practically vertical, but I should hit it an upward, forwardly glancing blow which would impart, as Professor Thomson expresses it, "spin about a horizontal axis to the ball."

Professor Thomson goes so far as to show by diagram the travel of a ball which has been hit so as to impart top-spin to it, but even in this diagram he is absolutely wrong, for he shows that immediately the ball has been hit with top-spin it begins to fall, but this is not so. In lawn-tennis the ball travels for a long distance before the spin begins to assert itself, and to overcome the force of the blow which set up the spin.

Professor Tait makes this same error in his article on "Long Driving," and it is quite evident to me that Professor Thomson is following, in many respects, the errors of his eminent predecessor.

Professor Thomson also says:

Excellent examples of the effect of spin on the flight of a ball in the air are afforded in the game of base-ball. An expert pitcher, by putting on the proper spin, can make the ball curve either to the right or the left, upwards or downwards; for the side-way curves the spin must be about a vertical axis; for the upward or downward ones, about a horizontal axis.

There are no particular laws with regard to the curves of a base-ball. The same laws regulate the curves in the air of every ball from a ping-pong ball to a cricket ball, and Professor Thomson, in saying that "for the side-way curves the spin must be about a vertical axis," is absolutely wrong. Every lawn-tennis player who knows anything whatever about the American service, will know that Professor Thomson is utterly wrong in this respect, for the whole essence of the swerve and break of the American service, which has a large amount of side-swerve, is that the axis of rotation shall be approximately at an angle of fifty degrees, and any expert base-ball pitcher will know quite well that he can get his side-curve much better if he will, instead of keeping his axis of rotation perfectly vertical, tilt it a little so that it will have the assistance of gravitation at the end of its flight instead of fighting gravitation, as it must do if he trusts entirely to horizontal spin about a vertical axis for his swerve.

Professor Thomson says:

If the ball were spinning about an axis along the line of flight, the axis of spin would pass through the nose of the ball, and the spin would not affect the motion of the nose; the ball, following its nose, would thus move on without deviation.

The spin which Professor Thomson is describing here is that which a rifle bullet has during its flight, for it is obvious that the rifle bullet is spinning "about an axis along the line of flight," and that the axis of spin does pass through the nose of the bullet, but we know quite well that in the flight of a rifle bullet there is a very considerable amount of what is called drift. It is, of course, an impossibility to impart to a golf ball during the drive any such spin as that of the rifle bullet, although in cut mashie strokes, and in cutting round a stymie, we do produce a spin which is, in effect, the same spin, but this is the question which Professor Thomson should set himself to answer. He states distinctly that a ball with this spin would not swerve. If this is so, can Professor Thomson explain to us why the rifle bullet drifts? As a matter of fact, a ball with this spin *would* swerve, but not to anything like the same extent as would a ball with one of the well-recognised spins which are used for the purpose of obtaining swerve.

PLATE XI.

JAMES BRAID

Finish of drive, showing clearly how Braid's weight goes on to the left leg.

Professor Thomson proceeded to prove by the most elaborate experiments the truth of those matters stated by Newton centuries ago, but it will not be necessary for me to follow him in these, because these principles have been recognised for ages past.

It is curious to note that in the reference to Newton, who was aware of this principle of swerve so long ago, we are shown that Newton himself did not quite grasp the method of production of the stroke, although he analysed the result in a perfectly sound manner. Writing to Oldenburg in 1671 about the Dispersion of Light, he said in the course of his letter: "I remembered that I had often seen a tennis ball struck with an oblique racket describe such a curved line." The effect of striking a tennis ball with an oblique racket is, generally speaking, to push it away to one side. The curve, to be of a sufficiently pronounced nature to be visible, must be produced by the passage of the racket across the intended line of flight of the ball.

This matter of the different pressure on one side of the ball from that on the other is very simple when one thoroughly grasps it. Professor Thomson gives in his paper an illustration which may perhaps make the matter clearer to some people than the explanation which is generally given. He says:

It may perhaps make the explanation of this difference of pressure easier if we take a somewhat commonplace example of a similar fact. Instead of a golf ball let us consider the case of an Atlantic liner, and, to imitate the rotation of the ball, let us suppose that the passengers are taking their morning walk on the promenade deck, all circulating round the same way. When they are on one side of the boat they have to face the wind, on the other side they have the wind at their backs. Now, when they face the wind, the pressure of the wind against them is greater than if they were at rest, and this increased pressure is exerted in all directions and so acts against the part of the ship adjacent to the deck; when they are moving with their backs to the wind, the pressure against their backs is not so great as when they were still, so the pressure acting against this side of the ship will not be so great. Thus the rotation of the passengers will increase the pressure on the side of the ship when they are facing the wind, and diminish it on the other side. This case is quite analogous to that of the golf ball.

Even in this simple illustration it seems to me that Professor Thomson is wrong, for he is pre-supposing that which he does not state—a head wind. It is quite obvious that these passengers might have to face a wind coming from the stern of the ship, and in this case the analogy between the passengers circulating round the deck of a ship, and his golf ball would receive a serious blow. In stating a matter which is of sufficient importance to be dealt with before such a learned body as the Royal Institution of Great Britain, it is well to be accurate. If Professor Thomson had stated that his Atlantic liner was going into a head wind, or, for the matter of that, even proceeding in a dead calm, his analogy might have been correct, but it is obvious that he has left out of consideration a following wind of greater speed than that at which the liner is travelling.

Professor Thomson has not added anything to the information which we already possessed with regard to the effect of back-spin on a ball; rather has he, as I shall show when dealing with the question of impact with the ball, clouded the issue. At page 12 of his remarkable lecture he says: "So far I have been considering under-spin. Let us now illustrate slicing and pulling; in these cases the ball is spinning about a vertical axis." We here have a very definite statement that in slicing and pulling the ball is spinning about a vertical axis, but it is not doing so.

Professor Thomson has "an electromagnet and a red hot piece of platinum with a spot of barium oxide upon it. The platinum is connected with an electric battery which causes negatively electrified particles to fly off the barium and travel down the glass tube in which the platinum strip is contained; nearly all the air has been exhausted from this tube. These particles are luminous, so that the path they take is very easily observed."

These particles, I may explain, take, in Professor Thomson's mind, the place of golf balls, and by an electromagnet he shows us exactly what golf balls do, but it seems to me that if Professor Thomson is not absolutely clear what is happening to the sliced ball and the pulled ball, there is a very great chance that, like Professor Tait, he may induce his particles to do the thing that he wishes them to do, and not the thing that a real golf ball with a real pull or a real slice would do. This, as a matter of fact, is exactly what Professor Thomson does, for, as I shall show quite simply and in such a manner as absolutely to convince the merest tyro at golf, Professor Thomson is utterly wrong when he states that in the slice and the pull the ball is spinning about a vertical axis.

I shall not need any diagrams or figures to bring this home to anyone who is possessed of the most rudimentary knowledge of mechanics. It should be quite evident to anyone that to produce spin about a vertical axis it would be necessary to have a club with a vertical face, or to strike a blow with the face of the club so held that at the moment of impact the face of the club was vertical. Now this does not happen with the slice at golf, for the very good reason that if one so applied one's club, the ball would not rise from the earth. The club which produces the slice is always lofted in a greater or less degree, and quite often the natural loft is increased by the player designedly laying the face back during the stroke. It is evident that in the impact with the driver or brassy, the ball, especially the modern rubber-cored ball, flattens on to the face of the club and remains there whilst the club is travelling across the line of flight. This naturally imparts to the ball a roll—in other words, as the club cuts across the ball it rolls it for a short distance on its face.

It is obvious that this rolling process will, to a greater or less extent, give to the ball a spin about an axis which is approximately the same as that of the loft on the face of the club. Therefore, it is clear that in all sliced balls the axis of spin will be inclined backward. It seems likely, also, that as the axis of spin is inclined backward and the ball is rising, there will be some additional friction at the bottom of it which would not be there in the case of a ball without spin. This probably helps to produce the sudden rise of the slice. In all good cut shots with lofted clubs, the angle of the axis of spin is to a very great extent regulated by the amount of loft on the face of the club.

Professor Thomson's error with regard to the slice being about a vertical axis is beyond question, but his error in saying that the axis of rotation of the pull and the slice is identical, is, from a golfing point of view, simply irretrievable. Print is a very awkward thing—*it stays*. The merest tyro at golf knows quite well that the pulled ball and the sliced ball behave during flight and after landing on the ground in a totally different manner from each other. If Professor Thomson knows so much, it should unquestionably be evident to so distinguished a scientist that there must be a very considerable difference in the rotation of these balls. The slice, as is well known, rises quickly from the ground, flies high, and is not, generally speaking, a good runner. The pull, on the other hand, flies low and runs well on landing.

It is not merely sufficient to contradict Professor Sir J. J. Thomson in these matters, so I shall explain fully the reason for the difference in the flight and run of the slice and the pull. The slice is played as the club head is returning across the line of flight, and therefore is more in the nature of a chop than is the pull. Frequently the spin that is imparted to the ball is the resultant of the downward and inwardly glancing blow. This not only leaves the axis of rotation inclined backward, but sometimes inclined also slightly away from the player, but it is obvious that even if the ball had, as Professor Thomson thinks it has, rotation about a vertical axis, which is the rotation of a top, such rotation would, on landing, tend to prevent the ball running, for, as is well known, every spinning thing strives hard to remain in the plane of its rotation, but the slice is more obstinate still than this, for the axis of rotation being inclined backward, frequently at the end of the flight, coincides with the line of flight of the ball, so that the ball is spinning about an axis which, to adopt Professor Thomson's term, runs through its "nose." This means that the slice frequently pitches in the same manner as might a rifle bullet if falling on its "nose," and the effect is, to a very great extent, the same. The ball tries to stay where it lands.

Let us now consider the flight and run of the pull. The pull is played by an upward, outward, glancing blow. The ball is hit by the club as it is going across the line of flight away from the player and this imparts to the ball a spin around an axis which lies inward towards the player. This means that the pull goes away to the right, and then swerves back again towards the middle of the course if properly played, and upon landing runs very freely. The reason for this run has not been clearly understood by many, and it is quite evident that Professor Thomson does not know of it, so I shall give an extremely plain illustration.

Nearly every boy has at some time played with a chameleon top, or some other top of the same species, that is to say, a disc top. Every boy who has played with such a top will be familiar with the fact that when the spin is dying away from the top, it rolls about until one edge of it touches the earth or whatever it is spinning on. Immediately this happens the top runs away as carried by the spin.

That is about the simplest illustration which it is possible to give of the plane of spin of the pulled ball during its flight and of its run after it has touched the earth, but from this very simple explanation it will be perfectly obvious to anyone who gives the matter the least consideration that not only is the axis of rotation of the pull and the slice dissimilar, but as a matter of fact the rotation of the pull and the slice is almost diametrically opposed the one to the other.

Professor Thomson says:

Let us now consider the effect of a cross wind. Suppose the wind is blowing from left to right, then, if the ball is pulled, it will be rotating in the direction shown in figure 26 (from right to left); the rules we found for the effect of rotation on the difference of pressure on the two sides of a ball in a blast of air show that in this case the pressure on the front half of the ball will be greater than that on the rear half, and thus tend to stop the flight of the ball. If, however, the spin was that for a slice, the pressure on the rear half would be greater than the pressure in front, so that the difference in pressure would tend to push on the ball and make it travel further than it otherwise would.

I have not given this aspect of the question a great amount of thought, but it seems obvious that in playing for a slice in the circumstances mentioned by Professor Thomson, it is extremely unlikely that the greater pressure would be, as he says, on the rear half. If, indeed, this were so the slice would, in my opinion, not take effect; also on account of the tremendous speed of the golf ball it seems to me utterly improbable that in any ordinary wind which one encounters on a golf links it would be possible to obtain on the rear half of a golf ball a greater pressure than that on the forward spinning half, or, to be more accurate, quarter of the ball. I cannot help thinking that Professor Thomson in saying that in such a case as this the greater pressure would be on the rear half of the ball is falling into an error, for it seems to me that he is overlooking the tendency of the ball to set up for itself something in the nature of a vacuum which will undoubtedly tend to protect the rear portion of the ball from the force which must assail it in front during its passage through the air.

Professor Thomson says that "the moral of this is that if the wind is coming from the left we should play up into the wind and slice the ball, while if it is coming from the right we should play up into it and pull the ball."

That is Professor Thomson's theory. I shall give my readers the benefit of my practice, which is that whenever there is a cross wind of any description whatever, hit the ball as straight as it is possible for you to do it, right down the middle of the course from the tee to the hole, and forget all about pulls or slices. On a windy day avoid anything whatever in the nature of side-spin because once you have applied it to a ball you never know where that ball is going to end, and if you want any confirmation for this practice you may get it from Harry Vardon in *The Complete Golfer*, for there can be very little doubt that a side wind has nothing like the effect on the ball that golfers seem to imagine, provided always, of course, that the ball be hit cleanly and without appreciable spin. It is not given to one golfer in a thousand to know how to use the pull and slice to obtain assistance from the wind and also to be capable of executing the strokes. As a matter of practical golf these strokes should, for at least ninety-five per cent of golfers, be rigidly eschewed.

At the beginning of Professor Thomson's article he said:

I shall not attempt to deal with the many important questions which arise when we consider the impact of the club with the ball, but confine myself to the consideration of the flight of the ball after it has left the club.

It would, indeed, have been well if Professor Thomson had carried out his expressed intention of leaving this matter alone, for in dealing with it he has shown most conclusively that he has no practical grip of the question which he has attempted to deal with. At page 15 of his article he says:

I have not time for more than a few words as to how the ball acquires the spin from the club, but if you grasp the principle that the action between the club and the ball depends only on their *relative* motion, and that it is the same whether we have the ball fixed and move the club, or have the club fixed and project the ball against it, the main features are very easily understood.

I can readily believe that this statement of Professor Thomson's is absolutely accurate. The only thing which troubles me about it is that I think the person of ordinary intellect will find it absolutely impossible to "grasp the principle" which Professor Thomson lays down. If we have the club fixed and project the ball against it, we know quite well that the ball will rebound from the club, but if we are to have the ball fixed and move the club against it, nothing will happen unless we move the club fast enough, in which case we should simply smash the club.

This is a most amazing illustration of looseness of thought—such an astonishing illustration that I should not have believed Professor Thomson capable of it if it had not been published broadcast to the world with his authority. Of course, I know perfectly well what Professor Thomson means to say, but I have not to deal with that, and as a matter of fact what he means to say is quite wrong, but it will be sufficient for me to show that what he *does* say is wrong.

Professor Thomson then goes on to say:

Suppose Fig. 27 represents the section of the head of a lofted club moving horizontally forward from right to left, the effect of the impact will be the same as if the club were at rest and the ball were shot against it horizontally from left to right.

Here Professor Thomson shows that he is quite under a misapprehension as to the production of the golf stroke. He pre-supposes that the club is moving in a horizontal direction at the moment it hits the ball. In a vast majority of instances, probably in about ninety per cent of cases, the club is not moving in a horizontal direction—in fact, it would be hardly too much to say that it never moves in a horizontal direction. It is nearly always moving either upwards or downwards in a curve at the moment it strikes the ball, so that it stands to reason, especially when the club face is travelling upwards, which is what it does in the great majority of cases, that the blow is never delivered horizontally, but is always struck more or less upward through the ball's centre of mass.

Practical teachers of golf know how extremely hard it is to induce the beginner, and for the matter of that many people who are far beyond beginners, to trust the loft of the club to raise the ball from the earth; so many players never get out of the habit of attempting to hit upwards.

It stands to reason that if the blow in golf were delivered as with a billiard cue, any blow struck in that manner, provided the face of the club had sufficient loft, would tend to produce back-spin, but practically no blow in golf is struck in the manner described by Professor Thomson; nor is the beneficial back-spin of golf obtained in this manner, in fact the loft of the club has comparatively little to do with producing the back-spin which so materially assists the length of the carry. There can, of course, be no doubt that loft does assist a person in producing this back-spin, or, as Professor Thomson calls it, under-spin, but to nothing like the extent which is imagined by the worthy Professor. The beneficial back-spin of golf is obtained by striking the golf ball before the head of the club has reached the lowest point in its swing; in other words, the back-spin is put on a golf ball by downward cut—by the very reverse to that cut which is put on a ball when a man tops it badly. In the one case it is up cut, or, as it is called in lawn-tennis, top, which is a misleading term which has led many people, besides Sir J. J. Thomson, astray, and in the other case it is downward cut, which is exactly similar in its effect to the chop at lawn-tennis.

Professor Thomson, for the purpose of illustrating the fact that the golf ball obtains the beneficial spin, which influences its carry so materially, from the loft of the club, shows us a club face with a loft much greater than that of a niblick, and proceeds to demonstrate from this loft, which it is unnecessary to tell a golfer does not exist on any club which is used for driving, that the ball acquires its back-spin from the loft of the face of the club.

I have already referred to the Professor's fundamental fallacy that the golf stroke is delivered in a horizontal line—in effect that the force of the blow proceeds horizontally, but he is guilty of another very great error from the point of view of practical golf when he shows a club such as he has done, in order to explain how the beneficial back-spin of golf is obtained. Such a club as he shows might be useful for getting out of a bunker, but it certainly would be of no use whatever in practical golf for driving. As every golfer knows, the face of the driver is, comparatively speaking, very upright, and firing a ball at a wall built at the same angle as the loft of a driver would certainly not produce on that ball much in the way of back-spin. The idea of a modern golf ball which flattens very considerably on the face of the club, rolling up the face of a driver on account of its loft, is too ridiculous to be considered seriously by a practical golfer.

The trouble is that Professor Thomson always takes for his hypothesis something which does not exist in golf, so that in the great majority of cases it does not really matter to us what he proves. As a matter of fact, there is in golf only one horizontal stroke, and that is the stymie stroke introduced into the game by me, and which I have hereinbefore fully described. This stroke shows us conclusively how the power goes mostly into elevation instead of into propulsion. It is an absolute answer, if one were required, to Professor Thomson's theories. Professor Thomson's error is of such a fundamental nature that I must quote his sentence again in giving my readers the full paragraph wherein he exposes the delusion under which he is suffering. He says:

Suppose Fig. 27 represents the section of the head of a lofted club moving horizontally forward from right to left, the effect of the impact will be the same as if the club were at rest and the ball were shot against it horizontally from left to right. Evidently, however, in this case the ball would tend to roll up the face, and would thus get spin about a horizontal axis in the direction shown in the figure; this is under-spin and produces the upward force which tends to increase the carry of the ball.

This is the rock upon which Professor Thomson has split. He is under the impression that the beneficial back-spin of golf is obtained by loft, whereas it is perfectly possible to obtain the beneficial back-spin of golf with a club having a vertical face, and being at the moment of impact in a vertical plane, but in order to do this it would be necessary that the ball should be teed very high, as indeed one of the most famous professionals in the world is in the habit of doing when he is playing for a low ball against the wind.

When in *Modern Golf* I stated that a high tee for a low ball was practical golf, it was considered revolutionary, if not incorrect, doctrine, but players now understand that by using the high tee for a low ball they are enabled to cut down beyond the ball more than they could do if the ball were lying on the earth, and that they are, in this manner, enabled to obtain much more of the back-spin which gives the ball its extra carry, and also to play it with less loft.

This is a very serious error for a man of Professor Thomson's attainments to make, and indeed it is to me a wonder how he could possibly make the mistake of thinking that the force in the blow at golf is administered horizontally. This is one of the worst errors which he has made, but the idea that the back-spin of golf is obtained mainly by the loft of the club is utterly unsound and pernicious. It is so unsound, and the correct understanding of the method of producing this stroke is so important to golf, especially to the golf of the future, that I must explain fully how this stroke is obtained.

I have already shown that it is played by a downward glancing blow which hits the ball before the club reaches the lowest point in its swing, and I have already shown the delusion under which many players labour, even including so eminent a player as Harry Vardon, that the ball is struck down on to the earth. Although the ball is struck a descending blow, there is in the blow much more of the forward motion than the downward, so that all the ordinary principles with regard to getting the ball up into the air, apply with equal force to this stroke as to any other, and it is a matter of prime importance that the ball must be struck below the centre of its mass—that the loft of the club must get in underneath what is popularly called the middle of the ball. If this does not take place the ball will not rise from the earth, and to show as Harry Vardon does, at page 170 of *The Complete Golfer*, that the ball must be struck at or above the centre of its mass, and with, as he indicates at page 106, a vertical face, is utterly unsound golf.

I cannot emphasise too strongly that in this miscalled push shot, which is answerable for all back-spin, the loft must be allowed to do its work in the ordinary manner, otherwise the stroke will be a failure.

Having now made it perfectly clear how this stroke is obtained, I must explain a little more clearly the wonderful character of this ball which is without any doubt whatever, in my mind, the king of golf strokes in so far as regards obtaining distance and accuracy and direction. On account of the downward glancing blow the ball has been struck, it leaves the club with a very great amount of back-spin. The hands are always forward of the ball at the moment of impact in this stroke when it is properly played. It stands to reason that this, to a certain extent, decreases the loft of the club with which the stroke is played. The result is that the ball goes away on the first portion of its journey with a very low flight, keeping very close indeed to the earth. All the time it is doing this, however, the ball, as we know, is spinning backwards, which means that the lower portion of the ball is spinning towards the hole, and that it is on the lower portion of the ball that the motions of progression and revolution conspire.

It is equally obvious that on the upper portion of the ball the progression through the air is at the same rate, but in so far as regards its frictional-producing result on the air, it is lessened by the fact that the upper portion of the ball is revolving or spinning backwardly towards the player. The result of this is that the ball is getting much more friction on the lower portion than it is on the top, but as speed can always dominate spin, this is not very apparent until about two-thirds of the carry.

As the speed of the ball begins to decrease, the friction of the spin gets a better grip on the air, and the result is that with the continual rubbing of the air on the lower portion of the ball, it is forced upward and so it continues until the lifting power of the combined propulsion and revolution is exhausted. By this time the ball has arrived at the highest point of its trajectory and it then begins in the natural order of things to fall towards the earth.

It is obvious that by this time much of the back-spin will have been exhausted, but there still remains a considerable amount of rotation, and as the ball begins to fall towards the earth this back-spin which has hitherto been used for forcing the ball upwards into the air, still exerts its influence, and as it is travelling towards the earth the remnant of the back-spin exerts its influence to extend the carry of the ball, because the main frictional portion of the ball has, to a certain extent, on account of the dropping of the ball, been altered and shifted probably a little more towards the lower side of the ball.

The result of all this is that by the time this ball, in a well played drive, comes to earth, most of the beneficial back-spin which obtained for it its long flight, will have been exhausted, and that portion which remains and has not been exhausted will, in all probability, be killed on impact, for the ball pitches on one point, and naturally the top portion tends to throw forward so that the ball will run along the course. It stands to reason that it would require an enormous amount of back-spin to stay with the ball during the period of its low flight, to lift the ball then to the highest point in its trajectory near the end of its carry, to stay with it still in its descent, and then to be strong enough to resist the shock of landing so as to check the run of the ball. The result is that on account of the low trajectory of this ball and of the phenomena explained by me, it is frequently, when well played, and particularly in dry weather, a good runner, so that we see that in this ball we have practically the ideal golf drive; a drive with which no other can compare; a drive which is as good, although it is called the wind-cheater, for a still day as in a gale.

From this explanation it will be seen what a poor chance anyone would have who follows Professor Thomson's ideas of obtaining the beneficial back-spin of golf from the loft of the club and a horizontal blow.

Professor Thomson gives some illustrations of the pull and the slice. In two of his figures he shows horizontal blows being produced in a straight line with the line of flight. Both of these, I may say, are absolutely impossible in golf. He shows a slice in Fig. 29 which would be much more likely to result in a pull, and he shows a pull in Fig. 31 which would almost certainly result in a slice even if the shots were possible, which, as he shows them, they are not.

Professor Thomson shows by diagram an ordinary slice which he says is produced by "such a motion as would be produced if the arms were pulled in at the end of the stroke." This in itself is an utterly loose definition. What Professor Thomson evidently means is if the arms were pulled in during the stroke or at the moment of impact, but as I have shown the slice is not produced by the arms being pulled in at the moment of impact. It is produced by the club head travelling across the ball at an angle to the intended line of flight of the ball. Professor Thomson shows the slice in this case by diagram, and correctly, but he says that if the club were fixed rigidly and the ball were fired at the club down the same line as the club made in its previous stroke, the ball would come off the club in exactly the same manner as when it was hit by the club, but in this he is making a very grave error, as I think I shall be able to show.

I shall quote Professor Thomson with regard to this matter. His proposition is so simple that although I give his indicating letters it will not be necessary for me to reproduce his diagram. He says:

Suppose, now, the face of the club is not square to its direction of motion, but that looking down on the club its line of motion when it strikes the ball is along P Q (Fig. 28), such a motion as would be produced if the arms were pulled in at the end of the stroke, the effect of the impact now will be the same as if the club were at rest and the ball projected along R S, the ball will endeavour to roll along the face away from the striker; it will spin in the direction shown in the figure about a vertical axis. This, as we have seen, is the spin which produces a slice.

This, as we have already seen, is not the spin which produces a slice, but we need not waste any further time going into that matter. We can, however, deal with what Professor Thomson meant to say when he wrote

... but if you grasp the principle that the action between the club and the ball depends only on their *relative* motion, and that it is the same whether we have the ball fixed and move the club or have the club fixed and project the ball against it, the main features are very easily understood.

For the purpose of analysing what Professor Thomson evidently meant when he wrote this, let us take the ordinary case of a slice. We all know now quite well that a slice is produced by a glancing blow coming inwardly across the intended line of flight, and Professor Thomson tells us it is exactly the same thing whether we hit the ball with the club or fire the ball against the club. Let us see how this works out in the slice.

We will consider, for the sake of argument, that the slice has been produced by a stroke which has come across the intended line of flight at an angle of 30 degrees. We shall now fasten our club rigidly and fire the golf ball out of a catapult against its face so that it hits it dead in the centre, and so that it travels down a line at an angle of 30 degrees to the face. Now most of us know enough elementary mechanics to know that in hitting a still object such as the face of the golf club, the ball will come off it at the same angle at which it hit it—in other words that the angle of reflection is the same as the angle of incidence, allowing always, of course, for the slight alteration which will be made by the loft of the club. In this case, of course, we have one object which is absolutely still, and all the motion during impact is confined to the ball.

Now let us consider the impact in the slice. In this case the club strikes the ball a violent blow. The ball, to a very great extent, flattens on the face of the club, and both the ball and the club travel together for a certain distance across the direct line of flight to the hole, and during the time that they are thus travelling together the club is imparting spin to the ball and influencing its direction, so that instead of the ball doing anything whatever in the nature of spinning off the face of the club at a natural angle, it is driving, during its initial stages, very straightly for a long distance before the spin begins to take effect.

It seems to me that the slice may be taken as a very good illustration showing that what Professor Thomson meant to explain is quite incorrect from a golfing point of view. It is quite evident that before we could accept as authoritative the explanations which have been given by Professor Thomson of these somewhat abstruse problems, it would be necessary for us to have, as he puts it, "a new dynamics."

I have already dealt very fully both in England and America with this remarkable lecture by Professor Thomson. I have criticised it in the leading reviews and magazines of the world, and the authoritative golfing paper of England—*Golf Illustrated*—in a leader, invited Professor Thomson to make good his assertions, but he has not been able to do so. One can understand fallacious matter being published under the names of professional golfers when one knows quite well that the majority of the work is done by journalists hired for the purpose, but it is almost impossible to understand how such utterly false doctrine could be put out by so eminent a man, and under the auspices of the Royal Institution of Great Britain.

The flight of the ball has always been a fascinating and for most people a very mysterious subject, but except in one or two matters there is no mystery whatever about the flight of the golf ball, but even amongst practical golfers there is an amazing lack of accurate information. For instance, we find Mr. Walter J. Travis, in *Practical Golf* at page 139, saying:

With a very rapid swing, the force or energy stored up in the gutta ball is greater than in the Haskell. The latter, by reason of its greater comparative resiliency does not remain in contact with the club head quite so long, and therefore does not receive the full benefit of the greater velocity of the stroke in the same proportion as the less resilient gutta. It flies off the face too quickly to get the full measure of energy imparted by a very swift stroke. This responsiveness or resiliency, however, asserts itself in a greater and more compensating degree in the case of the shorter driver. It makes up, in his case, for the lack of speed, and he finds his distance very sensibly increased.

This is a remarkable error for a golfer like Mr. Travis to make. It is abundantly plain that the rubber-cored ball stays on the face of the club much longer than the old gutta-percha ball did. Provided that there were such things in the world as incompressible balls, the impact in the drive would be of the least possible duration with them, but the more compressible the ball becomes the longer it will dwell on the face of the golf club.

That the rubber-cored ball does dwell for a greater period on the face of the club is responsible, to a great extent, for the fact that the modern ball swerves much more when sliced or pulled than did the old guttie in similar circumstances, and the reason seems to be that on account of the fact that the ball stays longer on the face of the club during the time that the club is going across the intended line of flight, it is able to impart to the ball a much greater spin. This spin, as we know, exerts its influence principally towards the end of the ball's flight, and in all probability it gets to work now approximately at the same place where the spin in the old gutta-percha ball began to assert itself, but probably a little further in the carry.

We all know that once the spin has begun to assert itself so as to make the ball swerve, its deflection from the line, particularly with a suitable wind, is extremely rapid, and we all know equally well that the carry of the rubber-cored ball is much longer than that of the old gutta-percha. It stands to reason that the ball having a much greater distance wherein to swerve will execute a correspondingly larger swerve than it would if its carry were shorter.

We find some amazing statements made by authors who profess to deal with golf. For instance at page 167 of *The Mystery of Golf*, we are informed that

... another important thing about the follow-through, surely, is this. As Mr. Travis has pointed out, such is the resiliency of the rubber ball that club and ball are in contact for an appreciable period of time—the impact, that is, is not instantaneous. It is highly probable that the trajectory of the ball is largely influenced by this period of contact. If you follow through your club head travels in precisely the same line as the ball, and the flight of the ball is by this rendered straighter, steadier, and longer.

This, truly, is a wonderful instance of analytical thought by one who is attempting to explain the mystery of golf. He has come to the conclusion that "it is highly probable that the trajectory of the ball is largely influenced by this period of contact."

I have seen many goals kicked at Rugby football, and have kicked a few myself, and I am almost sure that in every case when a goal was scored the boot had a good deal to do with the direction. Marvellous *analysis* this!

We may, however, discard these wonderful efforts of analysis and deal with the remark made by the author that "if you follow through, your club head travels in precisely the same line as the ball," for this is absolutely incorrect in the case of many strokes wherein one desires to influence the flight of the ball by applying spin. For instance, at practically no time of its travel, no matter how good the stroke is and how perfect one's follow-through, is the club head in the slice or the pull "in precisely the same line as the ball." This is merely one of hundreds of instances of confused thought for which the poor golfer has to suffer.

I have before referred to the idea of pulling and slicing to counteract wind. It is astonishing how deeply rooted this idea is. At page 53 of *Concerning Golf* Mr. John L. Low says: "There is no shot which produces such straight results as the sliced shot against a right hand breeze," to which I reply that there is no shot which gives such straight results as the straight shot in itself without slice or pull of any description whatever, and that as a matter of fact it is practically impossible to calculate within twenty yards, and that means double the distance, where one will land if one starts pulling and slicing in a cross wind.

PLATE XII.

GEORGE DUNCAN

A characteristic stroke, showing Duncan's perfect finish in the drive.

This is a matter of such importance that I must quote Harry Vardon in support of my statement. He says at page 92 of *The Complete Golfer*:

Now, however, that this question is raised, I feel it desirable to say, without any hesitation, that the majority of golfers possess vastly exaggerated notions of the effect of strong cross winds on the flight of their ball. They greatly over-estimate the capabilities of a breeze. To judge by their observations on the tee, one concludes that a wind from the left is often sufficient to carry the ball away at an angle of 45 degrees, and indeed sometimes when it does take such an exasperating course and finishes on the journey some fifty yards away from the point from which it was desired to despatch it, there is an impatient exclamation from the disappointed golfer, "Confound this wind! Who on earth can play in a hurricane!" or words to that effect. Now I have quite satisfied myself that only a very strong wind indeed will carry a properly driven ball more than a very few yards out of its course, and in proof of this I may say that it is very seldom when I have to deal with a cross wind that I do anything but play straight at the hole without any pulling or slicing or making allowances in any way.

If golfers will only bring themselves to ignore the wind, then it, in turn, will almost entirely ignore their straight ball. When you find your ball at rest the afore-mentioned forty or fifty yards from the point which you desired to send it, make up your mind, however unpleasant it may be to do so, that the trouble is due to an unintentional pull or slice, and you may get what consolation you can from the fact that the slightest of these variations from the ordinary drive is seized upon with delight by any wind, and its features exaggerated to an enormous extent. It is quite possible therefore that a slice which would have taken the ball only twenty yards from the line when there was no wind, will take it forty yards away with the kind assistance of its friend and ally.

These are, unquestionably, words of wisdom. There can be no doubt whatever that the straight ball is the ball all the time in golf, and it is absolutely certain that what Vardon says about the effect of the wind on the golf ball is true. Wind has remarkably little effect on the golf ball which is driven without spin. I have had no doubt on this subject for at least seventeen years. I had my lesson in one ball during the course of a match played over my home links in New Zealand. One of the holes was on top of a volcanic mountain at a place where New Zealand is only a few miles wide, and there was a howling gale raging from ocean to ocean right across the island. I can remember as if it were yesterday, the champion of New Zealand, as he was then, playing this hole. He drove a very high and perfectly straight ball from tee to green, and the ball travelled to all appearances as directly as if there had been no wind whatever, whereas had there been the least slice on the ball it would have been picked up by the wind and carried away into the crater which lay sixty or a hundred yards off the course.

Speaking of Mr. Low reminds me that he makes some extraordinary statements with regard to spin. At page 35 of *Concerning Golf* he says: "I have said that a ball with left to right spin swings in the air towards the left in exactly the opposite direction from a sliced ball and from contrary causes." It is obvious that this is wrong, for the spin of the slice is from left to right, and of course, as every one knows, that spin makes the ball swerve towards the right, which is the swerve of the slice.

At page 32 Mr. Low makes the same error. He says there: "Now a pulled ball comes round to the left because the sphere is rotating from left to right, or in the direction contrary to the hands of a watch." This, of course, is a contradiction, for the hands of a watch as we look at them do rotate from left to right, but in any case Mr. Low's explanation is quite incorrect, because the spin of the ball is not in a direction contrary to the hands of a watch laid face upwards on the ground, as Mr. Low affirms.

Mr. Low says at page 31:

Every child nowadays seems to know how to slice a ball; you have only to ask the question and the answer will come quickly enough, "Oh, draw the hands in when you are hitting," or, in other words, spin the ball in the direction of the hands of a watch laid face upwards on the ground. The ball advancing with this spin finds it is resisted most strongly by the atmosphere on its left side, and therefore goes towards the right in the direction of least resistance. The converse is the case with a pulled ball in the sense of a ball which curves in the air from right to left.

We have already shown in dealing with Professor Thomson's article that this statement is quite incorrect. In passing I may also refer to the fact that Mr. Low's idea of the production of the slice, viz. by drawing the hands in when one is hitting, is also wrong. There is no drawing in of the hands at the moment of impact in the properly played slice. It is the drawing in, if we may use the term, of the head of the club in its travel across the intended line of flight, but not anything which is done intentionally during impact. However, that is by the way.

Mr. Low is evidently under the impression, as was Professor Thomson, that the spin of the ball in the slice is about a vertical axis. This is an error in itself, as we have shown, but it is not nearly so bad an error as it is to say that the pull is the converse of the slice in this respect, for, as we have seen, if the ball were merely spinning about a vertical axis it could not possibly have the running powers which it possesses, to say nothing of its low flight. Although Mr. Low has got somewhat mixed in describing his rotation, it is evident from his reference to the hands of the clock that his ideas are correct in so far as regards the general direction of spin, but where he is at fault is in stating the axis of rotation of his ball.

If we accept Mr. Low's statement about the axis of rotation we shall have the pulled ball, when it lands, striking the earth with a spin equivalent to a sleeping top, but that is not what we want in the pulled ball, for neither would it give us the low trajectory which we desire so much, nor would it give us, on landing, the running which we desire, if anything, still more. The spin which we desire to produce and which we must have in our minds to produce when we are playing the stroke, is such a spin as will give us, when the ball lands, approximately the spin of a disc top as it falls to earth when its spin is nearly exhausted. I am speaking now, of course, not of the question of degree, but of the plane of spin. We must have our ball spinning in such a plane that when it touches the earth it will behave in the same manner as the disc top does when its side comes into contact with the floor.

In dealing with "The Science of the Stroke," James Braid in *Advanced Golf* goes into an analysis of the effect of spin on flight. He says early in the chapter:

At the present time most players know how they ought to be standing, and what the exact movements of their arms, wrists, and body should be in order to swing the club in the right way and make the ball travel as far as possible, but they do not all know, and in few cases one suspects have ever troubled to think, what is the process by which these movements, when properly executed, bring about the desired effect.

I do not know how Braid can truthfully say that at the present time most players know how they ought to be standing, when we are confronted with the fact that his own book, *Advanced Golf*, and practically every book which has been published on the game, tells the unfortunate golfer to stand as he ought not to be standing instead of giving him the simple truth and sound golf, and it is incomprehensible to me how Braid can say that they know "what the exact movements of their arms, wrists, and body should be in order to swing the club in the right way," when he himself has confessed in *Advanced Golf* that, particularly with regard to the wrists, which unquestionably have a most important function to fulfil in the golf drive, he absolutely does not know where they come in. It is useless in a work on *Advanced Golf* to assume on the part of one's readers a knowledge superior to that which the author of the book himself has given as his own limitations. Braid says:

They have the cause and also the effect, but they do not often see the connection between the two. Of course, the ball in a ball game moves always according to scientific laws, but it has seemed to those who have studied these matters that the scientific problems involved in the flight of the golf ball are more intricate, but at the same time more interesting, than in many other cases.

Of course this is quite stupid, because, as I have frequently explained, there is no special set of mechanical laws for golf—or the golf ball.

The golf ball follows in all respects exactly the same laws as those which govern the flight and run of any other ball. The only difference in connection with the golf ball is that it is probably the most unscientifically constructed ball in the world of sport. Braid continues:

The chief matter of this kind that it is desirable the golfer should understand is that concerning the character and effect of the spin that is given to the golf ball when it leaves the club. This spin is at the root of all the difficulties and all the delights of the game, and yet there are some players—one might even say many—who do not even know that their ball spins at all as they hit it from the tee.

I may pause here to note that James Braid says that spin is at the root of all the difficulties and all the delights of golf. This is in many respects quite an exaggeration, but I am giving it exactly as he says it, for the simple reason that it emphasises the fact which I have always insisted on, that a proper knowledge of the application of spin to the golf ball is essential for one who would attain to the greatest success or who would obtain the greatest enjoyment from the game.

Braid quotes the work of the late Professor Tait very extensively. Referring to the most important subject of back-spin, he says:

It appears to be the proper regulation of the under-spin given to the ball when applying it from the tee and through the green, at all events when length is what is most required, that makes success, and it is in this way that players of inferior physical power must make up for their deficiency and drive long balls.

I may say at once that any idea whatever of the proper regulation of back-spin in the drive is, from the point of view of practical golf, merely nonsense. In so far as regards obtaining extra distance by driving a low ball with back-spin, whose properties I have already fully described, there is nothing whatever to be done but to get back-spin and as much of it as one possibly can. The golfer has yet to be born who in driving can obtain too much back-spin. Braid says:

It is in the long drive that the principles of spin are most interesting and important, but it must be remembered also that they are very prominent in their action upon the flight of the ball in the case of many other shots, and the peculiarities of different trajectories can generally be traced to this cause after a very little thought by one who has a knowledge of the scientific side of the matter, as explained by Professor Tait. This is particularly the case with high lofted approach shots.

One may remark here, perhaps, that there is no more unsuitable stroke in which to study the peculiarity of the application of back-spin to the trajectory of the ball than in the high lofted approach shots, for it is in such shots as these practically an impossibility, if one may so express it, to locate the influence of the spin on the flight of the ball. It is quite a different thing in the wind-cheater class of stroke where one sees the ball travelling low across the turf and can absolutely mark the place where the back-spin begins to get to work and give the ball its upward tendency towards the end of the drive, and, when the velocity of the ball has become sufficiently reduced, to allow the back-spin to exert its lifting power.

I now come to a matter which is of very great importance in the application of back-spin to the ball. It is quite evident to me that Braid is falling into the same error as that which was originally made by Professor Tait, and followed fifteen years later by Professor Sir J. J. Thomson. On page 226 he says:

Therefore the great authority concluded that good driving lies not merely in powerful hitting, but "in the proper apportionment of quite good hitting with such a knack as gives the right amount of under-spin to the ball"; and one of his calculations was to the effect that, in certain circumstances, a man who imparted under-spin to his ball when driving it might get a carry of about thirty yards more than that obtained by another man who hit as hard but made no under-spin. There would, of course, be a great difference in the comparative trajectories of the two balls. In the case of the short one there is no resistance to gravity, and consequently, in order to get any sort of flight at all, the ball must be directed upwards when it is hit from the tee or, to use a scientific term, there must be "initial elevation." This may be only very slight, but it is quite distinguishable, and in fact a player, who is only at the beginning of his practice, and has little knowledge of the principles of the game, will generally be found trying to hit his ball in an upward direction, and by that means will make it travel farther than it would have done otherwise. On the other hand, the ball that is properly driven by a good player is not only not consciously aimed upwards, but, according to Professor Tait, is not hit upwards. For some distance after it has left the tee it follows a line nearly parallel with the ground, and eventually rises as the result of the under-spin which is forcing it upwards all the time.

We may pause here to consider a few of the statements in this remarkable passage. I may say again that the idea of driving a ball with the "proper apportionment of quite good hitting with such a knack as gives the right amount of under-spin to the ball" is simply a wild guess at what takes place during the execution of a correct drive with back-spin. The proper playing of this stroke is a matter of very considerable difficulty, and it is practically a certainty that no golfer has ever lived or ever will live who could regulate his back-spin in the drive to any appreciable extent; all that he ever thinks of doing—all that he is ever likely to do—is to obtain his back-spin, *and as much of it as he can.*

It is, of course, quite wrong to say that in the ball hit without back-spin there is "no resistance to gravity," for if there were no resistance to gravity the ball would be on the earth. However, we know quite well what is meant, although, when we are dealing with a matter which is absolutely a matter of science, we do not expect such loose statements as these. I should probably have passed this remark, but for the fact that it is emphasised by the statement that in order to get any sort of flight at all the ball must be directed upwards when it is hit from the tee, which again, as a matter of practical golf, is what nine of ten golfers do, although we are told that "a player who is only at the beginning of his practice, and has little knowledge of the principles of the game, will generally be found trying to hit his ball in an upward direction."

It is astonishing how few players, even of quite a good class, are content to leave the question of elevation entirely to the club. It probably would be no exaggeration to say that quite ninety per cent of the players make an attempt, however extremely slight it may be, to assist the club in lifting the ball from the earth. According to the best theory in golf, this is quite wrong, for the blow should be at least in a horizontal direction, which practically it never is, and preferably in the line of the arc formed by the club head in its travel through the air on its downward path. The latter case, of course, would produce back-spin, and a considerable amount of it. The former would probably produce slight back-spin, but a very slight amount. However, the very great majority of golfing hits are at the moment of impact proceeding upwardly, and it is this fact which puts any idea whatever of the unconscious application of back-spin by the ordinary golfer quite beyond serious consideration. The amount of back-spin which is unconsciously applied to the golf ball is practically negligible.

We see that, according to Professor Tait, the ball which is properly driven by a good player is not only not consciously aimed upwards, but that it is actually not hit upwards. Indeed we are told that for some distance after it has left the tee it follows a line nearly parallel with the ground and eventually rises as the result of the under-spin that is forcing it upwards all the time. This statement is not in accordance with the experience of practical golfers. It is evident that Professor Tait was under the impression, in which, as I have stated before and now emphasise, he has been followed by Professor Sir J. J. Thomson, that the beneficial back-spin in golf is obtained by the loft of the club. There can be no doubt whatever that if a golf ball were struck a blow by a golf club having any considerable degree of loft and proceeding at the moment of impact in a straight line, the result would be to impart some degree of back-spin, but this is not what happens in practical golf. At no portion of the travel of the head of the club in the golf drive is it proceeding in a horizontal direction, and in the vast majority of cases, at the moment of impact, even with the very best of stroke players, the club is going upward. If this were not so it would be impossible for many of our greatest drivers to get the trajectories they do with the comparatively straight-faced clubs which they use.

Braid quotes an experiment which was made by Professor Tait in the course of his investigations with regard to the qualities of under-spin. It appears that the Professor laid a ball to the string of a crossbow, the string being just below the middle of the ball, so that when it was let go it would impart a certain amount of under-spin to it. When he shot the ball in this way he made it fly straight to a mark that was thirty yards distant; but when he shot it a second time, pulling the string to the same extent and laying it to the middle of the ball so that no under-spin would be given to it, the ball fell eight feet short of the same mark.

It is impossible to accept such a rough and crude experiment as this as evidence in any way whatever of the influence of back-spin in the drive; rather it would seem to show beyond a shadow of doubt that the extra carry was obtained because the power of propulsion was applied to the ball at a lower portion, and therefore tended to give it a greater trajectory. It should be obvious that this result would be obtained even disregarding the question of back-spin, which in such an extremely short flight as thirty yards would certainly not have any opportunity whatever to make such a difference in the length of carry as that suggested.

It is, however, when we come to deal with questions of practical golf that we find that the ideas of the late Professor Tait will not bear looking into.

Braid says:

However, it is well to bear in mind one thing that the Professor said, "The pace which the player can give the club head at the moment of impact depends to a very considerable extent on the relative motion of his two hands (to which is due the 'nip') during the immediately preceding two-hundredth of a second, while the amount of beneficial spin is seriously diminished by even a trifling upward concavity of the path of the head during the ten-thousandth of a second occupied by the blow."

Here we have plain evidence of the fact that Professor Tait is under the impression that there is some particular snap which he calls "nip" imported into the stroke immediately before impact. We have already dealt fully with this matter. We remember what Vardon has said in condemning the idea, and we know that Braid himself has confessed that he knows nothing about the matter, so it will not seem disrespectful if we come to the conclusion that we can disregard this vague statement about the "nip" in the blow. We can then proceed to notice the really important remark made that "the amount of beneficial spin is seriously diminished by even a trifling upward concavity of the path of the head during the ten-thousandth of a second occupied by the blow." It seems to me that this last statement is absolutely accurate, and it is the thing which I have always contended for in dealing with the practical side of golf driving, as contradistinguished from the purely theoretical, which has been put before us by Professor Tait, and following him, by Professor Sir J. J. Thomson. It will be observed that Professor Tait said that the amount of beneficial spin is "seriously diminished by even a trifling upward concavity of the path of the head during the ten-thousandth of a second occupied by the blow."

Some of my readers may remember that when I was dealing with Professor Sir J. J. Thomson's lecture before the Royal Society in an article which appeared in *The English Review* in February 1911, I stated that what actually did happen was that there took place in practically every drive at golf exactly this "trifling upward concavity of the path of the head during the ten-thousandth of a second occupied by the blow," and that therefore the amount of beneficial back-spin obtained from the loft of the club was practically negligible.

It is quite clear that Professor Tait was under the impression that back-spin was got from the loft of the club proceeding in a horizontal direction, but it is well known now to golfers who give the science of the game any attention whatever, that back-spin is not obtained in this manner, and that back-spin so obtained would be practically ineffectual as an aid to distance, for the loft of the driver and the brassy is not sufficient, even if the golf drive were played in the manner suggested, to produce any considerable amount of back-spin. As we have already seen, the beneficial back-spin in the golf drive is obtained by the club striking the ball *long before the beginning* of the "upward concavity of the path of the head," that is to say, in its arc *as it is proceeding downwards* to the lowest point in the swing from which it then starts that "upward concavity."

I have emphasised and re-emphasised this matter, for it is evident that when famous men like Professors Tait and Thomson start out with an absolutely erroneous idea, an idea which is *fundamentally* wrong, it is quite natural for less gifted men to be led astray. Braid says, and it must be remembered that this is in *Advanced Golf* (page 229): "So far as I know, it cannot be stated in accurate scientific terms and figures, and by lines drawn on paper, what is the proper scientific swing in order to get the best drive." This seems to me, especially in a book like this, to be a wonderful statement, particularly when we are dealing with the scientific results arrived at by men of the greatest eminence, results which I may say have been known for more than two hundred and fifty years.

There is no doubt whatever which is the best way to swing in order to get the best drive, and it can be explained in scientific language and shown by diagram and by figures, and in fact it has been so shown again and again.

Braid says:

What golfers have done, therefore, in the past has been to find out gradually which is the best way in which to hit the ball in order to make it travel far, and thus they have groped their way to the stances and swings which, if the truth were known, would probably be set out by science as the best possible ones for the purpose.

This very well expresses what has taken place. The golfers have "groped their way" to what they have found out, without a glimmering of the scientific reasons for doing it, and the consequence is that, as they got their practice first, and were not informed of what they were doing by that theory which is the best of all theory, the concentrated essence of the practice of experts, they have signally failed to impart their science to those who have come after them.

At page 229 Braid says:

However, there are certain things that the player should know about his drive when it is right, and which he should aim at producing, and they have been very well set forth by Professor Tait as the result of his investigations into the trajectories of golf balls hit under varying conditions of club-force, wind, and so forth. One of the first things to say, and this is really important in estimating their chances of making certain carries that are constantly set to them in the course of their play, is that some golfers have a delusion to the effect that the ball is at its highest point in the middle of its flight—that is to say, they think that just about half-way between the point from which it was hit and the point at which it will touch the ground again, the ball is at its highest, and after that commences to fall again. In this belief when they have, say, a 140 yards' carry to make, they will reckon that their ball must then be coming down very fast towards the turf, having been at its highest, some 50 or 60 yards before. They may think in such circumstances that they ought to hit up a little more and try to hit harder to make up for doing so. They would be wrong entirely, and that because they did not know what the under-spin was that they gave to the ball, or what effect it had on its flight. Thus in the case just quoted, assuming that the ball had a total carry of from 150 to 160 yards, it would be at its highest point when it had travelled about 130 yards, and there would be no occasion to hit up, unless the object to be carried were very high.

It is obvious that in such a case as that given no practical golfer would in any way whatever consider the question of the *amount* of back-spin on his ball, for he would know that he has no possibility whatever of gauging its effect in the air in such a shot, and he will leave that to regulate itself and to act when the ball strikes the earth.

It is unquestionable that theoretically this may be done, and it is well known that I am a strong advocate of the use of back-spin, but in the case quoted by Braid there is nothing whatever to show that the ball has been played in such a manner as to produce an appreciable quantity of serviceable back-spin, or that such a method of play is necessary or advisable.

Braid continues:

The fact is that a well-driven ball that has a total carry—that is, from the tee to the point where it touches the turf again, and not the distance of the obstacle that it clears—of about 165 yards, under normal conditions of wind and weather, is at its highest about 135 yards from the point where it was struck, and after that it begins to fall rapidly. This is chiefly the result of the under-spin which is given to it when it is struck by the driver in the proper way, and it shows the importance of under-spin to the golfer, for if there were none, then all our courses would have to be shortened, hazards brought closer to the tee, and the principles upon which the game is played would have to be altered in many respects. If there were no under-spin, then the ball would have no help against the force of gravity, and the result would be that the highest point of its flight would be half-way between the point from which it was driven and that at which it alighted.

We see here again strong evidence of the fact that Braid is under the same impression as Professor Tait, and that is that the back-spin of golf is obtained from the loft of the club, whereas the loft of the club has one function, and that is to raise the ball from the earth, and there will be no particular necessity to alter our courses, for in ordinary every-day golf, back-spin is practically not used, except when it is intentionally applied by the golfer by means of the stroke suitable for its production.

Braid gives a series of diagrams taken from Professor Tait's lecture which illustrate various trajectories of golf balls driven in varying circumstances. Many of these are so entirely theoretical that I need not consider them, but in referring to one of them Braid says:

The ball which has travelled farthest, or rather the one that has been given most carry, is that which has been hit in the right way, and to which has therefore been imparted the right amount of under-spin. This is, in fact, the ideal trajectory of a well-driven ball. It starts low, rises very slowly and gradually, the line of flight bending upwards slightly, and does not come down too quickly after the vertex has been reached.

This is, on the whole, a sound but very general description of an accurately played wind-cheater, but the remarkable thing is that although Braid expresses himself in such terms of admiration for this particular ball he does not anywhere in *Advanced Golf* show us how to produce the stroke which gives this beneficial back-spin. This surely is a very great oversight. Nor so far as I have been able to see does he explain clearly how the beneficial back-spin of golf is obtained.

Braid shows clearly by his quotation from Professor Tait's article that in the Professor's mind was the deep-rooted idea that it was possible to drive golf balls by a stroke delivered at the moment of impact in the same manner as is a blow from a billiard cue, but, needless to say, this is in the golf drive utterly impracticable. Professor Tait, in his paper, used a considerable number of diagrams to show that too much back-spin is bad in the drive, but as I have already pointed out, although this is very well in mere theory, it does not work out in the slightest degree in golf. It is easy to take light balloons and give them back-spin and show that it influences their trajectories to such an extent that they will go behind the point where they were struck, but a golf ball is a very small, hard, and heavy thing, and by the time that its back-spin begins to exert its influence in a marked manner on its flight it has travelled a considerable distance and the rate of spin will have materially diminished, so that no golfer need ever be afraid of applying too much back-spin to his drive.

Braid proceeds:

Of course, as already indicated, the golfer does not know, and in one sense does not care exactly how much under-spin he gives to his ball when he drives it, only being aware that he has given too much or too little according to results, and knowing also that in either case excess or otherwise was due to faulty stance or swing—most frequently this—or both. In the present case of this high trajectory, the exact amount of under-spin given to the ball is half as much again as that given to the properly driven ball, and under the same normal conditions these would be the relative flights of the two balls.

Now it is obvious that if Professor Tait was under the impression that the beneficial back-spin of golf was obtained merely from the horizontal blow delivered through the centre of the ball's mass, so that the ball took some slight spin by its roll up the face of the club, he had no very accurate idea of the rate of spin of that ball at the moment it left the face of the club, so that any attempt whatever on his part to measure the respective rates of spin of the different flight of these balls must be received with very great caution. As a matter of fact the rate of spin of the golf ball at the moment it leaves the club in a well-played drive with back-spin would be immeasurably faster than anything supposed by Professor Tait, who based his calculations on the ball obtaining this back-spin *from the loft of the club*, which is undoubtedly a grave error, and Braid wholly subscribes to this error, which is not to be wondered at, for Professor Sir J. J. Thomson, one of the most eminent scientists, has fallen into the same trap.

Professors Tait and Thomson and James Braid talk much about the possibility of obtaining too much back-spin in the drive. This is scarcely theoretically possible in golf, and it is practically impossible. I will give an example taken from practical golf which will, I believe, quite convince any golfer that the possibility of obtaining too much back-spin in the drive need never be considered.

Let us imagine a very badly sliced ball. By a badly sliced ball I do not necessarily mean an extremely quick slice where the ball leaves the line of flight to the hole quite suddenly, nor do I mean a ball pushed away to the right of the line to the hole; what I do mean is a ball which has been so sliced that it takes a tremendous curve from left to right, beginning to develop that slice in a pronounced manner at, say, half to two-thirds of its carry, which is quite bad enough for a slice. We frequently see in such a case, particularly on a windy day, and even on a still one, the great power which the spin has to deflect the ball from the line to the hole. It must be remembered that in this curve the spin is assisted by gravity—the ball is falling much of the time as it is being edged away—and even then it will be apparent that it is easy to get much greater spin in the slice than it is in the wind-cheater, for the simple reason that in the slice one has an unrestricted cut across the ball, whereas one has not this opportunity with the wind-cheater, for one hits the ground immediately one passes the ball.

Now although it is possible to apply an infinitely greater cut to the slice than one can possibly do to the wind-cheater, the deflection from the line, except on a very windy day, is, comparatively speaking, gradual. That is to say that if, for the sake of argument, the trajectory of the slice could be turned upwards there would be no possibility whatever of the ball showing such a thing as a curl backwards towards the hole, which is shown by Professor Tait and, following him, by Professor Thomson. This is clearly so in any slice which is not an extremely exaggerated specimen, so it stands to reason that in the wind-cheater, where one's opportunity for applying cut is so restricted, and where the ball in its effort to climb upwards has to fight the direct pull of gravity, there is no possible chance of applying too much back-spin to the ball.

At page 239 Braid says: "It may be of interest to mention that Professor Tait found that a well-driven ball turns once in every 2½ feet at the beginning of its journey." If Professor Tait found that a golf ball, obtaining this back-spin in the way in which he thought it did, turns "once in every 2½ feet at the beginning of its journey," he would probably have found, if he had realised how back-spin really is obtained, that the number of revolutions at the moment that the ball is leaving the club are at least three or four times as many as he asserted. It is unnecessary to enlarge upon the fact that this would mean a lifting capacity infinitely beyond anything that Professors Tait and Thomson ever ascribed to back-spin in the drive.

Braid continues:

We have so far only been considering the effect of the spinning of the ball in the case of long shots with wooden clubs. As a matter of fact, and as suggested at the outset, it has also very great influence on the play in the case of the shorter shots with iron clubs, as may be understood after a very little consideration of the circumstances. It is the excessive under-spin that is given to the ball by the angle at which the face of the club is laid back, and the peculiar way in which the stroke is played, that make the ball rise so quickly and so high in the case of a short pitched approach, and then make it stop comparatively dead when it comes to the ground again.

It is obvious here that Braid is under the impression that the loft of the club is largely responsible for the back-spin in the approach shots, but this is quite an error, for not one player in a hundred does apply back-spin to his lofted approaches unless he has been specially taught how to do it, for, curiously enough, the more lofted the club is, the greater chance is there that the player will at the moment of impact impart into his stroke that little bit of "upward concavity" which Professor Tait says, and truly says, is the enemy of back-spin. The fact is that very little under-spin, or, as I always prefer to call it, back-spin, is obtained from the loft of the club unless the blow is delivered as the club is travelling downward. That is the whole essence of the secret of back-spin, but it is not mentioned by Professors Tait or Thomson, or by James Braid. Any attempt whatever to obtain back-spin from the loft of the club will be practically useless. It must be obtained by the method of playing the shot, and the only way to obtain it effectually is to hit the ball before the club has arrived at the lowest point in its swing. By this means, and this means alone, is it possible to obtain the beneficial back-spin of golf, and I cannot say too often or too emphatically that anyone who trusts to the loft of the club to produce back-spin will be disappointed.

Braid seems to have a glimmering of this, for he says:

However much a club were laid back it would be impossible to play these shots properly if no under-spin were given to the ball, and it seems to be a great advantage of having the faces of iron clubs grooved or dotted that it helps the club to grasp the ball thoroughly while this under-spin is being imparted to it, so that the full amount is given to it, and none is wasted through the ball slipping on the face.

This is unquestionably sound mechanics. But even here, although Braid is so close to the heart of the matter—although he says, as I have shown repeatedly in many places, that "however much a club were laid back it would be impossible to play these shots properly if no under-spin were given to the ball," thus stating explicitly that something more remains to be done to produce back-spin than merely to hit the ball with a lofted club,—he does not get really to the essence of the stroke and show that it must be played by the club *as it is descending.*

There is a very important matter which Braid refers to in this chapter on the science of the stroke. Speaking of the follow-through and the impact, he says:

One or two other calculations that were made by Professor Tait may be briefly mentioned at the close of this chapter, each of them seeming to convey an idea to the golfer. The first is, that owing to the speed at which the ball leaves the club, the total length of time during which ball and club are in contact with each other is between one five thousandth and one ten thousandth of a second, and the total length of that part of the swing when the two are together—the length of impact—is half an inch. It has been pointed out that it by no means follows from this that because the time and space of impact are so short that follow-through is of no real account, after all, in the making of the drive. When the follow-through is properly performed it shows that the work was properly done during that half an inch of the swing that was all-important. If the follow-through were short and wrong it would indicate that the work during the impact was wrong too. What it comes to is this, that it is impossible for any man to swing his club round with so much force and regulate exactly what he will do, and be conscious of the fact that he is doing it as he regulated, during such a short space of time as from one five thousandth to one ten thousandth of a second. That is quite clear. What the golfer has to do, then, is to make sure that his swing is right at the beginning, that is, in the back-swing and the down-swing, and also in the follow-through. He knows from instruction and experience that if all these things are properly done the ball will go off well; and what it amounts to is that the beginning being right and the end being right, control being exercised over each, the middle is right also, though in this case there is no control over it.

This quotation emphasises strongly the fact which I have always insisted on, that the matter of impact with the golf ball is an incident in the travel of the head of the club, and that it is practically impossible for the player to consciously perform anything which will affect the flight of the golf ball during impact. Braid has insisted upon this in other places, and it should quite settle any idea which many people have, of juggling with the golf ball during impact, but it is a remarkable thing to see James Braid claiming that at the moment of impact there is "no control over" the swing although there is both in the downward swing and the follow-through! I need not criticise this.

The point, however, which I wish to refer to here specifically is in connection with the follow-through. Braid says, finally:

What the golfer has to do, then, is to make sure that his swing is right at the beginning, that is, in the back-swing and the down-swing, and also in the follow-through. He knows from instruction and experience that if all these things are properly done the ball will go off well; and what it amounts to is that the beginning being right and the end being right, control being exercised over each, the middle is right also, though in this case there is no control over it.

This, it seems to me, is a very bad presentment of the case. Although we admit that the impact is merely an incident in the travel of the club head, it is the most important incident, and it is on that incident that the mind should be concentrated, so that the idea of cumbering one's mind with any thought of the follow-through is very bad golf. The only portion of the stroke which should be on the player's mind at all is that which leads up to impact, for it is obvious that if that has been correctly performed, one need not trouble much about the follow-through, as that will come quite naturally. Also we will observe that Braid says here "control being exercised over each." This, of course, includes the follow-through over which Braid now speaks of exercising control, but it will be fresh in our minds that in describing the moment of impact, he says "Crack! everything is let go," and that really is what should happen after impact has taken place. There should be no thought whatever of the follow-through. That should produce itself, if one may so express it, and the player who encumbers his mind by any thought whatever as to how his club is going to end is simply adding another anxiety to his game.

PLATE XIII.

J. SHERLOCK

This plate shows Sherlock's stance and address in his favourite iron-shot. He addresses the ball so that it is nearly opposite his right heel.

Braid explained most graphically how the follow-through should be allowed to take care of itself, so that I cannot understand why he should now endeavour to split his pupils' mental idea of the golf stroke into halves with the golf ball in between. This is surely a bad conception of the stroke, and one which is likely to lead the pupil into grave error, for it shifts his mind forward on to the finish of the stroke, whereas it has no business to be anywhere else but on the ball.

Before concluding this chapter I must refer to what Braid has to say with regard to a topped stroke. At page 238 he says:

A final thing to remember in connection with this question of the rotation of the ball is, that when the ball is what we call topped, the stroke is applied in such a way that a motion exactly the reverse of under-spin is applied to it, that is to say, the front part of the ball is made to move in a downward direction. On the principle already explained, there is then an extra air-pressure upon that ball from the top, pressing it down, so that even if the ball that is topped is somehow got up into the air from the tee, as happens, it cannot stay there long, but comes down very suddenly—"ducks," as it is called. However, a ball that ducks for this reason nevertheless gets some benefit from this over-spin when it does come down, for the spin acts in just the same way as "top" does in the case of a billiard stroke, that is to say, it makes the ball run more. If there were no rough grass and no bunkers between the tee and the hole this over-spin might be an exceedingly useful thing, and the principles upon which the game of golf is played might be entirely different from what they are; but as there is rough in front of the tee, and generally a bunker at no great distance from it, topping and over-spin are more frequently fatal than not, the ball coming to grief either in the rough or the bunker.

This quotation makes it quite evident, I think, that James Braid is not very well acquainted with the principles which govern the flight and run of the golf ball. If this were his "knowledge" which we are considering, I should be more loath to deal with it so plainly as I am doing, but as he expressly states that he is indebted to another for much of his "knowledge" on this subject I have no hesitation whatever in criticising it and showing that it is absolutely impracticable from a golfing point of view.

It is not too much to say that top-spin has absolutely no place in golf, for it is there utterly useless, and would be so were golf links like billiard tables, for no ball with top on it can travel any appreciable distance through the air, and to speak of a ball being driven with top is simply to show one's utter ignorance of the game, for even if there were no rough grass and no bunkers between the tee and the hole, this over-spin could never be "an exceedingly useful thing," nor could it ever, by the greatest stretch of one's imagination, alter the principles upon which the game of golf is played, for no stroke in golf could ever supplant the drive with back-spin.

It is nonsense such as this which does much harm to the game. To speak of the possibility of over-spin being such that the "principles upon which the game of golf is played might be entirely different from what they are if the course had no rough grass and no bunkers" is one of the greatest absurdities which I have ever seen put in any book, and when one finds matter of this sort in a book called *Advanced Golf*, it calls for the severest possible criticism.

The nearest approach to top-spin which exists in golf is the spin of the pull, and there because the axis of spin is turned over to a certain extent, we get the beneficial run at the end of the drive, but anyone who knows the first principles of the flight and run of the ball would know that if the golfer in his drive obtained pure top instead of this much modified over-spin, his drive would be entirely ruined, for the thing which produces the low flight of the ball is that the ball does its ducking sideways, if we may so express it, and the chances are that quite frequently the shock of landing alters the plane of its spin, so that it is converted into pure running, but this latter point, of course, is a matter which we can only theorise about and regard as almost proved from the nature of the run of the ball on many occasions.

We need not here bother about top-spin. The only place where top (not top-spin) is of any use in golf, so far as I can remember, is on the putting-green, and there it is unquestionably useful, and it is not used so much as it should be. The point of outstanding importance, which I venture to think is made fairly clear by this chapter on the flight of the ball, is that the beneficial back-spin of golf is by far the most important spin which it is possible for a golfer to apply to his ball, and that that spin is not obtained in the manner stated by Professor Tait and, after him, by Professor Thomson, but is obtained by the method which I have indicated, viz. by a downward glancing blow, and, so far as regards this statement, we have the corroboration of James Braid to the extent that he says that "no matter what the loft is upon the club, it is impossible to obtain by loft alone the back-spin which one requires in golf."

It may seem that I have been unnecessarily emphatic in dealing with this question, but as a matter of practical golf it is absolutely impossible to lay too much stress upon the value of a complete understanding of the method of obtaining this most valuable and serviceable spin, and unless a player most perfectly understands the theory of the stroke, it is the greatest certainty possible that he will waste many years of his life endeavouring to acquire the practice, whereas if he knows perfectly well what he is trying to do, he may acquire it in as many months as he would otherwise waste years in not getting it.

CHAPTER XI

THE GOLF BALL

It is remarkable, when one considers the vast number of scientific men who play golf, how little attention has been directed by them to the form and make of the golf ball. Many golfers are under the impression that the golf ball which is now used represents the limit of man's inventive genius. Probably the leading maker of the best feather ball in the days before the gutta-percha ball was known would have thought the same. As a matter of ascertained fact the vast majority of golf balls which are made to-day are imperfect in a variety of ways. There can be no doubt whatever that the ball which is marked by what are commonly called pimples, or bramble marking, is a most imperfect production.

If one were to suggest to a billiard player that it would improve the run of the balls if they were covered with little excrescences similar to those which are on many golf balls, he would be pitied or maltreated, yet Mid-Surrey greens are not many removes from a billiard table, and putting is quite half the game of golf, as I think has been remarked by a great number of people, but is nevertheless not sufficiently considered by golfers, especially in the matter of choosing golf balls.

It is not necessary, in considering the question of the golf ball, to bore people, as is usually done, with the history of the evolution of the golf ball, from the time when prehistoric men used a knuckle bone or something like that, right down through the feather ball period up to the present time. It will not be necessary for me to go back any further than the period of the gutta-percha ball. Most golfers will remember that the guttie was not a perfectly smooth ball; it was marked with grooved lines running round it. These crossed each other at various angles, producing, generally speaking, squares, although, naturally, some of the markings, where the lines did not cross at right angles, were irregular, but the principle of the marking was by indentation.

The bramble marking, or marking by excrescence, is an idea which has obtained a hold more recently, and it is certain, from a practical and scientific point of view, that it is a very imperfect marking.

It is a curious thing that in golf, where a very great amount of accuracy is demanded, particularly when one is playing a short put on a fiery green, the ball should be, so far as I am aware, the only ball which is deliberately constructed on principles which if applied to a billiard ball would make the ball what billiard players call "foul," that is, a ball which runs untruly.

It is unquestionable that sufficient thought has not been given to this matter. Very few people understand that it is practically impossible to place a ball with bramble markings on a perfectly true surface so that it will remain in the exact place where it was put, even if it were deposited on this spot by mechanical means. It is not hard to understand that this is natural when we remember that a golf ball which is marked by the excrescences called pimples or brambles comes to rest on a tripod of excrescences, and indeed it sometimes requires to find a base of four of these excrescences before it settles down.

Any thinking golfer will be able to understand very easily that this must make for instability, and he will see clearly what it means when a ball is rolling very slowly. Let us imagine, for instance, that a golfer is playing an approach put of twenty yards. It is evident that while the main force of the blow is behind the ball it will enable it to overcome much of the untrueness of the ball, but it is equally apparent that as the force is dying away at the critical time when one wishes the ball to run truly on its course to the hole, it is most prone to waver. It is at times like this that the golfer blames the "beastly green," whereas if he knew as much as he should about the make of a golf ball he would know that he had only himself to thank for playing with such an extremely imperfect thing as the golf ball which is marked by excrescences.

It is of course clear that on a putting-green the ball with excrescences sinks into the turf, and whilst it is running with any considerable force behind it, it makes for itself what may be termed a trough to run in, which is equivalent in depth practically to the hole which the ball would make when lying at rest on the green. This is the only thing which saves the ball marked with excrescences from being a much worse failure than it is. It is, however, when one comes to put with it over a hard, keen, or bare green that its wonderful imperfection is shown.

Many golfers, on account of the fact that an ordinary putting-green does assist this imperfect ball to this extent, are inclined to maintain that the ball is sufficient for the needs of golf. They forget, of course, that a ball with these excrescences must necessarily be more inaccurate off the face of the putter than would be a ball marked by indentation, for when a ball is marked by indentation, either of the dimple pattern, which has come into vogue more recently, or of the lines which were used in the old days, it undoubtedly will run more truly than if marked by excrescences, for the reason that the indentation is bridged in such a manner that it is not felt to the same extent as is an excrescence.

I may illustrate this by applying the marking of an old guttie to a billiard ball. Let us consider for a moment that the billiard ball has been marked by having lines sawn in it similar to those on a gutta-percha ball; these lines would not affect the trueness of the running of a billiard ball to a very great extent. But let us, on the other hand, imagine that instead of lines being sunk in the ball, these lines had been put in a network on the ball, so that they were raised from the surface of the billiard ball. It is obvious that such a ball would be absolutely impossible, and it would be an extremely foul-running ball.

There is another point to be considered in connection with this matter of marking by indentation or by excrescences. It would be almost a matter of impossibility to stand a ball marked by excrescences so that it balanced on the point of one of the pimples. On the other hand it would be perfectly natural for a ball marked by a dimple of corresponding diameter to the base of the pimple, to come to rest on the "ring" formed by that dimple. We have already seen that the ball marked by excrescences requires three or four of those excrescences to rest on before it becomes stationary. Roughly, therefore, the instability of the ball marked by excrescences is at least three times as great as that of the ball marked by indentation, and if we contrast the ball marked by excrescences with the ball marked by the old gutta-percha marking, the difference would probably be very much greater against the bramble marking.

We have already seen that the putting-green assists, to a certain extent, to make up for the defects of the ball with bramble marking, but it must not be forgotten that although the putting-green does this, the greater tendency to instability is there the whole time, and must put the golfer who uses the bramble-marked ball at a disadvantage.

Putting, especially near the hole, is a very delicate operation, and it is apparent that in many cases the blow will be delivered on the point of one of these excrescences. It is equally apparent that in many cases that excrescence will not be in such a line with regard to the putter that the force of the blow will pass clean through the centre thereof, and also through the centre of the ball's mass in a line to the hole. When it does not do this it is certain that there is an element of inaccuracy introduced into the put (particularly the short put) which the wise golfer will not have in his stroke, for not only is the ball with excrescences more inaccurate off the face of the putter, but it is, particularly for short puts and on keen greens, much more inaccurate in its run than is the ball which is marked by indentations.

This question of hitting one of the pimples of the golf ball might be considered to be theoretical, but it is a matter of the most absolutely practical golf, and I have seen the force of it exemplified not only in golf, but in lawn-tennis. I must give here a very interesting illustration of the point which I am making.

Some time ago a lawn-tennis racket was produced which had a knot at the intersection of the strings. The idea of this knot was that it would enable the racket to get a better grip on the ball, and so to produce a much greater spin. This, to a certain extent, was correct. There was no doubt that the racket did get a very good grip on the ball, although personally, as a matter of practical lawn-tennis, I never regarded the invention very seriously; but it was useful in emphasising the point which I am now making with regard to the marking by excrescences of the golf ball. It was found that when one attempted to play delicate volleys with this racket that it was impossible to regulate the direction, for the simple reason that the ball, on many occasions, was struck by one of the knots on the racket, and this frequently spoilt the direction of the stroke.

What happened with that racket and the lawn-tennis ball is what is happening every day on hundreds of greens with the golf balls which are marked by excrescences, and the golfer who is wise will have nothing whatever to do with any ball which is marked otherwise than by indentations.

It was in the year 1908 that I first put forward these ideas in an article in *The Evening Standard and St. James's Gazette*. I had written many articles which were of much greater importance to the game from the scientific point of view, but this particular article eclipsed them all in interest. I had started the idea that the golf ball should be made much smoother than it was at that time, and for four months the controversy as to the merits of the rough ball or the smoother raged. I caused the leading manufacturers of golf balls to be interviewed. The manager of Messrs. A. G. Spalding & Bros., the well-known manufacturers, gave it as his opinion that the idea was perfectly ridiculous. He was quite convinced that the rough ball was the better ball. The manager of another company was of opinion that the smoother ball would not drive straight. Many of them traced this to the fact that a smooth ball would not fly straight, but we were not concerned with the question as to whether the smooth ball would fly straight or not; golfers, generally, are well aware of the fact, and even in 1908 were well aware of the fact, that a perfectly smooth ball will not fly straight. The whole point of the discussion was to ascertain if it would not be better to have a much smoother ball than that with the bramble marking.

I was interested in having the opinion of the golf ball manufacturers, for I have never thought that they have dealt with the matter in a scientific manner. It seemed to me that the evolution of the marking of the golf ball had been entirely haphazard, and it is, I believe, still in the same condition, but it certainly shows some signs of improving.

In order to put the matter beyond doubt I asked Mr. Rupert Ayres, of the famous firm of F. H. Ayres, Ltd., to have made for me a golf ball with an extremely fine marking; in fact I gave instructions for the ball to be marked with what I considered the least possible indentations which were likely to be serviceable. Mr. Ayres took a very great amount of trouble in connection with this matter, and he produced for me a ball similar, in all respects, to that which I wanted, with the slight exception that the marking was finer than I had desired. The result was that when the ball was painted the interstices were filled up to a very considerable extent, so much so indeed that I doubted if the ball was sufficiently marked to ensure its flying correctly. I tried this ball at Hanger Hill, both personally and by submitting it to a considerable number of drives by George Duncan, and it always gave unsatisfactory results—indeed its flight was so remarkable that it might well have been christened "the butterfly." It zigzagged and soared and ducked in a most remarkable, and to a very great extent, inexplicable manner.

I knew, of course, that what I had to do was to increase the indentations a little in depth, for my object was to obtain the mean between no marking whatever and the ridiculously exaggerated marking by excrescences which is now so common, and my experiments were not in the direction of obtaining any marking whatever by excrescences, for I was following on the lines which were accidentally discovered by those who found that the old feather balls, and particularly the gutta-percha balls, flew better after they had been indented by the golf clubs. My idea, therefore, was, starting from the least possible indentation, to proceed by marking the ball more deeply and yet more deeply until I found that it would fly as accurately as a ball marked by excrescences.

Mr. Ayres helped me in my experiments with remarkable patience and ability. I found that there are a hundred and one different markings, all of which are practically of equal service in so far as regards affecting the flight of the ball, but in every case I came to the conclusion that the marking by indentation is the best. This led me to get Mr. Ayres to produce for me a ball which he ultimately put on the market under my name, which was marked in identically the same manner as the old guttie. I believe "The Vaile" was the first rubber-cored ball with the old guttie marking to be placed on the market, and this marking was found to be satisfactory in every respect. The ball, as indeed one might imagine, both flew and ran perfectly, but it was met by golfers with a strange objection. They said it was too much like the old guttie. Personally, I did not care what they said about it. I had not caused the ball to be made from any commercial interest I had in the matter.

It had been stated that a ball marked like this would not be so good for golf as a ball marked with excrescences. I had proved beyond a shadow of doubt that the ball was better for golf than the ball which was marked by excrescences, and I was content to leave it at that, although as a matter of fact later on Messrs. Ayres did produce for me a ball with a more distinctive marking which gave us equally good results in so far as regards flight and run, but which I did not like nearly so well as the old guttie marking.

At the time this ball was produced I stated emphatically that I believed that the result of the agitation and discussion would be to knock the pimples off the golf ball. This statement was, of course, ridiculed by the makers of golf balls, and quite wisely too, for they had tens of thousands of pimply golf balls which they had to dispose of, and it was not their business to agree with my ideas of altering the make of the golf ball until they had disposed of their stock. They have, however, now no prejudice whatever in the matter, and the leading manufacturers both here and in America are pushing balls which are marked by indentation. They certainly were a long time after my manufacturers in realising the importance of the principle, but they are now endeavouring to make up for lost time. One firm, Messrs. A. G. Spalding & Bros., is pushing three balls as their leading lines. These are the Glory Dimple, the Midget Dimple, and the Domino Dimple. All these balls are what are now called dimple balls, and they meet with great favour in many quarters, although there are still a number of golfers who swear by the bramble-marking.

During the course of this long controversy I suggested that it would be a good idea if the balls which were marked by excrescences and those which were marked by indentations were subjected to a test by being mechanically propelled. Sir Ralph Payne-Gallwey, the famous wild-fowler and author of *The Projectile Throwing Engines of the Ancients*, wrote to me and very kindly volunteered to carry out the experiment if I would send him the balls I wished him to test. I naturally accepted his very kind offer, and sent him a variety of golf balls to be tested. Sir Ralph is the possessor of some very remarkable catapults built on the principles of the old Roman engines of war, and with these he conducted a series of experiments, which were so interesting that they deserve to be permanently recorded for the benefit of future generations. His conclusions were published in two articles which occupied about three columns of *The Times*, and they are of such an instructive nature that I propose to quote somewhat fully from them.

Sir Ralph showed quite clearly that in a very great number of cases the centre of gravity of the ball is untrue. Quite a number of golfers would think that it is not a matter of very great importance if the centre of gravity of a golf ball is untrue. Anyone who thinks this may speedily undeceive himself by a small experiment suggested by Sir Ralph. Let him cut a hole in the side of a golf ball, insert a piece of lead or half a dozen shot and fill the hole up with wax or soap and then put with that ball. He will be astonished to find what a peculiar course it takes.

Of course, not many golf balls are loaded like this, but it is beyond any doubt whatever that in many cases the gutta-percha covering of the rubber-core is of very uneven thickness. This in itself and quite apart from the defect of marking by excrescences which I have already referred to, is sufficient to account for the very bad running of many golf balls.

I may say, too, that I believe this untrueness of the centre of gravity is responsible for the double swerve which one frequently sees in a truly hit golf ball. A swerve which is obtained from the application of spin to the golf ball, almost invariably is continuous and in the one direction, but I have frequently seen well-hit drives by the most famous players swerve to the right, back again to the left and resume their original course. This has happened with such perfect regularity in many cases that there must unquestionably be a definite reason for it, apart from rotation applied by contact with the club, and the only explanation which I can give of it in any way at all is that it is caused by an untrue centre.

The shape, resiliency, and centre of gravity of the golf ball are of vital importance to the player, but the golfer accepts all these matters with a blind faith which is touching in the extreme. A golfer should not accept from a golf ball manufacturer a ball which is not truly spherical, or one which does not fly truly when truly hit, but as a matter of fact almost fifty per cent of the golf balls supplied by the leading makers come within this category. One may take fifty golf balls of any specific sort, and test these for shape, centre of gravity, and weight, and it is an even chance that twenty-five of them will be quite different from the other twenty-five.

It is very easy indeed to test the rubber-cored balls as regards the correctness of their centre of gravity. Sir Ralph Payne-Gallwey found that none of the rubber-cored balls was correct as to its centre of gravity, though some were much more incorrect than others, and he found that not one of them was truly spherical in shape. I may say that in a large number of cases I have verified his experiments. Sir Ralph Payne-Gallwey's method of testing them for correctness of centre of gravity is so simple that I may give it here for the benefit of any player who desires to see that he is getting a ball which will serve him truly in so far as regards this important particular.

Sir Ralph placed the ball which he desired to test in a basin of water and waited until it came to rest. When the ball had come to rest, there was naturally a small portion of it protruding from the water. Sir Ralph marked the centre of this spot with a pencil dot and he found that however carelessly he put the same ball into the water, however much it was rolled about, that the portion of the ball marked with the pencil dot always came upwards out of the water again, and that the actual spot with the pencil mark on it always came to exactly the same place. It was evident from this that the centre of gravity of the balls tested in this manner was considerably untrue.

Sir Ralph found, as might be expected, that the old guttie ball was much truer as regards its centre of gravity than the rubber-cored balls. He tested the gutta-percha ball and the miniature ball which would not float in plain water, in a solution of salt and water.

The experiments which he conducted in connection with these balls were really quite exhaustive. He found that with some of the balls, especially the smaller ones, the dot appeared in two seconds, while some of the others took from four to six seconds to come upward. He arrived at a comparative idea of the error in centre of gravity by placing the dot downwards in the water, and then noting with a stop-watch the time occupied by it in appearing out of the water on top of the ball. He thus took the time in each case from the moment of release to the moment that the pencil dot again came uppermost, and by these means he obtained as accurately as he could with a stop-watch the comparative error of one ball with another in regard to its centre of gravity.

The testing of the balls for true spherical shape was, of course, easy, and was done by means of callipers. It can be done either by callipers or by a parallel vice which may be opened just wide enough to allow a ball to be passed between its jaws. If one has not a vice or callipers available, it is, of course, easy to cut a circle in a piece of cardboard and gradually increase the size of the circle until a ball will just get through. The circle, of course, must be made truly, but this can easily be done by a pin and a string if compasses are not available.

Of course, it would be advisable in testing a golf ball through a ring such as this to obtain in the first case a ball which is as near a true sphere as any rubber-cored ball can be. This may be done by fixing any two objects in a similar position to that suggested for the jaws of a vice, as for instance the opening of a drawer. One may open a drawer and fix the drawer firmly so that the ball can just pass in at the opening. Once this is done, it is almost as effectual as either callipers or the jaws of a vice.

Sir Ralph found that the gutties were as near true spheres as possible, and also that these balls showed very slight error in centre of gravity. This, of course, from the solidity of the matter and their original formation in the mould might naturally have been expected, for in the nature of the modern ball it stands to reason that its centre of gravity could never be so consistent as that of a ball which is made entirely in the one piece as was the old gutta-percha ball.

Sir Ralph has some remarkable projectile engines which gave him exceptional facilities for testing the flight of the golf balls which I sent him. He has one engine which weighs about two tons and is capable of casting a stone ball of twelve pounds a distance of a quarter of a mile. The catapult which he used for the purpose is a small reproduction of this big engine. His small model of this engine weighs about forty pounds and will pitch a golf ball from 180 to 200 yards, the distance of course depending upon the amount of tension used and the angle of elevation.

The power of the engine is obtained from twisted cord, and the arm of the machine used by Sir Ralph is two feet eight inches long, and is provided with a cup at its upper end to hold the ball. It is so arranged that the balls can be thrown any intermediate distance required up to 200 yards, and at any elevation. Sir Ralph conducted experiments with balls thrown by the catapult, and also with balls hit away by it in a manner similar to a golf club, and, as might be expected, no spin whatever was imparted to the ball. It was thrown in a straight line every time with unvarying accuracy, and there was not the slightest sign whatever of slice, pull, or cut. This, of course, is exactly what one who knows the principle of the catapult would expect.

Sir Ralph found, however, that the accuracy of flight of the ball was very remarkable, and he gives as an instance the fact that a ball which had been marked as having a particularly accurate flight was pitched twenty times in succession within a few feet of a stick stuck in the ground 180 yards from the machine.

It is interesting to note the weights of the balls used in these experiments. They varied from 22 drachms to 23 drachms avoirdupois, and their diameters from 53 to 54 thirty-seconds of an inch. The guttie ball used by Sir Ralph weighed 24½ drachms, and one of the miniature balls 24 drachms 6 grains. Sir Ralph threw a dozen balls of various makes from his small engine at a mark 160 yards distant, and he threw each ball twenty times before another was tried. He employed a fore-caddie to mark the indentations each ball made where it fell. A peg was put in at the spot where each ball landed, and these distances were all subsequently measured, and the records kept for purposes of comparison.

After this had been done with one ball the same was done with another, and it is almost unnecessary to say that the angle of elevation and the force used in each case was the same. Sir Ralph found that in propelling the balls with the wind there was very little difference in the length of carry or the steadiness of the flight, though, as might have been expected, the guttie beat all of them in distance, being six times in its first series of twenty throws a few yards farther than the longest carry made by any of the other balls. This, of course, was quite natural, for the old guttie was heavier, harder, a more correct sphere and more correctly marked than the ball which is now in common use. Therefore it was quite reasonable to expect that it would go farther when propelled from the catapult. It is, of course, just as easy to understand that this superiority would not exist when the ball was struck with a golf club, for then the question of resiliency comes into the matter.

It is interesting to note that Sir Ralph found that the miniature golf ball more nearly approximated to the guttie than to the rubber-cored balls. The miniature being harder and heavier than the other rubber-cores, when thrown by the engine gave the longest flight of all the rubber-cores, although it did not get so far as the guttie. Its superiority, however, when struck from the engine in a manner as nearly as possible resembling the blow with a golf club, was non-existent, and its carry was then found to be the shortest of all the rubber-cores, and the guttie ball was, when hit away by the machine, shorter yet than the miniature golf ball.

Sir Ralph found, as I had confidently asserted would be the case, that against the wind the balls with the roughest markings always carried the shortest distance, and that they tended to rise too much in their flight. This was most apparent at about two-thirds of the carry. Sir Ralph found that there was a distinct difference in this matter of soaring between the very roughly marked balls and those which were a little less so. He proved to demonstration the fact which I had confidently maintained, that the less roughly marked balls, owing to the small amount of air friction which they set up, and naturally in consequence thereof, their lower parabola, always carried farther against the wind.

I have referred elsewhere to Harry Vardon's remark about not attempting to regulate the flight of the ball in a cross wind, or indeed, for the matter of that, in any other wind by applying spin to it. Sir Ralph Payne-Gallwey's experiment put this matter beyond a shadow of doubt, so that we may be absolutely certain that the idea of trying to slice against a wind to get a straight ball, or to pull into a wind to get an extra run, is for ninety-five per cent of players not practical golf. Sir Ralph found that with a fresh side wind from the left, all the balls, except the guttie, landed from eight to twelve yards to the right of the mark at a range of 130 yards. He states emphatically that in this case it was clearly shown that the more roughly marked balls consistently showed the greatest deviation from the correct line of flight. We have, however, gained a very strong argument in favour of the ball with the less pronounced marking.

Sir Ralph also discovered another thing which is of very great importance indeed to the practical golfer, but a thing which is not considered in the slightest degree by one golfer in ten thousand, and that is that the balls which were most untrue in regard to their centre of gravity, not only always dropped the farthest to the right, that is, were most affected by the cross wind, but that they also ran at a more acute angle in the same direction after contact with the ground. Thus we see that in 130 yards the most roughly-marked ball in a cross wind is deflected twelve yards. We see also that this ball was the one which was most incorrect as regards its centre of gravity. We therefore have a specimen of the worst ball which could be used for this purpose being carried twelve yards off its line, and we may reasonably take this to be the extreme of error for that distance.

It is easy to understand when we consider such an illustration as this what a tremendous handicap the golfer is suffering from when he uses the ball which allows the wind to get such a grip of it as the bramble-marked ball does, and moreover one with a centre of gravity which is so bad that it assists the work of the wind in carrying the ball away as it does, and not only assists the wind to this extent, but even carries its vices to the extent of still further fighting against the player by exaggerating its error when it lands by running away from the line.

These are all bad enough, but we must remember that there is also to be considered the error which is unquestionably a matter to be reckoned with, which inevitably takes place when the ball marked by excrescences is struck by a club.

I had sent Sir Ralph Payne-Gallwey the ball which I had had made for experimental purposes with very slight marking, and he was good enough to experiment with this for me. He says of it: "This ball was quite smooth, as smooth indeed as a billiard ball, the idea being that having no markings on its outside it would not present so frictional a surface to the air in its flight, as a ball with markings, and that being without this it would also be very accurate from the putter. I tried this smooth ball from the engine, and it 'ducked' every time in an extraordinary manner, its length of carry being seldom more than eighty yards."

Sir Ralph is most accurate, generally speaking, but he is in error by stating that this ball is as smooth as a billiard ball. The ball which I sent Sir Ralph was called by me "The Ruff," merely as a distinctive name, for it was the nearest approach to a perfectly smooth ball that I could make. It is evident from Sir Ralph Payne-Gallwey's description of it that it is, as compared with the golf balls now in use, very smooth, but it is pitted all over with remarkably small indentations so that it appears to be chased, but, as I explained, the paint to a certain extent covered up the interstices so as to prevent the ball giving me the test which I expected to get from it. It is, however, not accurate to say that this ball is perfectly smooth.

It is obvious that from this I was trying to work to the mean which I felt perfectly certain existed between the old golf ball, whose erratic flight was well known, and the modern golf ball with its exaggerated marking.

Sir Ralph thought that the form of this ball might not, for some unknown reason, suit a projectile engine. He continues:

... and as I could not drive it further than about eighty yards with a golf club, I engaged the well-known professional, Edward Ray, to play a round of the green with this ball at Ganton. As Ray is an exceptionally long and accurate player with driver and cleek I felt the ball would have a fair chance of going, if it could go. From the first tee the ball did not carry a hundred yards, though, to all appearances, struck clean and hard. I thought that for once in a way Ray had missed his drive, but as the same thing occurred from every tee and through the green for the next six holes, there was no disputing that a smooth ball was quite useless for golf.

I then proceeded to nick the ball slightly with the point of a knife, spacing the small raised nicks about one-third of an inch apart, the ball being still a very smooth one in comparison to any of the usual kinds. After this slight alteration the ball flew splendidly, whether off wood or iron clubs, neither too high nor too low, but quite straight, and with the very slight rise towards the end of its carry that is the essence of perfect flight in a golf ball, some of the carries when measured from the tee being well over two hundred yards.

Sir Ralph Payne-Gallwey continues that when he returned home he shot this ball from the small engine, and it then several times out-distanced the best records made by any of the balls previously tested. After this he chipped up many more little raised nicks on the same smooth ball as a further experiment, but he then found that this not only reduced its length of flight by several yards, but also caused it to soar too much upwards when projected against a head wind as is the case with the ordinary rough-marked golf ball.

It will be seen here that Sir Ralph continued with the ball sent by me to him, the experiment, which I had started, as it was my intention to proceed from a ball as nearly as could be, smooth, towards the present exaggerated ball, by the least possible steps, so that the moment that I had arrived at a ball so marked that it would not give me any extra carry, I should desist at once.

Sir Ralph's summing up is as follows. He says: "From such practical tests it is evident that the surface of a golf ball is far too rough, and that it would fly with more accuracy and farther, especially with a head or a side wind, had it much less numerous and prominent markings on its cover." This is exactly what I contended for in my original article on the subject, and it is exactly what has to be realised by the makers of the golf ball of the future. Many of the balls which are now being produced with the dimple marking are moving in the right direction, but they still have the grave errors of bad centre of gravity and excessive marking. When these two matters have been adjusted we shall have a very much better ball.

It will be interesting now to refer to the results which Sir Ralph Payne-Gallwey obtained when he fitted his catapult with an arm provided with an enlarged head similar in shape to the head of a golf driver. Sir Ralph says:

This striking arm hit the ball away just as it is hit by a golf club. The ball I suspended by gossamer silk from the projecting beam of a little gallows fixed over the engine, and so positioned that the enlarged upper end of the arm struck the ball fair and true and with its full force and at the same angle every time.

I was not present when Sir Ralph made these experiments. He, however, was kind enough to send me a copy of his most interesting work entitled *The Projectile Throwing Engines of the Ancients*. This book gives many illustrations of the catapults used by the Romans and others.

I find it somewhat difficult to follow Sir Ralph Payne-Gallwey when he says: "This striking arm hit the ball away just as it is hit by a golf club," for it seems to me that as the ball was suspended above the striking face of the club which was fixed to the upper end of the arm, that the arc described by the arm of the catapult would be exactly opposite to that described by the head of the golf club, and it is of course conceivable that this would in some way affect the carry of golf balls struck by the machine in this manner.

I need not, however, go into that here, for whatever the results obtained by Sir Ralph Payne-Gallwey were each ball was hit in exactly the same manner, and therefore we have, in so far as regards distance and the effect of the side wind, fairly accurate comparative tests. Sir Ralph says: "Though I could not obtain the same length of carry by making the engine strike the ball as I could when the ball was thrown by it—not by about fifteen yards—yet the individual results in distance and in deviation with a side wind exactly corresponded with the behaviour of the various balls when they were thrown and when carries of from 180 to 200 yards were obtained from them."

Sir Ralph found that in this experiment the carry of the guttie was invariably about eighteen yards shorter than that of the ordinary rubber-cored balls. He therefore carried out an interesting experiment by fixing a pad of rubber on the face of the head of the arm, and the guttie, when struck by this, travelled as far as any of the balls. He found, as I have previously indicated, that of the rubber-cored balls the small one carried the shortest distance when struck by the engine, and he found also that its length of flight was not increased by using the rubber pad. This, of course, is what we might have expected.

There is one very interesting matter which Sir Ralph Payne-Gallwey notes. He says: "Another curious thing, the ball with the most untrue centre of gravity usually made one, and occasionally even two, swerves in the air when hit against the wind, though this eccentricity in its line of flight was less noticeable when it was thrown from the engine." This is a very interesting statement to anyone who devotes attention to the flight of the ball, and it goes very far indeed to confirm my own impression that the double swerve of the golf ball which I have noticed so frequently, is produced by defective centre of gravity.

PLATE XIV.

J. SHERLOCK

Top of swing in iron-shot. Note the position of the ball, and the upright swing of the club.

These experiments are of very great value, and should be carefully noted by golf ball makers, but Sir Ralph Payne-Gallwey was not content with testing the golf balls for their flight. After having put in several days doing this, and having fired fully 500 shots, he continued his experiments with these balls with the object of ascertaining their relative merits on the putting-green. He says:

I obtained a piece of lead three-quarters of an inch thick, two inches wide, and three feet long, in which I cut a straight and smooth groove one inch wide. One end of this piece of lead I rested on the cushion at the baulk end of a billiard table, and directed its other end towards the spot on which the red ball is placed in the game of billiards. The forward end of the grooved lead I tapered off so that a ball ran evenly and smoothly from the groove on to the table without any drop or deviation as it left the piece of lead, which from its weight, when once set, could not change its position. I now placed a thimble on the spot at the far end of the table and rolled an accurately-turned wooden ball the same size as a golf ball down the sloping groove. After a little adjustment of the lead piece its line of fire was correct, and I was able to knock the thimble off the spot fifty times in succession. The ball travelled with sufficient speed just to reach the cushion beyond the thimble when the latter was moved aside, and the shot at the thimble nicely represented a slow put of eight feet in length.

This is a most interesting way of testing the golf ball. I may say that I have myself carried out experiments on similar lines, and that the results which I obtained practically confirm the accuracy of those which Sir Ralph Payne-Gallwey got. He found that on testing various golf balls the results were widely different. He tried each ball several times in a series of twenty tries at the thimble. He found that individually they seldom hit it more than three or four times in a series, and that some of the balls, particularly those which he had found to be incorrect so far as regards their centre of gravity, rolled away from the thimble as much as two feet to the right or left, and that they sometimes actually went into the corner pockets of the table. This would seem to be incredible, but I can vouch for the accuracy of Sir Ralph Payne-Gallwey's statements.

It is an amazing thing to think of, but it is perfectly true, that the modern golf ball is so badly constructed that in a straight roll down the middle of the table such as that described by Sir Ralph Payne-Gallwey, the ball will absolutely roll as far off the line as the corner pockets, and indeed sometimes farther even than this. That is what the golfer has to contend with when he tries to put with a bramble ball on a golf green, but, of course, as he does not know it, he blames himself for an off day, or the green for being "beastly," but he never by any chance whatever gives a thought to his horribly defective golf ball.

Sir Ralph says that the guttie was a notable exception to the inaccuracy of the rubber cores. He found that in its different series of twenty tries it often struck the thimble from fourteen to fifteen times, and when it missed was usually within an inch of the mark. This shows clearly the wonderful difference which I have already emphasised between marking by indentation and marking by excrescence. Sir Ralph also emphasises a point to which I had already directed attention as to the ball marked by excrescences running truly when hit hard. It is when the ball has no great propulsive force behind it that its inherent vice is most surely shown. Sir Ralph says:

Any of the balls if played fairly hard from a cue could be made to strike the thimble every time; but then such a hard hit ball would go far beyond the hole in golf, and probably overrun the putting green! The smooth billiard-table cloth may be taken to represent the hard, bare and fast putting green of a dry summer.

That is a very fair comparison, with the exception that the hard, bare and fast putting-green of a dry summer would present infinitely greater inaccuracies to the already sufficiently inaccurate golf ball than would the billiard table. Let the unthinking golfer ruminate a little on this subject, and the day is not far distant when we shall never see such a thing as an excrescence on a golf ball.

Sir Ralph was very ingenious and thorough in his experiments. He desired to obtain the nearest possible approximation which he could to a natural putting-green, so he stretched a strip of rough green baize on the billiard table and tested the balls on this. He made a chalk mark on which to place the thimble, and its distance from the lead gutter was the same as in his other experiments. He then found that the balls, with the exception of those which had been marked as having their centre of gravity much out of place, ran with far greater accuracy. Most of them hit the thimble from eight to ten times in their individual series of twenty shots, but the guttie was, as usual, an easy winner. Sir Ralph found that on the billiard table if the balls were played fairly hard from a cue, although too hard for golf, the thimble could be knocked over every time.

I consider that these experiments prove beyond a shadow of doubt, as I personally never doubted, that the ordinary bramble-marked golf ball will not run truly unless it has a considerable amount of force behind it, and that for short puts, and particularly on anything like a fast green, it is a most treacherous ball. Sir Ralph Payne-Gallwey says:

All this goes to prove that, although a ball may be of inaccurate make, it keeps its line to near the end of its course when hit hard along the ground, as for instance, in a long running up approach to the hole from the edge of a putting green. It is also clear that a ball with an incorrect centre of gravity will very seldom run true off the putter if the ground is hard, fast and smooth and the distance it is required to travel is only a few feet. For this reason manufacturers should consider the accuracy of a ball for short puts—accuracy that can only be gained by making it a perfect sphere with its centre of gravity in the exact centre of the ball; for short puts must lose many more matches than short drives.

As Sir Ralph Payne-Gallwey truly says, with a badly balanced ball the easiest of short puts may fail, especially on a downward slope, though the player rarely suspects that his ball and not his skill is to blame.

It is not, as I have already pointed out, only the question of the badly balanced ball which is of such vital importance in short puts, but it is the question of the untrue running of the ball marked by excrescences; also there is the equally important matter, which I have referred to, of the untrueness of the ball marked by excrescences in coming off the face of the putter. I am firmly convinced that there is no more perfect marking for a golf ball than that used for the old guttie ball, that is a marking by indented lines, but even here I believe that equally good results, both in flight and run, would be obtained if the gutta-percha ball were marked in a similar manner but with fewer lines.

Some of Sir Ralph Payne-Gallwey's conclusions are important. He suggests that a golfer should carefully test a ball before using it in an important match, and this is, unquestionably, from a scientific point of view, a very sound and good suggestion. I have already indicated his method of testing a ball for its centre of gravity, and I have shown how the ball may be tested for its spherical shape. There is no necessity to apply any test whatever to the ball in so far as regards its marking. There is one maxim with regard to that—avoid anything in the shape of a golf ball marked by excrescences.

Sir Ralph Payne-Gallwey's advice to golfers with regard to the balls need not be given here in full, valuable as I believe it to be in the main. But there is one matter which is worth repeating. He says:

Select a ball with as smooth a cover as you can find, for though all golf balls require to be roughened in order to steady their flight, those most deeply scored travel the shortest distance, and are most affected by a head or side wind.

This is very sound and important advice, and it should receive the attention not only of golfers, but of the golf ball manufacturers, for even those balls which are now marked by indentation are, in my opinion, too freely marked, and I am inclined to think that the dimples on the golf balls which are so marked, are, if anything, too large and too frequent. I think it is extremely probable that the balls which are so marked would fly and run better than they do now if they were marked by lines as the old guttie was marked, but with fewer of these lines. Probably if they were marked with one-third of the number of lines which were used on the old guttie, we should have a perfect flying and running ball.

Before closing this chapter on the make of the golf ball, it will be interesting to refer once again to the results obtained by Sir Ralph Payne-Gallwey when throwing the smooth ball from his machine and also when having it driven by Edward Ray. He obtained results similar in all respects to those which George Duncan and I obtained when trying "The Ruff." It is very curious indeed that so far there have not been any definite scientific experiments made to show exactly where the serviceable degree of roughness ends and the prejudicial begins, though much has certainly been done since I started the controversy about the relative merits of a smoother ball.

Some golf ball makers have gone so far as to produce a dimple ball with a small pimple in the dimple. This, in effect, reduced the dimple to a ring, and these balls have been found to fly and run very well, but all that has been so far done has been a matter of experiment, of rule of thumb work. I do not think that there is a firm of golf ball makers in England which is in possession of a proper mechanical driver. We are assured that at least one firm in America is in possession of such a machine, but so far as I am aware there is no efficient machine of such a nature in England. This is very remarkable, as with such a machine a firm of golf ball manufacturers could obtain results which would probably give them a big advantage over their competitors.

I was quite astonished to see it stated by a firm of golf ball makers the other day that, although they were making a ball marked by indentations, they had come to the conclusion after much experimenting that the bramble pattern was the best for all-round excellence. In the face of the remarkably conclusive experiments conducted by Sir Ralph Payne-Gallwey, whose results I may say bore out up to the hilt everything which I had said about the defective construction of the golf ball, I should like to know how this manufacturer comes to the conclusion that the bramble marking is the best.

One point which has not been made very strongly is that it was not necessary for the old balls to be badly knocked about before they would fly well. Comparatively little damage improved the flight of the ball. This, in itself, should be sufficient to convince manufacturers that they are still in many ways marking their balls excessively. It is quite evident that no particular kind of marking is required on the golf ball, although it is conceivable that a certain kind of marking might possess some slight advantage over another. It would be interesting if an exhaustive set of experiments on the lines of those already conducted by Sir Ralph Payne-Gallwey could be carried out under proper supervision by some eminent scientist or by a leading firm of golf ball makers, or by some prominent paper interested in golf. The matter would undoubtedly be of very great interest to golfers generally, and would probably result in a great improvement of the balls at present on the market.

The phenomenon of the uneven flight of the smooth golf ball has never, so far as I am aware, been satisfactorily explained. We all know, of course, that practically nothing which has not a tail flies well. A tail is necessary for an arrow, for an aeroplane, for a bird to steer itself with, and even the rifle bullet would not fly well until it was, in effect, provided with a tail. It has always seemed to me that there was a possibility of an explanation of the defective flight of the smooth golf ball in this fact. It stands to reason that in the passage of the ball through the atmosphere there is a considerable compression of the air in front of the ball, and it is equally obvious that this compressed air is, if we may so express it, flowing backwards over the ball, and therefore running between the bramble markings. Of course, we are aware that it is not really a question of the air flowing backwards, but of the ball driving through the atmosphere, but we have merely to consider what may possibly be the effect of this action.

It seems to me that the air, in passing back and round the ball in the manner described, is also in a state of compression until it has passed backwards and, to a slight extent, behind the golf ball, so that we have, if we may so express it, attached to the ball a tail of compressed air which is constantly striving to resume its normal density at a slightly varying distance behind the ball in its passage through the air.

If my idea, which is expressed now in an extremely unscientific and popular form, is correct, it would seem that the roughened ball holds more straightly into this tail of compressed air than it would be possible for a smooth ball to do; in other words, it seems to me that there would be a greater possibility of the smooth ball slipping the pressure which would be accentuated on that portion of the ball which Professor Thomson describes as its nose, and it seems feasible, although I do not care to be dogmatic on this point, that if the centre of gravity of the smooth ball were untrue, as indeed the centre of gravity of nearly every smooth ball is, the effect of the pressure of the condensed air on the front of the ball would be much more pronounced with the smooth ball than it would in the case of the ball marked by excrescences or indentations.

I am aware that this idea of mine is open to argument, and I do not say for one moment that it is absolutely correct. It is undoubted that there is much uncertainty in the minds of extremely scientific men as to the cause for the uncertain flight of the smooth golf ball. Even so distinguished a scientific inquirer as Professor Sir J. J. Thomson assured me that he did not understand the reason for the erratic behaviour of the smooth ball. There is possibly another explanation, but again I put this forward tentatively. Even when a ball is driven by a golf club without appreciable spin, as indeed most golf balls are, it seems to me quite possible, especially in the case of the balls with defective centres, that before they have gone far on their journey they will proceed to acquire spin on account of the tendency of one side to lag more than the other.

It seems, then, that if this spin is set up in the manner which I described, it may, and indeed quite likely will, influence the path of the ball sufficiently to deflect it from the original line of flight, but as this spin has no very great power behind it, it seems quite likely that when it has deflected the ball from the line of flight it may be checked to such an extent that the atmosphere has a chance to get to work on the ball again and produce that which is practically a reverse spin. In this way, and in this way alone, can I see any reason for the double swerve which I have already referred to, in the carry of the golf ball. It must be understood that in the case of double swerve which I am referring to, the deflection from the straight line has always occurred at a point in the carry where one would not expect to see it if it had been occasioned by spin administered by the club, and it is always very much less indeed than the swerve would be if it had been obtained by spin produced by the club.

Also there is this other fact against the hypothesis that the swerve is produced by spin imparted at the moment of impact. In the swerve which I am referring to, both the first swerve and the return swerve which takes the ball back again into the line of flight are very slight, and in most cases practically of the same length and degree. If the original deflection from the straight line were due to rotation of the ball acquired at the moment of impact, the swerve and return to the straight line, if there were any such return, would never be so symmetrical as they are.

I can quite easily understand the double swerve of a golf ball from spin produced by the contact between the club and the ball, although I must admit that I have never seen a swerve of this nature in golf which I could put down unhesitatingly to spin acquired at the moment of impact. I must, however, when I say this, except one instance. This was in the case of a ball hit with back-spin, and although it is in a sense improper to refer to it as double swerve because it only affected the trajectory and did not alter the plane of the ball's flight in any way, it was, in a sense, a case of double swerve. It was a wind-cheater struck by a very good player at Hanger Hill. The ball flew very low and looked as though it was about to hit a bunker, when suddenly, on account of the tremendous amount of back-spin which the player had put on his ball, it rose with the ordinary rise of the wind-cheater and soared straight away for thirty or forty yards, when it began to tower in the ordinary manner of the wind-cheater. This was such an extraordinary shot that I illustrated it in *Modern Golf*, but I have never, in the course of fifteen years' acquaintance with the game, seen another shot of the same description.

There is no doubt whatever that double swerves may be obtained by the axis of rotation of the ball altering during the flight of the ball. I can remember quite clearly at a meeting of the All-England Lawn-tennis Club at Wimbledon, a player informing me quite seriously that a lawn-tennis ball would swerve two ways in the air. At that time I was under the impression that I knew all there was to be known about the flight of the ball. I did not contradict him, but inwardly I pitied him; but at the same time I made up my mind to watch for this phenomenon, little as I expected to see it, for in the course of at least seventeen years' practical acquaintance with the game of lawn-tennis wherein one has a splendid opportunity of observing the action of spin on the ball, I had never seen, or perhaps it would be more correct to say I had never observed, any ball swerve two ways.

It was not many days after this that I distinctly saw an American service, delivered by one of the players in the All-England Lawn-tennis Championship, swerve two ways. Since then I have looked for this phenomenon, and I have seen it happen both in lawn-tennis and golf, but I am satisfied that in golf it is not due to spin acquired at the moment of impact, as undoubtedly it is in lawn-tennis. It seems to me that with the lawn-tennis ball, which offers a very large frictional area in proportion to its weight, that it is quite feasible that during its travel, particularly in the American service, it may alter its axis of rotation on account of encountering a heavier bank of air, or for some other reason. It naturally follows that immediately this takes place the arc of the original swerve is interfered with, but in no case have I seen in lawn-tennis, as I have in golf, the original swerve of the ball exactly compensated for by the swerve back into the straight line, which is the peculiarity of the double swerve at golf.

There is no doubt that there is a considerable amount of mystery in this matter. It may appear that it is not of much importance to golfers, from a practical point of view, whether it is solved or not, but it is hard indeed to say how useful a proper understanding of the higher science of the game may be in the practice of it; and in the experiments carried out by Sir Ralph Payne-Gallwey with so much patience and ability we have a very good example of the value to golfers of the scientific investigation and consideration of matters appertaining to the various implements of the game.

CHAPTER XII

THE CONSTRUCTION OF CLUBS

In my last chapter I dealt with the construction of the golf ball. In many respects the golf club is more perfectly made than the golf ball, although it is, of course, hard to compare two objects so entirely dissimilar. In making the comparison I am, however, thinking mainly of the amount of exactness which has been brought to bear on the manufacture of the respective articles in so far as they have developed in accordance with the best of modern thought. It cannot be denied, however, that from a mechanical point of view, the golf club is still a very imperfect implement, for the simple reason that the striking point of the club is not in a line with the handle. This, of course, is, from the point of view of one who desires to obtain the maximum of strength and accuracy, a glaring fault. It has been remedied to a very considerable extent in the Schenectady putter, to which I shall have occasion again to refer.

Golf is a very old game, and, as I have shown, it has been simply festooned with the cobwebs of tradition, and in no respect, probably, is this truer than it is in regard to the golf club. Originally, almost every implement made for playing a game by striking a ball was curved or so crooked that the ball was struck off the line of the shaft. The cricket bat was originally a crooked implement, so was the lawn-tennis racket, lacrosse, and even the billiard cue, but these have all been straightened, so that at the moment of impact the ball is in a straight line with the handle or shaft of the striking implement. It would indeed seem exceedingly strange to see a batsman furnished now with a curved bat, but that, in effect, is what we have in golf. It is certain that to obtain the best result from one's strength, it is necessary that the forearm, the ball, and the shaft of the striking implement shall be, at the moment of impact, in one and the same straight line or plane. This is a fundamental rule in athletics which is too much ignored by many players, both at lawn-tennis and in golf.

Ignoring this principle in lawn-tennis has cost England her supremacy—not only, indeed, has it cost her her supremacy, but it has relegated her to the back ranks of the world's lawn-tennis players; for instead of having the handle of the racket and the forearm in one and the same straight line at the moment of impact, the English player, both with the forehand and the backhand, introduces between his racket and his forearm a considerable angle. He thus, instead of confining his force to one line, diffuses it over a triangle, and causes the weight of the blow to fall on his wrist in such a way that it offers least resistance.

The golf club, although naturally to a less extent, embodies this fundamental error in mechanics, for instead of hitting the ball dead in a line with the shaft, it gets it in the middle of the face which projects from one side of the shaft. A moment's reflection will show that this is a very imperfect method of striking the ball.

It will, of course, be said by the slaves of tradition that it is a horribly revolutionary thing to suggest any alteration in the shaft of the golf club, but it must be borne in mind that the golf club has to go through a process of evolution before it will become perfect, also that it has for generations past been going through a process of evolution which has materially altered its structure. Originally the head of the golf club was much longer than it is now. Gradually the head has been shortened so that the point of impact has come nearer to the shaft, and no less an authority than Harry Vardon has said that this tendency is well justified, for one can undoubtedly obtain greater power and accuracy the nearer the blow is brought to the shaft.

Following Vardon's reasoning to its logical conclusion, we have very little difficulty in arriving at a decision that we could undoubtedly obtain better results if we struck the ball in a line with the shaft. This seems at first glance a revolutionary idea, but, as a matter of fact, it is nothing new in the game of golf. The old St. Andrews putter, which had a pronounced curve in its shaft, was so built that if the line of the upper half of the shaft were continued it would run practically on to the centre of the face of the club. The lower portion of the shaft curved very considerably. Sometimes, indeed, this curve was spread over almost the full length of the shaft. The object of this curve, which I may say is even now in the handle of all scientifically constructed wooden putters, is to bring the hands in a line with the point of impact at the moment of striking, but in this year of grace, 1912, we find the Royal and Ancient Golf Club barring on its own links, but, as it states now, *nowhere else*, such a well known and proved club as the Schenectady putter.

The Schenectady putter is not a centre shafted putter, and in my opinion is open to several grave objections, for it is made with a head shaped on the general principle of the wooden putter, which it resembles more than it does the ordinary metal putter. I have a rooted objection to any putter which has a broad sole, for it is simply importing into the stroke an unnecessary element of error. If the swing is untrue, there is much greater risk of soling with a broad-soled putter than there is when one is using one of the metal putters.

I have besides this two other objections to the Schenectady putter. It does not go far enough, in that it is not a centre shafted putter, and therefore the point of impact and the shaft are not in the same straight line; and thirdly, the shaft enters the head of the club some distance back from the face of the club.

Some years ago, when in America, I invented and patented the "Vaile" clubs. These are centre shafted clubs and they are built exactly on the principle of the time-hallowed St. Andrews putter. For example, the only difference between the "Vaile" putter and the revered St. Andrews putter in principle is that in my club, instead of spreading the curve over the full length of the handle, I have gathered it all at the neck, and instead of allowing the shaft to run into the head of the club, as in the Schenectady, some distance from the face of the club, I have turned the neck away in a curve to the heel of the club, so that the club is much more like the ordinary golf club than is a putter built on the lines of the Schenectady. The same principle is used in the wooden clubs.

Now it is absolutely incontestable that this principle is scientifically more accurate and will deliver a stronger blow than the golf clubs which are at present used. James Braid in 1901 said of this putter:

I consider this putter very good for direction, as, the shaft being practically centred, you get the effect of the driver headed putters with inserted shafts, without losing the advantages which the ordinary putter head possesses over the large headed clubs. The principle, from a scientific point of view, is certainly right, and I have no doubt that any player who suffers from bad direction will find this a valuable club.

In passing, I may draw attention to the fact that James Braid himself considers that the ordinary putter possesses advantages over the large headed clubs, and I think myself that there is very little doubt that this is so for the vast majority of golfers. Arnaud Massy, in his recent book *Le Golf*, says of my clubs: "Certes, au point de vue scientifique, cette théorie est inattaquable." Notwithstanding the opinion of three such men as Vardon, Braid, and Massy on a matter of practical golf like this, the Royal and Ancient Golf Club of St. Andrews has declared that my clubs are illegal on their links, but in response to questions which they have been asked with regard to this matter they assert that the club is barred only on the links of the Royal and Ancient Club!

It seems a very great pity that this famous Club should have taken this action with the Schenectady and the Vaile, for it has undoubtedly led, as I pointed out in *The Contemporary Review* for August 1910, would be the case, to the passing of the great Club as a world power in golf. It is impossible for any club or body of persons to stand in the way of the progress of a great game such as golf, and anybody or any club endeavouring to do so must inevitably, as I clearly indicated at the time, pay the penalty for doing so.

I have very little doubt that in the future, and at a by no means distant date, golf will be played with clubs constructed on an infinitely more scientific principle than those which are now used. It is quite plain to anyone who gives the matter a little thought that the longer the head of the club the greater must be the inaccuracy in the stroke. It stands to reason that the inertia at the toe of the club is greater than at the heel, and every fraction of an inch which one goes farther from the shaft must increase the inertia in the head of the club. It follows quite naturally that if one is using a whippy shaft, the tendency must be for the head of the club, especially if it is at all long, to exert a very considerable amount of torsional or twisting strain on the shaft of the club in the downward swing. It has been asserted that this torsional strain, by reason of the recovery of the shaft at the moment of impact, adds something to the force of the drive in golf, but this is quite an error, as at the moment of impact the club is travelling at its fastest. It follows, therefore, that if there is any inertia in the toe of the club, it will be very apparent at the time when the club is travelling at its fastest, and the result is that the torsional strain, instead of providing any beneficial spring at the moment of impact, only tends to lay back the face of the club and contribute materially towards slicing. It will, therefore, be seen that it is very inadvisable to have a long head when one is using a whippy shaft.

I may, perhaps, illustrate this question of keeping the impact in a line with the striking implement by instancing the sword cut. Most people have seen at military tournaments the competition known as lemon-cutting. In this event a mounted man gallops past a certain number of lemons suspended on strings, and as he passes he endeavours to sever them with his sword. It will be seen that at the moment when his sword enters the lemons his forearm and the sword are, in both cuts, in the same plane, and it seems so obvious as to need no emphasising that if the line of his blade were even an inch or two off the line of his forearm there would be introduced into his stroke a very great degree of inaccuracy, but although this may be so obvious, it is practically what we are doing every day in golf.

If the golf club were made in such a manner that the point of impact was absolutely in a line with the forearms at the moment of impact, tradition, instead of being outraged, would really be honoured. Not long ago a friend of mine came to me and showed me an old driver, saying, "I cannot understand how it is, but I can always get twenty or thirty yards farther with this driver than I can with any other." I took the club and ran my eye down the shaft. I noticed at once that it was warped considerably so that it threw the shaft inwards in such a manner that it resembled very much the shaft of an old St. Andrews putter—in other words, it put the golfer's hands and forearms in a line with the shaft of his club and the shaft of his club in a line with the point of impact at the moment the stroke was played. I pointed out to him that his club was, in effect, a centre-shafted club, and that this was the reason why he was getting a longer and, as he stated, a straighter ball with this club than with any other club he used.

While I am on this question of the construction of clubs, I may as well state that under the recent ruling of the Royal and Ancient Golf Club there is not a legal golf club in use in England to-day, for one of the essentials of a legal club now is that the head must be all on one side of the shaft of the club. Passing by, as too technical an objection, the question as to whether a circular object may be said to have a side, we are confronted with the fact that many of the best-known clubs have the shaft inserted in the head. All the socketed clubs technically are illegal, because the head is certainly not all on one side of the shaft. Many cleeks are illegal because the shaft goes through the socket and right through the heel of the club to the sole thereof, so that a considerable portion of the head of the club is on the hither side of the shaft, and every ordinary golf club is so constructed that it is more correct to say that the head of the club, instead of being all on one side of the shaft, is either at the foot of the shaft, or at least that there is, without any doubt, a considerable portion of the head which goes beyond the one side of the club whereon the head is supposed to be.

It is a very great mistake indeed to attempt to introduce any standard golf club or to lay down any regulation whatever as to how the golf club shall be made. The good sense and sportsmanlike instincts of the golfer should be sufficient to govern the question of what may and what may not be used. It is an absolute certainty that if any man were to endeavour to use an implement which was not in accordance with the best spirit of the game, he would speedily provide his own punishment, but it is a wonderful thing to find the greatest Club in the world barring on its own links clubs which embody in their formation the well-recognised principles of the most revered implements of the game.

The principle which I have referred to of endeavouring to get the point of impact as near to the shaft as possible is being shown also in the hockey stick, which has not now anything like so great a curve in it as it originally had, and the striking-point has been brought much nearer to the shaft. The tennis racket, as distinct from the lawn-tennis racket, has stood for many years as a lob-sided instrument, but about eighteen months ago I was with a tennis player who ordered from Messrs. F. H. Ayres, Ltd., six straight tennis rackets, saying that he believed the soundness of the principle which I am now advocating to be absolutely incontestable and of universal application in ball games.

I mention this matter because I believe it is of historical interest, for I do not think that prior to the time mentioned by me, tennis rackets were ever made straight. We all know how, when aiming a stone, playing a billiard ball, firing a gun, shooting an arrow, or pulling a catapult, one instinctively tries to get one's eye into the line of flight of the object to be propelled. It is evident that one can aim better thus. This is denied one in golf, where the ball is practically the smallest played with, to a greater extent than in any other game. It follows that a greater degree of mechanical accuracy is called for in golf than is required in other games. Very few golfers realise that they are deliberately handicapping themselves by playing with the clubs at present used. The weight and leverage of the head of the club is on one side of the shaft, and the angle of error is there. True, it is small, but a very slight initial error in the flight of a golf ball becomes in 200 yards serious, perhaps fatal. The golf club of the future will inevitably follow the march of scientific construction, and fall into line with the straight-handled implements wherewith the ball is struck in a line with the shaft.

It is clear that at the moment of impact with a golf club, as they are now constructed, there is a very great tendency for the club to turn in the hands. This is shown very clearly when one happens to hit with the toe of the club a little lower than it ought to be, so that the toe strikes the earth. This is absolutely fatal for the club will be turned in the hand, but it is otherwise if by chance one happens to strike the ground with the heel, for as the force of the club is transmitted in a straight line down the shaft, the blow is very frequently, particularly with iron clubs, not interfered with to any very great extent. It is clear that if the club is centre shafted, greater strength and accuracy are obtained, for the club has an equal weight on each side of the shaft. There is thus no torsional or twisting strain on the shaft as there is at present with every golf club, and, as I have already shown, this torsional strain cannot be considered as a negligible factor in a club. I must repeat, however, that it is an error to think that this torsional strain can, by its recovery, contribute anything to the length of the drive, for the recovery from the torsional strain does not take place until long after the impact has ceased and the ball has gone on its way. This, it seems to me, even from a theoretical point of view, is undoubted, but I have proved by practical experiment that one can obtain a longer ball with a centre-shafted club than one can with an ordinary golf club.

There is another matter in connection with the construction of clubs which should receive the attention of manufacturers. We know that the clubs are of varying lengths, descending from the driver to the putter according to the length of the shot which is required of them. The difference between a driver and a mashie is frequently as much as six inches. The difference between a mashie and a putter is roughly, say, three inches. It has always seemed to me that in proportion to the work demanded of it the putter does not continue in the decreasing scale of length as it should, particularly for short puts. Many very fine putters get quite low down to their put and grip the putter a long way down the shaft. It is undeniable that for short puts there is some advantage in this method, but it is open to the objection that it leaves too much of the shaft free above the hands, thus not only destroying the balance of the putter, but risking striking some portion of the player's body with the free end of the shaft.

I believe that the putter should, generally speaking, be made much shorter, but, if this is not done for approach puts, I am sure that it would be worth one's while to experiment with a short putter for short puts. I have had such a putter made for me, and I have no hesitation whatever in saying that it is a very valuable club and one that should be better known than it is. It is necessary, of course, to readjust the balance in such a club, but when that has been done, I firmly believe that one is very much more accurate with this club than with an ordinary putter when playing short puts. The putter which I am referring to is, if I remember, little, if any, more than twenty-six inches.

While I am on the question of the construction of putters, I may say that I am inclined to think that all these putters which are made with heads such as the Schenectady, the ordinary wooden putter, or those putters with aluminium heads, are a mistake. The sole of the club is too broad, and to use such clubs as these is simply providing a greater chance of error. There is nothing which can be done with one of these large-headed putters which cannot be done as well, or better, by an ordinary metal putter.

111

There are many fearful and wonderful putters on the market at the present time. Lately there has been produced a putter with a very shallow face, which is now being largely used because a man who has won the open championship frequently is using it. For ninety per cent of golfers a putter with a narrow face is a very great mistake, and I believe that in saying ninety per cent I am fixing the percentage low. I do not think that any putter should be built whose face is so narrow that at the moment of striking the ball properly with the putter the top edge of the putter is below the top of the ball. I am firmly of opinion that a putter which is so built that it delivers the main portion of its force below the centre of the ball's mass is absolutely defective. I go even so far as to say that I believe that in a scientifically constructed putter the face should be made much broader than the face of the average putter, and that the weight, instead of being massed at or near the bottom of the putter, should be reversed, and put, if anything, nearer the top. The whole essence of true putting is that the ball shall be rolled up to the hole, and not at any portion of its journey played with drag, or as one is sometimes told to do, slid along the green. Any attempt whatever to put with drag, or by tapping the ball, must cause inaccuracy.

I saw, a short time ago, one of the finest golfers in England, Mr. A. Mitchell, lose an important match on the putting-green, or, to be a little more accurate, on quite a number of putting-greens. He was then, and I believe still is, making the same mistake as James Braid made when he was such a bad putter, viz. tapping his puts, and finishing low down on the line after the ball. It is almost impossible for anyone to be a good putter with this stroke, and his chance of being a good putter is rendered remoter still if he attempts to do putting of this nature with a shallow-faced putter.

A putter should have very little loft indeed, if any. It is questionable, from a scientific point of view, if the putter should be lofted at all, but in practice a very slight degree of loft is generally used, and there may be something to be said in favour of this slight loft if one is playing the put as it should be played, as nearly as possible by the wrists, for if that is done it stands to reason that the putter with a very slight loft will tend, in, of course, an extremely small degree, but still to such a degree as to be perceptible, to deliver its blow upwardly through the ball's mass, and this naturally tends to give the ball a truer roll off the club than would be the case if the putter were perfectly vertical.

If one were using a putter with a vertical face, it seems fairly clear that at the moment of impact, when one is endeavouring to roll the ball forward, it is held simultaneously at two points. There must then, it seems, be some slight dragging on the face of the club and also on the green, but when the putter has some small loft on it and the blow is delivered, to a certain extent, upwardly, the ball will naturally get a truer roll from it, and for this reason perhaps the smallest degree of loft on a putter is advisable.

Shallow faces and broad soles in putters have nothing whatever to recommend them, and there is very little doubt that golfers will, in due course, find this out, and will use a putter so made that it will carry the weight where it is most wanted, and that certainly is not at the base of the ball, for, unnecessary as it may seem to mention the fact, the put is the one stroke in golf which we always desire to keep as close to the green as possible. We know quite well that in all other clubs, when we want to get the ball off the ground quickly, we take a club which has its weight thrown into the sole, but as we want exactly the opposite thing on the putting-green, it seems reasonable to think that we should alter the adjustment of our weight when constructing a putter which has any claim whatever to being considered a scientifically made club.

I have referred to the defect of the broad sole, and I have in a previous chapter of this book indicated that the perfect put should bear as close a resemblance to the swing of a pendulum as the player can give it. Let us now for a moment imagine that we have as the weight on the pendulum the head of an ordinary metal putter, and let us so adjust this metal head that in the swing of the pendulum it will barely clear a marble slab placed underneath it. Let us now remove the metal putter and substitute in its place such a club as one of the ordinary aluminium-headed clubs, or a Schenectady, and hang this club on the end of the pendulum so that when the pendulum is absolutely vertical the front edge of the sole of the club clears the slab by exactly the same space as the metal putter did when at rest. We shall now find that this club will swing freely back in the same manner as the metal putter did, but we shall get a very striking exemplification of the fact that the breadth of the sole of this club will prevent it swinging forward at all, for the rear portion of the sole will foul the marble slab. This, of course, is sufficient to absolutely prevent a proper follow-through, for even when this happens on a good green the delicacy of the put is such that it is more than likely the stroke will be ruined.

This is an illustration of what I mean when I say that the golfer is importing into his game an unnecessary risk when he uses a broad-soled club. It will be seen from the example which I have given that there is an infinitely greater danger of soling with such a club than there is when one is playing with an ordinary metal putter.

The same error with regard to breadth of sole is very frequently seen in the mashie. Indeed, the sole of the mashie is so broad and taken back at such an unscientific angle that very frequently the player strikes with the back edge of the sole before the front. It stands to reason that when he does this he is cocking up the front edge of his club, and so robbing himself of a great portion of the loft of the club. Many players lay the face of the mashie back in order to increase the natural loft of the club. In nine cases of ten when they do this, instead of increasing the usefulness of their clubs they diminish it, for they insist then upon the front edge of the face of the mashie striking the ball higher up than would be the case if they played with the club in the ordinary way.

PLATE XV.

J. SHERLOCK

Finish of iron-shot. Note carefully the upright finish following the swing back, and the position of the hands, a characteristic of the finish of this shot. Sherlock gets a lower ball than the ordinary iron-shot.

Most mashies are constructed in a very unscientific manner. It is the function of the mashie to get as far underneath the ball as possible. To do this a mashie should always have its front edge very clearly defined, and almost immediately the sole leaves the front edge it should begin to curve upwardly—in other words, a mashie should practically never have a sole. When the mashie is made like this it is astonishing how much easier and more accurate it makes one's work with the club. Not only does the curving sole to the mashie allow one to get more in underneath the ball and prevent any jar of a square edge behind the front edge of the sole, but if it is a question of taking turf, which involves cutting down behind the ball, one is able to do this with a mashie having the sharp edge and the curved sole such as I describe, much more easily than one could with the flat sole, for the simple reason that one is enabled to pass the ball on the downward stroke much more rapidly than one could possibly do with the broad-soled mashie. It is obvious that in playing a ball with heavy back cut, the essence of obtaining that cut must be the speed at which the mashie passes down behind the ball, and it must be also equally apparent that if one is playing that shot with a club whose sole is as broad as is that of the ordinary mashie, that the pace of the blow must be arrested to a very great extent long before the club has had an opportunity of absolutely clearing the ball. This means that the club is hampered in the execution of its natural duty.

113

While I am on the subject of the construction of the mashie, and particularly with regard to the curving sole, I may mention that I have such a club. It was made for me in accordance with a specification which I furnished, but it did not in any way carry out what I wanted; in fact, my instructions were very much exaggerated, but the moment I saw that club I knew that it would be, for short approaches and for playing stymies, a wonderful club; and so it has proved. It would take a good deal more than its weight in silver to induce me to part with it, for that club led to the making of history in golf—in other words, its construction caused me to see the great advantage which could be got by using it in playing the stymie shot which I have described in a previous chapter, and it was while playing this particular stymie shot that I came to the conclusion that for the usual stymie shot at or about the hole the ordinary mashie is far too long, as in the case of the short putter, because when one tries to get down on the club as low as one really ought to do for playing a shot of the delicacy required in these strokes, one finds that one has too much free shaft above one's hands. If I had any doubt whatever as to the advisability of having a short putter for short puts, I have absolutely none with regard to the benefits which are to be obtained from having a short mashie for playing close stymies, and I may say that at the time of writing I have never handled such a club—I have never seen such a club, nor have I ever heard of such a club, but before this book is published I shall have one.

Stymies were once upon a time a perfect terror to me, but with the club which I have referred to, and whose construction was practically an accident, they are no trouble, and I firmly believe that nine stymies of ten would be no trouble to a golfer of ordinary skill if he had the proper club with which to play them, but it seems not unreasonable, when we consider the descending scale of the clubs which I have before referred to, to think that a club which we use frequently to get eighty yards with should not be the most suitable implement for playing a stroke of nine inches to a foot.

While I am on the subject of iron clubs, there is another matter which I should like to refer to, and that is that, in my opinion, the communion, if I may use the word, between the club and the ball is not as intimate as it should be. In the lawn-tennis ball and racket one gets a wonderfully firm grip, and it is astonishing with what accuracy one can place a lawn-tennis ball by means of cut, but the vast majority of iron clubs which are used are insufficiently and unscientifically marked. I can remember the time when iron clubs, generally speaking, were innocent of any indentation whatever on their faces. Marking is fairly general now on iron clubs, but it is done in an utterly unscientific manner. It is frequently done by great deep straight lines, and, particularly in the mashie, nearly always by lines which run from heel to toe. Now in the great majority of mashie shots when one is putting on cut one requires lines running in an exactly opposite direction. We do sometimes see, of course, lines on these iron clubs running at right angles to each other, but in nearly every case the marking is too large and too coarse to be of the practical benefit which it ought to be.

Quite recently I saw a very skilful golfer playing with rusty clubs, and somebody who did not understand what it meant commented rather strongly on his untidiness. He did not understand until he was told that the idea of the man who was using these clubs in keeping them rusty was that he got a better grip on his ball, and there can be no doubt whatever that this is the case, but a scientific maker of iron clubs would not be satisfied to leave it to his customer to make up for his deficiency by allowing his clubs to become unsightly. He would produce a club marked as nearly as might be in a similar manner to a club which was heavily rusted.

I have experimented with various means for establishing a better grip between the club and the ball, and I have, I believe, found an almost perfect medium for establishing effective contact. Let us consider for a moment how little use the cue would be to us at billiards were it not for the medium of contact which is commonly used; to wit, the chalk. Now it is inconvenient, and, moreover, would be ineffective to a great extent, to chalk one's iron clubs in golf, but it is an absolute certainty that something which answers to the chalk should be on the face of every iron used in golf. What that is to be we must leave to the ingenuity of our scientific club makers, but it is an absolute certainty that we shall see a very great improvement in this particular matter within quite a short time.

CHAPTER XIII

THE LITERATURE OF GOLF

It will be readily understood by those who have followed me that I consider that golf has been badly served by those who have essayed to teach it by books. The main, if not indeed the whole, cause of the trouble is the manner in which writer after writer has allowed himself to be influenced by the work of those who have preceded him. This is neither amusing nor instructive. The essence of progress is research. We cannot progress in anything by repeating parrot-like the fallacies of those who have preceded us.

I want to make it particularly plain that this book aims at absolutely dispelling the fog and mist, the obscurity and the falseness which now clusters about the game of golf. One dear old chap was explaining to me how he tries to drive. He said,

"When I get to the top of the swing I have so many things to remember that I get all of a dither and mess it up hopelessly." Could anyone express it better?

About seventy-five per cent of the golfers who follow the usual tuition are "all of a dither." The whole trouble is that they are given too much to think of *during the stroke*. I am certain that the secret of success in golf is to eliminate the necessity for thinking *and theorising* on the links. This, I contend, can be done by *knowing*, not merely by *reading*, the contents of this book.

So strongly do I feel in this matter that I consider that every beginner who desires to succeed at golf should know what is here set out, while every misguided golfer who has been jumping from his right leg to his left, and putting his left hand in command instead of his right, should lose no time in getting the truth and so revolutionising his game.

I have stated in my Preface that this book is a challenge. So, in effect, it is. It stands for truth and practical golf, instead of the nonsense which is generally published about one of the greatest and simplest of games.

I must here refer to a book entitled *Practical Golf*, published by Mr. Walter J. Travis, the Australian who perfected his golf in America and won the Amateur Championship of England.

Mr. Travis' book is very interesting in many ways. He calls it *Practical Golf*, and it ought to be, coming from him, but Mr. Travis falls into nearly all the mistakes of those who have followed the time-worn fetiches of the people who handed down to us "the traditions of golf." I was much astonished at this, for Mr. Travis tells us himself that he worked out his own salvation, at the same time as he remarks that "as a general rule the average professional, while he may be a good player, lacks the faculty of imparting proper information to beginners."

This, unquestionably, is true, but one cannot expect too much theory from the professional, who is not, generally speaking, a very well educated man, but from a man in Mr. Travis' position one has a right to expect a fairly good grip of fundamental principles. He says that "All good players work practically on the same basic principles." This is, of course, right. The trouble is that most good golfers, like Mr. Travis, work on the same correct basic principles, but advertise to their unfortunate readers and pupils those which are utterly opposed to their practice.

Mr. Travis absolutely subscribes to the fundamental but common error with regard to the distribution of weight. He says at page 30: "In the upward swing it will be noticed that the body has been turned very freely, with the natural transference of weight almost entirely to the right foot." At page 7 he says: "The ease and rapidity with which the weight of the body and arms is transferred from the left leg to the right and back again, joined to wrist action—concerning which reference will later be made—are largely, if not wholly, responsible for long driving."

It is obvious from this that Mr. Travis thinks that one's weight ought to be on one's right leg at the top of the swing. It is also obvious that he thinks he throws his weight about from one leg to another when he is playing. It is, notwithstanding this, certain that he tells us, as does every man who writes a book about golf, that the head must be immovable during the operation of driving. We must wait for Mr. Travis to tell us how this conundrum can be solved, as none of the famous golfers of the world have yet been able to do it. If the stance has once been taken with the weight equally distributed between the legs, it is impossible, if the head be kept still, as Mr. Travis and everybody else says it should be, to get the weight on to the right leg at the top of the swing, but it is not impossible to get it on to the left leg, where it should be, and where, indeed, it goes quite naturally.

In speaking about the palm grip Mr. Travis says: "This style is more affected by cricketers and base ballers, but it is open to the objection that it introduces a tendency to hit the ball with tautened muscles, and discourages the proper follow-through."

Personally, I cannot see that there is any objection whatever to hitting the ball with tautened muscles—in fact, it absolutely must be done in that way, and in no other, or the result will be dire failure. James Braid himself says that at the moment of impact the muscles are in a state of supreme tension, and as a matter of practical golf there can be no doubt whatever that this is so. Mr. Travis also comes into line with the general body of golfing opinion with regard to the fetich of the left. He says on page 14: "As a general rule the left hand should grip somewhat more firmly than the right." I may say that Vardon and Taylor do not agree with Mr. Travis, and the mere idea of putting the left to exert a firmer hold on the shaft is a reversion to primeval fables.

Mr. Travis tells us, speaking about the waggle: "Do not on any account in this preliminary address *lift* the club up. Lifting the club pre-supposes stiffness and rigidity of muscles and the resultant stroke cannot be thoroughly satisfactory."

It will be obvious that as the club is at the lowest portion of its arc it is necessary to lift the club. This is done by an easy action of the wrists, and the waggle, of course, then becomes a swing worked almost entirely from the wrists, but it is absolutely essential to lift the club for the ordinary waggle.

At page 19 Mr. Travis says: "When the top of the swing is reached, without pausing, bring the arms and body around as swiftly as possible and *swish* the ball away." We see here that Mr. Travis is also an adherent of the fetich of the sweep, but we must in his case call it the fetich of the "swish." In golf it is now realised that the golf drive is a hit of the very finest order.

Mr. Travis says at the same page "Do not seek to artificially raise the left foot on the toe. Strive rather to keep it rooted— the natural turn of the shoulders and body rotating to the right will bring it up and around. Keep the right leg as stiff and as straight as possible. And whatever you do, do not move the head." If one is going to pivot on the left toe in any way whatever, it is fatal to the rhythm of the swing to wait until the arms pull the left heel off the earth. The left heel should leave the earth almost simultaneously with the club leaving the ball. If this is not done it will be impossible to maintain the rhythm of the swing. Mr. Travis shows himself in nearly every case pivoted on the *point* of his left toe at the top of the swing. This is now universally admitted to be bad form, as one should put the weight on the ball of the toe, and forward from that at the side of the shoe.

It is, of course, possible to play the drive practically flat-footed, in which case one's swing will naturally be much flatter than the ordinary swing, but this is not generally done. For those who pivot on the left toe, Mr. Travis' advice to wait for the arms to pull the heel up is, I think, absolutely bad. His advice to keep the right leg stiff and straight is quite good, and, of course, there can be no doubt of the correctness of his advice when he says "do not move the head," but will he tell us how, with a perfectly stiff and straight right leg, and no movement whatever of the head, he is going to transfer his weight to his right leg? for, as he truly says on page 20, "If the head is kept still, no swaying of the body can be indulged in."

There is a very remarkable statement on page 20. Mr. Travis says: "Any doubt as to whether the head is moved may easily be satisfied by the player assuming a position with the sun immediately at the back of him, and watching the shadow of the head during the swing. If the head is shown to move, the swing should be persistently practised until this fault is remedied." If I were not now writing practical golf myself, I might suggest putting in a peg on the ground to watch whether one's shadow impinged on this peg or not, but as a matter of practical golf if I considered anything of this nature necessary, I should prefer a string stretched across by my right ear so that swaying would be bound to make me touch it, but as a matter of *intensely practical golf* neither of these expedients is in the least degree necessary if the player will only get it firmly rooted in his mind that his weight must be on his left leg at the top of his swing, and he will then find that he has no temptation whatever to sway.

On page 23 Mr. Travis says: "It is not really the length alone of the downward swing that contributes distance so much as the rapidity with which the club head is moving at, and just after the moment of impact." It is almost unnecessary to draw attention to the fact that what happens "just after the moment of impact" does not much matter to the ball. It is what happens during the impact which is of importance, although it stands to reason that if the speed during impact has been sufficient, just after impact it will still be the same, minus the force expended on the golf ball.

Mr. Travis makes a terrible error in *Practical Golf* when he says, speaking of the downward swing: "Let him resolve to centralise the power of the stroke immediately the ball is reached."

This is an idea fatal to good golf. As I have frequently pointed out, and as James Braid in *How to Play Golf* also emphasises, the meeting between the ball and the club should be *merely an incident*. Any attempt to try to do anything during impact in the drive is futile.

Mr. Travis at page 24 makes the same error with regard to the speed of the club after the ball has been hit. He says: "A great deal more depends upon the maintenance of speed after the ball is struck than is commonly supposed. This part of the stroke is known as the follow-through, and plays a very important part in the length of the drive as in straightness." Mr. Travis evidently does not perfectly realise that the follow-through is of no importance whatever except as the natural result of the correctly played first part of the stroke, and the maintenance of speed after the ball has been struck is of no importance provided that the first portion of the stroke has been properly executed and at a sufficient pace. The only importance of the maintenance of speed in any way whatever is that this indicates that the first half has been correctly performed.

Mr. Travis seems to be very hazy as to the causes of slicing and pulling. A ball being hit slightly to the right of its centre would not necessarily produce a slice, although it would probably deflect it from its intended line of flight. A slice is produced by the amount of rotation which is imparted to the ball by the glancing blow. He says: "With a pulled ball it is just the opposite—the ball is hit to the left of its centre, that is, nearer the player, producing a spin from right to left." This is not in any way necessary. The ball may be hit absolutely at the point farthest from the hole, and with the club at a perfect right angle to the intended line of flight, but the point which Mr. Travis does not mention is that the club is travelling upward across the intended line of flight and outward from the player. This it is which produces the beneficial spin of the ball in the pull.

At page 31, Mr. Travis says: "Every golfing stroke describes a circle, or a segment of a circle." This is an egregious error, for the golf stroke, quite naturally from the method of its production, bears a far greater likeness to an oval than to a circle. Anyone endeavouring to produce the golf stroke as a circle would certainly not get either a very graceful or a very accurate result. Mr. Travis falls into the astonishing error for a man who plays golf so well as he does, of thinking that it is possible to juggle with the golf ball by means of a golf club during impact. Speaking of brassy play, he says: "The lofted face, joined to the slight whipping up of the hands at the proper time—that is after the club meets the ball—will produce the desired result. Don't on any account seek to bring the hands up too quickly, otherwise a top will assuredly result."

Mr. Travis here falls into the common error with regard to using the wrists during impact. It will be observed that he avoided it in dealing with the follow-through, but in this matter he makes the usual error. This turning up of the wrists which he refers to comes long after the ball has been hit, and is the natural turn up which follows any slice or any cut played to raise a ball suddenly.

At page 41 he makes the same error, for he says: "By striking the ball slightly towards the heel of the club, and immediately after bringing the arms somewhat in and finishing well out, a slight spin is imparted to the ball which causes it to rise more quickly." Here it is clear that he thinks that one may, after impact, do something with the hands to affect the manner in which the ball leaves the club. There could not possibly be any greater fallacy in golf than this. That this is a rooted fallacy of Mr. Travis I shall show later on when I deal with his remarks about bunker play.

Mr. Travis says at page 49: "Hitting with the heel of the club meeting the ground after the ball is struck will cause the ball to rise more, and, joined to the spin imparted by drawing in the arms and turning the wrists upward, will produce a very dead ball with hardly any run. The science of the stroke consists in hitting very sharply, and turning the wrists upward immediately after the ball is struck."

Here we see the same delusion. The essence of this stroke is purely a matter of practical golf which I have not seen mentioned in any book or essay on golf. When one plays a ball off the heel of one's mashie, it stands to reason that one gets the ball on the very narrowest portion of the blade, and that therefore one hits the ball as far beneath the centre of the ball's mass as it is possible to do—so much so, in fact, that a very considerable portion of the ball overlaps the top of the face of the club. This puts a tremendous amount of undercut or stop on the ball. This is the practical golf of the shot which Mr. Travis is attempting to describe, but his idea of putting cut on it by juggling with it during impact is fatal.

In speaking of approach puts, Mr. Travis gives some wonderful advice. He says: "You should aim to hit the ball as if it were your intention to drive it into the ground.... This will cause the ball to jump, due to its contact with the ground immediately after being struck." This is practical golf of a nature which we may very well pass without discussion. I think that there are very few golfers who will desire to bounce the ball off the earth when they can play it off the face of the club.

This is Mr. Travis' advice as to how to cut the put. At page 65 he says: "Put cut on the ball by drawing the arms in a trifle just at the moment of striking." The drawing of the arms across the ball is not to be done at the moment of striking. It starts at the beginning of the swing and finishes at the end thereof. This is how cut is put on a put by practical golf. Mr. Travis advises for putting that people should select "a particular blade of grass" on the line to the hole. He then says: "Take your stance and square the face of the putter at perfect right angles to the blade of grass you have picked out." As a matter of practical golf I may remark that blades of grass have a remarkable family likeness.

Mr. Travis says: "Close observation of all missed puts discloses the interesting fact that by far the large majority go to the left of the hole, thereby indicating the presence of the pull, due to the arms being slightly drawn in just after striking." This is what is called a sliced put in England, but again as a matter of practical golf I may say that many of these puts are simply misdirected, such misdirection being due to the turning over of the wrists *too soon* in the action of striking the ball. Unless one determinedly follows through well down the line the natural tendency is to hook one's put across the line, but this does not indicate any pull. It merely indicates, if of frequent occurrence, ignorance or carelessness.

Speaking of stymies, Mr. Travis says: "Occasionally you will be confronted with an absolutely dead stymie by having your opponent's ball just on the edge of the cup, your own being so close, say seven inches to a foot away, that it is impossible to negotiate the stroke by either curling around or lofting. In such extremity there is only one way of getting your ball in the hole unaccompanied by your opponent's, and that is by what is technically known in billiards as the follow shot." As a matter of practical golf the stymie stroke introduced by me is far more likely to prove successful in this case than the follow shot, for we are dealing with very tricky things when we try to play billiards with golf balls covered with numerous excrescences or dimples. If the stymie described by Mr. Travis is played by my stroke, it should be got five times out of six, and I very much doubt if Mr. Travis or anybody else could get anything like this with the run through stroke.

Writing of "Playing out of hazards," Mr. Travis says: "Then bring it down again on the same line with all the force you can controllably command, consistent with accuracy. As it sinks into the sand its course may then, but not until then, be slightly directed towards the ball."

Coming from a practical golfer this is an absolutely amazing statement. The idea of attempting to deflect one's niblick from the line originally mapped out for it as it enters the sand is too amazing and too utterly unsound to merit any further comment or notice, except to say that it would be impossible to deflect the club head from the line of travel mapped out for it at this moment without materially reducing the force of the blow, and when one is hitting into heavy sand, to get underneath the ball and in many cases to get it out of the bunker without even touching it with the club, every pound of force that can be put into the club is necessary.

There is another thing which Mr. Travis tells us that certainly is not practical golf, and it does not seem to me to be practical carpentry, but he says at page 126, speaking of the brassy: "The screws which hold the blade sometimes work loose. This trouble may easily be remedied by putting glue in the holes before inserting the screws." One is never too old to learn, and I think that in any future efforts I may make at amateur carpentry, I shall glue my nails!

Mr. Travis makes a very remarkable statement at page 139, speaking of the guttie ball as opposed to the Haskell: "The latter, by reason of its greater comparative resiliency does not remain in contact with the club head quite so long, and

117

therefore does not receive the full benefit of the greater velocity of the stroke in the same proportion as the less resilient guttie"; but surely the greater the resiliency of the ball the longer it will remain in contact with the club. It should be obvious that one of the reasons for the greater swerve in the sliced or pulled rubber-cored ball as compared with the guttie, is that on account of the longer period of impact the ball acquires a greater amount of spin.

Speaking of the waggle, Mr. Travis is delightfully indefinite. He says "With the club gripped pretty firmly with both hands in the manner already described, it is well to see that the whole machinery is in good working order by waggling the club a few times over the ball, allowing the wrists to turn freely, without, however, relaxing the grip. The waggle should be entirely free from any stiffness, which simply means that the wrists should be brought into active play."

This is certainly delightfully vague, and is not, I am afraid, of much use to anyone as a matter of practical golf. The waggle is unquestionably of importance in the game of golf, otherwise it is quite improbable that we should see it employed by so many of the famous players. The curious thing about this waggle is that it seems to be confined to games wherein one plays a stationary ball. The same operation is gone through at billiards with the cue, but is there known as cueing at the ball. With a very great number of players the waggle may be described as moral cowardice—an excuse for putting off the evil moment. Many players convert the waggle into a performance which is both tedious and stupid, and which instead of giving them a better chance of hitting the ball, has a very great chance of absolutely putting them off their stroke.

I do not know that I have ever seen the necessity for the waggle explained, nor have I seen the waggle of any of the famous players illustrated. There can, however, be very little question that in the majority of cases the address and waggle is unnecessarily exaggerated and prolonged.

In *Modern Golf* I have illustrated George Duncan's waggle. So far as I am aware, this is the only time that such a thing has been done. Duncan is probably the quickest player living, so that it will not be necessary for us to assume that every one will be satisfied with so little preliminary work as Duncan puts in before hitting the ball. His method of playing is to take his line to the hole as much as he can as he approaches the ball. He then marches straight up to it and takes his stance, at the same time swinging his club head out so that it is roughly on a level with his waist and pointing towards the hole, but being at the same time almost above the line of flight to the hole. He then brings his club back to the ball, and addresses it in the usual way, soling his club close behind the ball. Now he lifts the club practically straight up for six or nine inches and carries it forward of the ball in a gentle curve for about six inches. From here he carries the club head back along the plane of flight produced through the ball as far as it will go without turning his wrists over. The club then is swung easily and naturally back to the ball almost in the same manner as it would come to it in the drive, until it arrives close behind the ball, but about two inches from the turf, when it sinks to rest by dropping straight down behind the ball. It is now soled again as in the original address.

This sounds like a somewhat lengthy process, but as a matter of fact it is probably the shortest waggle used by any golf player who is in the front rank. In fact, so rapid is Duncan in his play, that very frequently spectators who are not accustomed to his methods, do not see him play the ball, as they allow for the more deliberate style generally followed by the other leading professionals. In Duncan we have a player who in my opinion is as good a golfer as anyone in the world. We see clearly that he wastes very little time in addressing his ball, either through the green or on the putting-green. On the other hand, we see some men of greater fame than Duncan whose deliberation is tedious in the extreme, although it must be admitted that in so far as regards the waggle in the drive, the great players do not overdo this nearly so much as do amateurs of an inferior class.

I am not aware that anybody has yet explained the reason for the waggle. It seems that it is a natural movement, or in some cases a very unnatural movement, which players fall into in endeavouring to readjust their distance from the ball and their position with regard to the line of flight. Very many players who waggle, produce most remarkable flourishes with their club. The club is made to describe curves in the air which it could not possibly do in any other operation at golf than the waggle. The whole object of the waggle seems to be to allow the player to get his eye in, as it is commonly called, at the ball, to loosen his joints, and, which is a point that I have not seen previously made, in a measure to produce in anticipation the motions of his wrists and club immediately before, at, and after impact with the ball.

If this view of the object of the waggle be accepted as correct, it is obvious that in nine cases of ten the attempted waggle is force hopelessly wasted—in fact, worse than wasted, for it has been occupied in describing weird geometrical figures in the air, figures which can have no possible reference whatever to the work which the club is expected to do. In Duncan's waggle it will be observed that firstly he swings his club head out down the line towards the hole, and secondly that he carries it back for a considerable distance from the ball in the plane of flight produced through the ball. It will be seen from this that to a great extent he produces in the waggle the same motions as his forearms and wrists go through immediately before, at, and after impact with the ball. On examining the photographs of Duncan's hands in the drive, we find that for the space of nearly two feet before he reaches the ball, and probably for quite that distance after the ball has been struck and he has continued the follow-through, there is no turning over of the wrists—that during this space of roughly three feet, the space wherein James Braid says that the wrists *have it all their own way*, Duncan's wrists are practically quiescent, and that during the whole of this time the club is travelling at almost its maximum speed, but the arms and wrists are doing very little more to it than to withstand the centrifugal force developed in the earlier part of the swing and to keep themselves braced to withstand the shock of impact.

These are merely a few instances taken haphazard from a book called *Practical Golf* by one who is, undoubtedly, in so far as regards his own play, a practical golfer. This does not, however, prevent him from furnishing another and a very striking example of the curious fact that nearly all good golfers teach the game in a manner entirely different from that in which they play it, and that their tuition, if followed out, must result in their followers learning to play in very bad form, and probably also learning much which has to be painfully unlearnt later on when they have discovered the truth.

AFTERWORD

It would be very easy for me now to begin to explain in the ordinary manner of golf books how the game is played, but to do so would be going outside the scope of this work, and interfering either with the proper functions of the professional, or the proper practice of the intelligent golfer.

I have, in this book, taken my readers through all those matters which are of the most vital importance to the game, and practically everything which is contained between the covers of this book may be better studied and digested by the golfer, be he a champion or a beginner, in his arm-chair than on the links. He who wishes to know golf to the core, must know what is in this book, all of which he can thoroughly understand without taking a club in his hands.

The whole fault of the false doctrine which has been so plentifully published about golf in the past, is that it has given the unfortunate people who have taken notice of it an incalculable number of things to think about. The truest and best tuition in golf is that which advances by a process of elimination and so proceeds that it gives the learner a minimum number of separate circumstances to think about during his game; in fact, if the tuition has been properly carried out the golfer will have astonishingly little to think of at the moment when he is making his stroke. This is the ideal condition of mind. The remark which the puzzled golfer made to me that when he started on his downward swing he had so many things to think of that he was "all of a dither" expresses marvellously accurately the condition of mind of about ninety per cent of golfers who think they have studied golf.

The golfer who studies this book soundly and intelligently will learn what he will learn from no other book on golf, and that is what a vast number of things there are in connection with the golf stroke which it is expedient to forget at the moment one is making it.

Let me give an illustration of what I mean. The golfer is told now that at the top of his swing he must get his weight on to his right foot, and that he must keep his head still. The merest attempt to do this produces a conflict at once. Then he is told that his left hand must dominate the right: here is conflict again. But when he learns that in order to keep his head still he must put his weight at the top of his swing on his left foot, the conflict vanishes, he finds that it is natural and easy to do; and he forgets to encumber his mind with the fact that it has to be done, so that it becomes just as habitual with him to put his weight in the right place as it is when he is walking. The same thing applies with regard to the instructions which he has always had drilled into him to allow the left hand and arm to usurp the position of the right. Here again he is distinctly exhorted to encourage these two members to enter into conflict during the stroke. Although I explained to him most clearly that this idea about the left being the more important member of the two is utterly wrong, and that the right is, and always must be, the dominant member in the golf swing, I did not tell him to remember this during the golf swing, and he is indeed a very foolish person if he attempts to remember it. All he has to do is to cut the false doctrine out of his mind, and nature will attend to the rest. So it will be seen that when one has grasped the truth in connection with golf one has advanced by such a process of elimination that there is left for the happy golfer when he addresses his ball very little to think of but hitting that ball.

Golf in the past has suffered from the multiplicity of false directions. It is by recognising these for what they are, and by forgetting them that the golfer will ultimately arrive at *The Soul of Golf.*

Made in United States
Orlando, FL
12 December 2021

11590274R00067